New York Times **bestselling auth**
writes "smart, sexy entertainment

D0196548

Praise for

The Marcelli Bride

"Although humor is one of Mallery's biggest strengths, the deep resonance of her dramatic storytelling is a close second. The highs and lows of the Marcelli family saga have made this series extremely compelling and quite unforgettable. The bonus: Joe finally gets his due!"

—*Romantic Times* (Top Pick, 4½ stars)

The Marcelli Princess

"Longtime readers will be thrilled to catch up with the whole Marcelli clan and see Mia finally come into her own in this series finale. This family drama has been heartwarming and filled with complex emotions."

—*Romantic Times* (4 stars)

"Charming . . . series fans will find much to enjoy in the family dynamics."

—*Publishers Weekly*

Raves for Susan Mallery's acclaimed women's fiction

"Complex and creative and definitely addictive."

—Romance Reviews Today on *The Best of Friends*

"Mallery skillfully conducts an intense emotional journey . . . in this richly textured, poignant tale."

—Booklist on *Sunset Bay*

"This heartwarming novel . . . perfectly shows off Mallery's beautiful writing. It will evoke emotions from tears to laughter."

—*Romantic Times* on *Sunset Bay*

Also by Susan Mallery
from Pocket Books

The Best of Friends
Sunset Bay
The Marcelli Princess
The Marcelli Bride
The Sparkling One
The Seductive One
The Sassy One
Married for One Month
Sweet Success

A Marcelli Wedding

The Marcelli Bride
&
The Marcelli Princess

SUSAN MALLERY

GALLERY BOOKS
New York   London   Toronto   Sydney

Gallery Books
A Division of Simon & Schuster, Inc.
1230 Avenue of the Americas
New York, NY 10020

This book is a work of fiction. Names, characters, places and incidents are products of the author's imagination or are used fictitiously. Any resemblance to actual events or locales or persons, living or dead, is entirely coincidental.

The Marcelli Bride copyright © 2005 by Susan Macias Redmond
The Marcelli Princess copyright © 2007 by Susan Macias Redmond

All rights reserved, including the right to reproduce this book or portions thereof in any form whatsoever. For information address Pocket Books Subsidiary Rights Department, 1230 Avenue of the Americas, New York, NY 10020

This Gallery Books trade paperback edition May 2011

GALLERY BOOKS and colophon are registered trademarks of Simon & Schuster, Inc.

For information about special discounts for bulk purchases, please contact Simon & Schuster Special Sales at 1-866-506-1949 or business@simonandschuster.com.

The Simon & Schuster Speakers Bureau can bring authors to your live event. For more information or to book an event contact the Simon & Schuster Speakers Bureau at 1-866-248-3049 or visit our website at www.simonspeakers.com.

Manufactured in the United States of America

10 9 8 7 6 5 4 3 2 1

ISBN 978-1-4516-1237-0

These titles previously published individually.

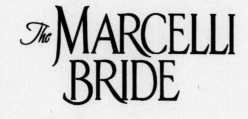

The MARCELLI BRIDE

1

❧

*I*f Darcy Jensen had known she was going to be kidnapped, she would have worn better shoes. Or at least more sensible shoes. As it was she'd dressed in black strappy sandals that weren't all that comfortable for walking, let alone being dragged across a parking lot and thrown into the back of a van.

She did her best to resist. Screaming was out of the question because they'd already gagged her. And the resisting part went badly, what with her hands tied behind her back, although she did nail one guy with a decent head butt.

Even as she landed hard on the metal floor of the van, she wondered how it all had happened. She'd been in Ann Taylor checking out the new clothes for fall. She'd told Drew she needed to use the restroom.

Traveling with two Secret Service agents meant rarely using a public restroom. Drew had consulted with the manager of the store, who was all too happy to have the president of the United States' daughter peeing in her private bathroom. Darcy had done her business, washed her hands—not only because she always did, but also because people checked on things like that when one was in the public eye—and had started back through the stockroom toward the dressing rooms, where she had a pile of clothes waiting for her.

That's when the men attacked. Four guys in Halloween-type demon masks grabbed her. Before she knew what was happening, they'd slapped tape on her mouth. The hand tying came next, then the dragging.

One of them even remembered to pick up her purse, she thought grimly as she stared at her now-scratched Maxx bag bought on QVC lying next to her on the floor of the van.

The rear doors slammed shut, and the vehicle sped out of the parking lot.

Darcy braced herself as best she could on the ribbed floor as the van bounced, swerved, then turned onto what felt like a main road. Two of her abductors had taken the front seats—she could see them through the small grille—while the other two must have had their own transportation. She was alone in the back of the van.

Alone with her purse.

There were no windows, no way to get anyone's attention. And no one to watch her retrieve the panic button that would signal the Secret Service and send them rushing to rescue her.

She inched her way toward the purse, only to have the van take another corner, causing the bag to go sliding out of reach. Two more slip-slides across the dirty metal floor and she was within reaching distance of her purse . . . except for the small problem of her hands tied behind her back. Could she open the zipper with her teeth? Probably not with the gag in place.

Darcy had done her best to stay focused in the moment. If she anchored herself in the now, the terror wasn't so bad. She could function. But if she allowed herself to think about what they could do to her, how it was national policy to never negotiate with terrorists, then fear would explode inside of her, making her want to scream and beg, despite the tape across her mouth.

No! She wouldn't go there. She wouldn't give in. She was strong and determined, and by God, she would get her panic button and push it until dozens of armed agents came storming through the walls of the van.

She didn't have much choice. Drew had been assigned to her long enough to know that the "trying on" part of a shopping trip could take at least an hour, which meant he wouldn't notice she was missing until the van had enough time to cross a couple of state lines.

If only it wasn't so hot, she thought as she went to work on the zipper. August in D.C. maintained the average temperature of a blast furnace with plenty of humidity thrown in for good measure. The front of the van might have AC, but here in the prison part of the vehicle, no such luck.

She ignored the heat, the sweat, the scrapes and bruises, and bent over her purse. Several more turns, some speeding and three failed attempts later, Darcy had discovered she could *not* open the damn zipper with her teeth. Which left her to scoot the purse into a corner, turn her back, and try to open it that way.

Easier said than done, she thought as she discovered she couldn't even hold on to the purse, although she did a lovely job of scraping her arm and banging her head. Why did this stuff always look so easy in the movies?

She tried again, carefully lodging the purse against the wheel well, then rolling onto her back and grabbing for the bag with her fingers. This time she got it and turned it slowly until she felt the zipper.

Don't make a turn, don't make a turn, she chanted silently, knowing if they did, she would slide across the van and have to start all over again.

The vehicle stayed mercifully straight.

Inch by inch she pulled the zipper down. Sweat poured down her back and made her fingers damp. Her bare legs stuck to the floor of the van and to whatever crumbs and icky things were scattered there. At last the purse was open. She plunged both hands inside and felt around for the familiar plastic case. Lipstick, wallet, cell phone, pen—

Cell phone? Nearly as good as the panic button. She would have to dial, of course, but she could call the operator and asked to be put through to her father. She could—

Darcy swore. Right. The tape across her mouth would make it difficult to hold a conversation. Back to digging for the panic button.

At that exact moment, the van suddenly came to a stop. Both she and her purse went sliding, although not at the same rate of speed. She had no way to get back to it before the bad guys opened the rear door to find her sprawled in a corner, her skirt up to her waist and the contents of her purse spread all over the floor of the van.

"You didn't take her handbag?" one of the guys asked

the other. "Goddamn it, Bill, I thought you were smarter than that."

The recipient of the scolding, a smallish man in a vampire mask, stiffened. "You used my name. Now she knows my name."

The other one, demon-guy, snorted. "Yeah, because there's only one guy named Bill in the whole country. Come on, Einstein, let's get her inside."

Darcy tried to scramble away from her kidnappers, but as she was already in a back corner of the van, there was nowhere else to go. They half carried, half dragged her into what looked like a large warehouse.

She did her best to fight, lashing out at them with her feet. The action caused them to hold on tighter to her upper arms and made her break a heel on her new sandals.

Now she was mad, she thought as they put her into a straight-back chair and began tying her down. They'd screwed with her day, bruised her, thrown her around the inside of a disgusting van, scratched her new leather bag, and ruined the black sandals she'd just bought after waiting four weeks for them to go on sale. There was going to be hell to pay.

She told them so, although the tape on her mouth interfered with the intensity of her message.

"I don't think she likes us," Bill said, stepping back as she tried to kick his shin.

"Gee, I wonder why. Most people love a good kidnapping."

With that, the two men walked off. Darcy tried to hold on to her anger by reminding herself how much the sandals had cost, even on clearance, and how little money she had coming in these days. It worked for nearly a minute, then the fear set in. What were they going to do to her?

She told herself that torture was unlikely. Either they wanted money or something they thought they could only get from the president of the United States. Unfortunately that was a big pool of possibilities, everything from sovereignty to nuclear weapons.

Then there was the matter of the no-negotiation policy. The one that told her she could be stuck here for a very long time, and then she could be killed.

Darcy might not love everything about her life at this moment in time, but she wasn't ready for it to be over. Terror tightened her throat and made it impossible to breathe. She had the sudden thought that she was going to throw up.

Stay calm, she told herself. If she vomited, she could drown in a really gross way. She had to find her Zen center. Not that she'd ever studied Zen, but she could imagine what it was like. A tranquil place. A place where reality was an illusion and all that mattered was the slow, steady beating of her heart.

Deep breaths, she told herself. In and out. No hurry in the air department. Just nice slow—

"Did you hurt her?"

The question came from somewhere behind her as she heard several people approaching. Panic joined fear as she tried to figure out if, in this man's opinion, hurting her would be a plus or not.

"She got banged up in the back of the van," Bill said. "But that's all."

She looked around for some kind of escape. But the

huge, empty warehouse didn't offer any places to hide, and being tied to a large, heavy chair limited her options. She tried to scoot and only succeeded in wrenching her back.

"Good. We don't want any unnecessary bloodshed."

Darcy exhaled in relief. Speaking as the kidnappee, she was delighted to know that bloodshed was to be avoided until necessary. Not that she wanted to know what would be considered necessary.

Their footsteps got closer, then three men were standing in front of her. She recognized her two kidnappers, who stood with a new guy, also in a demon mask. He was taller than the other two, and stronger. Something he proved when he turned on the non-Bill one and grabbed him by the throat.

"What the hell were you thinking?" he demanded, shaking the smaller man like a dog shakes something tasty just before he kills it.

Bill danced from foot to foot, although he didn't rush in to help his friend. "We got her, boss. Just like you said. The president's daughter. This is her."

The leader released non-Bill and curled his hands into fists. He stared at Darcy through the slits of the mask and growled.

"Not *this* one, you idiot. The other one. Lauren. No one cares about this one."

Less than thirty minutes later the van came to a stop. Darcy was still too stunned to react, even as the rear doors opened and the two men reached in to pull her out. One of them cut the bindings on her wrists while the other collected her purse and tossed it on the ground next to her. The broken sandal followed. Then they ran back to the front of the van, jumped inside, and sped away.

She had enough functioning brain left to look for a license plate—there wasn't one—and to note the color and make of the van. Then she sank down on the curb of the deserted loading area at the rear of the mall and rested her filthy arms on her scraped and bloodied knees and her head on her arms.

This hadn't happened, she told herself, even as the truth of it settled around her like a hot, sticky fog. She'd been rejected by kidnappers, which made the event a new high in a lifetime of lows.

Talk about a photo opportunity, she thought grimly. Here she was, battered, bruised, cut up, scraped. Her clothes were dirty and torn, her shoes broken, and she'd just been tossed aside like a used tissue.

Darcy straightened, pulled the tape off her mouth, then gasped as skin tore with the adhesive. That wasn't going to be pretty as it healed. She felt around on the cement until she found her purse and pulled out the panic button. Better late than never, she thought as she pressed down on the bright red button and waited for the cavalry.

Lieutenant Commander Joe Larson had always considered the admiral a reasonable, if distant, commanding officer. All that had changed at 9:18 the previous evening. The admiral wanted someone's head on a stick, and he was gunning for Joe's.

"What kind of half-assed, goddamn asshole . . ."

The tirade continued, but Joe didn't bother listening

as his captain got reamed. He could figure out the highlights without hearing them. Besides, the captain would be passing them along personally to Joe soon enough.

Such was the chain of command. The admiral chewed out the captain, the captain chewed out him, and he, well, Joe hadn't decided what he was going to do. Like they said—shit rolled downhill.

He crossed to the window of the office foyer and stared at the activity below. There was plenty of it at the Naval Amphibious Base. And just beyond the building, the Pacific Ocean sparkled in the bright summer morning. Other careers might offer better pay, but none could beat the location on Coronado Island.

Given the admiral's temper, there was every chance Joe could soon be exploring those other careers. Or stationed on a naval base in Greenland. Screwups came in all shapes and sizes. This one had all the potential firepower of an aircraft carrier. Explaining to the captain that it hadn't been his fault wasn't going to change a damn thing.

Fifteen minutes later, the door to the captain's office opened and the admiral stormed out. Joe stood at attention as the angry man stalked by, then he looked at his commanding officer.

"Come on in, Joe," the other man said in a weary voice.

Joe entered then closed the door behind him. "Sir."

Captain Phillips waved to the empty chair in front of his desk. "You hear all that?"

"Yes, sir."

Phillips, a tall man in his early forties, sighed. "He loved that boat."

Joe didn't respond. The information wasn't news. The admiral had been restoring his nearly eighty-year-old boat for the past five years. The engine was new, and the electronics state-of-the-art, but the rest of it was original, lovingly sanded and varnished by the admiral's own hand.

The man's wife had left him, claiming she refused to come in second to a floating hunk of wood, and his children rarely visited, knowing they would be put to work on the boat. Six months ago the admiral had decided to live aboard.

Then, last night, at 9:18, the admiral's pride and joy had been accidentally blown up by men under Joe's command. They were lucky the admiral hadn't been on board at the time.

"Want to tell me what happened?" the captain asked.

Joe shrugged. "The team was celebrating being back," he said. The Navy SEAL team in question had just returned from six months of hazardous duty out of the country. "They'd all made it out alive. Even Grayson."

"How's he doing?" the captain asked.

"Lieutenant Grayson is still in the hospital, sir. He's recovering from his injuries."

Grayson had been shot on their last op. His men had brought him back and kept him alive until he'd been evacuated to the hospital ship, then brought back home.

Joe remained perfectly still as he continued. "I spoke with the men on the team yesterday afternoon. They'd had six missions back to back, with minimal downtime in between. I suggested they burn off some steam."

Phillips nodded. "They decided on boat races."

"Yes, sir." Made sense. To a SEAL, the water was a second home. "They used small boats and kept within the marina speed limit." Sort of. "Unfortunately their racing course took them over a BUDS training exercise."

The future SEALs had been in their second round of training, learning to dive and work with explosives underwater.

"Last night the explosives were live. Apparently the movement of the boats racing overhead confused a few of the trainees. They're not allowed to surface to get their bearings. Instead of putting their explosives on the target, they placed them on the admiral's boat."

Talk about plain bad luck, Joe thought grimly. "The explosives were small and shouldn't have caused much damage. Unfortunately the admiral had recently refueled his craft. There was a small leak in the engine. When the explosive went off, it triggered a chain reaction that turned the admiral's pride and joy into kindling. At least that's the preliminary report."

Captain Phillips didn't speak for several seconds. "Aren't you going to tell me that the admiral tied up in a restricted area? That he shouldn't have been there in the first place?"

"No, sir." What was the point? Joe had been in the navy long enough to know excuses only made the situation worse. Besides, who would have told an admiral to move his boat?

"You have a great career," his captain told him. "You've worked hard, moved up the ranks. I was confident you'd make it to admiral yourself, before you retired."

Joe had walked into some of the most dangerous situations in the world and lived to tell the tale, but nothing he'd experienced prepared him for the sense of fury that gripped him as he sat there and heard his career talked about in the past tense. The navy was all he knew, all he'd ever wanted.

He'd told the men to go have fun. It was *his* responsibility. Technically, he could pass the punishment on down, but next in line was Lieutenant Grayson, currently missing most of his right leg and facing a long road to recovery.

No. This time the chain of command stopped here. With Joe.

Phillips flipped open a file. "You've been with the SEALs nearly ten years, Joe. You're a fine officer and one of the best men I've ever worked with. The admiral wants you punished, and I want to save your career if I can."

"Thank you, sir," Joe said, feeling the first hint of relief.

The captain smiled. "You might want to hold off on your thanks. The best way I know to punish you is to temporarily reassign you to a special project that has nothing to do with the SEALs. The best way I know to save your ass is to get you the hell out of here for a few weeks and let the admiral cool down. As an interesting point of fact, my brother-in-law is fairly high up the chain of command in the Secret Service. I don't think you knew that."

"No, sir," Joe said, not sure what the information had to do with anything.

"You've mentioned you have family here in California," Phillips said. "The Marcellis. They own a winery just north of Santa Barbara?"

"Yes, sir." Joe had no idea what was going on, but he

didn't like it. Technically he was related to the Marcelli clan, but they weren't his family.

"What you don't know," the captain said, "is that the president's daughter was kidnapped yesterday."

Joe stiffened as he pictured the attractive, curvy blonde who frequently served as the president's hostess. "Lauren?"

"No. The other one. Darcy. Apparently they grabbed her by mistake—Lauren was their actual target."

"How could they screw that up?" Joe asked. Darcy was nothing like her sister in looks or temperament.

"No one knows. The point is, both women are being taken out of Washington and sent to different locations. Safe houses, if you will. They'll have their usual Secret Service protection, but until the kidnappers are caught, they need to lay low. This is all confidential, Joe. You aren't to discuss this information with anyone."

"Of course not, sir." Joe had no problem keeping quiet. What he didn't understand was what any of it had to do with him.

Captain Phillips leaned forward. "There is some concern about Darcy. She's not generally cooperative, and frankly no one wants to be locked up in a safe house with her. The thought is if she can be kept safe but still have a semblance of a life, it will be easier for all concerned. Basically a place that is isolated but not solitary. I thought of what you've told me about your family's winery. There's a large house, plenty of room for the team and Darcy. I wasn't sure how I was going to convince you to take this assignment. After last night, I don't have to."

Joe put the rest of the pieces together and didn't like

the finished picture. That was to be his punishment. To babysit the president's daughter *and* spend time with the Marcellis.

"I have a SEAL team heading out in two months," he said. "There's important work to be done."

"Someone else can take care of that, Joe. Right now the president's daughter is your responsibility."

"Sir, sending her to the hacienda is an interesting solution," he said, "but the winery is not easily guarded. There are hundreds of acres, employees, staff. Plus my relatives would have to be cleared for security purposes."

"Already done. You're right about the winery being an open space, but who would think to look for her there? The navy is cooperating with the president at his request," Phillips told him. "Unless you want to call the president and explain why you're unwilling to protect his daughter?"

Joe felt the doors of the prison swing closed. "What is my assignment, sir?"

"Coordinate with the Secret Service. Their job is to protect Darcy, but you are to facilitate what they need. Be another pair of eyes. Use your tactical skills to their advantage. When the kidnappers are caught, you'll return here and we'll see if the admiral has cooled off enough for you to resume your duties. In the meantime, do what you can to keep Darcy Jensen happy."

Joe rose and saluted. "Yes, sir," he said and left.

He was completely and totally screwed, sent away in disgrace, his career in jeopardy. He would be lucky to come back as an ensign.

As for keeping Darcy Jensen happy—from what he'd heard, that was a task even a SEAL couldn't pull off.

2

❧

*D*arcy heard the murmurings of her temporary Secret Service team before she heard the knock on the door. The whispered "Swan is here" warned her of her sister's approach.

She stayed in her apartment bedroom, one of the guys in suits would get the door, and continued her packing. In less than four hours she would be whisked away to an undisclosed location for however long it took to find the crazies after her sister. Based on the Secret Service's current level of competency, she could be gone for months.

Not knowing where she was headed made packing a problem. All she knew was she was staying in the continental United States and that she was expected to stay very low-key when she arrived.

News flash—she didn't want to walk around flaunting herself. One kidnapping in a lifetime was more than enough.

She grabbed a handful of shorts, some T-shirts and jeans, and tossed them on the bed.

The bedroom door opened and Lauren entered. The

two Secret Service agents with her hovered in the hall then nodded at the single agent standing in the corner of Darcy's bedroom.

Lauren crossed to Darcy, grabbed her upper arms, and stared into her eyes.

"Are you okay?" she asked, sounding near tears. "Did they hurt you?"

Darcy had a few bruises from her ride in the back of the van, some sore muscles, and several raw spots around her wrists from the ropes. She hadn't slept at all the previous night and couldn't imagine ever not feeling afraid again. But the agent in the room kept her from saying all that.

"I'm fine," she said.

Lauren didn't release her. "Are you sure? I was so worried."

A change, Darcy thought. In the past year, *she'd* been the one worried about Lauren.

"If anything had happened to you . . . ," Lauren said, those threatening tears finally making an appearance. "I couldn't stand to lose one more person I love."

Darcy appreciated the sentiment, knew it was true, and told herself neither of them had time for a breakdown. Lauren had finally surfaced from the emotional devastation of the shocking death of her young husband, and Darcy refused to let her sink back into despair over a botched kidnapping. Darcy might be hearing things go bump in the night, but she refused to let her sister be afraid.

She drew in a deep breath as she took in Lauren's outfit. The aqua and pink sundress just grazed generous curves in unwrinkled perfection. Delicate pearls graced her sister's tiny ears. Her sling backs matched her purse, and a narrow woven silver and pearl bracelet completed the ensemble. She wore her long, wavy blond hair pulled back in an elegant clasp. She would fit in equally well having lunch at the club or hosting an afternoon charity event.

"Why do you always have to dress like an Easter egg?" Darcy asked. "Do you own anything in a primary color? I know you could never wear black. How scandalous. The heavens would open and weep."

Lauren's intense gaze never wavered. "At least I don't dress like a former rock groupie in mourning. Does every single outfit have to be tone-on-tone black? It's summer, for heaven's sake. Lighten up and wear a color."

Darcy felt the corners of her mouth turn up slightly. Lauren began to giggle. Laughter escaped, and then they were hugging each other tight. Darcy hung on tighter than usual.

"When they told me what happened, I nearly died," Lauren whispered in her ear. "I'm so sorry. I wish it had been me."

Darcy straightened. "No, you don't. Trust me on that."

"But they wanted me instead of you."

"Don't they all. That's the world in which we live. I've gotten used to it."

"Darcy, don't." Lauren sighed. "I feel horrible."

"Don't. Do you know where they're taking you?" she asked.

"No. You?"

"I want to be safe. Something I'm not sure the moron brigade can do."

Lauren shot the agent in the room an apologetic

glance then turned on her sister. "Darcy, no. You can't be mad at your team."

"Why not? If they'd been doing their job, I wouldn't have been taken." From the corner of her eye she saw the agent flinch. Well, too bad. If they'd been doing their job, she would never have realized that she was at risk.

She'd had Secret Service protection for years and had never considered it more than an annoyance. She'd always known that she and Lauren were technically possible targets, but she'd felt safe surrounded by the grim-faced agents. Not anymore.

"It's not completely their fault," Lauren said. "No one was expecting you to be kidnapped."

Darcy snorted. "It's their job to expect the unexpected. They're professionals."

"I know, but they didn't mean for anything bad to happen to you."

"Oh. They didn't *mean* it. Then that makes it all right."

Lauren might technically be the firstborn, but she had the personality of a middle child—always seeing the other person's side of things. It was a trait Darcy found annoying on occasion, even as she admired it.

"Darcy . . . ," her sister began.

Darcy waved her off. "Don't sweat it. They'll be on their toes now. That's what matters. So we'll head off to our separate but equal locations and wait for the crazies to be caught."

And then what? She'd tried to live a normal life, but it was impossible while her father was in office.

"There was so much to cancel," Lauren said. "I had two benefits, and I was going to be at a state dinner." She frowned. "Weren't you flying to New York?"

"Yeah." Darcy didn't want to think about that either.

Lauren groaned. "Your interview. When is it?"

"Monday."

Being the president's daughter put her in the unique position of being unemployable in her chosen field. She was a graphic artist with a master's in marketing. But, as the dozens of companies she'd applied to over the past couple of years had told her, no client wanted to turn down a presentation by someone so close to the president. It could be very bad for business. Rather than put their clients in such an awkward position, she'd been passed over time and again.

A small firm in New York *had* been willing to take a chance on her. Now she was unlikely to make her second interview, and telling them why wasn't going to make them want to hire her.

"Maybe if you explained," Lauren said, looking so earnest Darcy actually laughed.

"What? That I was recently kidnapped and have to lay low until the culprits are found? I don't think that will win me employee of the month."

Lauren sighed. "I know this life is hard for you."

"And I know you love it," Darcy said without rancor. It was true—public life suited her sister. Lauren was never happier than when she was cutting a ribbon at some hospital wing opening, or serving as their father's hostess for a formal dinner for three hundred. Darcy would rather be staked naked in the desert on top of a nest of fire ants.

"I'll be fine," she said before tender-hearted Lauren started to cry again. "Don't worry about it. Have you met your new security team?" she asked, to change the subject to something more neutral.

"No. Have you?"

"Just one of them. Alex Vanmeter. He's downstairs. He looks competent, but I'll be grilling him later to make sure he knows what he's doing."

Lauren stared at her. "The incredibly hunky guy who looks like a street fighter? I'm sure he'll keep you safe."

"I wish I was sure." Darcy shook her head. "You know, I'm actually *not* interested in his looks right now. He could be a troll, as long as he's a troll who knows what he's doing."

She crossed to her dresser and pulled out bras and panties, then tucked them into the suitcase. She'd already packed up her art supplies and her laptop.

Lauren walked to the window and stared down at the Secret Service team below. "What happened to the two guys assigned to you?" she asked.

"I don't have a clue." Darcy didn't think they were in a good place for having lost her. "Don't worry. I doubt they were taken out back and shot." Although in her mind, they more than deserved a good beating. Or maybe a kidnapping. Let them feel what she'd experienced. Toss them in the back of a filthy van driven by demon-headed guys named Bill and force them to open a purse with their teeth.

"Don't even joke about that," Lauren said. "I feel bad for them. And you, of course."

"Of course. Doesn't seeing both sides ever make you tired?"

Lauren rolled her eyes. "Desperately. I mostly do it to make you crazy."

Darcy grinned. "You usually succeed."

"I'm glad." Lauren turned serious. "You'll be all right, won't you?"

Darcy figured that in time she would be able to sleep and the flashes of terror would recede. Until then, she would simply fake her way through it. That had always worked for her before. "I promise."

"I guess we'll be able to talk by phone on secure lines. I want to hear about everything."

"Me, too."

Lauren moved close, and they hugged again. "I love you," her sister whispered.

"I love you, too. Be good."

"That's my line," Lauren said as she stepped back and waved.

Darcy watched her go then turned back to her packing. For the moment, the fear was gone, but in its place was a dark and lonely space.

Joe arrived at the Marcelli winery shortly after four in the afternoon. He'd put off leaving as long as he could, which had meant all of the morning, but he'd known better than to linger much past noon. He might be entering hell on earth, but he was still a naval officer. His job was to follow orders.

As he turned onto the road that led to the three-story hacienda, he studied the pale yellow stucco structure as he might an enemy target, or a place he would have to defend.

Too many windows and exits, he thought grimly as he took in the French doors leading to balconies and the decorative wrought iron that would allow someone in reasonable shape to climb from flower beds to the tile roof. Trees that others would think provided comfortable shade in the August heat showed him places snipers could hide.

Beyond the house was a multicar garage that could conceal at least fifty armed men, and less than a quarter mile beyond that were the various buildings of the winery.

Perfect, he thought grimly as he pulled his truck up behind the house and turned off the engine. Maybe someone could call in one of those entertainment networks to announce Darcy Jensen's location to add to the challenge.

The rear door of the house opened, and a man stepped onto the porch. Joe recognized Marco Marcelli, his biological father.

"Joe! You're here."

Marco hurried to the truck and met Joe as he closed the driver's door behind him.

Marco studied him for a second before wrapping both arms around Joe in a welcoming hug. Joe accepted the embrace—to do otherwise would invite conversations he didn't want to have, then when he was free, he stepped back and glanced around.

"A lot of grapes," he said, motioning to the vines heavy with fruit.

"A good year," Marco said. "Brenna and Grandpa Lorenzo are excited about the harvest. More wine means more excuses for Colleen and me to travel as we sell the wine. I'm not complaining."

Joe nodded, as if the information had meaning. The Marcellis *were* wine. Marco's children were the fourth generation to grow grapes on this stretch of land. He and his wife, Colleen, were responsible for sales.

Marco patted the side of the truck. "You usually travel light."

"I don't know how long I'm going to be here," Joe said, wishing that wasn't the case. "I couldn't fit everything on my motorcycle, so I rented the truck."

"They haven't told us much," Marco told him. "But several people from the government have been all over the property and have spoken with everyone in the family. They picked you to help."

Joe heard the pride in Marco's voice and thought about telling him that the only reason any of this was happening was because Joe's men had screwed up.

"I thought I'd brief everyone at once," Joe said. "I guess we should do that first, before I unpack."

Marco patted his shoulder. "It's good that you're staying here for a while, Joe. We want . . ." The older man hesitated. "We're helping because of you."

Joe knew what he was trying to do—show that the family would be there for him. Marco, like every other Marcelli, had spent the past three years doing his best to convince Joe he was one of them.

Joe knew different. He might share bloodlines, but they had nothing else in common, and they would never be his family.

"Tessa made up your room," Marco said.

"I appreciate that." He looked at the man who thought of himself as Joe's father. "You know this is temporary. I'm only staying until the job is done."

Marco nodded. "Of course. You're still a navy man."

The back door opened again. A small, elderly woman

with gray hair piled on her head walked onto the porch. "Joseph? Is that you? So that's what they're teaching officers these days? That it's polite to keep an old woman waiting?"

Despite his dislike of the assignment and the pressure he felt being back at the winery, Joe couldn't help smiling as he crossed to the house and climbed the three back stairs.

"No, Tessa, that's not what they teach me," he said as he bent down to gather her close. Too late he remembered her need to pinch every cheek in range. Her forefinger and thumb closed over his skin with enough strength to snap steel. He might have survived a gunshot wound and a couple of knife fights, but man, could she make him wince.

"Let me look at you," she said, grabbing him by the hand and dragging him into the kitchen. "The government has sent people here. They talk to us and ask questions. They say we need clearance, but they won't say for what." She humphed. "As if we would be a danger to anyone. Now."

She stopped in the center of the kitchen and studied him from head to toe. Her dark eyes missed nothing as she frowned and poked him in the stomach. "You're not eating enough. You look skinny."

"I weigh exactly the same as I did the last time I was here," he told her.

"You were too skinny then, too. All that exercise. It's not good for you. I'm going to feed you while you're here. You'll eat good food. What do you have at the place you live? Junk food? A man your age on his own. It's not a good thing." Her expression softened as she took his hand in hers and rubbed his fingers. "Joseph, you need to be married, eh? A wife would know how to take care of you."

It was a familiar conversation, one he refused to participate in. "Who else is at the hacienda?" he asked.

Grandma Tessa narrowed her gaze. "Your mother and Lorenzo. They'll be here in a few minutes. So what is this all about?"

Just then Colleen Marcelli walked into the kitchen. She was a well-dressed, petite woman a year or so shy of fifty. Her stylish clothes and unlined face made her look much younger, but Joe could do the math. He'd just turned thirty-three, which meant Colleen had had him when she was still in high school.

"Joe," she breathed when she saw him. Her expression blended hope and longing in a painful combination. He could deal with the rest of them, but seeing Colleen always made him feel guilty. He couldn't shake the sense of being a real bastard every time he held her at arm's length. He knew what she wanted—what they all wanted.

Rather than deal with the guilt, he stepped forward and hugged her. Before he straightened, Lorenzo Marcelli, the aging patriarch, strolled into the kitchen.

"So, you're back," the elder Marcelli growled. "They're snooping around here like we're a bunch of terrorists. Send them away."

"Not in my job description," Joe said as he released his mother and shook hands with Marco's father. "You're looking well."

"I'm old," Lorenzo said. "This is all a bunch of nonsense."

"Pop, it's not so bad," Marco said.

"You don't even know what's going on," Lorenzo

complained. "None of us do. If those agents trample even one grape, there will be hell to pay."

"Lorenzo!" Tessa reached into her apron pocket and pulled out a rosary. "Don't say that."

"It's true." Lorenzo thumped the cane he'd started using about a year ago and made his way to the large kitchen table in the center of the room. "Well, get on with it. Tell us why we've been taken over like an enemy country."

Joe nodded at Marco, who led Colleen and Tessa to chairs by Lorenzo's. When they were seated, he began.

"What I'm about to tell you is classified information. You are not to discuss it with anyone outside of the immediate family."

Tessa reached for Lorenzo's hand, and Colleen shivered. "That sounds so serious," she said nervously.

"It is," he told her. "Two days ago the president's daughter was kidnapped. She got away, but the kidnappers are still out there."

Tessa gasped and clutched her beads tighter. "Who would do that? She's a lovely girl. So pretty and always helping with those little children."

Colleen nodded. "It was so sad when she lost her husband. Their wedding was so beautiful. They'd barely been married a year when he was killed in that car accident. She got so sad afterward." She reached for Marco. "I can't imagine what she must have gone through, missing him so much."

Lorenzo frowned. "What does this have to do with us? What do we care about his daughter?"

"Lorenzo!" Tessa glared at him. "We care. Lauren Jensen-Smith is a lovely girl." She turned her attention to

Joe. "How can we help?" Even as she asked the question, her breath caught. "Oh! Is she coming here?"

"Not exactly," Joe said, wondering why they'd done the same thing he had—jumped to the conclusion that it was Lauren who was in trouble and not Darcy.

"You'll have the president's daughter here, but it won't be Lauren," he said. "It will be the other one. Darcy."

There was a moment of silence. Colleen released her husband's arm and smoothed down her skirt. "I'm sure she's very nice, too."

"That other one?" Lorenzo asked. "I don't know anything about her. Except she never bothered to get married and have babies to make her family proud."

With that he pushed to his feet and used his cane to help him turn. "This is all a waste of time if you ask me," he grumbled as he slowly limped out of the room.

Tessa rose as well. "Are you sure they're not sending Lauren? A nice, pretty girl like that needs to be married." She smiled at him. "Maybe to an officer."

Joe held in a groan. Right. Because his life wasn't hellish enough already. Fortunately a knock on the back door prevented him from responding. He crossed the kitchen and opened it.

"Lieutenant Commander Joseph Larson?" the woman on the other side asked.

He nodded.

"I'm Special Agent Paige Newberry. I saw you arrive and thought I would introduce myself to you and meet the family."

She stepped inside and shook his hand. Paige was tall, only a couple of inches shorter than his own six feet. She wore a dark pants suit and a concealed sidearm. Short hair framed attractive features.

He was used to judging people in a matter of seconds. Joe's first impression of Special Agent Newberry was that she was intelligent, competent, and ready to play on a team. Thank God he wasn't in this alone.

Joe had been briefed early that morning. While the Secret Service was in charge of Darcy and her protection, Joe was there to act as liaison with the family and to offer any expertise the Secret Service might require. As he doubted they wanted or needed his help, he was little more than a glorified babysitter. None of which was the agent's fault.

Joe led her into the kitchen.

"This is Special Agent Paige Newberry," he said. "She's in charge of Darcy Jensen's personal security."

"Actually Special Agent Alex Vanmeter is in charge of this operation," Paige said with a smile. "He's with Darcy right now. They'll be arriving in the morning. I am, however, one of the agents who will be in close contact with Darcy at all times."

Tessa nodded. "You call her by her first name?"

"Yes, ma'am. At her request."

"This is Tessa Marcelli," Joe said by way of introduction. "Marco Marcelli and his wife, Colleen."

Paige shook hands with all of them. Colleen moved to the ever-present coffeepot and began to pour. "This is really difficult to take in. The president's daughter. Here. What are we supposed to do? How do we act? What do *we* call her?"

Paige smiled. "I think she'd like Darcy best. In fact I would prefer that you use first names with all of us. That way we don't call attention to ourselves."

Colleen looked at her dark suit. "I don't mean to be rude, but you're not exactly fitting in with the locals."

"I know. I brought more casual clothes with me. I thought I'd wait until Special Agent Vanmeter arrives before changing."

Joe stared at Paige. There was something about the way she said "Special Agent Vanmeter." He couldn't put his finger on the inflection, but he would bet it meant something.

"You've worked with him before?" he asked.

Paige nodded. "He's excellent. Very thorough. Darcy will be safe, as will your family, Lieutenant Commander."

"We agreed on first names," Joe said.

"Of course."

Tessa began pulling food out of the refrigerator. "Sit. Sit. You need to eat. Marco, bring Paige some wine."

"Oh, no thanks. I can't drink on duty."

Tessa waved away her words. "You said Darcy won't arrive until the morning. Be on duty then."

Joe led her to the table and sat across from her. In a matter of seconds, seemingly from nowhere, food appeared. Salads, fixings for sandwiches, three kinds of cookies, bread, cheese, and of course pasta. He was used to the quantity of the spread, but Paige looked stunned.

Joe grinned. "You'd better eat, or they'll get surly."

"Of course you'll eat," Tessa said as she set wine-glasses in front of them. "So, Paige, are you married?"

Thirty minutes later, Paige and Joe escaped the clutches of Grandma Tessa, as she'd insisted on being called, and stepped out in the sunset. Paige had enjoyed the home-cooked food, even if it came with a pretty big side of matchmaking.

"Interesting family," she said.

"She's determined to get me married," Joe said flatly.

"Yet you've stood strong against her all these years. Impressive."

He shrugged then glanced around at the vineyards, which stretched for miles.

"Do you really think you can protect Darcy Jensen here?" he asked.

Paige wasn't sure if his question was simple conversation or a genuine concern. "The location is a compromise, but I think it's a good one. Who knows how long it will take to track down the kidnappers? I understand Darcy's need to be in a place where she won't get claustrophobic."

"Better claustrophobic than dead."

"Agreed, but we're going to keep her alive." She walked toward the guesthouse, which would serve as both her sleeping quarters and temporary headquarters. "Darcy will be kept close to the house for the first few days. We'll have agents in the tasting rooms and other tourist areas to keep them from getting anywhere near the hacienda. I've already spoken with Brenna Marcelli about that. She was more than cooperative." She glanced at the naval officer at her side. "Your sister?"

"One of four," Joe said. "She runs this winery, along with a smaller one. Her husband owns Wild Sea."

"Right." Paige remembered her briefing notes and the interview she'd had the previous day. "Nic Giovanni. He's cooperating as well. In fact everyone has been more than helpful."

"Lucky us."

She turned to Joe. He was tall, good-looking, and had a service record that would make anyone proud. But she would bet her next three paychecks he didn't want to be here.

"You're acting as our liaison with the family," she said. "We appreciate that."

"I live to serve."

The fine hairs on the back of her neck rose. She felt like an angry cat trying to puff up to look more intimidating. She might be a hell of an agent, but Joe Marcelli had been a SEAL. In a one-on-one situation, she didn't stand a chance. Still, that wouldn't stop her from taking him on.

"Lieutenant Commander Larson," she said, keeping her voice steady and firm, "I cannot stress the importance of this assignment enough. We are protecting the life of the daughter of the president of the United States. Two days ago someone got close enough to abduct her. She was forcibly taken, tied up, and threatened. Do you think there was even one moment in her life that prepared her for that kind of terror?"

Joe didn't look much more than bored with the conversation. "I'm a naval officer, Special Agent Newberry. I'll do my job."

"Not good enough. I'm willing to take a bullet for her. If you can't offer that same level of commitment, I don't want you here."

"You don't have the authority to get rid of me."

She leaned in slightly. "Want to test that theory? Nothing is going to happen to Darcy Jensen on my watch. I don't care what I have to do or who I have to offend to keep her safe. If you're not fully on this team, then you're in my way. Do I make myself clear?"

His expression didn't change, but she saw something flash in his eyes. Respect, maybe. However grudgingly given, she would accept it.

"You like her," he said, sounding surprised.

"I do. I've worked with Darcy before. She's funny, smart, and not interested in being the center of attention. That makes my job easier, and I appreciate that. So are you on board?"

He nodded. "A hundred percent."

Paige accepted his word because she had to, but she vowed to keep an eye on him. SEAL or not—if he got in her way, she was taking him down.

Darcy had spent the previous night in a small house on the edge of Baltimore. This morning, after a short flight to Florida, she'd been delivered to another nondescript location on the edge of what looked like a massive swamp. She'd been warned not to leave the house, not to make phone calls, and not to answer the door under any circumstances.

Oh, right. Because she *wanted* to make a general statement, announcing her location to the world.

Someone knocked on the bedroom door. Darcy refused to be seen as a coward, so she uncurled on the bed and sat up.

"Come in," she said, expecting Alex Vanmeter, the special agent in charge of her security and Drew's replacement.

Alex stepped in and nodded at her. "Your father will be here in fifteen minutes."

Darcy blinked at him. "My father? He's in Chicago."

"He's flying back to D.C. tonight and is stopping by to see you."

Before Darcy could say anything, Alex touched the ever-present earpiece and then nodded. "Falcon is on the ground."

Meaning her father had landed and was being driven to the safe house.

She stood. As Alex excused himself, she entered the bathroom attached to the bedroom and ran a brush through her short, dark hair. She looked tired and either sick or shell-shocked. Makeup could help, but there wasn't much time.

Exactly fourteen minutes later, President Ryan Jensen walked into her temporary bedroom.

"Darcy," he said when his assigned agent had swept the room then left them alone. "How are you feeling?"

"I'm sure the doctors faxed you a medical report. You tell me."

Ryan Jensen had served as vice president for four years before running for the head job. He was eighteen months into his first term. The stresses of the office aged some men, but not her father. Oh, there were a few more gray hairs at his temples, but that only made him more attractive. Last year he'd had to deal with the embarrassing reality of being named the country's most eligible bachelor.

Right now, though, the leader of the free world looked annoyed and frustrated. "Darcy, I'm on a very tight schedule. I changed my flight plan to come by and see you. That has to mean something."

"It does, Dad. Really. I hope you're not keeping anyone

important waiting. I mean it's been nearly forty-eight hours since the kidnapping. I wouldn't have wanted you to rush to my side or anything."

His gaze narrowed. "I phoned when I was informed about the kidnapping."

"You did, and it was a very touching call. Did I thank you for it? I meant to."

"You're impossible," he muttered. "Fine. Be angry with me or whomever you'd like. Regardless, I'm glad you're all right and I want you to stay safe. For once, listen to what the agents tell you to do, will you?"

The unfairness of the request took her breath away. She'd *always* listened. They were the ones who had let *her* down.

But what was the point in trying to explain anything? Ryan Jensen had stopped hearing her years ago.

"Be grateful you got away without getting hurt," he added.

Darcy thought about the still-healing scratches on her legs, the rope burns on her wrists, and the pain in her heart. There had been plenty of wounding, but it wasn't the kind he meant.

Someone knocked on the closed door. Ryan Jensen glanced toward it, then back at her. "I need to get to Washington. You'll have a secure line up and running at your safe house in a day or so. Check in and let me know how you are."

"It's what I live for," she told him.

"Dammit, Darcy." He looked at her, started to speak, then caught himself. He turned away and was gone.

When she was alone again, Darcy crawled back onto the bed and pulled her knees to her chest. He was a busy man. She should be grateful he'd diverted to Florida to see her. It could almost mean something.

But instead of convincing herself, she remembered a dark night ten years before. When he'd glared at her and yelled that she wasn't his daughter. She never had been.

Later, he'd apologized. He'd spoken in anger and grief. He hadn't meant it.

Regardless of his contrition, he'd spoken the truth. Ryan Jensen *wasn't* her father. That long-ago night the lies fell away, and his words had changed her forever.

3

*T*he plane left Florida shortly after daybreak, which, with the time difference, meant an early arrival in California. Darcy hadn't known their destination until an hour into the flight, when Alex Vanmeter had informed her they would be landing at a naval base north of Los Angeles.

As she stepped off the plane usually used to transport the vice president, she saw three black SUVs parked on the tarmac. Secret Service agents flanked her, making it difficult to get down the steep flight of stairs. The second her feet touched the ground, Alex moved in, took her arm, and hustled her to the middle SUV. He opened the door and slid in beside her.

"Pigeon is safe," he said into the microphone at the inside of his left wrist. "Move out."

Seconds later, all three vehicles drove away from the plane.

"At least you're taking my security seriously," she said as she gazed out the window.

"We always have."

"Really? I have a kidnapping that says, not so much."

"The other team screwed up. That won't happen on my watch."

"I really want to believe you, but you're going to have to earn my trust. If that sort of thing matters."

"It does. A comfortable subject is more likely to cooperate."

She glanced at the man sitting next to her. Late thirties, she would guess. About five ten and strong. She could see the ripple of muscles through the suit jacket he wore. There was something about him. Something not quite civilized. As if he hadn't grown up in the company of polite society.

Bad boy turned good guy? She wouldn't want to bet against him in a street fight, a thought she found comforting.

"Do you really think after what happened I'm going to be difficult?" she asked.

"You have a reputation for being a pain in the ass."

Darcy knew all about that. The press wasn't fond of her because when her father had been running for vice president, she'd traveled in the press bus as part of an internship project for one of her college classes. Instead of reporting on the campaign, she'd written an exposé on several members of the press corps, detailing who had substance-abuse problems, who was having an affair, and who had a thing for underaged campaign workers.

She also didn't play the political game very well. But she'd never screwed with her Secret Service team.

"Get back to me with exactly one time when I ducked out or escaped them," she said, holding her temper in check. "Or when I did something they told me not to do. I might have a reputation for being difficult, Alex, but I'm not stupid."

Darcy turned to look at the SUV in front of theirs. To the casual observer, their little convoy was nothing more than three vehicles on the same road. No one else would know there were a total of seven agents and one relative of the president leaving the navy base that morning.

"Where's Lauren going?" she asked.

Alex glanced at her. His dark blue eyes never wavered. "I'm not at liberty to say."

"Because I'm a security risk?"

"Because the fewer people who know, the better. You don't want anything happening to your sister."

He made it a statement rather than a question, but it was still true.

Darcy leaned back in the leather seat and wondered what would happen now. How long would she be kept isolated for her own good, and when could she get back to her regular life, such as it was? She'd already called and canceled her interview in New York. There was no way she could make it, and she wasn't allowed to explain the reason why. Normal was something the rest of the world took for granted. What she wouldn't give to be one of them, even for a little while.

Alex glanced at her. "Have you slept since the kidnapping?"

"Of course," she lied, not wanting to talk to him about it. Alex Vanmeter might be exactly the right person to keep her safe, but he wasn't the warm and friendly type. Besides, she didn't generally confide in people she'd just met. With enough concealer and the right light, she could keep her lack of sleep a secret until she was able to close her eyes without feeling the fear.

The lead SUV signaled a turn. Darcy glanced out the window and realized they were leaving the freeway and heading into what looked like a very picturesque part of Tuscany.

"They grow grapes here?" she asked as she stared at acres and acres of vineyards.

"Yes. The Marcelli family has owned this land over eighty years. Four generations of winemakers."

"Marcelli." The name was vaguely familiar. "As in Marcelli Wines?"

He nodded.

"This is where I'll be staying?" she asked.

"Yes. The family was pleased to cooperate. You should be safe here."

Darcy looked at the heavy, lush grapevines, the tall trees lining the road, and the vineyard sparkling in the distance.

"Not bad duty," she said, picturing an old-style bed-and-breakfast with a view of the ocean. No doubt she and her Secret Service team would take over a wing of the building. There wouldn't be much to do, but she could catch up on her reading. Lying low had never looked so good.

Fifteen minutes later they turned off the road and onto a long driveway. Darcy didn't see any signs for a hotel or a bed-and-breakfast. Instead she saw what looked like a large, pale yellow, three-story house decorated with wrought iron balconies. There were several outbuildings, plenty of trees, and a colorful garden complete with a path and small benches.

"What's with the house?" she asked as the SUV pulled to a stop.

"The Marcelli family has lived here since it was built in the late twenties," Alex said.

They must own the B and B, too. Made sense.

Alex stepped out of the SUV and waited for her to do the same. Darcy climbed out and looked around. The air was still and warm, scented with fruit. Make that grapes, she thought as the back door opened and several people hurried down the stairs to the driveway.

There was an older couple, a not so old couple, an amazingly good-looking guy, some Secret Service agents—easily recognizable by the sunglasses and the dark suits—and Special Agent Paige Newberry.

"Paige," Darcy said, grateful to see at least one familiar face. "At least one person here knows what she's doing."

"Hi, Darcy." Paige stepped forward and smiled. "How was your trip?"

"Good. Long."

Darcy was conscious of everyone watching her. She smoothed the front of her casual black and white sundress. Aware that first impressions mattered, she'd dressed carefully, using makeup, putting on sandals, and digging out another of her bargain handbags that matched.

She knew her sister would have had something disarming to say, and that in a matter of minutes the entire cast of the Make Room for Lauren ensemble would have been delighted to be a part of her life. Darcy hadn't received the gift of small talk. Still, she would play the professional political family member, even if she wasn't that good at it.

"Good morning," she said, telling herself to smile to cover her nervousness as she spoke. "I'm Darcy Jensen."

"Of course you are," the older man said as he thumped his cane on the ground. "This is all a bunch of nonsense if you ask me. She's here. We're here. Now let's get inside before someone gets sunstroke."

"Lorenzo!" The elderly woman at his side scolded him. "She's the president's daughter. Show a little respect."

Paige stepped between them. "Darcy, allow me to present Mr. and Mrs. Lorenzo Marcelli. They own the winery and all the property here." Paige pointed to the slightly younger couple. "This is their son, Marco, and his wife, Colleen. And Lieutenant Commander Joe Larson." Paige hesitated. "He's a former SEAL and our naval liaison with the family."

"Because I'm in danger of being kidnapped and taken out to sea?" Darcy asked. "That's comforting. Be sure someone stocks me up with Dramamine. Any other surprises?"

"That's not why I'm here—" the lieutenant commander said, but he was interrupted when Mrs. Marcelli senior stepped forward.

"I'm Tessa," she said with a smile. "You should call me Grandma Tessa. Everyone does." She grabbed Darcy's upper arms as she studied her. "You're much prettier in person than in the pictures. You should smile more. Welcome. It's good to have you here."

Then, before Darcy could react to the comment or the advice, the small, elderly woman reached up and pinched her cheek. The squeeze sent pain shooting through her entire face and made her eyes water.

"Mama, not so hard," Marco said, putting his arm

around his mother and pulling her back. "Don't scare our guest off." He smiled. "Paige said we were to call you by your first name. Are you comfortable with that?"

Darcy nodded, still caught up in the pain in her cheek. That little old lady could twist wood with that grip.

Darcy shook hands with Marco, his wife, and most of the Secret Service team. Last up was Joe Larson.

He was tall—maybe six feet—and muscled. Not as big, pound for pound, as Alex, but still a lot of man. He might be navy, but she would bet he could give any member of her team a run for his, or her, money.

A former SEAL was good, she thought. He'd probably killed bad guys before. She would have to remember to stick close to him.

"Lieutenant Commander," she said as she stared into eyes as dark as a storm. They shook hands.

"We should probably get inside," Paige said.

The elder Marcelli led the way, followed by his wife. Darcy motioned for Marco and Colleen to follow.

Darcy paused at the bottom of the steps. "I don't get it. Are we staying here?"

"Yes," Paige told her. "You'll be in the main house with the family. Alex and I are in the guesthouse."

Darcy couldn't believe it. "Here? Have you looked around? Open fields. How are you going to keep me safe? There have to be a thousand places for people to hide."

"They're not open fields, they're vineyards," Alex said.

She glared at him. "Thanks for the clarification. I'll be doing a crossword puzzle later. You can stop by and help."

Paige touched her arm. "Darcy, this is a good location

for you. There's plenty of protection, but you won't feel trapped or isolated. Plus the family is pretty cool."

She wasn't interested in the family or anything but not feeling afraid.

"I don't like it," she said.

"Tough. Until I hear otherwise from the president, this is where you're staying," Alex said sharply.

"Alex, no." Paige turned to Darcy. "Let's give it a couple of days. I think you'll like it here."

Darcy ignored her. "You're the agent in charge?" she asked Alex.

"Yes."

"Then you better do your job. Because I will take this up with my father."

A bluff, but Alex didn't know that.

Alex shook his head. "Take care of her," he told Paige, then stalked away.

Paige looked at Darcy. "You're in a mood. What's going on?"

Darcy grimaced. "I know. I'm sorry. I'm tired, I'm scared. My team let me be kidnapped. I'm a little wary of that happening again."

"Alex is the best," Paige told her. "We're all here to keep you safe."

"The words sound good, but I'm not much of a believer."

The back door opened, and Joe Larson stuck out his head. "You two coming?"

"Right away," Paige said easily. "I was explaining to Darcy that there are even more Marcellis in her future."

"How many more?" Darcy asked.

"Dozens," Joe said as he stepped out onto the porch.

"Four sisters, three spouses, three and a half kids. More grandparents, too. Or at least one more. Mary-Margaret O'Shea, better known as Grammy M."

Darcy didn't know what to do with all that information. There was no way she could keep that many people straight.

"Have they all been checked out?" she asked Paige.

The Secret Service agent smiled. "Yes, and they're all cleared. I've met most of them, but not Grammy M a.k.a. Mary-Margaret O'Shea." She pulled a small notebook out of her jacket pocket and flipped through the pages. "She's living just south of Santa Barbara with Gabriel Reese. He's the grandfather of one of the Marcelli granddaughters' husbands."

Darcy blinked. "I'll never keep this straight."

Paige grinned. "You'll have time to study before the quiz."

Joe held open the back door. "Food's waiting."

Darcy hesitated, then stepped past him and entered a massive kitchen and was confronted by what had to be three tons of food.

Grandma Tessa and Colleen carried trays to a huge kitchen table by a row of windows. There were platters of meats, bowls of pastas, mounds of salads, along with at least three different kinds of bread. The scent of simmering sauces competed with the fragrance of cinnamon and fruit.

The elderly Marcelli walked into the kitchen. "It's ten-thirty in the morning," he grumbled. "Only a fool would eat now."

"Lorenzo, stop. We have company. Darcy, come." Grandma Tessa took her arm. "You must be hungry. All that travel."

As tempting as it all looked, Darcy couldn't imagine keeping down food. She felt too unsettled. But before she could say anything, Lorenzo limped over to stand in front of her.

"How old are you?" he demanded.

"Twenty-six."

"Ha." He grabbed her left hand and looked at her bare fingers. "No ring. No husband, no babies. What is it with you women today? Listen to your parents and grandparents. Get married and have babies." He dropped her hand and poked her in the stomach. "You need babies."

Darcy took a step back. "I'll get right on that."

Colleen sighed heavily. "Lorenzo, please. Stop torturing Darcy. At least let her get settled." She looked around the kitchen and waved at Joe. "Would you take her upstairs and show her around? We've put her in Katie's old bedroom. Brenna and Francesca's is just too frightening." Colleen smiled at her. "You can unpack, then come back down and have something to eat. How does that sound?"

For once Darcy didn't have a snappy comeback. Not knowing what else to do, she smiled and said, "That would be very nice. Thank you."

She followed the naval officer out of the kitchen and down the hall.

"This way," Joe said as he headed for a flight of stairs.

The house was large and well kept. She liked the blend of colors, the earth tones that offered welcome. Although a hotel would have made her feel more safe, she could see the charm of the Marcelli home.

He led the way down a long hallway and stopped at the end. "You have your own room," he said. "It hasn't been decorated since Katie was in high school, but it's comfortable enough. You also have your own bathroom."

She stepped into a large and airy room decorated in shades of lavender. Before she could take in much more than the white eyelet bedspread and the striped wallpaper, a Secret Service agent entered her room, carrying a large suitcase. Three more followed, each with at least one bag. Paige came last. She handed Darcy a wristband.

"Automatic transmitter," she said. "So we know where you are at all times."

"I live to be a blip on a monitor." Darcy took it and snapped it into place. The cold metal was comforting. At least if someone tried to take her away, her team would be instantly alerted.

When Paige had left, Joe glanced at Darcy. "So much for being a regular person."

Surrounded by luggage, security, and wearing the human version of a homing beacon, she wasn't in a position to argue.

"Why on earth would I want to be?" she asked. "Talk about boring. So how exactly does a naval liaison know so much about the Marcelli family?"

"Colleen and Marco are my parents."

If he'd meant to surprise her, he'd succeeded. "But you have a different last name."

He shrugged. "True enough. If there's anything you need, just ask. The Marcellis lead with their hearts. The Grands will do their best to feed you to death. Colleen will hover and mother you, and the sisters will seduce you with wine, chocolate, and girls' night out."

All of which sounded like fun, but she knew better than to admit that. "Whatever," she said as she picked up one of the smaller bags and put it on the bed. "So what are you doing here? Why aren't you on a ship some- where?"

"I'm part of the team."

"You're not Secret Service."

"I'm the liaison with the family."

But why would they need one? "The navy doesn't get involved with the personal security of the president's family."

"They do now."

She looked at him. "You were a SEAL?"

"Until I got promoted out of active duty and into logis- tical planning, yes."

"At least you'll know what you're doing if the kidnap- per returns."

As the bedrooms in the guesthouse were identical, Paige had figured it was safe to claim one for herself without waiting for the special agent in charge to okay the deci- sion. She'd unpacked the night before and begun to familiarize herself with the area around the house. Now she listed all the sections that would have to be checked on a regular basis, such as outbuildings, tree groves, and storage sheds.

The front door opened. Paige sucked in a breath to brace herself then glanced up as Alex Vanmeter stalked into the small living room.

He'd gotten older, but then they both had. He was still good-looking, in a rugged, street-fighter kind of way.

Barely contained energy radiated from him, making her remember how much heat the two of them had once generated.

"She's going to make this a hell of an assignment," he said as he crossed to the refrigerator, pulled open the door, and checked the contents. "I heard she's a bitch on wheels, but I thought the other agents were lying. Obviously not."

"Yes, they were," Paige said. "Darcy isn't difficult at all." Or she hadn't been until today.

Alex grabbed a bottle of iced tea. "So you think this attitude of hers is temporary?"

Paige leaned back in her chair. "She's scared, Alex. She was just kidnapped because our department failed to keep her safe. You might want to cut her a break."

She used his first name deliberately. He might be in charge and able to pull rank, but she'd seen him naked, and she wasn't about to let him forget it.

"You've worked with her before," he said. "What do you know about her?"

"That her reputation is a lot more about the press wanting a story than about Darcy herself. She'll cooperate."

"She's not going to have a choice. Nothing is going to happen to her on my watch. I want to meet with the team in two hours. We'll review the location, set up a schedule. I want you working the house. I'll be here, mostly, coordinating everyone. The team will work in eight-hour shifts."

Paige made notes as he spoke. "Anything else?"

"Just one more thing." He moved close to the table and loomed over her. "Are you going to have a problem with me being in charge?"

"We've worked together before," she said.

"Not in quarters as close as these, and not with me running the op."

She stood, dropping her pen on the table. "I asked to be assigned to this team," she said slowly and deliberately. "I care about Darcy and I want to be a part of keeping her safe. As long as you do your job, I don't give a rat's ass who's in charge. You might be a good agent, Alex, but in private, you're not all that."

4

Darcy unpacked three pairs of linen slacks, jeans, several shirts, and five pairs of shoes, all black. As she held up her third black T-shirt, she felt her lips twitch. Dear God, she really *did* dress like a rock star groupie in mourning.

Not the best time in the world to notice, she thought as she carried her clothes to the closet. What with her being abducted the last time she'd gone to the mall, she had a feeling she would be doing all her future purchases online. But maybe she could try a color other than black. Maybe—

A knock on the door interrupted her mental list. "Come in," she called.

The door opened and a very pretty, very pregnant woman entered. She had long, dark wavy hair, olive skin, and huge brown eyes. She held a bottle of wine in one hand and a glass in the other.

"Hi, I'm Brenna," the woman said. "I can't have wine, but I figured you'd need some."

Darcy glanced at the bedside clock. "It's barely eleven in the morning."

"Sure, but you're still on East Coast time." Brenna grinned. "Trust me. With my family, you need all the help you can get. Drink early and often." She set the bottle and glass on the dresser. "Wow. You have a lot of clothes. And they're gorgeous. I'm currently shopping in the tent department of the sporting goods store. What a nightmare. Nic and I both really want kids, but I have to tell you, unless he plans to carry the next one, this is the end of the line for me."

Brenna lowered herself into the room's only chair, then sighed. "Better. Now, you look confused. What didn't I explain?"

Darcy sank down on the edge of the bed. "Who the hell *are* you?"

Brenna grinned, then started to laugh. "Sorry. Brenna Marcelli. Well, technically Brenna Giovanni. I live in the next house over, which is about two miles away. I'm one of Marco and Colleen's daughters. I run Marcelli Wines. I have my own winery, too. Four Sisters. It's doing great, but that's another story."

Darcy felt as if she'd been caught up in a tornado. "Okay. Am I in your room?"

"Nope. You're in Katie's. She has much better taste. I shared a room with my twin, Francesca, and let me tell you, you don't want to stay there. Very scary wallpaper."

"You're one of four sisters?"

Brenna nodded. "Katie's the oldest. She's married to Zach, and they have one daughter, Valerie. Francesca is my fraternal twin. She's married to Sam. They have a fifteen-year-old, his from a previous marriage, and twins who are nearly two and a half. Mia, the youngest of us, has just graduated from Georgetown with a master's in world domination. She starts her job with the State Department in September. Currently, she's traveling with friends, enjoying her last summer of leisure. And you've already met Joe."

"Yes." The good-looking naval officer. "I thought being in a political family was complicated, but we're easy compared to your relatives."

Brenna rested her right hand on her swollen belly. "Don't worry. They won't quiz you on the various relationships for at least a week. But this can't be tough duty. You're used to hanging out at state dinners. I could never do that. I'm way too opinionated."

"I avoid state dinners. That's more my sister's idea of a good time."

"Still, I can't imagine what it must be like to be the president's daughter. Everything would be so public. I mess up enough in my life that I really appreciate being anonymous."

"There are advantages to no one knowing who you are," Darcy said lightly.

Brenna's expression turned sympathetic. "They told us about the kidnapping. How terrifying. Are you doing okay?"

"I'm fine," Darcy said. "They didn't hurt me."

Brenna glanced at the marks on her wrists. "I would think they did. But you'll be safe here. There are tons of us to protect you. Not that I could really do much. Except maybe sit on the guy until he screamed for mercy. But Joe's burly. All that SEAL training. Just toss him a Q-Tip and he'll take on any enemy."

"A Q-Tip, huh? What could he do with an actual weapon?"

"Conquer the known civilized world. Oh!" She pressed down on her belly. "Someone's awake. It's time for soccer practice." She felt around on both sides of her stomach. "Just the two feet, I think. There can only be two. I couldn't take more."

"Are you expecting more?"

"I'm terrified I'm having twins. The doctor swears there's just the one heartbeat, but they've been wrong before. I'm a twin, my twin had twins, and I firmly believe God has a sense of humor. Plus, I'm huge. Francesca didn't even show until fifteen minutes before she gave birth, and Katie gained exactly twenty-seven pounds. I am a freak of nature."

Darcy wanted to be sympathetic, but she couldn't help laughing. If Brenna was an example of the Marcelli sisters, she couldn't wait to meet them all.

She heard footsteps in the hallway. Grandma Tessa appeared. "Brenna, there you are. How are you feeling? Are your feet swollen?"

Brenna raised a foot. "Pretty much all the time since late June."

"When are you due?" Darcy asked.

"The end of September. Another seven weeks. I don't think I can stand it. Can someone just knock me out until after the delivery?"

Grandma Tessa reached in the pocket of her dress and pulled out a rosary. "Don't talk like that. Babies are a blessing."

Brenna leaned toward Darcy. "It's never good when Grandma Tessa takes a trip around the beads. Just so you know."

Darcy grinned. "Thanks."

Tessa sniffed. "You're already teaching our guest to be disrespectful. What will your mother think? What will the president think?"

"You don't have to worry about him," Darcy said. "I won't tell."

Grandma Tessa returned her rosary to her pocket. "Lunch is at twelve-thirty. Brenna, you're staying. I called Nic, and he's joining us. Darcy." The old woman reached for her hand. "We're so happy to have you here with us. I'm going to put you across from Joseph. A pretty face like yours will help his appetite. He doesn't eat enough. Plus, an officer, eh? Think how nice everyone would look at the wedding." She winked, released Darcy, and left.

Darcy stared after her. "Am I being set up?"

Brenna chuckled. "Oh, yeah. Big time. Get used to it. Grandma Tessa's been trying to marry Joe off for the past three years. Matchmaking is a way of life in this family. As the president's daughter, you're something of a catch."

She wasn't sure about that. "If Joe's your brother, why does he have a different last name?"

"Ah, that's one of our more interesting stories." Brenna tucked her hair behind her ears. "My parents met and fell in love in high school. Neither set of their parents approved—young love never lasts and all that. So when my mom turned up pregnant, the families pressured her to give up the baby for adoption. Which she did."

Darcy had expected to hear about a child from a previous marriage. "So he was raised by someone else?"

Brenna nodded. "It's really sad. His adoptive parents were great, but they were killed when he was pretty young. He went into foster care. My sisters and I never knew about him. My parents married right out of high school and are obviously really happy together, but they were crushed to find out what Joe went through. But we found him, and now he's one of us." Her smile faded. "At least that's the goal."

Darcy shifted on the bed. "I didn't mean to pry, I just wondered."

"Makes sense. Grandpa Lorenzo gets on him to change his name to Marcelli, but Joe resists. He's still holding back, not ready to be one of us. Which is probably more than you wanted to know, huh?" Brenna slowly pushed to her feet. "I'm going to leave you to unpack. I have some wine I need to check on. See you at lunch."

"Okay. Thanks for the information on the family."

Brenna smiled. "There's so much more, but I don't want to scare you off on your first day. But I'm sure Katie, Mia, and Francesca will be visiting before long. Brace yourself. Remember what I said about drinking wine. It really helps."

Joe did his best to duck out of lunch. The last thing he wanted was a big family meal and a lot of questions about his career—as in why wasn't he leaving the navy to move to the winery—and his love life—had he met someone, when was he getting married and having babies? But when he opened the back door to make his escape, he saw Grammy M and Gabriel arriving, and he could no more run out on her than he could back a car over a puppy. Tessa might perform the strongest cheek pinch on three continents, but Grammy M's warm smile and lilting Irish voice got him every time.

"Joe," she said warmly as she climbed out of the large yellow Cadillac. "I'd heard you'd come home. It's been far too long since we've set eyes on you."

He walked down to hug the tiny, old woman. "I've been busy."

"Too busy for those who love you most?" she asked gently. "'Tis a sad thing when a grandson stays away."

"I'm here now," he told her.

"So I see. Along with the president's daughter. Who would have thought. Is she pretty?"

Joe didn't want to think about Darcy Jensen or the fact that he'd been *aware* of her from the first second he'd seen her. "She's okay."

Gabriel got out of the car and reached for his cane. "That Lauren's a real looker. I can't say much about her sister. Still, a kidnapping had to take some of the starch out of her sails."

He limped up to join Grammy M, then took her arm. "Step aside, sonny," he snapped. "I'll be escorting my woman to lunch if you don't mind."

Grammy M giggled. "Oh, Gabriel. Don't talk like that in front of the young people. You know it makes them uncomfortable."

"My grandson doesn't mind," Gabriel said with a cackle. "He likes knowing the family plumbing still works at my age."

Joe winced. He was with Grammy M on this particular topic.

He followed the older couple into the kitchen, where he found it in the usual Marcelli chaos. Tessa and Colleen carried huge bowls and platters of food to the dining room. Nic had arrived. He managed to call out a greeting to Joe as he helped a very pregnant Brenna out of a chair. Marco carried in several bottles of wine, then paused to kiss his mother-in-law on the cheek. The action caused Tessa to notice that Grammy M had arrived.

"So you're here," Tessa said in a chilly voice.

"I wanted to meet Darcy," Grammy M told her serenely. "So she could see we weren't all rigid and judgmental."

Tessa bristled. "I'm not sure you should be around a young woman like that. You could send her down the dark path to hell."

Marco headed for his mother while Joe took Grammy M by the arm.

"Let's get you and Gabriel seated," he said, leading her into the dining room.

"Nowhere near the likes of her," Grammy M said. "She's turned cruel and difficult. It's amazing what old age will do to a body."

Gabriel leaned close. "She's jealous."

Grammy M smiled and patted his hand. "Perhaps. I just . . ." Her voice trailed off. "No use crying over spilled milk, as my nana used to say. 'Tis her loss."

Brenna waddled into the room. "You're both stubborn," she said as Nic wrapped his arm around her thick waist. "You two have been friends for what, thirty-plus years? Why let things get in the way now?"

Grammy M picked up her napkin. "Ask Tessa. She started it. Tellin' me I had to choose between her and Gabriel. As if she resented my happiness. That's not friendship."

Nic patted Brenna's shoulder. "Did I tell you not to get involved? Did you listen?"

"I hate that they don't talk. It's not right."

Tessa bustled into the room. "Sit everyone. The food's all ready. Brenna, you're there, with Nic beside you. No, save that seat. It's for Darcy. She'll be across from Joe."

Everyone turned to look at him as he held in a groan. Shit. He'd been home less than twenty-four hours and this was Tessa's second attempt at matchmaking.

Marco came in with a tray of pasta. Colleen followed with baskets of bread. Joe retreated to the kitchen, thinking if he helped carry things maybe he could escape being the center of attention for once.

An unnecessary plan, he realized when he returned and found everyone focused on Darcy Jensen as she entered the dining room.

She still wore the fitted sundress she'd had on when she'd arrived. The black and white fabric hugged slender curves. He preferred women on the lush side of the scale, but she wasn't bad-looking. And she smelled good. He'd always been a sucker for that.

"If this is lunch, I'm not sure I can face dinner," Darcy said into the silence. "It, um, looks delicious."

"It is," Brenna told her. "And you're probably one of those disgusting women who can eat what she wants without gaining a pound. It makes me want to hate you, but I won't." She waved toward Grammy M. "Darcy, I don't believe you've met my maternal grandmother and Gabriel. We call her Grammy M, short for Mary-Margaret O'Shea. Gabriel Reese is her—"

"Paramour in sin," Tessa snapped. "That's right. They're living together without the benefit of marriage." She made a quick sign of the cross. "So have a seat."

Marco jumped to pull out Darcy's chair. Brenna introduced Nic while Colleen hustled her mother-in-law into the kitchen, no doubt to warn her to back off. Joe made himself busy at the buffet, opening bottles of wine.

Lorenzo walked into the dining room and took his place at the head of the table.

"Damn fool idea to have a big meal in the middle of the day," he snapped. "No one will want to work later."

"I was planning to take a nap anyway," Brenna said cheerfully. "I have to, what with not sleeping at night. Here's my question. Why nine months? Why can't pregnancy last three months, or four? Isn't that enough? I know *I'm* ready."

"Your time will come," Grammy M promised. She turned her attention to Darcy. "Welcome, child. How was your journey?"

"Good. I came here via Florida. Traveling in secret takes longer than regular travel." Darcy hesitated, as if not sure what to say. "I, um, appreciate your family taking me in. You've all been very kind."

"We're happy to have you," Colleen said as she walked back into the dining room with another tray. This one contained a roast and potatoes. After setting everything on the table, she motioned for Joe to take his seat. She did the same, with Tessa following close behind.

Lorenzo make a great show of tasting his glass of wine, then nodding. "Brenna, this is one of yours."

"That merlot-cab blend you didn't want me to bother with," she said smugly. "It's perfect, isn't it? I told you it would be." She gazed longingly at the bottle. "I swear the first thing I'm doing after I'm done breast-feeding is getting drunk. I miss wine. I can give up caffeine and processed foods and other alcohol, but I really, really miss wine."

"You'll get there," Nic said as he kissed the top of her head.

"Easy for you to say," she complained. "You get to drink what you want."

Lorenzo waited until everyone had a glass, then raised his. "Welcome, Darcy Jensen. Welcome to the family."

Brenna raised her water, everyone else picked up their wineglass. "Welcome."

Joe looked across the table at Darcy. She looked startled by both the words and the gesture, although she raised her glass and smiled.

He remembered his first reaction to the Marcelli family and had an idea of what she was feeling. Overwhelmed didn't cover it. The Marcellis tended to suck people up and make them their own. Once branded, it was difficult to escape.

As the platters and bowls were passed around, he glanced at her. She listened to the conversation around her but didn't speak much. He would have expected her to claim all the attention, but she seemed content to observe. She took small portions and didn't finish them. He could see her collarbone and the hint of ribs where her dress dipped between her breasts. Did she avoid food because of fashion or something else?

Too skinny. Not his type. And yet . . . He felt it—the subtle tension between them. A precursor to attraction.

Not to worry, he told himself. What he felt didn't matter. As long as he didn't act on it, he was fine. No woman was worth his career, certainly not this one.

"Brenna," Lorenzo said loudly. "You ordered too many barrels. We have no use for them."

"Oh, they're not all for us," she told him. "The extras are for Nic."

Nic looked at his wife with an expression of long-suffering. "I have more than enough barrels."

"No, you don't. You need to age more of your chardonnay in wood, not stainless steel. Then you blend the two together."

"Brenna, Wild Sea is my winery."

"Yes, my love, but that doesn't seem to prevent you from doing it all wrong. Take the extra barrels and use them. You'll see a big increase in the quality of the reserve chardonnay."

Darcy leaned toward him. "Why does it matter what they're stored in?" she asked.

Joe shrugged. "I haven't a clue."

As soon as he spoke, he knew he should have kept his mouth shut. But it was too late. Lorenzo set down his fork.

"You should know," he growled. "You are the first-born grandchild. The only boy. This could have all been yours. But no. You resist. Why? So you can play soldier?"

"Pop, stop it," Marco said.

"Don't worry about it," Joe told him. He was used to the old man's complaints. They didn't bother him.

"If he would just try. Give it a chance."

"Not interested," Joe told him.

"I don't know anything about wine," Darcy said. "Except that you're supposed to have red with beef. How big is the Marcelli winery?"

Joe narrowed his gaze. Had she stepped in to deflect the attention from him? Why the hell would she bother?

"More acres than you'd want to walk. I can take you

on a tour," Brenna said. "In a manner of speaking. We'll have to use carts, what with me being unable to waddle very far, but there's still a lot to see."

"Sounds like fun," Darcy said. "If it's not too much trouble."

Brenna grinned. "Are you kidding? I love the chance to show off everything I know about wine." She patted Nic's hand. "I'll explain the difference between the quality we shoot for here at Marcelli Wines and the volume they're so proud of at Wild Sea."

"Bite me," Nic said with a grin.

"I believe that's what got us into trouble in the first place," his wife told him. She turned back to Darcy. "Does tomorrow morning work for you?"

"I'm not exactly filling my social calendar these days," Darcy told her. "Name the time."

That evening, Alex walked into the small guesthouse. He'd been avoiding it for the past couple of hours, but he'd run out of work and been forced to return.

The space itself wasn't too bad. He'd turned the dining room into a command center. Computers and monitors covered the table and spilled onto the chairs. A large map of the Marcelli and Wild Sea property covered most of one wall. That left the living room as the only place to sit outside of the two bedrooms.

The rest of the team would be housed at a nearby hotel, but he and Paige would share the house and the single bathroom. He'd suffered through worse, of course. He'd slept in tents, cars, and out in the open, all in the name of getting the job done. The difference was he hadn't done it in such close quarters with Paige.

The bathroom door opened and she walked out. Her hair was damp, and she'd traded in her dark suit for a loose pair of pajama bottoms and a tank top. No bra. Her nipples were clearly visible through the thin, ribbed fabric.

It had been a long time since they'd shared a roof, and he expected her to run for cover when she saw him. When she didn't do anything but nod, he was determined to show he didn't care, either.

"They're in for the night at the house," he said. "Richards had the first shift. He'll let us know if he spots anything."

"I don't think there's going to be trouble, but it's best to be sure," she said as she walked into the kitchen and opened the refrigerator. "Did you taste the pasta Grandma Tessa sent over? It's spectacular. I'm going to have to add a couple of miles to my run every morning or I won't fit into my clothes."

As she spoke, she bent over and pulled out a covered bowl. He wasn't so much interested in the food as in the way the pajama fabric stretched over her ass. He couldn't figure out if she was just being herself or if this was all a carefully constructed plan to drive him insane.

"We need to clear the air," he said, hating how stiff he sounded.

She straightened and faced him. "Is there a problem?"

"You tell me. We started out in the same training class."

"Ah." She reached for a bowl and scooped pasta into it. "You're worried that I'm bitter. Don't sweat it, Alex. You had a couple of lucky breaks, where you got to strut your stuff. You're good, and I'm okay with that."

He hated her causal acceptance. "You used to be driven. You used to want it all." He remembered it had been a mutual decision for them to end things. They'd both been more interested in their careers than in each other.

"Not anymore." She put the small bowl in the microwave and punched in a time. "I guess I've mellowed with age. These days I'm looking for more balance in my life."

She was saying all the right things, and he hated that. "You get that from your husband?"

Her green eyes narrowed. "Yes. Not so much from his life as from his death."

Alex instantly felt like a jerk. "I'm sorry," he said.

"Thanks, but I'm okay with it now. I still miss him, but I mostly remember the good times."

With that she took her pasta from the microwave and walked to her room.

He watched her go and wondered what she remembered from their time together.

5

*D*arcy had been on plenty of tours in her time. There had been the factory that made shipping boxes—a thrilling journey into the world of cardboard—and a company devoted to the production of thread. She'd seen cheese being made, tractors, tires, microchips, and miniblinds. But never wine. Wine seemed a whole lot more interesting.

She dressed in black cargo pants and a black tank top, then carefully slathered on sunscreen. Somehow over the past couple of years she'd gotten incredibly pale. Unfortunately the lack of color only emphasized the dark circles under her eyes. Another couple of nights without sleep and even her concealer wouldn't work.

It wasn't that she didn't want to sleep, it's that the second she closed her eyes, she felt them grabbing her again. Her wrists throbbed as she remembered the rope. Fear tightened her throat and left her unable to breathe. Far better to give up sleep than face the demons in the dark.

After slipping on sandals, she hurried downstairs

where she found Joe waiting in the kitchen. There were no other Marcellis around. Just Joe sitting at the kitchen table and a tempting pot of coffee on the counter.

He glanced up from the paper. "Morning."

He looked neither friendly nor happy to see her, so she nodded a greeting and beelined for her morning jolt of caffeine. After adding the right amount of milk and sweetener, she joined him at the table and gingerly took the entertainment section of the paper.

"Not interested in what's going on in the world?" he asked from behind the paper.

"I already did a half hour of CNN while I was getting ready," she said. "That's about as much current events as I can stand. Besides, if it's really important, the White House sends me a briefing."

He set down the paper and raised his eyebrows. He'd showered and shaved. His hair was military short, his skin tanned, and his shoulders broad enough to carry the weight of the world on them. He looked good. Capable.

A plate of Danish sat between them. Joe pushed it toward her. "You should eat something."

The dull ache of acid in her stomach told her she should eat a lot, but she couldn't. "I don't remember hiring you as my personal nutritionist. Did we sign a contract?"

"You're too skinny." He reached for his mug. "It's not healthy."

"I'm not sure I care about your opinion. Let me think." She sipped her coffee. "Nope. Don't care."

"Is this a chick thing? Do you want to look like a supermodel or something?"

"Why does it matter?"

"I'm curious."

"And that impacts me how?"

He leaned back in his chair. "Is it because it's morning, or are you naturally unpleasant all the time?"

"I'm naturally unpleasant."

One corner of his mouth twitched in an almost smile. "Good to know. Why aren't you eating?"

"Are you going to dog on me all day until you get an answer?" she asked, more intrigued than frustrated.

"Probably. I don't have a lot to keep me busy. I could use the distraction."

"Fine. I'm not a good stress eater. I wish I were. I understand it's very comforting. But when I'm tense or upset, I can't stand the thought of food."

His gaze slipped to her too-skinny arms. "Been upset a lot lately?"

Darcy shrugged. She knew she'd lost weight in the past year or so. Too much weight. "I've had stuff on my mind."

He returned his attention to the paper. "Brenna should be here in half an hour. Your Secret Service agents want me to come along on the tour, too."

His flat tone told her all she had to know about *his* enthusiasm level. It annoyed her that once he'd gotten his answer, he'd dismissed her.

"Let me guess. You're not dying with excitement at the thought of the winery tour."

He raised his head. "Something like that. But it doesn't matter. I'm here and I'm going to do my job. Never question the chain of command." He pushed the plate of Danish toward her. "Eat one."

"I'm not hun—"

His gaze narrowed. "Try."

She sighed heavily, then picked up a cheese Danish. "Fine. I'll try. Although Yoda said there is no try. There is do, or do not. Or was it do or not do? I can never remember."

Joe's expression didn't change. Nor did he offer an opinion.

"*Star Wars*," she mumbled as she took a bite and chewed. After swallowing she said, "The second one. *The Empire Strikes Back.* My personal favorite of the first three."

He returned his attention to the paper.

"You're not very friendly," she said.

"Do you need me to be?"

"It wouldn't kill you to make an attempt. Or should I apologize? Oh, Joe, I'm terribly sorry my kidnapping is interfering with your regular life. Silly me. I should have arranged it for a different month."

"I heard you were a pain in the ass," he said.

The words meant nothing, she told herself, even as she felt their sting.

"But you're not a victim," he added. "Good for you."

Not sure what to say to that, she reached for another Danish and tore it in half.

"Did you fight them?" he asked.

It took her a second to figure out he meant the kidnappers. "Yes, but there were four of them, and I'm not exactly buff. I did get in a good head butt though." And she hadn't allowed the fear to control her. When it got bad at night, she reminded herself of that.

"You're tougher than you look," he said.

She wasn't sure what that meant, or what it had to do with him being friendly.

"How was it?" he asked.

She glanced down and realized that she'd finished the second Danish. She pressed one hand to her stomach. The acid burn was gone.

"Delicious," she said.

"Have another."

"Don't push me, sailor. I have connections."

He chuckled. "I bet you do."

A car pulled up out front.

"Brenna," Joe said as he stood. "I'll alert the security team."

Darcy finished her cup of coffee and carried it to the sink. She rinsed it and set it in the dishwasher as the back door burst open and Brenna stepped inside.

"Oh my God, I've gained three pounds in the past *week*," she announced as she entered. "Is that fair? Is it right? I hate being pregnant more than I can tell you. It seriously sucks. I'm huge. Oh, no. Danish. No, no. I can't. The sugar will give me heartburn." She turned to Darcy. "Did you eat one? Was it fabulous? Let me live vicariously through you, I beg you."

Darcy laughed. "It wasn't bad."

"I knew it. And you're so damn skinny. Look at you." She stopped and covered her mouth with her finger. "Oh, can I say *damn* in front of you? Have I broken the law?"

"You can say anything you want. I'll say *damn*, too, if it makes you feel better."

"It does. Okay, let's go. I hear the Danish calling my name, and if I stay here, I'll give in."

Darcy followed her outside, where she was greeted by a large golden retriever.

"This is Max," Brenna said as the huge dog sniffed and licked and wagged his tail so hard his whole back end shook. "He likes everybody."

"I guess." Darcy bent down to hug him and received a quick doggie kiss for her efforts. "Are you a handsome boy?"

Max yelped in agreement.

"This is going to be a modified tour," Brenna said as she patted her belly. "We'll take carts, which limits where we can go. But you'll get a feel for things. Plus, if you're interested, you can go exploring on your own."

Just then two golf carts came around the house. Joe drove one, while Alex piloted the other. Paige sat beside him.

"Or not," Brenna said. "Will they let you go out on your own?"

"Not anytime soon." Darcy hated that protection was necessary, and even worse, that she wanted it. She hated being afraid.

"Ready?" Joe asked as he stopped beside Brenna.

"Yes, but I'm driving," she said. "If you argue, I'll take you down."

He grinned. "You can drive."

"Men like it when we take charge," Brenna said. "I don't know why, but I accept it as a secret of the universe."

Darcy appreciated the advice, but she was more intrigued by her Secret Service agents. She'd only ever seen them in suits—black, navy, dark gray. But today both Paige and Alex were in jeans and T-shirts. Paige looked great, but Alex seemed awkward, as if he wasn't comfortable in his own skin.

"Wow, casual," she said, strolling over to their cart. "What gives?"

"We're blending in," Paige said.

Darcy turned to Alex. "You need to relax a little. You're not blending."

"We haven't completed our reconnaissance of the property. There are areas that aren't secured."

"Don't worry," Brenna said as she slid behind the wheel of the other cart. "We won't go anywhere unsecured."

"You don't know where that is," Alex said between clenched teeth. "I haven't told you."

Brenna patted the seat next to her. "Come on, Darcy. Let's get a move on."

Five minutes later they were bouncing along the edge of a massive vineyard. Max trotted ahead, then turned back and barked, as if urging them to keep up. Joe sat in the rear of their cart, while Paige and Alex came up behind.

"So these are chardonnay grapes," Brenna said. "Note the pale color. They're nearly ripe and will be picked first. The cabs are last to ripen."

"Cabs?"

"Cabernet sauvignon. Our pride and joy. Red wines are the gift of the gods. Whites are nice, too, but honestly, not my favorite."

"Katie only drinks white wine," Joe said.

Brenna glared at him. "He's making trouble. Can you believe it? He disappears for weeks at a time, and when he returns, he makes trouble."

"Just sharing. You women like that."

"Slap him for me," Brenna said. "Slap him really, really hard."

Darcy laughed. The morning was perfect—the coolness of the night had faded, but it wasn't hot yet. The sky was clear, the company enjoyable.

"We grow different kinds of grapes here," Brenna said. "Chardonnay, merlot, cabs, some voigner for blending. We also have vineyards up in Northern California. The grapes are brought down here, and everything is blended together. I hope you're here when we start picking. It's very exciting. The grapes are pressed on the property and put into huge barrels for fermenting."

"I'd like to see that," Darcy said.

Brenna continued to talk about grapes and winemaking, but Darcy found herself focusing more on the family than their wine.

What a wonderful place to grow up, she thought. So much space, so much love and acceptance. Except Joe hadn't known about any of this. What would it be like to find out he had this whole other family who wanted nothing more than to make him one of them? Was he angry about what he'd missed? Hurt his parents had given him up?

They turned around and headed for the barrel rooms.

"Running two different wineries is tough," Brenna was saying. "Mine—Four Sisters—is pretty small, but it still takes a lot of time. Plus, working here has the added thrill of dealing with my grandfather. In theory, I'm in charge. In reality, he argues with me about everything. What wine should be used for the reserve and what should be blended. How long to ferment, whether or not to use oak barrels or stainless steel. Don't even get me started on labels. I've been trying to get him to approve new ones for over three years. But does he? No. We're using the same old crappy labels. He makes me insane. Truly he does."

Lorenzo might annoy his granddaughter, but Darcy heard the love in her voice, too.

They left the carts and walked into the main buildings of the winery. Brenna showed her the pressing room, the fermenting room, and the equipment that delivered ready wine into bottles. Paige hovered by the main entrance while Alex stalked from room to room, checking for terrorists in all the shadows.

"I need to talk to my manager," Brenna said. "I'll just be a second."

Darcy nodded and crouched down to pat Max as she examined the bottling equipment more closely.

"This is interesting," she said. "My peak tour experience had been watching them manufacture M&M's, but this is just as good." She stood. "You must love being a part of it."

Joe shrugged, as if it didn't matter.

She faced him. "You don't care about this?"

"No."

"But they're an amazing family."

"We're related. That doesn't make us family."

She couldn't have been more surprised if he'd morphed into a giant moose.

"But that's crazy," she told him. "Why on earth would you walk away from all this? It's your heritage, it's who you are."

"I'm not interested in their money."

"I'm not talking about money. I'm talking about belonging to something bigger than just you. There's history here, and love. People who care about you."

He turned away. "I'm here because of my job. Nothing else."

She could hear Lauren's voice in her head telling her this was a really good time to change the subject. She didn't want to alienate someone on her security team on her first day. There were probably at least fourteen different, polite ways to handle the situation. Darcy ignored them all.

"I thought you had to be smart to be a SEAL. I guess not."

Brenna returned, and they completed the tour. Joe stayed in the background, watching Darcy as she interacted with everyone she met.

He hadn't thought about her as a person before. To him she'd been little more than the slightly attractive reason he was stuck here instead of back on base. Not that there was any guarantee that he would have been allowed to stay on base after the incident with the admiral's boat.

Now he saw her as an individual—one with a temper. She liked dogs, had a smart mouth, and was shy with strangers, although she forced herself to act otherwise. She was also afraid.

Brenna opened her car door and Max jumped inside. She turned to Darcy.

"I had fun," she said.

"Me, too." Darcy smiled, then leaned in to hug her. Brenna's large stomach got in the way.

"I'm huge," Brenna said with a sigh.

Darcy touched her belly. "You're lucky."

Her voice had a wistful quality that made Joe feel as if he'd stumbled onto something personal. Before he could turn away, Brenna reached for him.

"All right, big guy. I'm outta here. Take care of our guest." She lowered her voice. "I like her. Based on what I read in the paper, I thought I'd hate her, but I don't. So be nice to her."

"You're not the boss of me."

"So you like to think."

Brenna moved to the car and climbed in. Darcy stood there and waved until she disappeared around the corner.

"That was fun," she said when they were alone. "Your sister's great. I really like how she bullies you."

"I let her think she bullies me."

"Oh. Right. That's how it is."

Her eyes were bright with humor, her mouth smiling. She was pretty, he thought, as heat tumbled in his gut and moved south. And as much as he hated to side with Brenna—if she found out she would never let him forget—he agreed with her assessment of Darcy. From what he'd read in the paper, she was supposed to be a class A bitch. So far, no real sign of that.

Paige strolled up. "Hey, Darcy. What's up for the rest of the day?"

"I'm not sure. I'd like to head out and sketch the vineyards."

"Sure. Give us about a thirty-minute heads-up. We'll send you out with a team of three."

Darcy's smile faded. "Sure. Thanks."

Paige wandered back to the guesthouse. Joe turned to Darcy.

"Not in the mood for an entourage?" he asked.

"I don't mind that. Sometimes I forget why I need them. I'm not excited to be reminded."

"You were kidnapped. They want to be careful."

"And I want them to be careful."

She turned toward the house, but he grabbed her arm to stop her. Her skin was soft against his fingers.

"What?" she demanded. "Did I disobey? Do I have to get down and give you twenty?"

He studied her face. The shadows were darker today. "You're not sleeping."

Instantly her expression closed, and she jerked free of his hold. "I'm fine."

"You should talk about it to someone."

"Are you volunteering?"

"Maybe Paige could help."

"Don't worry about me."

He knew what she was going through—not the particulars but what it was like to be unable to come down after an assignment. "There are ways to handle post-traumatic stress—"

"Don't you dare psychoanalyze me," she told him. "You don't know what the hell you're talking about."

"Actually I do. And while you're already pissed off at me, I'm going to tell you to start eating better. And exercising. It will help you sleep."

She headed for the house. "Go away," she called

over her shoulder as she ran up the stairs and ducked inside.

He wanted to, but there was nowhere to go. Like her, he was trapped here for the duration. Also like her, he had ghosts haunting his sleep and things he didn't want to remember.

6

∾

*T*wo days later Joe heard a commotion in the driveway. As Darcy had stuck close to the house, he'd been trapped inside as well, and he was happy for an excuse to get outdoors. As he stepped outside, a familiar battered Jeep pulled up. Instantly several Secret Service agents appeared and surrounded the vehicle.

"Don't shoot," Mia said as she got out of the driver's side and held up both hands. "We're unarmed."

Joe felt himself smile. When Mia was around, life was never boring.

She spotted him and squealed. "Joe! You're here! Did you know about the Secret Service? They stopped us at the turn-off to the driveway and searched the car. Now I think they're going to take Ian out back and shoot him."

As she spoke a tall, lanky blond guy climbed out of the Jeep and also held up his hands.

"I don't get it," the kid said, looking both confused and scared. "What I do?"

Paige took Mia's friend by the arm. "If you'll come this way," she said as she steered him toward the guesthouse.

Mia waited until the agents had walked away before lowering her arms and racing toward Joe.

"What gives?" she demanded as she launched herself toward him. He grabbed her and pulled her against him, then hugged her close.

"All these questions," he said, putting her down. "How about starting with a greeting?"

She grinned up at him. Mia was barely five foot three, with big brown eyes and brown hair she always had streaked blond. Too much makeup stained her face, and she insisted on wearing trashy cropped shirts and too-short shorts. But she was pure energy, and she adored him with a devotion that never wavered.

Her full mouth swelled into a pout. "You should be greeting *me*. You never answer my e-mails. Why is that? I'm very faithful about writing."

He patted her on the head, deliberately mussing her hair. "I don't consider 'hey, get any lately' correspondence I want to respond to."

"You're such a stick-in-the-mud." She glanced toward the guesthouse and then back at him. "What's up with the police brutality?"

"They're being careful."

"Who's they?"

Joe wasn't sure what to say. Of all his family members, Mia was the biggest risk to blab. "You didn't tell anyone you were coming to visit."

"This is my home, Joseph," Mia told him sternly. "I don't need permission to show up. So what did I interrupt? An alien landing? Secret nuclear experiments? Although Brenna won't like anything that messes with her precious wine. Why don't you—"

The back door opened. Joe heard it, and he knew who had appeared by the expression of total stunned disbelief on Mia's face.

"Holy shit," she breathed. "That's the president's daughter."

Joe glanced back at Darcy. "Meet Mia Marcelli, the youngest and least mannered of the four sisters."

Mia slugged him in the arm, then walked over to Darcy. "Wow. What on earth are you doing here? Are you lost?"

Darcy smiled. "No. I'm hiding out for a few weeks."

Mia turned on him. "That's why those government types came and asked all those questions. I thought it was about something else. This is so incredibly cool." She looked at the guesthouse and gasped. "Oh, no. Ian wasn't cleared, was he? That's the big deal. I brought an unknown enemy into sacred territory. Jeez. What will they do to him?"

Joe didn't have the answer, so he shrugged.

"You're no help," Mia said as she took off at a run toward the guesthouse. "Wait!" she yelled. "He's not a terrorist. We're just sleeping together. Don't hurt him!"

Joe watched her for a second, then turned to Darcy. "We're all so proud."

Darcy continued to watch as Mia entered the Secret Service headquarters. "She's great. I can't wait to meet your other two sisters."

"They're both a little more low-key. Although Francesca has a master's in psychology, which makes her think she knows more than she does."

"Then she must have a field day with you."

Joe hadn't seen much of Darcy in the past couple of

days. He knew he'd pissed her off, and he'd half expected her to report him to Paige or Alex, complaining that he'd crossed the line between the hired help and those who were part of the inner circle. But neither of them had said anything to him.

Now he took in the shadows under her eyes—they were darker than before. There was a wariness in her expression, as if she expected him to attack.

He told himself he didn't care if she never slept again, that his entire focus was on getting through this assignment and getting back to the base. Nothing else mattered. Not her, not his family, and especially not the awareness he felt whenever she was around.

"You're looking fierce about something," Darcy said. "I was teasing about your sister. You don't have to be so sensitive."

He stiffened as if she'd shot him. "I'm *not* sensitive."

Darcy held in a smile. Men were so predictable. Violate their sense of manliness and they got all prickly and defensive.

"Of course not. How could I have thought such a thing?" He glared at her but didn't speak. No doubt he wasn't sure if she was kidding. The last time they'd been together, he'd pissed her off, and she'd reacted. Maybe overreacted. She suspected Joe had only been trying to help.

"I like your family," she said as a change of subject. "Mia reminds me a lot of Brenna."

"They're alike," he admitted. "Katie and Francesca are similar, too. Less volatile."

She smiled. "Less interested in making you crazy?"

"Sometimes."

"You're a lucky man, Joe Larson," she said. "You have a family most people would envy."

His expression turned from wary to trapped. She sensed he did *not* want to be having this conversation with her. She also knew that he wasn't comfortable walking away from her. After all, she was the person they were all trying to keep safe.

"Oh, I have to admit I like that," she murmured.

His dark gaze lasered in on her face. "Like what?"

"Having power over an ex-SEAL."

One eyebrow rose. "Not in this lifetime or the next."

"Uh-huh. The thing is, you can't go anywhere, can you?"

She moved closer, then circled around him. Was it possible to make him do tricks? She grinned. His eyes narrowed.

"Ever married?" she asked.

"Once. You?"

She laughed. "You hardly have to ask. Nearly every detail of my life has been played out in the press. No engagements, no serious boyfriends. At least not in a while. Dating the president's daughter comes with restrictions most guys aren't willing to take on. Now back to you. What happened to the little woman?"

"I used to ship out for six, eight months at a time. Kind of makes it hard to keep the home fires burning."

Yet other men managed to do it. Why not Joe? He was good-looking enough. He had a body that was near god-like in its perfection. When he forgot to act as though he had a stick up his ass, he was okay to talk to. So why no entourage of women hanging on him? Why did he always act as if he would rather be somewhere else?

"You do like women, right?" she asked, pretending a seriousness she didn't feel.

Fury erupted in him. She felt both the energy and the heat, but his control was impressive. Not by a flicker of a lash did he react to the insult. "What do you think?"

"I think your past could make for a very interesting story. But don't worry. I won't ask you. There are plenty of folks around here who would like nothing more than to tell me all they know about you."

He groaned.

"Oh, yeah," she said with a laugh. "The hell of family. Why is it so hard for you to be with them?"

"This isn't a conversation we're going to have."

"Why not?"

"The subject doesn't interest me."

But it interested her. Why did he resist such a wonderful group of people? From what she'd seen in the past two days, all that the Marcellis wanted was the freedom to love him. What wouldn't she give to have a piece of that for herself.

"I can help you with this," she said.

"No, thanks."

"Oh, but you don't have a choice. We're trapped here, and I could use a distraction." She didn't mean any of it, but threatening him was fun.

"When did you get to be an expert?" he asked.

"I'm not. Those who can, do. Those who can't, teach. That's me. Your new instructor on getting along with your family. We'll have classes and everything. You can thank me later."

"Not likely." His gaze narrowed. "This is a joke, right?"

She arched her eyebrows. "Maybe. Maybe not."

The man actually growled. She had a feeling he was thinking that he would rather have an arm cut off than deal with her *and* the Marcellis. Not that he had a choice. Neither of them were going anywhere, and she was in a position to force her will on him.

For once being the president's daughter didn't seem like such a bad thing.

Mia Marcelli didn't sit still, Paige noted. She squirmed, hunched over, straightened, then bounced to her feet.

"I didn't know what those agents wanted when they came to see me last week," Mia said as she took the mug of coffee Paige offered. "I thought it was about the spy stuff."

"What spy stuff?"

Mia rolled her eyes. "They keep asking me to be a spy. Is that crazy or what? I mean look at me. Do I blend in?"

"Why you?" Paige asked. "Do you know?"

Mia shrugged. "I do languages. Give me a good instructor and a few weeks and I can function using that language. Give me three months and I can talk like a native. It's my brain. I'm really smart about other stuff, too, but languages are my thang. I try to pick up a couple every year, you know, just for fun."

As Paige had struggled with high school Spanish and barely passed, she didn't know what to say. "Good for you. Did you accept any of the offers?"

Mia wrinkled her nose. "No. I just graduated from Georgetown, and I'm starting with the State Department in September. This is my last summer of freedom, and I was going to spend it traveling with Ian. Are you guys going to kill him?"

Paige laughed. "No. We want to find out more about him, though."

"Because of Darcy." Mia's eyes got wide. "Why is she here?"

"There was a kidnapping attempt on Lauren. They took Darcy by mistake."

"Whoa—that's scary. I wonder how you guys picked this place to hide her. But it's good. I mean, the Grands will love her to death. I know they always make me feel better when I've had a bad day or something."

Alex walked into the kitchen. "We're nearly done," he told Paige, then he turned to Mia. "Your friend will be free to go in about an hour."

"So he's not dangerous?" Mia asked. "I could have told you that. Ian's fun, but not the least bit deep, and isn't depth of character required for true commitment to a cause?"

Alex stared at her without speaking. Paige was careful to hide her amusement.

Mia rose and walked over to Alex. "You obviously work out. Talk about muscles. So who are you?"

"Special Agent Alex Vanmeter. I'm in charge of this operation."

"Ooh, our fearless leader." She glanced at Paige and grinned. "I just love military types. And guys into security. There's that whole 'take a bullet' mentality. The ultimate sacrifice. Of course it doesn't measure up against Kyle Reese in *Terminator.* He traveled across time, but death is a close second."

Alex sighed heavily. "Ms. Marcelli," he began.

Mia moved in close and rubbed her palm against his upper arm. "Mia. Call me Mia. And I'll call you Alex."

She stared into his eyes. "Ian's just a summer fling. It's not serious at all. I mean, he's fun, but I can't imagine living with him for the next sixty years. He talks too much, and I'd be forced to kill him. Then I'd need to be punished. Would you want to be the one to punish me, Special Agent in Charge Vanmeter?"

Paige had a feeling that if Alex had been drinking, he would have spit. Color darkened his cheeks as he jerked free of her touch and stepped back.

"Perhaps you would like to return to the house until we're finished questioning your friend," he said firmly.

Mia sighed. "All right. But if you change your mind, let me know."

She waggled her fingers at Paige and sauntered out of the guesthouse.

Paige began to chuckle as soon as Mia left.

Alex glared at her. "You think that's funny?"

"That you have a groupie? Absolutely. She's just playing with you, Alex. She doesn't mean it."

He grabbed a bottle of iced tea from the refrigerator. "If she gets in the way of my job, I want you to talk to her."

"Oh, no. If you have a problem with Mia, you take it up with her. She's not a threat, and if you can't handle a little flirting from a twenty-one-year-old grad student, then you're not the man I thought you were."

Alex's glare deepened. "You *like* her."

"Of course. She's fabulous."

"Then she's your problem."

"Sorry, no. I'm busy with Darcy." She moved close and batted her eyes. "But I'm sure a big, bad agent like you can handle little Mia."

Alex set the bottle on the counter and grabbed her upper arms. There was nothing challenging about his hold, or threatening. But the second he touched her, everything changed.

For a moment, time shifted and Paige found herself slipping back to her weeks in training. When Alex had been so much more than a fellow recruit. The heat of his hand burned through to memories she'd thought she had forgotten. The scent of his body reminded her of being naked and in bed and never ever having enough of him.

Wanting slammed into her like a shot from a .45. Need joined it, making her hungry and weak and suddenly afraid.

Then time righted itself and she was back in the kitchen, a very different person than she'd been before.

"This isn't a game, Paige. This is deadly serious."

She nodded, not sure if he meant the situation with Darcy, the trouble with Mia, or what was happening between him and her.

He dropped his hand, grabbed his iced tea, and walked away. She was left alone in the kitchen, shaken, aroused, and confused as hell.

Darcy sat in front of the window, doing her best to draw the vineyard. The problem was her view was limited by a couple of large trees. As much as she would like to walk outside and find the perfect spot for an afternoon of drawing, she wasn't sure she was willing to put up with the security entourage that would accompany her. Their silent but very real presence wouldn't do much for her creativity.

Before she could decide if the pain was worth the price, someone knocked on the door. Before she could say anything, it burst open and Mia bounced into the room.

"I can't believe you're here," the younger Marcelli said as she jumped onto the bed and stretched out. "It's very exciting. I'm the youngest. You knew that, right? Mom made one last attempt to have a son, and I came along. They've hidden their disappointment pretty well. And now they adore me, so they're stuck, right? Plus they have Joe. So, you're here. Wow. How are you adjusting? Was it too horrible being kidnapped? I'll bet you were brave. You look like the brave type. I would have screamed and begged and really embarrassed myself, I just know it. Do you like having Secret Service agents all around? I met Alex. He's hunky." She glanced around, as if checking that they were alone, then lowered her voice. "Do you, like, get to have sex with the agents? Is that too personal? Should I wait a couple of days before asking that?"

Darcy put down her pencil and stared at her visitor. "Honest to God, I have no idea what to say to you."

Mia tucked her hands behind her head and beamed. "I know. I often have that effect on people, but they love me anyway."

"I can only imagine."

Mia sat up. "They searched the car. I turned into the driveway, and these men appeared from nowhere. They had guns and ordered me to stop. I had to show them ID, then they searched the car. I think they were look-ing for a bomb or something. Then they said we could drive up to the house but not to get out of the Jeep until we were instructed to. It's like being in a spy movie.

And the worst part is I can't tell anyone. That seriously sucks."

Darcy felt as if she could barely catch her breath. She'd thought that Brenna was high energy, but Brenna had nothing on Mia.

"I guess I can talk about it with Ian," Mia continued. "Of course I can't talk to him about Alex." She grinned. "You didn't answer my question about sex with the agents, did you?"

"No. And that's my answer. No. Haven't, wouldn't, don't want to."

"But he's very hunky."

"Maybe. I can't imagine him naked, though. He's too uptight."

Mia sighed and flopped back on the bed. "Oh, I can clearly see him naked, and it's a very nice picture, let me tell you. Yum." She raised her head. "You know I'm just playing, right? I say a lot of stuff to make people nervous, but I don't really mean it. Ian and I are together—at least for now. I wouldn't cheat on him or anything."

"I'm sure Alex will be relieved to hear that."

Mia grinned. "You're not going to tell him are you?"

"Nope. Let him suffer."

"Good. So what do you think of us?"

"I like the family," Darcy said and meant it. "Everyone has made me feel really welcome."

"We're like that. The Grands are so cool, and my folks are, too. Are Grammy M and Grandma Tessa still not talking?"

"They don't seem to get along."

"I hate that." Mia scooted around so her head was at the foot of the bed, then she flopped over onto her stomach. "I wish they'd make up. But they're both so stubborn. Maybe having Joe here will help. They adore him. We all do. Not that he's so crazy about us."

The bright light in her eyes faded. "Have you heard how he came to be here?"

"I know that he was given up for adoption and then found years later."

"Yeah. It's totally horrible that my mom had to do that. Now Joe's here, but he's not a part of us, you know. He won't let anyone get close. I make him crazy, which is fun, but it's not the same as being, you know, emotionally intimate. Brenna's the one he gets along with the best, but he holds back from everyone. He doesn't have a girlfriend."

She paused expectantly.

Darcy did her best to look innocent. "Oh. Should I be taking notes?"

Mia giggled. "No, but are you interested?"

"I barely know the man."

"What does that matter?"

"Amazingly enough, it matters to me."

"Oh, well. Maybe next time. You should think about it, though. I'll bet he's great in bed." Mia wrinkled her nose. "You know, I don't think I can talk about Joe's sex life. As intriguing as it would be, he's my brother, and there's a serious ick factor."

"I'm sure your family will be delighted to know you have limits."

Mia sat up. "I don't want limits. But there it is. The thought of my brother having sex is gross. So if you guys do it, I don't want to know."

Darcy made an *X* over her heart. "My lips will be sealed."

"He's probably gorgeous," Mia added thoughtfully. "Joe naked. I wonder if he has any scars, you know, from wounds and stuff."

There was a noise in the hall. Both Darcy and Mia turned toward the open door. Joe stood there. Darcy couldn't read the expression on his face, but it seemed to be an intriguing combination of horror and fear.

Mia sighed. "He heard the naked part," she said in a mock whisper.

Darcy did her best not to laugh. "Possibly even the sex part." She cleared her throat. "Hi, Joe. We were just talking about you."

Joe's dark gaze locked with her own. For a second, she would have sworn he'd vowed payback. Then he turned on his heel and left.

Mia started to laugh. Darcy joined in. She laughed until tears filled her eyes and she could barely breathe. Until that minute she would have said getting kidnapped was one of the worst things that had ever happened to her, but suddenly, she wondered if maybe it hadn't been so bad after all.

7

⤶

*D*arcy was up early because, well, not sleeping had a way of making a person face the dawn. She stood at her bedroom window, watching pale light creep across the vineyards. Suddenly her fingers itched for a pencil. She wanted to capture the moment, the changing light, the way the dew sparkled on the leaves.

She would never make it as an artist, she acknowledged, pulling on jeans and a T-shirt, then quickly brushing her hair. It was the reason she'd studied graphic arts and advertising in college. But not having an abundance of talent didn't stop her from wanting to capture the world with a quick sketch on a perfect morning.

She collected her supplies, then quietly made her way downstairs. The house was still. Reasonable, normal people wouldn't be up for at least another hour. Which meant she could sneak outside and enjoy the morning in solitude.

As the thought formed, she felt a tendril of fear snake along her spine. Did she *want* to be alone? Was it safe?

"Not going there," Darcy muttered. She pushed the questions away, along with the chill, and focused on the chance to just *be* for an hour or so.

But when she stepped outside, she saw an unfamiliar Secret Service agent in a car by the back door. He got out of the car as soon as he saw her.

"Morning, Ms. Jensen."

"Morning. And it's Darcy."

He nodded. "How can I help you?"

Part of her wanted to forget it. To just go back into the house and wait until all this was over. But a stronger voice in her head told her that she couldn't wait much longer without going crazy. She had to start doing something.

"I want to draw the vineyard this morning," she said, holding up her sketch pad. "I'm guessing it will take about an hour."

"Okay. Give me a second." He picked up a walkie-talkie and spoke into it.

No doubt getting permission, she thought glumly. What if they said no?

Before she could decide on a course of action, she felt a slight prickling between her shoulder blades. She turned and saw Joe coming out of the house.

Contradictory emotions warred within her. Part of her wondered why she couldn't spend five minutes alone outside of her bedroom. Another part of her acknowledged that if someone had to disturb the quiet, she wouldn't mind if it was Joe.

"You're up early," she said.

"Old habits," he told her.

She waited for him to comment on her being awake as

well, but he didn't. Instead he nodded at the pad and pencils.

"Hoping for inspiration?" he asked.

"I was, but it's turning out to be a big deal."

The Secret Service agent put down the walkie-talkie. "Okay, I'm ready," he said, then spoke into his ever-present wrist communicator. "Pigeon is leaving. Repeat, Pigeon is leaving."

Joe raised his eyebrows.

"Don't say it," Darcy told him. "My father is Falcon, my sister is Swan, and I'm Pigeon. Does the Secret Service have a sense of humor or what?"

Joe stepped toward the other man. "Why don't you stay here," he told him. "I'll go with our bird friend while she draws."

The agent frowned. "I'm supposed to be with Ms. Jensen, ah, Darcy, as protection."

"Check with Paige," Joe said. "She'll clear it." Then, without waiting for approval, he returned to Darcy's side and pointed toward the vineyard. "Let's go."

"Pretty smooth," she said when they were out of earshot and walking through vines heavy with grapes. "You said to contact Paige, not Alex, knowing she's the softer touch."

"Uh-huh."

"What makes you think it's easier for me to have you along than the other agent?"

"I don't call you Ms. Jensen."

She smiled. "Good point." And in truth, she didn't mind having Joe around.

"Where are we going?" he asked.

"Not a clue. We'll walk until I find inspiration."

They continued walking, she in front, he right behind. Dew spattered her arms and soaked her jeans. There was a peacefulness to the quiet, and a sense of safety. As if nothing bad could ever happen here.

At the other end of that plot of grapes they found a narrow dirt track. Darcy paused to survey the miles of grapes and a cluster of trees to the west.

"That way," she said, pointing. As they followed the path, they were able to walk side by side.

"I talked to my sister last night," she said. "They're holding her on some farm in the Midwest. She's surrounded by cornfields. When I told her about the wine, she was very jealous."

Joe looked at her. "You shouldn't discuss your location, even on a secure line."

Darcy grinned. She liked messing with him—it was a little like pulling a tiger's tail—dangerous but very exhilarating.

"You think?" she asked with a grin. "Don't worry, my little SEAL friend. I told her I was in Washington state. They make wine there, too. But as you're a part of all this, I'm guessing you already know that."

He shrugged.

She studied him. "How much, exactly, do you know about wine?"

"I'm a beer drinker myself."

She winced. "That can't be good. Aren't you interested in wine?"

"No."

"But it's your heritage. It's in your blood."

"I want salt water in my blood."

The man was nothing if not consistent, she thought.

Still, to have so much right there for the taking. "I envy you," she said quietly. "It's just my father, my sister, and me. And I don't get along all that well with Mr. President." For reasons she had never discussed with anyone. "Which means it's pretty much Lauren and me. We're close, although we're not that much alike. She's perfect and I'm—"

As she spoke, she stumbled on a loose rock in the road. Before she could catch her balance on her own, Joe grabbed her arm and pulled her upright.

They stood there, in the center of the road, his hand on her arm, his fingers touching bare skin. They were close enough for her to feel the heat from his body and his slow, steady breathing. She could see the various colors of brown that colored his irises and the faint scar on the edge of his jaw.

Her stomach clenched in anticipation, which was crazy. Nothing was going to happen.

But for the moment, that single heartbeat of time, she wanted it to. She wanted him to . . . oh, who knew. Kiss her? Say something sweet? She wasn't particularly picky, as long as he acknowledged the connection between them.

But he didn't, and she started to feel awkward. She pulled free of his grasp.

"Obviously Lauren is the perfect one," she said with a laugh that didn't exactly sound real. "I'm the clumsy one."

"You're still not sleeping."

"I know. Some. A little."

"Hardly at all."

Annoyance replaced her awareness of him. "Haven't

we already had this particular conversation? If you recall, it didn't end well."

"If the objective isn't achieved on the first mission, the team doesn't give up."

She glared at him. "There are so many things wrong with that statement, I don't know where to begin. For one thing, you're not a team, and I'm sure as hell not a mission."

He shifted uncomfortably. "You know what I mean."

"I do, and it's insulting."

"Darcy, you can't avoid what happened forever. It's not going away until you deal with it. The longer you wait the harder it gets."

She didn't want to hear that. She wanted to continue to think that the fear would one day just be gone.

"Go away," she said, turning her back on him.

He put his hand on her shoulder and moved her until they were facing each other again. "No can do. Look, I understand. You think I don't, but you're wrong. I've been scared and alone and bad things have happened to me, too. I can help."

She refused to cooperate. Instead of speaking, she pressed her lips together.

He looked at her. "You're stubborn."

"It's one of my best qualities."

"Want to take a poll on that?" He lowered his hand from her shoulder and sighed heavily. "Here's the thing," he said. "I've had years of training and experience. You didn't have any. When I walk into a dangerous situation I expect trouble, but you were just minding your own business at the mall. Those bastards grabbed you with no warning, and the people whose job it is to protect you screwed up. They weren't there and they didn't notice. You were totally and completely alone."

She honestly hadn't believed anyone could understand what it had been like, but with a few words, he showed her that he got it.

"Tell me what happened," he said gently.

She hesitated, then the words came tumbling out. "I w-was in the back of the store and walking to the dressing rooms. They grabbed me. I didn't have time to scream. They put tape on my mouth and tied my hands behind me, then threw me in the back of a van."

She didn't want to talk about it, she told herself, but she couldn't stop the words from spilling out. Somehow she was walking and telling him everything. About the van and how dirty it was, how she'd tried to get to her panic button but couldn't. About the warehouse and being tied to the chair and scared, so scared, they were going to kill her.

"I tried to get away," she said. "But there was nowhere to go, and the chair didn't make things easy. Then I tried to stay calm. I was afraid I was going to throw up, and I didn't want that. Then the guy in charge showed up. He looked at me and he said—"

She stopped in the middle of the path. Suddenly it was too hard to hold on to her pencils and sketch pad. They dropped to the ground. She rubbed at her still-healing wrists and wished away the rest of the pain.

"What?" Joe asked, his voice more gentle than she'd ever heard it before. "What did he say?"

Oh, God. Tears burned. Weak, stupid tears. She would *not* give in. Not now.

"I—He said that I wasn't the one they wanted." She

summoned anger and glared at him. "There. Are you happy? He said not this one. No one cares about this one. I was a mistake. Then they took me back to the mall, dumped me on the loading dock, and drove away."

Jesus. Joe didn't know what to say to that. What could anyone say? Darcy stared at him, her expression defiant. She was angry, but it was a thin veneer that could crack at any time, and he sure didn't want to be around when it did.

Before he could figure out how to respond, she started talking again.

"I love my sister," she said, her voice shaking. "Lauren is my best friend. She understands me and loves me. I admire her so much. But the thing is . . . the very worst thing is, sometimes I hate her." More tears filled Darcy's eyes. "I hate her because I'm weak and small and jealous. And then I feel so horrible, because I want to be like her and I don't know how and everyone loves her best. I'm jealous of my own sister. What does that say about me? What?"

The last word came on a sob. Joe felt both trapped and deeply inadequate to the task. What was it about a crying woman that reduced most men to cowards? He wanted to bolt, but he couldn't, so he did the only thing that made sense to him. He pulled her close and kissed her.

The shock of Joe's lips on hers was enough to stop Darcy's tears. One second she'd been in an uncontrolled free fall of self-loathing, and the next she was pressed against a man made entirely of rock, his arms around her body and his mouth very much on hers.

She couldn't think, couldn't speak; she could only

react, tilting her head slightly so he could kiss her more. Because it felt good. *Better* than good.

His lips were an impossible combination of yielding and firm. He held her with just the right amount of possession. Heat surrounded her, melting all the hard edges and drying her tears. She raised her hands to his shoulders and allowed herself to be swept away by the soft pressure.

He didn't deepen the kiss, but she was okay with that. It had been a long time since she'd wanted a man, so long she'd almost forgotten what it felt like to feel the first fluttering of desire low in her belly. Her breasts went from simply a sticky-out part of her body to exquisitely sensitive, and her legs actually got weak.

When he stepped back, she didn't know what to say. Embarrassment battled with self-preservation. When in doubt, be a bitch. But before she could say anything to shatter the moment, she caught a glimpse of something dark and powerful in his eyes.

Need.

He hadn't just kissed her to stop her crying. He'd kissed her because he'd wanted to. The revelation kept her mouth shut and opened her mind to a thousand amazing possibilities.

"Hell," he muttered.

She nodded in agreement. Talk about a complication.

"I'm—" He shook his head, as if not sure what to say. Then he turned on his heel and walked away.

Darcy watched him go. When he had disappeared into the grove of trees they'd been heading for in the first place, she picked up her sketch book and pencils and started for the house. Around her, the morning stirred to life. She heard birds and someone driving up to the winery.

What on earth had just happened? She'd spilled her guts to Joe, and then he'd kissed her. Even more amazing, she'd felt it. She couldn't remember the last time she'd allowed herself to engage sexually. The few physical relationships she'd had in her past had all ended badly. It had seemed smarter to not go there again.

But now, with Joe, she found herself anticipating the next time she would see him. Oh, sure, it would be awkward, but they'd get over it. Besides, she would have the thrill of knowing he'd *wanted* to kiss her. Which made for a very good day.

Joe avoided the house for the next couple of hours, but he knew he couldn't stay away forever. What the hell had he been thinking? Talk about letting the little head run his life. Darcy was supposed to be under his protection, not in his arms. Was he looking for ways to screw up his career more? Because if he was, he'd found a hell of a good way to do it.

Angry with himself for being an ass, her for being so damn tempting, and the world in general because he was stuck here, he stalked into the house and found Brenna sitting in the kitchen. She had a plate of pasta in front of her and several slices of bread next to her glass of milk.

"Morning," she said cheerfully when she saw him.

He glanced at the clock. It was barely ten-thirty.

She followed his gaze. "Hey, I'm eating for the team. Don't you dare get coffee," she ordered when he started toward the pot.

"What? If you can't have any, no one else gets to?" he asked as he poured himself a mug.

"Exactly. Oh, man. It's great, isn't it?"

He took a long, slow drink. "Not bad."

She groaned. "Pig." Then she stabbed several pieces of penne and chewed on them.

"You'll be able to drink coffee soon," he told her.

"Not if I'm breast-feeding. And I plan to, for at least a while. I mean I think I can have a little, but it won't be the same. I miss my pot of coffee. And wine. And pretty much everything else I had to give up. This had better be an amazing baby, because if it's not, I'm writing a letter of complaint."

"I can't wait to see who you mail it to."

She grinned. "I'm Catholic, big guy. I have access to spiritual management you can only dream about."

"So I've heard."

He pulled out a chair and settled across from her. "Is this a late breakfast or an early lunch?"

"It's my meal in between. I've been starving for days. Not sure why. Maybe the baby's having a growth spurt. Do they do that?"

"Do I look like I know?"

"Not especially. I brought you something." She pointed to the stack of books on the table. "Since you're stuck here for a while I thought you'd like a chance to find enlightenment."

He glanced at the books and saw several of them were textbooks on wine making and grape growing.

This was Brenna—subtle as an explosion. Too bad he wasn't interested in playing the game.

"Not for me," he said.

"Oh, come on, Joe. You could look them over. Read a few pages. You might find yourself fascinated."

"Brenna, don't push me on this."

"Why not? I'm pregnant. It's not as if you can threaten me physically. Besides, it's time you accepted who you are—a Marcelli. Wine is cool."

He swore under his breath, then pushed to his feet. "I'm *not* interested and I'm never going to be interested. Not in this place, the land, or the wine. Just so we're all clear on the subject. This isn't my home, and you're not my family."

A flick of movement caught his attention. He turned and saw Grandma Tessa standing in the doorway that led to the dining room. Her eyes were wide and filled with pain.

Perfect, Joe thought grimly. The day was going just perfect.

He hesitated, not sure what to say, then he figured there weren't any words and he stalked out of the house.

Darcy wandered through the various rooms of the winery. Although Brenna had given a very detailed tour, she couldn't remember what all the equipment was for. The various barrels were marked, but not in any language she recognized. She supposed there was a code that explained what was inside, when it had been put in the barrel, and maybe even when it was supposed to come out.

All so interesting, she thought, breathing in the thick scent of grapes and wine and something yeasty—almost like bread. She found herself wanting to know more about the process and how the decisions were made.

"So you're intrigued."

She turned and found Grandpa Lorenzo standing behind her. "I'll admit it," she told him with a smile. "I didn't realize how much I didn't know about wine until I got here. I don't drink it much at home, and when I go out, someone else usually picks."

"Without wine, there can't be life," the elderly man told her. "Come. I will show you."

He leaned heavily on his cane as he led the way into another room filled with large, stainless steel vats.

"The white wines," he said. "Chardonnays and blends. Different kinds of barrels give a different taste."

"But how can metal give a taste at all?" she asked.

"You are right. The wine is different because it doesn't have the flavors of the wood. We play tricks with the grapes. We tease them and coax them. Sometimes they listen, sometimes they do not. Like children. We know what is best, but there are times everyone has to learn on his own."

He led her into a room filled with all kinds of equipment and a narrow conveyor belt that looked like a snake. "We bottle here. You will come and watch. It's very interesting. Brenna can't stand to be here. She says the treatment is too hard on the wine and it makes her sad to see it battered."

He pointed out where the barrels were emptied and how the liquid flowed into the bottles. Labels were applied, corks pushed in, then sealed with foil coverings.

"So many things can go wrong," Lorenzo told her. "The bottles don't move, the wine doesn't pour, the labels are crooked. But we persevere and then we have this. . . ."

He opened a door, and she saw cases of wine nearly stacked to the ceiling. They were everywhere, leaving only enough space for a small table, a phone, and an intercom.

"My retreat," he said. "When I want to be alone. I like the room when it's like this—crowded before the trucks come to take the wine away. In a few days it will be empty. I spend my afternoons out here. Tessa worries about me. I'm too old to be alone." He touched the intercom. "I call her from here. It buzzes in the kitchen. But still she worries. An old woman."

Darcy heard the love in his voice, and it made her feel warm inside. They had to have been married fifty or sixty years, yet there was still caring, still affection.

"You're very lucky," she said.

"You would think so, eh, but look at this." He opened one of the cases and pulled out a bottle of chardonnay. He pointed at the label. "The same one for too many years. But can we get a new one? No. Brenna brings me designs. They're so bad. Animals and flowers. We are Marcelli Wines. We have a proud tradition."

His voice lowered and his expression softened. "Now she has a baby of her own to keep her busy. So the labels will stay, and we will go on."

"I can't believe she runs two wineries," Darcy said. "That's pretty amazing."

"Yes. Too much, sometimes, but she's stubborn. When I wouldn't let her run Marcelli, she started her own label. Foolish girl. But the first releases are out. She scored high and sold everything within a week."

There was pride in his voice. Darcy understood that Grandpa Lorenzo would be an exacting boss, but she wouldn't mind dealing with the old man. For him, family was everything.

"You have a sister?" he asked.

"Yes. Lauren."

Lorenzo nodded. "And your mother?"

"She died when I was sixteen. My father never remarried. In politics it's difficult to find the time to have a personal life."

"Still, a man shouldn't be alone. It's not right. Look at my Joe. Alone for too many years."

Darcy laughed. "You're not subtle, are you?"

"I'm an old man who wants to see his only grandson married. He's a handsome fellow. Strong. He would be a good provider."

Darcy grinned. "Yes, and he seems to have very nice teeth. I'm sure he'll be a good breeder."

Lorenzo smiled. "You tease me."

"A little. I don't think Joe is interested in me that way." Although he had just kissed her. Hmm, the lip-pressing did sort of make things more intriguing.

"You could make him interested," Lorenzo said. "You have ways."

"Not as many as you'd think."

"Darcy?"

She heard someone calling her name. A familiar someone. Male, tall, and with good teeth.

"We're in here," she yelled.

Joe walked into the storage room. "Paige and Alex were going crazy. You disappeared."

"Oh, sorry. Your grandfather and I were just talking."

"About you," Lorenzo said. "About your heritage."

Joe shook his head. "Not now, old man. Let me get Darcy back to her Secret Service team."

"What about this family?" Lorenzo demanded, banging his cane on the wooden floor. "What about your duty to it? You should be married and having babies."

"Okay, gotta go," Darcy said, taking that as her cue to leave. She waved and hurried out of the room. Oh, yeah. Hanging with Alex and Paige was much less pressure than dealing with Joe's inability to get along with his family.

Joe watched Darcy duck out. Lucky her. She could simply walk away.

"I'm not interested in getting married," he said calmly.

"So we all know. And what will happen when you are? What will you call her?"

Joe frowned. "My wife?"

"Will she be a Larson? That is not your real name. You are a Marcelli. You should take back the family name. Be proud you are one of us."

"Not in this lifetime," Joe growled as he turned on his heel and walked out of the room. Change his name? He was Joe Larson, always had been. It was bad enough the old man pressured him about getting married, and now Brenna expected him to learn more about the winery.

The need to run, to bolt for freedom, quickened his step, but there wasn't anywhere to go. As long as Darcy Jensen was in residence, he was trapped.

He'd barely made it to the barrel room of the winery when he ran into Alex Vanmeter. The head of security didn't look happy as he glared at Joe and announced, "We have to talk."

8

$\backsim$

Alex led Joe around to the back of the winery and checked to make sure they were alone. Then he turned on Joe and let loose.

"What were you thinking?" the agent demanded. Fury tightened his features and sharpened his voice. "You are our liaison with the family. You're a goddamn trained SEAL. You're supposed to be protecting Darcy, not putting her in danger. You have no right to prance around here, sucking face with the president's daughter."

Joe groaned. Between his family and Darcy, he was in the seventh level of hell and sinking fast.

He didn't have to ask how Alex knew about the kiss. No doubt the agent on duty had followed them and seen the whole thing.

"Do you know what we're up against?" Alex demanded. "This is not an easy location to keep secure."

"Then you shouldn't have picked it," Joe told him. "I'm doing my job, and that's all you get from me. Darcy can kiss who she wants. It's not putting her at risk, so you can stop the lecture."

Alex's expression hardened. "You're right, Lieutenant Commander. Kissing her didn't put her at risk, but walking off and leaving her alone sure did."

Joe stiffened. Alex was right. Joe had reacted in the moment, both by kissing her and then by stalking off. He'd needed to get away, to figure out what he thought he was doing. In that moment he hadn't considered who Darcy was or why she was here. If that other agent hadn't been there . . .

He swore long and loudly.

"My thoughts exactly," Alex said. "I'll be e-mailing a report to your commanding officer. I don't imagine you'll be with us much longer."

Joe knew he'd more than earned the action. He heard a flushing sound, followed by the visual of his career slipping down the toilet. The hell of it was, this time he had no one to blame but himself.

"In your position, I would do exactly the same," he said quietly. "You're right. I left the subject unprotected. If your man hadn't been there, she would have been completely exposed and vulnerable. It won't happen again."

Alex didn't look convinced. "Why should I believe you?"

"Because I don't make the same mistake twice. Because I know my job."

Alex shook his head. "Fine. Then remember to do it the next time you're alone with Darcy."

He turned and walked away.

Joe stared after him. What was wrong with him? He *knew* better. Why had he reacted to Darcy? Why had he kissed her?

It wasn't just because she was a woman. He'd worked with women before. Dozens of times. A lot of them had been prettier, smarter, or sexier, and he'd never once lost sight of his objective. Enemy operatives had attempted to seduce him with some highly erotic practices, and he'd ignored them all.

So why Darcy?

"Joe! There you are."

Mia rounded the corner of the building with Ian in tow. Joe's bad mood worsened when he saw the tall, thin young man. There was something about Ian that got on his nerves. Reason number one surfaced the second the lanky blond caught sight of him.

"Hey, Joe," Ian said cheerfully. "How's it going? We've been walking around the winery. It's so great here. I've never been to a winery before." He chuckled. "I've never been much of a wine drinker. But yesterday afternoon Mia took me over to the tasting room. It's really nice there. I like the garden and all the grass around it. She said you guys have weddings there. It would be beautiful for a wedding. Anyway, we had lots of different wines. We tried all the merlots and had a couple of the Four Sisters pinots. Those were really great. Mia told me all about Brenna starting her own winery. That's really cool. That she would do that. You're in the navy, right? A SEAL? I saw that movie. Navy SEALs. It was great. Macho. Didn't that one guy get shot? Huh. I guess if they'd had you along, that wouldn't have happened? Oh, the Secret Service cleared me. But I guess you knew that. I'm still here."

When he paused for breath, Mia jumped in. "So how are things?"

Joe shrugged. "Fine." He stared at Ian. What did she see in the guy? Mia caught his gaze and grinned, as if she could read his mind. She mouthed something that looked very much like "he's really good in bed," which he didn't want to know.

"I haven't had a chance to talk to Darcy," Ian said. "What's she like? She's prettier in person, don't you think? Of course I really like Lauren. She's always helping with those sick kids and it was really sad when her husband died. It was in that ice storm, wasn't it? When D.C. was shut down and his car went off the road. I saw their whole wedding. I was in high school and my mom had this big party and all her friends came over and watched. She made these funny sandwiches and a little wedding cake. It was really good, with a chocolate filling."

Joe started backing away. "I, ah, gotta write a report," he said, interrupting Ian's flow of conversation. "See you guys around."

With that, he ducked into a rear door of the winery and wandered the halls as he headed toward the front of the building. As he rounded a corner, he saw Marco sitting in an office and knocked on the open door.

"Joe! Come in. What are you doing here?"

"Escaping Ian. Mia's had some interesting guys before but never anyone like him," he said, taking a seat.

"I know." Marco leaned back in his chair. "I'm never fond of anyone my youngest daughter is sleeping with, but Ian is worse than most. I try to tell myself that he's basically a nice guy, even though he never stops talking. Besides, your mother likes him, as does mine."

Joe didn't react to Colleen being called his mother, or

the guilt he felt over what had happened with Tessa. Instead he focused on the topic at hand. "Then they're too easy."

Marco nodded at the sales report posted on the wall by the door. "We're having a good year. My father has done a great job with the winery for many years, but Brenna brings a touch of magic to the wines. She knows what our customers want."

"She's working hard," Joe acknowledged, wondering if he was about to get nailed again.

Marco struck immediately. "She could use some help."

Joe regretted sitting down. "I'm sure she can hire a good manager to help after the baby's born."

"It's more than that," Marco told him. "Joe, I know you love what you do with the navy, but in time that will end. You'll put in your twenty and retire. Then what? Where will you go? We would like you to come here. You're a Marcelli, Joe. You belong here."

Joe stood. "Look, Marco, I know what you want, what the whole family wants. It's not going to happen. I appreciate that you're trying. It's great. You guys are terrific, but this isn't my world and you're not. . . ." He hesitated, not sure he could say they weren't his family again. Hadn't he hurt enough people already that morning?

"This isn't for me," he finished lamely.

Marco nodded without speaking, but Joe saw the pain in his eyes. Whoever thought families were a good idea, he wondered as he excused himself and escaped into the quiet of the hallway. Give him a nice armed insurgence any day. At least there he would know what to do.

*   *   *

Paige faced the special agent in charge and prepared to do battle. "You're not reporting Joe to his superior officer," she said, going for a calm, but forceful, tone.

"I am," Alex said flatly. "What he did is inexcusable."

"I agree he screwed up, but that's no reason to serve him up on a platter. I'm sure he was shocked by what happened." She'd been shocked. It had been a long time since the president's daughter had gotten involved with anyone, and if Paige were offering opinions, she would bet Joe was one of the good guys, but Joe and Darcy? It didn't seem very likely.

"He left her *alone,*" Alex reminded her.

"No, he didn't. Agent Briggs was with them."

"He didn't know that. It's my decision, and I'm not changing my mind."

He turned to leave, but Paige grabbed his arm to hold him in place. Temper flared in his dark blue eyes, but she had a feeling he wouldn't shake her off.

"It's not about Joe," she told him. "If you report him, you'll have to explain the circumstances. You'll have to talk about the fact that they kissed. Darcy will be humiliated. Give the girl a break."

"There are rules to follow," Alex began.

"Oh, and you've never once bent them?"

"No."

Figures. "Try being human," she said. "Just this once. You've already lectured Joe. He's not going to screw up again."

"He shouldn't have screwed up at all. He knows better. He can't walk around thinking with his dick. He needs his brain engaged."

She looked at him and sighed. "I don't remember you being this much of a bastard before."

"My only concern is Darcy's safety."

"What about her happiness?"

"She won't be very happy when she's dead."

He was right, Paige realized. They were talking about Darcy's life, and there was no room for error. She released him.

"Giving up?" he asked.

She nodded. "Darcy is my primary concern. I want her alive *and* happy, but if I only have one choice, I'll pick alive."

Darcy curled up in the library. It was a quiet spot in the Marcelli house, and she liked the view she had of the vineyards out the east-facing window. She also liked that she was completely and totally alone, and not scared about it. When she'd returned from her visit with Grandpa Lorenzo, she'd informed Paige she would stay in for the rest of the afternoon, which meant she didn't have to deal with any security.

Now, as she leaned back in the big leather chair, she breathed in a sense of peace. Maybe it was knowing there were so many people around to keep her safe. Maybe it was because her brain still buzzed with the memory of Joe's kiss. Maybe her astrological moon was rising into a better house. Whatever the reason, she didn't care. Feeling good was fabulous.

She picked up her book, then set it down again. She'd loved the feel of his body against hers. It had been a long time since a man had held her as if he meant it. She wouldn't mind a repeat of the kiss and maybe a little bit of time spent playing the bases with Joe. Not that he was likely to offer, but a girl could dream.

The door to the library opened and the star of her sexual fantasies walked in. He glanced around, then spotted her.

"Oh. You're here."

She smiled, not the least bit put out by his sullenness. From what she could tell, Joe hated everyone. His attitude wasn't personal. "I've always admired a man who handled his abundance of charm with such grace. It's so elegant."

"I'm having a bad day."

"Should I take that comment personally?"

"What?" He closed the door behind him then crossed to the window. "No. It's not about, you know."

You know? How interesting. The big, bad Navy SEAL couldn't say *kiss*? He prowled the room like a tiger, and she had the urge to tweak his tail.

"I don't know, actually. What are you talking about?"

He glared at her. "Our kiss."

"Oh. That."

His eyebrows drew together, and she had a feeling he was going to start yelling at her. All that energy, she thought, more intrigued than afraid. He must have been one fine soldier.

"I hate Ian," he grumbled.

The change of subject caught her off guard for a second. "He's not so bad."

"He's not sleeping with your sister."

"That's true." She tilted her head. "You've never claimed one of the Marcellis as family before."

"Don't read anything into it. It's just Mia's a baby. She thinks she's wild and tough, but she's not."

"And you worry about her."

He stopped in midstride and glared.

"Don't worry," she said. "My lips are sealed. Besides, even if I wasn't interested in keeping your secrets, I don't want to mess up a good thing. I like it here."

"Don't sound so surprised."

"I am. I didn't think I would. There are too many people and it's so wide open here. But I like the whole family. You should try to appreciate what you have."

"Look, I've heard enough of that to last a lifetime."

"If you were smarter, you'd realize how lucky you are to have found the Marcellis."

"They found me."

"And you've been fighting them ever since."

He returned to the window. "Can we change the subject?"

"We can, but I don't want to. Besides, if you hate what we're talking about, you could leave."

His silence told her he couldn't. But why?

"Are you hiding out here?" she asked.

"I'm running out of places to go."

A feeling she understood. She uncoiled her legs and rested her feet on the floor. "Okay. I'll stop torturing you for sport, but I won't change the subject. You have a terrific family. You're crazy if you don't appreciate that."

He looked at her. "Why does it matter so much to you?"

Because he had everything she'd ever wanted. "My family is small, and we're not so close," she said instead.

"Then you take 'em. I want to get back to base."

"So the navy is your real home?" she asked.

"Yeah."

"It must be nice to spend your day saving the world."

His gaze narrowed, as if he thought she might be teasing him. Darcy did her best to look innocent, although the excessive blinking might have given her away. But before Joe could get all macho on her again, the door opened and Grandma Tessa stepped inside.

"Joseph," she said tentatively, her expression fearful. "I thought you'd come inside." She nodded at Darcy. "I made sandwiches. You didn't come to lunch."

He looked at her, then back out the window. "I'm not hungry."

Darcy winced as the old woman seemed to shrink two inches. "All right, Joseph."

Tessa turned and left.

Darcy stood, walked over to Joe, and socked him in the arm as hard as she could. He looked at her.

"What was that for?"

"It's for whatever you did to Grandma Tessa."

Joe stared hard at the view. "Get off of me."

She socked him again. He didn't budge, but she really hurt her hand. "What did you do?" she demanded.

"Nothing."

"Tell me or I'll start talking about girl stuff."

He winced. "I can handle it."

Oh, no he couldn't. She searched her memories for something that would bring him to his knees.

"I was twelve when I got my first period," she began.

He swore. "Fine. I had a fight with Brenna. I told her the Marcellis weren't my family. Tessa walked in and heard me."

She sucked in a breath. "That bites. How could you do that to her? She's an old woman who loves you."

"I didn't do it on purpose," he yelled as he turned toward her. "Okay? I'm sorry. I shouldn't have said it."

She leaned toward him. "Well, don't apologize to me. And don't yell. Besides if you were really sorry, you would have taken her sandwich."

He opened his mouth, then closed it. "What?"

"The sandwich. *The sandwich.* Man, you might know a whole bunch about guns and rescuing people but you don't know anything about women, do you? Ever hear the expression 'food is love'? Tessa is old-world Italian. She shows her affection by feeding her family. Every time she offers you food, she's offering you love. When you reject the meal, you reject her."

"That's stupid."

She really wanted to hit him again, but her knuckles still hurt. "No, it's not. Just eat the food."

"I don't want to," he said as he walked out of the library. "This is all bullshit."

9

❧

*L*ife got ugly for Darcy when her favorite black cotton pants wouldn't zip up without her performing an inelegant shimmy on her back, on the bed. Once she sat up, breathing became impossible.

While she knew she had to put on a few pounds, she didn't think gaining them directly in her stomach and hips was anyone's idea of attractive. There was only one thing to do.

After rooting through one of her still-packed suitcases, she came across a pair of bicycle shorts, a black sports bra, and some serious-looking athletic shoes. They'd been designed by NASA or somebody equally scientific. Apparently if she put in some effort while wearing them, she could jump tall buildings and all that.

"Oh, yeah," she muttered as she laced up the shoes. "This is me—working out."

Ten minutes later she'd made her way to the Marcelli workout room. As all the equipment was relatively new and didn't look very used, she wondered if the space had been created for Joe's infrequent visits home. Somehow she couldn't see Grandma Tessa taking twenty on the treadmill.

She bypassed the running machine and went directly to the elliptical. There she punched in one of the existing programs, set the tension for as easy as possible, and pushed the On button.

Exercising was bad enough, but this room made it worse with four walls of mirrors. She got to watch her face turn bright red, then admire the drops of sweat as they formed and dripped off her nose. Talk about fashion forward.

Oh God, she thought nearly six minutes into her workout. She couldn't breathe. No way she'd gotten this out of shape. She was only twenty-six.

"On the outside," she wheezed. "On the inside, I'm a hundred and nine. Why does healthy have to be so h-hard?"

She sucked in a breath as the machine increased the tension. According to the heart monitor, she'd barely broken triple digits on her heart rate, but her chest felt tight, and her legs were ready to quit in serious protest. Flames licked up her thighs, and not the exciting, sexy kind.

"Lauren does this every day," she gasped. "And she runs. She's sicker than I thought."

At fifteen minutes into her twenty-minute program, she knew she was going to die. The Secret Service would come looking for her and find her sweaty but lifeless body bent over the machine. Paige would be sad, but everyone else would simply move on to the next assignment.

"I can't do this. I ca—"

The workout room door opened and Joe walked in.

Suddenly things like breathing and painful muscles didn't matter. Not when there was an entire buffet of eye candy, not only in person but reflected in the mirrors.

She instantly straightened so he wouldn't know how close she'd come to quitting and sucked in her gut. A deep breath and a lot of effort allowed her to say, "Morning. How's it going," as if she weren't completely winded.

Joe looked at her, then the door. He'd pretty much avoided everyone for the past twenty-four hours. Would he duck out now?

Apparently he needed the workout more than he wanted to be away from her. He grunted a greeting and walked to the treadmill. He, too, punched in a program, but he set his for warp speed. After about thirty seconds of a fast walk, he started jogging, then broke into a run.

Darcy had planned on doing her twenty minutes, then escaping to her room for some serious relaxation. But with Joe running so earnestly and his loose T-shirt flopping over thick, powerful muscles, she thought she might stay long enough to work with the set of free weights in the far corner.

Her machine beeped, freeing her from its torture. She patted her face with the towel she'd brought, then moved to the bench by the weights. It was in the perfect position, allowing her to see Joe from not only the front but also the back, which was reflected in the mirror.

"Missed you at dinner last night," she said as she picked up two ten-pound weights and raised them to shoulder height. "Grammy M stopped by, which meant Grandma Tessa was in a snit. She wasn't talking, but no one could tell because Ian babbled on and on about college and his studies and where he and Mia have been. He made Vegas sound boring, something I didn't think was possible."

Joe picked up the pace on the treadmill, which she took to mean that he was really enjoying their conversation.

"I'm here because of the pasta," she continued. "It's going all to my stomach, which is bad enough, but I know the next stop is my thighs."

"You're lifting wrong."

She paused in midpush, the weights just above her head, her elbows bent.

"What?"

"Start with your palms facing in, then turn them out as you push up."

She dropped the weights to her lap because it was too complicated to change position in midexercise. For a half second she considered ignoring his instructions. If she did it wrong again would he abandon the treadmill to sit next to her and show her how? Would he put his large, masculine hands on her damp, hot body and—

Whoa—stop that fantasy train right there. No more sexy thoughts about Joe, she told herself firmly. He wasn't for her. He didn't even like her. One kiss did not a relationship make.

She did a set of ten presses, then switched to bicep curls. He continued to run at a grueling pace designed to make her hurt just watching him.

"Why are you mad?" he asked.

"I'm not."

"You're scowling."

She glanced in the mirror and realized he was right.

She instantly relaxed her face and tried to think happy thoughts.

"Not a morning person?" he asked.

"I'm fine."

"You haven't had coffee yet."

She didn't ask how he knew. "I couldn't fit into my pants. I figured I'd better start working out."

"You need to gain weight."

"Thanks for the news flash, but you've already berated me for that. You don't get to do it again."

He grinned. "It's not like you can stop me."

She felt the scowl reappear.

"Yell at me," he said. "I can take it. Are you sleeping?"

"I'm not talking about that with you."

"But it's an interesting topic."

He was trying to make her mad, and he was succeeding. "Let's talk about you," she snapped. "I may be a skinny insomniac with post-traumatic shock or some such crap, but at least I don't go around hurting my grandmother's feelings."

"Good point."

It didn't feel like a good point. If anything, Darcy would say it felt small and mean-spirited. "I, ah . . ." Apologize, she told herself. The thing was, she didn't do it very often, so she wasn't very good at it. "I shouldn't have said that."

"Why not? It's true."

That stunned her, but the shock was nothing when compared with what he said next. "I've been thinking about what you said. The food-is-love connection. You might be right."

If she'd had any rhythm, she would have stood up and

done a little victory dance. Instead she contented herself with a smug smile.

"Gee, thanks for the endorsement. I won't let it go to my head. Besides, the concept is hardly revolutionary. Most mothers show love with food, mine always did. The Marcelli family is Italian, so they have that gene in spades." She considered his past. "Didn't your adoptive mother do the same thing?"

"I don't remember. I was a kid when my parents died. I barely remember what they look like."

The sadness inherent in the statement made her want to walk over and hug him. Both the jogging and her visceral reaction to him made that action impossible. Still, an ache settled in her midsection and made her more determined than ever to help him connect with his family.

"I'm sure she did the same thing," Darcy told him. "I'm not sure we as women can help it."

"Maybe," he admitted, with obvious reluctance. "My ex used to make cookies for her kids when they had a bad day."

"See?" She instantly wanted to ask more questions about his previous marriage but thought her obvious curiosity might destroy the moment.

She set down the weights and stood. "I know you're ambivalent about your family, but what I don't know is why. They only want to love you, Joe. What's so bad about that?"

He hit the Stop button on the treadmill and glared at her. "You're not going to let this go, are you?"

She shook her head as the moment died. "It's too important."

"Why do you care?"

"I'm a compassionate person, and don't you dare laugh. It's true."

Joe didn't doubt it. He might not enjoy his current assignment, but it wasn't because of Darcy. Somehow the press had become convinced she was a prima dona bitch with an attitude, and they slanted all their stories that way. But it wasn't true. Oh, sure, Darcy could use sarcasm like a weapon and she was verbally deadly when she was angry, but at heart, she was a complete pushover.

He wiped his face and neck, then stepped off the treadmill and headed for the mats covering the floor at the rear of the room.

"Come here," he said.

Her expression turned suspicious. "Why?"

He held in a grin. "Don't you trust me?"

"Not as much as you might think."

"I know I can't ask you to change the subject. For some reason you're convinced you can heal me and make me want to bond with my family. So I'm trying to distract you."

"Uh-huh. How?"

He crooked his index finger, beckoning her over. "Come on, Darcy. You know you want to."

"I'm not sure I want to at all," she said, but she began to move toward him. "Are you going to teach me some new exercises?"

"Nope. I'm going to teach you a few moves to ward off would-be attackers. Your Secret Service team should have done it already."

"I've been to a few self-defense classes."

"Not good enough. I'm going to teach you to fight dirty. Stand here." He positioned her in front of him. "I'm going to grab you. I want you to try and break free."

He leaned forward and wrapped both arms around her. The second he did, he knew he'd made a huge mistake.

She was hot and sweaty from her workout, which should have been a turnoff, but instead it made him think of other kinds of activity that could work up a sweat. He instantly pictured them rolling around together in bed, bodies sliding together, hands reaching, them both straining to—

He shook off the thought and did his best not to react. In nylon shorts there was no way he could hide a hard-on.

Focus, he told himself. He had to remember what was important.

"Elbow me in the midsection," he said. "As hard as you can. And don't worry, you can't hurt me."

She sucked in a breath, then rammed her elbow into his midsection. He barely felt it.

"Harder, Darcy. I'm the bad guy. Do it like you mean it."

She hit him again, but it wasn't much more than a slight blow. Her security wrist band barely moved. He released her. "Are you even trying?"

She huffed. "Yes. And let me say for the record—ouch." She rubbed her arm.

He couldn't help chuckling. "That was it? That was your big power play?"

Fury darkened her eyes and determination pulled at her mouth. Even all blotchy and damp, she was still pretty, he thought, amused by her temper. The sports bra and shorts left nothing to the imagination. She might be all female, but she was sadly lacking in curves. Still, he wanted her. Funny how it didn't matter that she wasn't his usual type.

"I want to do it again," she said, turning her back to him.

He obliged her by stepping close and grabbing her. One of his hands was right below her left breast. He felt the heat of the modest swell, and it was all he could do not to reach up and cup the feminine flesh. Would her nipple get hard right away? Would it—

Bam! She nailed him hard in the gut, and he'd forgotten to prepare. Her bony elbow connected painfully with a rib. At the same time she stomped down hard on his foot, then turned to face him, both hands raised in fists.

"Better," he said, ignoring the pain. "But don't take on your attacker. Run like hell. My point is, you can't use conventional methods to hurt a man who's bigger and stronger. That's what I wanted to demonstrate."

She looked disappointed. "I didn't hurt you?"

He ignored the fading pain in his midsection. "Do I look hurt?"

"I guess not."

He pointed to her face. "Go for the eyes. Or the base of your palm to the base of the nose. Push hard, toward the eyes." He explained a few other vulnerable points.

"What if there's more than one?" she asked when he'd paused. "What do I do then?"

He remembered the attack that had brought her here in the first place. "How many were there?"

"Four. They grabbed me and tied me up before I could do anything."

He reached out and put his hand on her shoulder. "You're not going to win against four guys, Darcy. There's nothing you could have done."

"But you could have held off four guys?"

He shrugged. "I have years of training."

"Could I learn?"

Would it help? Would it make her feel safer? "If you wanted to. First you need to get some muscle on your body. Those weights you were working with are fine to tone up, but you need to be pushing yourself." He glanced over her frame. "You should be able to bench-press a hundred pounds and leg press double that."

Her eyes widened. "Are you crazy? I'll look like some kind of freak."

"You won't bulk up. Women don't. Besides, muscle makes you tight and defined." He shook his head. "What is it about women and looking muscular?"

"It's cultural. As the half of the species rewarded for being bigger, you wouldn't understand."

"But you look fine."

"You said I was too skinny."

"You are."

She sighed. "Let me guess. You like lots of curves on your women."

He sensed this was a dangerous conversation and didn't respond with more than a shrug.

"I knew it."

"You look perfectly okay," he said.

"Oh, wow. I can hardly breathe from the excited beating of my heart. What a compliment. I'll treasure it always."

He didn't think she was upset, but he wasn't sure. "You know you're attractive, right?"

"I guess."

Her unenthusiastic response and the way she averted her gaze made him wonder if she did. He moved a little closer.

"Darcy, you are. You have a pretty face, great eyes, and when you smile, it's like you're sharing a secret with the world."

She ducked her head. "Thanks. I appreciate you saying that, but in my family, Lauren's the pretty one. Not that I mind," she added hastily.

"You need to get over your sister complex."

She looked at him and rolled her eyes. "Gee, Dr. Larson, thanks for the psychological evaluation. But it's not that simple. Life keeps getting in the way. For example, the first guy I ever slept with turned out to not be interested in me at all. He suffered through our relationship simply to get an invitation home for winter break where he hit on my sister. Lauren, being Lauren, refused to have anything to do with him, but that didn't take away the sting."

Why had he started this conversation?

"He's a jerk, and you're better off without him," Joe told her.

"I know that, but it's not the point. And at the time, it really hurt. There I was, heartbroken, and my sister was trying to make it better. She's just a nice person."

"She sounds perfect."

Darcy nodded. "She is. Pretty much in everything she does. Everyone loves her."

"Perfect can get boring."

Darcy glared at him. "Don't you say anything bad about my sister."

He held up both hands and took a step back. "You have a pretty complex relationship with Lauren."

"I know." She sighed. "Sorry for snapping. Sometimes . . ." She smiled. "I'm a multifaceted person."

And charming, he thought as he moved closer. Funny, vulnerable. And the president's daughter. He was just the hired help. Getting involved would be crazy.

"Oh, wow," she breathed as she stared up at him.

"I'm not going to kiss you," he told her.

"I can see that."

Darcy watched desire darken Joe's eyes. He might claim he wasn't going to kiss her, but she would bet a lot of money that he wanted to. She felt all shivery and hot and nervous. But she didn't move away. Not even an inch. If there was the potential for some lip-lock, she wanted to be there for the whole thing.

He reached out and touched her cheek with his fingers. "I could lose my career over this," he said quietly.

"No woman could ever be worth that."

"Agreed."

But he didn't step away, and the thought thrilled her. He wanted her. She could feel it in the tension in his body. He wanted *her*. Not Lauren, he wasn't interested in political favors. He was—

He leaned forward and claimed her mouth with his. There was heat and promise in that first brush of his lips. She relaxed into him, raising her arms to his shoulders, and let her body sag into his hardness. He pulled her close, angled his head, and swept his tongue against her bottom lip.

She parted without thinking. Need overwhelmed her, and the second he eased inside to claim her, she knew it wasn't going to be enough. She wanted more. She wanted all of it.

Hunger swept through her, causing her to run her hands up and down his back, urging him closer. Her breasts flattened against his chest, her thighs nestled with his. She wanted to rub against him like a cat—she wanted him touching her everywhere.

Instead she had to content herself with a deep, sensual, perfect kiss. He claimed her mouth with a mastery that left her breathless. His tongue circled hers, teasing, arousing, delighting. His large hands stroked her back before moving lower to cup her rear. When he squeezed, she arched forward, bringing her belly in contact with his erection.

Her breath caught as she realized he was hard. She'd made him want her. Need swelled as did her nipples. They ached. *She* ached.

Not knowing what else to do, she slid her hands under his T-shirt until she touched bare skin. He was hot and slightly damp, and she found herself wanting to explore him all over. First with her fingers and then with her tongue. She wanted to taste him and consume him.

He pulled back with a suddenness that made her gasp. They stared at each other, both breathing hard. Joe's eyes were dilated.

Silence filled the room. She waited for him to dismiss what had happened between them. Not because she believed he could, but because her luck with men just wasn't that good. He stunned her when he gave her a half-grin, half-grimace and said, "It wasn't supposed to be that great."

"Yeah?" she asked, unable to keep from smiling.

"Yeah. You're big trouble. Your father is my commander in chief."

"Does that really matter?"

"It should."

Which didn't answer her question.

"You go first," he said, motioning to the door.

Right. So they weren't seen together.

"I'll wait here," he continued. "Until it's safe."

"I doubt anyone is lurking in the hallway."

"That's not what I mean." He pointed at his crotch.

"Oh." He was obviously hard, and it was damned impressive. "Right. You don't want to flash that at Grandma Tessa."

He winced. "Talking about her will help solve the problem."

"I live to serve."

Mia caught up with Darcy late that morning. "You have to come right now," Mia said as she burst into Darcy's room. "I'm convinced there's something going on between Paige and Alex."

"What? That's crazy. Agents can't be involved."

"I don't know what the rules are, but they're always giving each other these smoldering looks. I've called a meeting of the Marcelli women and you *have* to be there. I mean, you're one of us, now."

Darcy didn't think that was true, but she was delighted to be asked. "I'm in."

"Cool." Mia grinned. "Francesca is coming, too, so you can meet her and the twins. They're at the insane age. Running around and getting into everything. There's two of them and only seven of us. I'm not sure we'll manage."

Darcy laughed. "I think we can handle it."

Mia shook her head. "Have you ever been around toddler twins? Trust me, every second is an adventure."

It turned out Mia was telling the truth. Eric and Haley were two and a half and too adorable for words. They both had dark hair, and blue, blue eyes. Haley had the kind of curls women sell their souls for. They were also bundles of energy who refused to be contained.

The Marcelli women gathered in the large living room where Darcy met Francesca Reese for the first time. Brenna's fraternal twin was tall and slender, with short, dark hair and beautiful features.

Brenna settled in a corner of the couch, then announced she would need help when it was time for her to stand up.

"Do you like her hair?" Brenna asked, pointing at Francesca.

Darcy nodded. "It's really cute."

"So typical. I cut my hair three years ago and I looked like a yak. She does it right after the twins were born and she's a supermodel." Brenna eyed the twins as they raced around the coffee table. "Please, God, no twins for me. I'd have to kill myself."

Grammy M picked up her cup of tea. "Brenna, darlin', be careful how you're talkin' to the Lord."

"But I'm sincere. I'm really worried about the twin thing. I can't have twins. I just can't. I'll be forced to send them back."

"Good luck," Colleen told her daughter. "They resist the process." She glanced around. "This is nice, having my girls here. Except for Katie. I miss her. If only she lived closer."

Grammy M smiled at Brenna. "See how a mother loves her children? You'll do the same, twins or not."

"I guess." Brenna didn't sound convinced.

Mia flopped down on the second sofa and reached for a cookie on one of the plates of food Grandma Tessa had brought into the room. There'd been a minor scuffle in the kitchen when Grammy M had shown up with brownies, but now Tessa's cookies and Grammy M's brownies sat at separate tables.

"Wouldn't it show up in an ultrasound?" Mia asked as she munched. "Wouldn't they see four arms or legs?"

"I've only had a couple to make sure things are all right. Nic and I don't want to know the sex of the baby, and if you keep going, someone is bound to slip. It's just that at one of the ultrasounds, the technician said there were two babies, but since then, we've only seen one." Brenna tried to lean forward, then sagged back and held out her hand. "Someone give me a brownie, please. I need chocolate."

Little Haley dove for the brownie Colleen picked up, slipped, and banged her head on the coffee table. She started crying, and Eric joined in, Darcy supposed, to be supportive. Francesca grabbed for one twin, Colleen took the other, and Brenna clutched her brownie.

Mia waited until the sobs had died down, then cleared her throat. "I'm sure you're all wondering why I called this meeting."

"You said it was because you thought Paige and Alex have something going on," Darcy said.

Francesca smiled at her. "They're your Secret Service agents, right?"

"Two of many," Darcy said with a shrug.

Francesca rocked Haley. "You must get tired of having so many people around."

"Yeah," Brenna said. "I had plenty of that when I lived here."

Tessa bustled into the room and scowled at her grand-daughter. "We're your family, and you're lucky to have us."

Brenna grinned. "I love you, too, Grandma Tessa."

The old woman's face softened into a smile.

"Hey, back to my agenda," Mia said. "Paige and Alex. I haven't actually seen them doing anything, but there are plenty of longing glances. It makes me wonder what's up. Darcy. You're the person most likely to know."

Everyone looked at her. Darcy held her mug of tea like a shield. "Time out. I don't know anything. I've had Paige on my security team before, but I've only just met Alex. To be honest, he's so by the book, I can't imagine him with a woman."

"Still waters," Colleen said. "Men like that can surprise you."

Brenna, Francesca, and Mia looked at one another, then Mia said, "Mom, if that is *any* reference to your sex life with Dad, I beg you to stop. No one here wants to know. Especially your daughters. Yuck."

Colleen's smile turned smug. "All right, girls, don't freak out."

"I'm totally freaked," Brenna said. "What about you?"

Francesca nodded. "It's an image I never want in my brain."

"Alex and Paige," Mia said. "Stay focused, people."

Darcy looked at her. "I don't understand. Do you want to help them get together?"

"Of course." Mia sat up straighter. "I figure we can trick them into being alone together."

Interesting plan, Darcy thought. "But they're already sharing the guesthouse. Doesn't that mean they're alone together every night?"

"Oh." Mia sank back onto the sofa. "Good point. I guess they don't need our help. So, Darcy, what do you think of Joe?"

Darcy immediately sensed the danger of the situation. Still, she faced the other women bravely and decided the best defense and all that.

"He's great. What can you tell me about his ex-wife?"

She'd expected a few murmurs about how lovely she was or maybe shrugs when they said they'd never met her. She didn't expect stunned silence, followed by forty-seven questions at once.

"Married?" Brenna asked. "When did he get married?"

"There's an ex-wife?" Francesca asked. "Do we know her?"

"Tell me she's dead," Grandma Tessa said as she pulled her beads out of her pocket. "Better that than a divorce."

"I wonder if she'll tell us what he looked like naked," Mia mused.

Joe wandered into the kitchen in the late afternoon. He crossed to the refrigerator before he realized Tessa was at the stove. She looked up when he entered but didn't say anything. Still, the hurt in her eyes was enough to make him feel like a slug.

Dammit, what was he supposed to say to her? He

couldn't give her what she wanted, but that didn't give him the excuse to be cruel.

He crossed to her and gave her a hug. "I'm sorry about what I said."

She held him with a fierceness that surprised him. "It's been three years, Joseph." She stepped back and stared up at him. "How long? When are we family?"

He didn't know how to answer that. He wasn't going to lie, but he didn't want to hurt her again.

She was so small and frail—she didn't even come to his shoulder. Funny how she seemed so much bigger when she was bustling in the kitchen or bringing a grown man to his knees with one of her deadly cheek pinches.

Finally she turned away. "I'll make you some pasta," she said. "You didn't eat lunch. You must be hungry."

His first instinct was to say no, but then he remembered what Darcy had told him. About food being love.

"I'd like that," he said and was rewarded with a glowing smile.

"Sit, sit. You'll have bread, too. And salad. Maybe some wine. You like the red, yes?"

"That would be great. Thanks."

She served the food, poured the wine, then sat down across from him. Later he would swear she waited until he'd taken the first forkful of food and his mouth was full.

"So, Joseph. Tell me about your wife."

10

❧

Still feeling the need to hide out after inadvertently dropping a bombshell on the family, Darcy retreated to her room and picked up the secure phone that had been installed the second day of her visit. She dialed a familiar number and was connected with her father's personal assistant.

"It's Darcy," she said. "Is he available?"

"No, honey. He's in a meeting with China. Want me to interrupt?"

Darcy glanced at her watch. It was nearly five here, which made it close to eight in D.C. As per usual, her father was working late.

"No. That's okay. Tell him . . ." What? That she missed him? That would make him laugh. "Tell him I called."

"Will do. Are you okay? Having a good time?"

Darcy looked around the room, at the familiar furnishings and the view of the vineyard just beyond her window.

"I'm having a great time," she said.

*   *   *

Darcy's bedroom door opened without warning and Joe stalked inside. She was about to point out that he should at least pretend to knock—what if she'd been naked—when she saw the slight twitch in his cheek and something that looked amazingly like the need to squash, beat, or maim in his eyes.

She put down the book she'd been reading and held up both hands in a gesture that some might take to be surrender.

"You never said it was a secret," she pointed out, speaking quickly. "It didn't occur to me they didn't know. I mean, come on. It's been three years and you never bothered to mention to your family that you'd been married? That's not my fault."

He closed the door and walked to the bed. She thought about scooting over and patting the mattress in invitation but doubted that was why he was here.

"You're right," he said, his voice tight and clipped, which could be caused by his clenched teeth. "I didn't tell them."

"And you didn't say I shouldn't say anything."

"Right."

"And you really should have mentioned it to them before this."

He crossed to the single chair in the room and sank onto the cushion. "Apparently."

"Are they hysterical?"

"Tessa's done her rosary twice and is begging me to tell her that my ex is dead, because a dead wife is a whole lot better than divorce in her book. Grammy M and Colleen are hurt, and Brenna and Mia are mad. I haven't talked with Marco or Lorenzo yet, but I'm sure they'll give me an earful."

He seemed surprised. Men, she thought. Sometimes they weren't all that bright.

"They're your family. You may not think of them as such, but they think of themselves that way. It's not like you stubbed your toe and forgot to mention it. You were *married*. You had a whole other life."

He shrugged. "I'm not married now. Haven't been in a while."

"What happened?" she asked. "I mean why did you guys split up?"

He stared at her without speaking. Darcy figured he was trying to intimidate her. While it kind of worked, she wanted to know more than she was afraid of him.

"It's a logical question," she told him. "You'd ask me the same thing if our positions were reversed."

"No, I wouldn't."

"Okay. Your loss. So what happened?"

Joe leaned back in the chair and rubbed the bridge of his nose. "She couldn't handle me having to leave without any notice and being gone for months at a time. I'd warned her what it would be like, and she said it was fine. But hearing about it and living it were different. One time I came home and she was gone."

Darcy's heart cracked a little in sympathy. "I'm sorry. That must have been horrible."

"It wasn't one of my best moments." He shrugged. "I got over her quicker than I should have, which says something about the state of our relationship, but I really missed the kids."

"How many?"

"Two. Eight and ten. They were great," he said with a smile that told her he had a lot of good memories. "Later, when I realized who I missed the most, I wondered if they were the real reason I'd wanted to get married. To have an instant family."

As soon as the words were out, he straightened, getting all stiff, as if he regretted the confession.

He'd wanted children in his life? She never would have guessed.

"That's just so sad," she told him.

"Whatever. I got over it." He looked at her. "My family doesn't need to know about the kids."

"Not a problem. I won't say anything. I didn't mean to spill secrets about your divorce."

"I know. I should have told them myself."

But he hadn't. Knowing him as she did, she could guess why. But what didn't make sense was why he'd told her.

Shortly after midnight, Alex found himself walking restlessly through the small guesthouse. He should have been getting some sleep. He wasn't on duty, and come morning there would be plenty to do. But he wasn't sleepy and the light still shining under Paige's door beckoned him like a siren's call.

She'd changed, he acknowledged. Softened, but not in a way that interfered with her doing her job. In that respect, she was as focused as always. She seemed more balanced, more connected with people. The drive had faded, maybe disappeared. He would have bet on her staying as career driven as she'd been when he'd first met her, and it pissed him off that the change was due to another man.

He paused outside of her door and put his hand on the

knob. Going in would be stupid and weak. Better to walk away. He'd managed to forget about her once before. In fact, after they'd split up and gone their separate ways, he'd barely thought about her at all. So what was the big deal now? He could—

He knocked on the door and opened it at the same time. Paige sat on her bed, reading. There was a glass of wine on the nightstand and soft music playing in the background.

She raised her eyebrows. "It's a little late for business," she said. "And we're officially off duty."

"I know."

He started to back out of the room, but she gestured to the open bottle of wine on the dresser. "Help yourself," she told him.

There was a second glass on the tray. Had she been expecting company? Expecting him?

After pouring himself a glass of chardonnay, he moved to the overstuffed chair in the corner of the room and sank down.

"The assignment's going well," he said into the silence.

Paige closed her book and set it beside her. She wore the same pajamas he'd seen her in before. A tank top over loose pants. No bra. The curve of her breast was clearly visible, as was the slight pucker of her nipple.

She picked up her wine and took a sip. "I agree. Darcy is relaxing, which is good. I had an interesting talk with Joe today. He thinks Darcy should receive some advanced self-defense training. Maybe get started in some form of martial arts. He also suggested I put together a workout program for her that will get her into some heavy weights."

Alex wasn't sure it would help. "She was taken by four men. Very few women would be able to stop that."

"Agreed, but the training and additional strength would give her more of a sense of control. That might help her sleep at night."

He worried more about the subject's physical safety than her emotional state of mind. Still it couldn't hurt.

"Whatever you want to do with her is fine with me," he said.

"How thrilled I am to have my leader's permission," she said with a grin. "I know Darcy will do the dance of joy."

He felt the teasing more than he should have. "Why were you telling me if not to get permission."

"I was having a conversation, Alex. You might remember them."

She thought he was too into the job. Not interesting enough. The assessment stung. He'd had to work his ass off to get his present assignment. She, of all people, should appreciate that.

"I know how to have a conversation," he said. "Let's have one. Do you miss being married?"

He wasn't sure if the question surprised her, but it shocked the hell out of him. He'd planned on saying something about the winery. Those other words had come from nowhere.

"I miss Ben," she said quietly. Her green eyes seemed to darken with what? Memories? Pain?

"A lot of people were surprised when you got married," he said. Mostly him. "What happened?"

"The usual." She smiled. "I met Ben and fell in love."

She'd claimed to love *him* but there'd been no talk of

marriage. No search for a happily ever after. Why? What had that Ben guy had that he, Alex, hadn't?

"It screwed up your career," he said.

"If you mean I didn't get ahead as quickly as I could have, that's true. On the other hand, I actually had a private life, and that was very important to me. Ben taught me life isn't an all-or-nothing sport. There are points of compromise, and sometimes that's even better than winning."

On what planet? Alex drank more wine and wished they were talking about anything else.

"When I met Ben," she continued, "I warned him I would work long hours and have to travel. He said he would rather have me around some of the time than not at all. It was a unique perspective."

Alex didn't know what to do with that information. "So, how did he die?"

"Lymphoma. He had it when we met, but he was in remission. Unfortunately, it came back and then he died."

Alex stared at her. "You knew he was dying when you married him?"

"I knew the disease was likely to reoccur and that the odds of us growing old together were slim."

"Why would you do that?"

Paige smiled. "Because I loved him. Because I would rather have had a short time with him than none at all."

Annoyance flared into something bigger and hotter. "You were willing to give up your career for some guy who was dying, but you broke up with me because your career was all-important?"

"I told you, Ben taught me to compromise. Besides, you never wanted to marry me."

"Oh, yeah? How do *you* know?"

One corner of her mouth turned up. "You never asked."

This was not how he'd wanted the evening to go. He stood and put the glass back on her dresser. "I won't bother you anymore," he said stiffly.

"You're not a bother."

Anger gave energy to his stride as he walked to the door. "I'll see you in the morning. Good night."

"Alex, wait."

But he didn't. Instead he stepped into the hall and closed her door behind him.

He stood there in the darkness, but she didn't come out. She didn't beg him to return. And then he didn't know why he'd left in the first place, but it was too late to change that now.

Joe walked through the winery. Funny how this was the one place he could usually find to be alone. No Grandma Tessa trying to feed him or talk about his ex-wife. No Brenna wanting to talk about grapes or his ex-wife, or Mia wanting to talk about God knows what, including his ex-wife, with Ian offering a hundred different opinions. No Darcy.

He didn't have a specific complaint about her, except he was an idiot where she was concerned. He wasn't supposed to even *like* her. She should be a nonperson. Simply the subject to be kept safe. Nothing more. But she was real and alive, and for some reason he'd yet to figure out, she got to him.

In an effort to distract himself, he walked into Lorenzo's office. The old man wasn't there—a good thing because Joe wasn't interested in going another round on inheritance, his future, or changing his name from Larson to Marcelli.

He glanced at the old ledger books, the charts that detailed production, and the big map on the wall—the one that showed all the Marcelli land, and most of Wild Sea next door. He moved closer and traced the line of the coast, then studied the elegant script that spelled out the family name.

He wasn't one of them, never had been, never would be. But no matter how many times he told them, they ignored him. It was as if they thought they could make him believe by their combined force of will. As if they could force him into what they saw as his destiny.

A familiar slow step caught his attention. He turned to the doorway and saw Lorenzo enter the room. The old man nodded at Joe, then made his way to his desk where he sat down heavily.

"There are too many women in this family," he announced as he rested his cane against the desk. "There always have been. God could have blessed me with five grandsons, but instead he saw fit to surround me with women." He leaned back in his chair and eyed Joe. "You had the right idea. Join the navy and leave the women behind."

Joe grinned. "They're letting women in the navy these days. Even on the ships."

"Fools. It was better before. When a man could be alone with his thoughts. Now—all the talking. If Tessa is awake her lips are moving, and not in prayer."

Joe held in his amusement. "At this point, she's not going to change."

Lorenzo nodded. "I know. She makes me tired. Of course you would know that. A man learns things when he takes a wife."

Joe groaned. "Not you, too."

"Of course me." The old man shook his head. "You didn't tell us."

"It didn't matter. The marriage was long over before I knew about the Marcellis."

Before Joe could respond, Ian popped his head in the office. "Hey. There you are. I thought I'd find you here. Hi. We're going to be heading out. Mia and I want to go down to San Diego for a few days before coming back here. Joe, you think you could get us on base? It would be really cool to see some of the ships and planes and stuff up close. I'd really like to."

Ian stepped into the office and looked around. "Great place. Marcelli is the best. Everything is so interesting here. I really like the wine stuff. Mia doesn't know much, but we've done tasting and watched the guys working. If I wasn't going into government work, I think I'd want to work with wine. But here. Not in Napa or up there. I grew up here." He spotted the map on the wall. "Cool. I know this part of the coast. My grandfather took me fishing out here all the time."

Ian traced a spot on the map and grinned at Joe. "There are some caves here. A few are really deep. You can get a big boat in them. Some fill up with every tide, so you don't want to be there at the wrong time. It could be really bad. But I liked the caves. You probably know all about swimming in caves, from being a SEAL. Right? Maybe you two could go fishing. Or if you wait until Mia and I come back, I could go with you."

Ian actually paused for breath. Lorenzo looked shell-shocked while Joe took advantage of the lull. "Is that Mia calling you?" he asked.

"What? Oh, she doesn't know I came in here. I'd better go find her. Thanks for everything. You guys have been great." He shook hands with Lorenzo, then turned to Joe. "Mia thinks you're terrific. She's always talking about you and—"

Joe pulled his hand free. "Thanks. You'd better go find her. You know how Mia gets."

"What? Oh, right."

Ian disappeared. Joe crossed to the chair opposite Lorenzo's and sank down. "Not my favorite guy."

Lorenzo frowned. "What does she see in him?"

"Nothing."

"Then why is she with him? I want Mia married and having babies, but not with that one."

Joe agreed. "Mia isn't interested in settling down right now. So she picks men who don't challenge her. She could never be with someone she didn't respect. That means she's protected—she won't fall in love with someone like Ian."

Lorenzo stared at him. "You have considered this."

He shrugged. "I've had a lot of free time since I got here."

"You have been around the women too long. They are changing your brain. Come. We'll go taste from the barrels. You can tell me what you think."

Lorenzo slowly rose to his feet. Leaning heavily on the cane, he led the way into the barrel room, where he motioned for one of the workers to come along. Small samples of wine were poured and glasses handed around.

Joe braced himself for a volley of criticism. There was no way he could survive a barrel tasting with his limited knowledge. Despite three years of visits to the Marcellis, he still preferred beer to wine.

"You taste what will be there in the future," Lorenzo said, swirling the liquid in his glass and studying it. "The hints of how the flower will blossom." He inhaled the smell of the wine. "It is still young. Like a child. But when it grows, what will it become?"

Joe took a sip and grimaced. The flavor was too sharp, too thick, too much of everything. Before he could say anything, Lorenzo also tasted the wine.

"You see," he said. "The blending has already begun."

"Uh-huh."

The old man's eyes narrowed. "What do you taste?" he asked sharply.

Joe shrugged and told the truth. "Really bad wine."

Lorenzo muttered something under his breath before saying, "You know nothing of us. Nothing of our wine. You should know. This should be who you are."

Joe was tired of the argument, tired of the criticism. "Who's fault is that?" he asked, allowing his temper to get the best of him. "If I remember correctly, you're the one who made sure I was sent away, so don't go blaming me for what I do and don't know. You're responsible, old man."

"That was a long time ago," Lorenzo snapped. "You know about us now. You should be here, married, having babies. You owe this family."

Joe set down his glass. "I owe you *nothing*. After thirty years I find out about you. So what? I have a whole life that doesn't include you or the Marcellis. You get that? I made my own way in the world. You came looking for me when it was finally convenient. You keep pushing, but I'm not interested."

Lorenzo narrowed his gaze. "So now you say you don't want your family. What kind of man thinks such a thing?"

"I do."

"Because the navy is so wonderful? What happens when you get old, eh? They won't want you anymore. But here, we will always want you."

"That's bullshit," Joe yelled, matching Lorenzo's rising voice. "You don't want me. You want some stud service to continue the family name because you have an out-dated concept of a woman's place in the world. Brenna's doing this a whole lot better than I ever could."

"Wow."

Joe turned and saw Darcy standing in the barrel room. She looked more amused than shocked by all the shouting.

"What do you want?" he demanded.

She folded her arms over her chest and leaned against the wall. "If anyone was curious about the two of you being related, this moment would satisfy them. You even yell the same. Anyway, Mia and Ian are packed up and leaving. I thought the two of you might want to say good-bye."

Lorenzo shook his head. "That girl," he said as he limped out of the room.

Darcy stayed where she was, watching Joe.

"I wouldn't have pegged you for a screamer," she said. "But you were matching him, decibel for decibel. It kinda kills my image of the cool, collected SEAL."

"He pisses me off."

"I guess." Her mouth curved into a smile. "Who would have thought Grandpa Lorenzo could take on the big, bad military guy and win."

He moved close and stared down at her. "I know forty-seven ways to kill you with my bare hands."

"Uh-huh." The smile widened. "And I can bring you to your knees with a single sentence."

No way, he told himself, liking how she wasn't intimidated by him or the argument.

"Prove it."

She rested one hand on his chest, drew in a deep breath, and then sighed. "Joe, I think we should talk about our feelings."

11

❧

"I don't think my stitches are even," Darcy said as she stared at the ten-inch square of fabric in her hands. "Aren't they supposed to be even?"

Paige leaned over and studied Darcy's work, then glanced at her own. "Hey, you're doing better than me. At this rate, the most they'll let me do is collect leftover scraps and throw them in the trash."

Darcy tugged at the thread, but it wouldn't pull through all the way, which left a little bit sticking up that didn't exactly match the rest of the pattern.

"This is for a good cause," she muttered. "Tell me it is, because I'm so not getting it."

"We're becoming better seamstresses so that when the next Marcelli bride gets her dress made we can help. Not that we'll be here, but it beats weeding the vineyards, right?"

Darcy smiled. "I don't think they'd make us do that."

So far the Marcellis hadn't asked her to do much of anything except show up for meals and be friendly. Grammy M had stopped by with the squares of fabric and had taught them a couple of basic quilting stitches, with the understanding that in time they would put their newfound skills to good use on a wedding gown.

While Darcy loved the idea of a family of women sewing each bride's dress, she had a feeling she wasn't going to be here long enough to see it happen. Although maybe they would invite her back when Mia got married.

"Have you talked to Lauren?" Paige asked, before she tugged too hard, broke her thread, and swore. "I'm not domestic. It's as simple as that."

"You and me both," Darcy said with a laugh. She tossed her square onto the coffee table in front of the sofa. "Yeah, I've talked to Lauren. I feel really guilty. I'm here and she's stuck in some farmhouse in the Midwest. Lately she seems to know way too much about growing corn, which is a little scary. I don't think she has anything else to do with her day but watch it grow and ripen."

Paige grinned. "She's fine. I promise."

"Hope so." Darcy glanced at the agent. "You know, Mia's convinced there's something going on between you and Alex."

Paige paused in the act of threading her needle. She blinked twice. "Really?"

The innocence was too studied, too forced. "Is there?"

"Special Agent Vanmeter and I are working on your security team," Paige said primly.

"And sharing a house. By the way, Mia told the entire family and wants us to help get you together."

Paige sagged against the sofa. "Tell me you're kidding."

"Not even a little. Of course now everyone is distracted by the news Joe was married before, if that helps."

"It doesn't."

Darcy was stunned. "There *is* something going on."

"No, there's not. But . . ." She hesitated. "There was. A lot of years ago. Alex and I met during our initial training and we developed a thing for each other. But when training was over, we both decided our careers were more important than any relationship and we went our separate ways."

Darcy hadn't had a clue. She supposed no one did, except Mia, and that was the point. "And now?" she asked.

"Now we're protecting you."

Darcy didn't think she believed that was the end of it. "Nothing else. No lingering sparks?"

Paige smiled. "Spark is too strong. There might be some heavy smoldering, but it doesn't mean anything."

"Because Alex is such a tight-ass?"

The smile turned into a grin. "You've noticed."

"Hard not to. The guy practically invented the word. He needs to lighten up."

"He wants to keep you safe."

It was a philosophy Darcy could get behind. Except, over the past couple of days, she'd found herself being less afraid. Less wary of every noise and person she met.

"Are you going to pursue it?" Darcy asked.

"Not a clue," Paige admitted. "What about you? Lieutenant Commander Larson looks very hunky."

Darcy leaned forward and grabbed her fabric square. At the mention of Joe her insides got all tight and her face felt hot.

"He's okay," she said quietly.

Paige laughed. "Honey, we all know he kissed you out in the vineyard. You were observed by an agent."

Darcy looked at her. "You're kidding."

"Sorry. No."

Great. One of the many joys of being related to the president. At least they didn't know about the kiss in the exercise room.

"He's cute and all," she admitted, "but I don't really have great luck with guys." The ones she'd met wanted her either for her sister or for her family connections.

"Are you worried he's only interested because you could help him with his career?" Paige asked.

Darcy hadn't considered that. "Could I?"

Paige looked at her. "Honey, with a couple of phone calls, you could practically get him his own ship. I doubt he'd be interested. Not in any command he didn't earn. He shares that with Alex."

Darcy chuckled. "Are you saying Joe's a tight-ass, too."

"Pretty much."

Darcy hadn't touched that particular body part, but she'd leaned against a lot of him, and he was rock solid everywhere. A quality she'd never considered in a man before but now found very desirable.

Colleen walked into the living room. She carried a tray heavy with sandwiches, cookies, and the inevitable bottle of Marcelli wine. This one was a cab-merlot blend.

"Now what are you two girls talking about?" Colleen asked as she set the tray on the coffee table and sat in the wing chair opposite the sofa.

Paige waved her scrap of fabric. "That I was never

very good at the domestic arts. All this lack of success is making me feel inadequate. I'm going to go clean my gun."

Darcy watched her go, then turned to Joe's mother. "I'm afraid I'm not any better at this. My stitches aren't even."

Colleen opened the bottle of wine and poured them each a glass. "I wouldn't worry about it. At the rate we're going, one of my granddaughters will have grown up and gotten engaged before Mia ever considers settling down." She handed Darcy a glass, then relaxed in her chair. "I love Mia so much, but too many days with her around exhausts me."

"She's sure full of energy."

"Among other things. I thought Lorenzo was going to have a heart attack when he realized Ian was sharing Mia's room. We'd given him his own, of course, but young people today. . . ." Colleen stopped and frowned. "My God. Did I actually say that? 'Young people today'?" She closed her eyes. "I'm turning into my mother, only without the charming accent."

Darcy laughed.

Colleen looked at her and smiled. "I suppose it was bound to happen."

"We're all getting older."

"I'm afraid you won't be able to claim that for some time," Colleen said. "On the one hand Mia wears me out, on the other the house seems quiet without her. I'm glad we have you here with us, Darcy."

The unexpected words surprised Darcy. She tried to be a good houseguest, but she knew she was a relative stranger here. "You've all been very kind."

"Trust me. We're not altruistic enough to be noble. We like having you around," Colleen told her. "Although I'm not sure being an honorary Marcelli is as exciting as the life you're used to. After all, you can go to the White House anytime you'd like."

Darcy nodded because it was expected, but in truth she didn't feel as if she could just drop in. Maybe to see Lauren, but not for any other reason. Certainly not to see her father. Appointments were required.

"It must be hard for the president," Colleen said as she set down her glass of wine. "He's been a widower for a long time, yet it can't be easy for him to date."

"Not really. There's a lot of speculation about his love life, but he has always said he won't get involved with anyone until he's out of office."

"I suppose that makes sense. How would he know if the woman was interested in him or what he could offer? Still, he must be lonely."

Darcy reached for a small sandwich but didn't bite into it. She'd never considered that her father also had to deal with hangers-on. Sure, in his regular life, but not romantically. Of course there would be women who would want to marry the president. A fair number probably wanted to just sleep with him, but she didn't want to think about that. Talk about an ick factor.

"Of course he has his girls," Colleen said. "Children are a blessing. And you're both so close. You in town and Lauren right there in the private quarters." She smiled. "I think you were smart to have your own place so you could keep your privacy."

"It is nice," Darcy said because she knew the truth was far less appealing. A part of her *had* been interested in living in the White House. She'd imagined a room across from her sister and plenty of moments to enjoy the once-in-a-lifetime opportunity. But she'd never been invited. When rooms had been assigned and living arrangements discussed, the assumption had been she would be staying in her D.C. apartment.

She'd kept her hurt to herself. She hadn't wanted to upset Lauren or put her in the awkward position of having to petition their father on Darcy's behalf.

"Do you go to many dinners and evenings there?" Colleen asked.

"Some. He hasn't really started entertaining much yet. I received invitations when he was vice president, but I was still in graduate school and had to refuse a lot of them."

Lauren had teased her about not wanting to come to anything but being unwilling to flat out say so. Lauren had said—

Darcy picked up her wine and took a sip. Was that what had happened? Had she said no so many times that they'd stopped asking? Did they think she wasn't interested?

No, she told herself. That wasn't possible. They *had* to know the truth. Didn't they?

The days stayed warm and sunny. Joe knew from his nighttime reading that warm sunny days were best right before harvest. That the heat and light brought out the sugar in the grapes. Or did it keep sugar from being in the grapes? Damn. He'd just read about it the other night. Why couldn't he remember?

Because this wasn't his thing, he told himself. He wasn't interested in wine or Marcelli land or grapes.

He rounded the corner of the house and saw Darcy in the shade, leaning against the back of a large jacaranda tree. Her eyes were closed, and her book had fallen off her lap. Just behind her were two agents, playing cards.

Joe nodded at them, then approached her. He crouched down at the edge of the blanket and waited until she opened her eyes and saw him.

"Hey," she murmured, her voice low and her skin slightly flushed.

She wore a loose tank top and shorts, both black. Flip-flops lay beside the blanket. Any makeup she'd applied that morning had faded, leaving her lips bare and only a shade or two darker than her cheeks.

She was gorgeous. Sexy, soft, and a thousand other things he shouldn't think. If he did, the physical manifestation of his thoughts would inform everyone in visual range exactly what he had on his mind.

"Hey, yourself." He sat next to her. "You're still not sleeping."

"Don't go there, big guy. I'm too drowsy to fight with you today."

"It's not a fight if you do what I say."

Her eyes widened as she laughed. "Do you think there's even the tiniest chance that's going to happen?"

"Not in this lifetime."

"Or on this planet," she told him. "I'm okay. And for your information, I'm sleeping better."

"How much?"

"Maybe fifteen percent."

"Not good enough." Her hand lay beside his. He wanted to pick it up and touch it, maybe lace their fingers together. Which meant his brain had failed and he was in serious need of some combat time.

"You should talk to somebody," he told her. "A professional. Even my SEAL teams need help now and then."

"Okay. Maybe. When this is over and I'm back in D.C."

He thought about pushing back, but if she saw someone sooner it would mean one more body who knew her location. That crowd was already too big for comfort.

"Brenna says the chardonnay grapes will be ready to harvest in a couple of weeks," Darcy said. "I kind of want to be here to see that."

He glanced around to make sure no one was listening, then lowered his voice. "I've been reading some of the books she left me. Harvest is a lot of work. There are—" He broke off at her smile. "What?" he demanded.

"Oooh, I could really blackmail you with the fact that you're studying up on wine."

"But you won't. We're in this together."

The second the words were out, he wondered what he was talking about. Darcy should have been surprised, too, but instead of calling him on it, she changed the subject.

"I've never spent any time in this part of the country, and I have to say I'm sorry about that. I really love it here. I could get used to this kind of life." She glanced at him. "I mean that at face value, so don't get all weird on me."

"I rarely get weird on anyone. I can see how it could be appealing."

She stretched out her legs, then drew a knee to her chest. "Really? So why are you so determined to get away from here as fast as you can?"

A legitimate question. "I love what I do," he said. "I make a difference every day. I trust my guys with my life, and they do the same with me."

Her dark eyes settled on his face. "And you can't trust the Marcellis?"

"Not the same way."

"That's unfortunate, because they are just as willing to give up their lives for you. They love you, Joe. More than you know and certainly more than you deserve. I wish you could see that."

He shrugged, not sure what to say.

"The good news is they're not going to give up," she told him. "You are so stuck with them."

"I've figured that out already. Brenna and Mia are easy, but I don't know what to do with the rest of them."

"You're letting Grandma Tessa feed you. That's something."

He shrugged. "It's just food."

"Not to her. My next goal is for you to start calling people by their actual names."

He didn't like the sound of that. "What are you talking about?"

"You avoid mentioning anyone by name. Probably because you don't want to call Colleen and Marco Mom and Dad, which makes sense, but what about the Grands. Even I'm calling them Grammy M and Grandma Tessa. It's who they are. The fact that they're related to you is beside the point."

He made a noise low in his throat. She laughed.

"Are you growling at me?" she asked, sounding more delighted than annoyed.

"Yes."

"I've never had a man growl at me before."

"They were probably all too scared of your Secret Service agents."

"And you're not?"

"I could take every one of them."

Darcy stood by the window in her room, but instead of the view, she saw questions. So many opportunities had seemed to slip through her fingers. Times when she could have said something, only to hesitate out of fear or concern or need. What had she missed because of that hesitation? What had been lost?

She crossed to the secure phone on the nightstand in the corner and dialed Lauren's number. Her sister answered in two rings.

"Hi, it's me," Darcy said.

"Hi, you. How's it going? Are you basking in your sunny days and sultry nights?"

Darcy smiled. "There's not much sultry here. Humidity is required for that."

Lauren sighed. "There's plenty here. Near record levels. The corn is growing, though. Growing and moving closer to the house. I'm beginning to feel like a character in a Stephen King novel. Soon I'll be slipping into insanity."

Darcy sat on the edge of the bed and battled guilt. "I'm sorry you're stuck wherever you are."

"Me, too, but I'll survive. The Secret Service guys are nice, and I'm teaching myself to cook. Nothing up to White House standards, of course, but I never really bothered before. Even when I was married . . ." Her voice trailed off.

Darcy knew her sister enough to know she was about to get lost in the past. Given that Lauren was trapped in the middle of nowhere and on her own, she didn't think that was a good idea.

"You should plan your welcome-home party," Darcy said quickly. "Start working on the guest list. You can put me on top."

Lauren laughed. "Hardly. You don't like all those fancy events, but I appreciate you making the effort for me."

"Is that what you think?" Darcy asked lightly. "That I don't like the White House social scene?"

"You don't. When Dad was vice president, he made sure you got invitations to everything, but you never came. I know grad school kept you really busy, but we both figured you were too polite to actually say you hated that kind of stuff."

Darcy wasn't sure what to say. Yes, she had been busy with school, but she'd also been confused and feeling unwelcome.

"I thought the kindest thing was to not ask you anymore," Lauren added. "Was I wrong?"

"No. Of course not." Darcy flopped back on the bed. "Maybe. I mean I know I kept refusing invitations, but I didn't want to be cut off from you two."

Lauren sucked in a breath. "Is that how you feel?"

"Sometimes."

"Oh, Darcy. I'm sorry. You know we don't want that."

Darcy's mouth twisted. "I know *you* don't want that."

"Stop it. Dad loves you. He talks about you and asks

about you, which he wouldn't have to do if you called him and came by sometimes. He's busy, but he's still your father and he cares about you."

Darcy wanted to believe that, even though it wasn't true. After her mother had died, she'd been so lost. Finding out the truth about her biological father the same day that her mother died had nearly destroyed her. Worse, the man who was her biological father was already dead, so she'd lost him before she ever found him. She'd been emotionally battered and unable to feel anything for months. Ryan Jensen had reached out to her time and again, only to have her walk away from him. Just about the time she'd been ready to reach back, he'd stopped trying.

"It's complicated," she said.

"It doesn't have to be," Lauren told her. "He wants you in his life."

Darcy wasn't so sure, but maybe she should find out before making any more decisions.

"All right," her sister said. "Change of subject. I'm so bored here. Tell me something exciting that's happening in your life."

Darcy opened her mouth to say there wasn't anything exciting, but what came out instead was, "I've met someone."

Lauren squealed. "You're kidding. That's so great. The petty, bitter side of me is complaining that you get to meet a guy while I'm stuck in a cornfield, but I will squash those evil thoughts and focus only on you. Who is he? What's he like?"

"He's . . ." Darcy curled up on the bed and grinned. "He's gorgeous. A naval officer and a former SEAL. I know nothing will come of it, but still, I really like him."

Lauren sighed. "Sounds fabulous. Okay start at the beginning and talk slowly. I want to know every detail."

"So you're reading the books," Brenna said. "Learning about the wine. What do you think?"

Joe held in a groan. "I'm sorry I said anything about them."

"I don't doubt that," Brenna said cheerfully, "but you did, and now I get to grill you on them. It's time to give in. Let the wine have its way with you."

They were in the storeroom in the winery. Brenna had gotten even bigger, which didn't seem possible. How far could one body stretch before splitting open?

As uncomfortable as it made him to look at her bulging stomach, his situation was made worse by the fact that he couldn't just walk away. Not from a very pregnant woman who looked as if she could go into labor at any time. No matter how much she bugged him.

"I'm not interested in the wine," he said, facing her and folding his arms over his chest. "I've told you."

"I only listen to about half of what you say. It's not personal—I deal with all men that way." She grinned. "You can't escape us. This is your destiny, Joe."

"Not in this lifetime."

The humor fled her eyes as she grabbed his arm. "I'm serious here. I'm pregnant. I'm going to have a baby. That's bound to cut into my time. Four Sisters is growing. Grandpa Lorenzo won't live forever. I need some help."

The walls instantly began moving in on him. He pulled away from her and moved toward the door. "Marco can take over."

"Whoa. Stop right there. No one is taking over from me. I said help. Like a partner."

"Like I said—Marco."

"Sorry, big brother. You're the one. You're the heir. Not just because you're male, although that's a big part of it, but also because you have the determination to make things happen. You have a lot to learn before you'll be of any help to me. So you need to start now. You have responsibilities."

He wanted to hit something or throw something. The barrels were too large and the desk behind him had been screwed down. He thought about tearing the intercom out of the wall, but what would that accomplish?

He glared at her. "It's not going to happen," he said, speaking slowly. "You can't make me want this. I'm not interested in you, in them, in the winery. In any of it."

"Is this why your marriage failed?" she asked softly. "Because you wouldn't let anyone in?"

"You don't know what you're talking about."

"Don't I?" She rubbed her stomach. "We're not leaving you, Joe. No matter how long you're gone or how much you push us away. It's been three years. What will it take for us to finally earn your trust?"

When he didn't answer, Brenna shook her head and walked out without saying a word. Seconds later Darcy appeared. Her knowing expression only made the need to destroy something even stronger.

"Go away," he growled.

"I wasn't listening in," she said. "You were yelling pretty loud until the end there. I'm guessing the whole back forty knows what you two were fighting about. Don't you ever get tired of having the same argument over and over again?"

"Yes. They need to give it up."

"Or you need to give in."

He threw up his hands. "Perfect. You want to run my life, do you? It's your fault it's screwed up in the first place."

"Oh, right. Because the sole purpose of the kidnapping was to mess up your career plans. I'm trying to help you here, you jackass. But you're too stubborn to see the truth. You keep pushing them away, and they keep coming back."

She moved closer. "You say the navy is your family, your life. But what do they care about you? You're a rank and a number. Someone capable of doing a good job. There are a dozen guys who could take your place. Even now someone else is doing your job, and that's what's killing you. But this is different. This is your family. They love you. It's specific and personal and you're blowing it."

He didn't want to hear any of this. "Don't call me a jackass."

"Why not? You're acting like one. You're such a typical male, wanting to be defined by what you do. But you're more than that."

He moved close and considered shaking her. "You're the most annoying woman I know."

"Maybe, but I'm trying to help you. You should be

grateful and offer me a small but tasteful gift. Flowers or chocolate."

He grabbed her and pulled her close. But instead of shaking her, he lowered his head and kissed her.

She let herself sink into him as she wrapped her arms around his neck.

"That works, too," she whispered before kissing him back.

12

&

Man, oh man, did Joe know how to kiss. Darcy closed her eyes and let herself get lost in the sensation of his warm mouth on hers. Despite the fact that they'd kissed before, he didn't attack or assume. Instead he coaxed her into responding. Gentle brushes of flesh against flesh had her wishing for more before he even offered.

He let her get used to the feel of his hard body, his arms around her. He let her inhale the scent of him and melt in his heat. Only then did he lightly nip her lower lip.

He followed the shape of her mouth, tracing the line slowly, so slowly that she finally grabbed him by the back of his head and pulled him close.

Even as he swept inside her mouth, he chuckled. She felt the rumble low in his chest and smiled in return. They were good together, she thought hazily, right before the passion exploded.

The need came without warning. One second she'd been enjoying his kiss, the next she was desperate. Hunger claimed her. Large, powerful, and nearly out of control, it made her cling, reach, seek. She wanted him touching her everywhere, she wanted him naked and ready. Right here, right now.

"Joe," she breathed, not sure what to say.

He raised his head slightly, and she saw the fire in his eyes. They stared at each other for two heartbeats, then fell together in a frenzy of wanting that left them both breathless.

He kissed her again, but this time he wasn't kidding. He claimed her, stroking the inside of her mouth with a fervency that made her shake.

She closed her lips and sucked on his tongue. He groaned, then lowered his hands to her hips, where he pulled her against him. She went willingly, wanting to know he was aroused. Her belly brushed against his erection and her insides clenched.

She clung to him, even as she tried to pull at his T-shirt. Bare skin, she thought frantically. She needed bare skin.

He pulled back enough to press his mouth to her cheek, then her jaw. He moved down the side of her neck until he reached her collarbone. The warm, damp trail of kisses made her tremble. At the same time he reached for the front of her sleeveless blouse and began to work the buttons.

"Yes," she whispered, giving up on his T-shirt and helping him get her undressed.

Even as they fumbled with tiny buttons and impossible fastenings, they kissed, noses bumping, lips missing. In the heat of the moment, perfection didn't matter.

When her blouse was finally open, he reached for the front clasp of her black bra and opened it one-handed.

She had a half second to be impressed with his technique before he bent down and claimed her left breast with his mouth.

The combination of hot, wet kisses, a sucking pressure, and her own building need nearly made her scream. She grabbed his head to hold him in place.

"Don't stop," she breathed. "Please, don't stop."

Ribbons of pleasure wove their way through her, circling around her breasts before heading to that growing ache between her legs. She felt herself swell and dampen. She wanted him inside her now. Right this second. She couldn't wait—

He moved to her other breast and flicked his tongue against the tight nipple. She gasped her pleasure. He did it again, then straightened. Before she could protest, he replaced his mouth with his very skilled fingers and kissed her.

Oh, yeah, she thought as she circled his tongue with hers and sank into the pleasure. This was good. Better than good. It was amazing.

He dropped his hands to the waistband of her shorts and unfastened them. Somewhere along the way, she'd already kicked off her sandals.

"I want you," he breathed into her ear. His breath was hot and tickled in the most erotic way possible. "I want you, Darcy. Hot, wet, and screaming when I make you come."

Her eyes widened. No one had ever talked to her during sex before. She'd always found the event to be silent and fairly unsatisfying. It looked as if all that was about to change.

A shiver of anticipation rippled through her.

"I can't promise to scream," she whispered as he pushed down her shorts and panties.

He pulled back a little and stared at her. His eyes were the color of stormy midnight, his expression predatory. He was a man who wanted a woman and meant to have her. Thrill joined anticipation.

"Can you promise to come?" he asked as he slipped his hand between her thighs.

Someone had given him a schematic, she thought happily as he went directly to her very favorite spot and began to tease it. Electricity shot through her, making her want to get to the finish right away as much as she wanted to make it last forever. He circled and rubbed and then slid his fingers inside of her while his thumb kept up the intimate dance.

"Darcy?"

She forced her eyes open. "What?"

"Can you come?"

The first flicker of promise tightened her muscles. "As long as you keep doing that."

He gave her a slow, sexy smile designed to bring her to her knees. But before she could stumble, he grabbed her by the waist and lifted her onto the desk.

"I'll go you one better," he said and slipped between her thighs.

Even as his arousal filled her, stretching her and touching nerve endings starved for a little attention, he returned his fingers to her most sensitive spot. As if that wasn't enough, he leaned in and kissed her. Talk about multitasking, she thought, as her brain began to shut down in a delicious overload of sensation.

There was heat everywhere. Heat and hunger and

the promise of perfect release. Muscles tensed in anticipation. Her body ached. She parted her legs more, then
wrapped them around his hips to bring him in closer
still.

In and out, in and out. The friction against her slick,
swollen center was exactly right. She could feel his tension and knew he was close, but he held back, waiting on
her.

"Almost," she breathed against his mouth. "Joe."

He stared at her, willing her to come for him. Willing
her to scream.

Brenna hauled herself up the back stairs and waddled
into the kitchen. She wanted to stalk, but it wasn't going
to happen. Until she gave birth to the planet-size baby
she carried, her stalking days were behind her. Along
with her dancing days, her running days, and her sleeping days.

"I hate gestating," she said as she leaned against the
counter.

Grandma Tessa smiled in sympathy. "The babies make
it worth it."

Brenna glared at her. "There are no babies. Just so
we're clear. There's the one baby. Singular."

Her mother crossed to her and touched her forehead.
"Are you feeling all right? You're flushed."

"I'm crabby. It's Joe. He's being stubborn and pig-
headed. I know they're the same, but it's annoying. He's
annoying. I hate him." She sighed. "Okay, not really."

Her mother offered her a glass of water and she took a
sip. Because she *needed* more pressure on her bladder
these days.

"We were talking in the storeroom. Arguing. He won't listen."

"He's stubborn," Colleen said.

Brenna looked at her mother. "He told Darcy his wife left because of the time he was gone."

Colleen and Grandma Tessa shared a glance. The older woman reached for her rosary.

"It could be true," Colleen said. "He believes it. I saw it in his eyes when he told us."

"That's not why," Brenna said. "She left because he wouldn't let her in. He wouldn't love her."

Grandma Tessa shook her head. "We don't know that."

"What if that's the way he is? What if he can't change." Her eyes burned with tears. Damn hormones. "I love him. We all do."

"And we're going to keep loving him," Colleen said.

"I know. I wish . . ." Brenna reached for the intercom. She wanted to tell him to get in here so she could sock him in the stomach, then hug him. Schizophrenic love at its best.

She pushed the intercom and heard a curious sound.

It wasn't conversation. Not exactly. It was . . . breathing. Hot, heavy breathing.

She released the intercom and jumped back.

Colleen frowned as Grandma Tessa reached for her beads.

"Dear Lord," her grandmother said. "What was it? Some giant beast in the storeroom?"

It didn't sound like an animal to Brenna. "I don't get it," she said. "I left Joe in there and passed Darcy on the way. . . ." Understanding dawned. But as soon as the thought formed, she pushed it away.

No. It wasn't possible. Her stiff-necked brother would never loosen up enough to—

She pushed the intercom again and heard Lieutenant Commander Joseph Larson say something very dirty.

"Oh my God," Brenna shrieked.

She backed away from the intercom. She looked from her stunned mother to her equally shocked grandmother and began to laugh.

Colleen grinned. "Guess Joe found himself a girl."

"In the storeroom?" Tessa asked, sounding outraged. "It's immoral."

"It's fun," Brenna said. "I always hoped he'd find someone, but the president's daughter? What on earth is he thinking?"

Darcy braced herself on the table and bucked against Joe. So close. So close. He rubbed her center, moving faster and faster until she had no choice but to fly into her release.

She wanted to warn him, to say something, but she couldn't speak. Her muscles convulsed as she came over and over again. Pleasure poured through her, a river of release. It was good. It was better than good—it was damn close to perfect.

Joe straightened and looked at Darcy. Her eyes were wide, and she was still breathing hard. He tucked her hair behind her ears then leaned in and kissed the tip of her nose.

"Not bad for somebody famous," he said.

As he'd expected, she grinned, then swatted his arm.

"Not bad for some macho, paramilitary type," she told him.

"There's no 'para' about it. I *am* military."

"Yeah, yeah, like that's going to impress me."

He touched her chin so she had to meet his gaze. "You screamed."

Color rose on her cheeks. "Did not."

She was right. She hadn't screamed. But she'd grabbed on to him as if she never wanted to let go, and she'd taken him on the ride of his life.

Reluctantly he stepped back and reached for his jeans.

"Ah, the postcoital cleanup," she said as she lowered herself to the floor, then reached for her panties and shorts.

He supposed he should feel awkward about what they'd just done. It hadn't been planned, and he didn't usually give in to impulses like that. If anyone found out . . .

He didn't want to think about that, even though he was going to have to—eventually. But right now there were other issues.

"You're looking serious." She finished fastening her bra, then started with the buttons on her blouse. "Regrets?"

"No." He pulled her close and lightly kissed her. She held on tight. "Questions."

"Such as?"

"You on any birth control?"

He watched her closely, knowing he would be able to

guess by her expression. Instead of panic, he saw something very close to smug victory.

"I'm on the Pill. Aren't you lucky," she said, leaning against him.

"Damn straight." He stroked her short hair. "I usually take precautions. You messed with my mind."

"Little ol' me?"

"No one else here." He felt her tremble. "Darcy? You okay?"

She nodded but wouldn't look at him. He touched his finger to her chin and raised her head.

"What?" he asked.

She looked defiant, shy, and embarrassed. An amazing trick.

"I'm being sophisticated and worldly," she said. "Don't mess that up."

And then he got it. He lashed out when he felt threatened; she used humor. He thought about her life—the public scrutiny, the Secret Service agents.

"Hard to date when you're the president's daughter?" he asked quietly.

"You have no idea."

He kissed her. "The guys in D.C. are idiots. And not just the ones in office."

"Thanks."

"I mean it."

She raised herself on tiptoe and kissed him. "I know." A smile tugged at the corners of her mouth. "You've just had sex with the youngest daughter of your commander in chief. I think you need to propose now. It's really the least you can do."

He wanted to pull her close again, but he respected her need to stay strong.

"Wouldn't you get nervous if I did?" he said. "It's almost worth it to see."

"Almost isn't the same." She stepped back and smoothed down the front of her blouse. "How do I look?"

"Sexy."

She dismissed him with a flick of her hand. "I don't care about that. Do I look normal? I don't want anyone guessing what just happened. We have your family to think of, and my security team. Trust me, none of them need to know."

"Agreed."

He studied her, taking in the swell of her breasts a whole lot more than the straightness of her clothes, then motioned for her to turn around.

When she'd completed a full circle, she held her arms out at her sides and said, "Well?"

"Perfect," he said. He moved in and claimed her in a hot, deep kiss that soon had his body ready for round two.

She moaned. "Good idea. Bad timing, but a great idea. We got lucky once. Do you realize the odds of someone walking in on us?"

Amazing how he almost didn't care.

"I'll go first," she said as she pushed away and started for the door. "Wait a few seconds before following." Her gaze dropped to his crotch, where he knew she could see he was hard again. "Or longer."

Darcy felt like the beautiful young princess in a classic fairy tale. It was only a matter of time until the birds broke into song and the little woodland creatures gathered supplies to make her a fabulous ball gown.

It was the sex. Parts of her body ached from the physical activities, but it was the kind of ache that made her smile and want to do it again. For that she could thank Joe.

He'd been great. Not just with the mechanics, although he could certainly earn a merit badge in technique and stamina, but with how he'd acted.

He'd made her feel comfortable, both during and after. He'd joked and he'd held her, and best of all, he'd wanted her again. Guys might be able to fake a lot of things, but not an erection that size!

Life was good, she thought as she headed toward the main building of the winery. Who knew getting kidnapped would turn out to be so beneficial for her personal life?

Still smiling, Darcy entered the main building of the winery. She felt more than saw the Secret Service agents behind her, but she ignored them. Today nothing could get in the way of her good mood.

"There you are," Grandpa Lorenzo said as she started down the hallway. He stood at the entrance to his office. "I've been looking for you, Darcy. Come in."

He sounded so stern and disapproving, she instantly felt guilty. It was all she could do to keep from rushing to his side, grabbing his arm, and promising she would always keep her room clean. Instead she followed him into his office and took the chair he pointed at.

He stared at her for a long time. Darcy stared back, noting the gray in his hair and how tired he looked. Then she ran through a list of possible infractions but couldn't come up with a single one.

"So, you like the winery," he said.

She hadn't had a clue as to what he wanted to talk about, but her liking the winery hadn't been on the short list.

"Yes," she said. "Of course. It's beautiful here, and the process of making wine fascinates me. I know I'm an imposition to your family, but I can't help hoping I'm here through part of the harvest. I'd like to see the picking and the pressing."

Lorenzo smiled. "You have the love in your veins. It's like that for some. You don't always have to be born into it. You're young, there's still time. You could study and be a part of all this."

She wasn't so sure about that. She had a feeling that as nice as the Marcelli family had been to her, they wouldn't be all that sorry to get their lives back. No one enjoyed having Secret Service agents running around on their property.

"Tessa cleaned your room the other day and found this."

He set something on his desk. It took Darcy a second to realize it was her portfolio. Lorenzo withdrew several large sheets from her sketch pad.

At least they were only drawings, she thought, surprised that Tessa had gone through her stuff and embarrassed that something so private had been viewed by others. Note to self—don't start a diary while in the Marcelli home.

She drew in a deep breath, preparing herself to take Lorenzo and his wife on about violating her privacy, when he said, "I like these. This one the most."

He tapped one of the designs, then turned it toward her. "You can make me more like this?"

She stared at the page of wine labels she'd been toying with. There were several incarnations, using the Marcelli name as the centerpiece in some and the house in the others. Lorenzo pointed to the one with the house.

"I like this one. I like the different colors. You've done pale for chardonnay, and darker for merlot. So the labels are all the same, but different, yes?"

She nodded slowly. "You like these?"

"Very much. The work Brenna brings me." He shook his head. "Amateurs. Yes, they draw, they design, but they don't feel the wine in their blood. They don't know the land, the work, the grapes. You, Darcy, you feel it in here." He pounded his chest. "We'll use these for the new Marcelli labels."

"W-what?"

"For the wine. Brenna will like them, too. She's a smart girl. She'll know how you have to draw them so we can turn them into labels. Stand up to her on the price. She'll try to talk you down, but this time, I think, we pay more, eh?"

He wanted her labels? On Marcelli wine bottles? "On all of them?" she asked tentatively.

"Yes. For all. You will be a part of us, then."

Darcy sprang from her seat and raced around the desk. She threw herself at Lorenzo, who gathered her close and hugged her. He was thin and frail under his loose clothes, but he still squeezed her until she couldn't breathe.

It felt good, she thought happily. It felt great.

When he released her, she grinned. "This is my first real design job. I've been trying to find work, but it's hard. No advertising agency wants to hire me. What client is going to be comfortable complaining about a design by the president's daughter? So I went back to college to get my master's degree. I thought that would help, but it hasn't yet. Until now."

Lorenzo squeezed her hand. "This isn't about your education, child. It's about what you feel in your heart. That's what's important. Never forget that."

Joe finished his afternoon briefing with the security team and headed back for the house. Marco joined him a few feet from the back door and asked him to wait.

"We have to talk," Marco told him.

Until that moment, Joe had been having a good day. Making love with Darcy might not have been the smartest thing he'd ever done, but it had been one of the best. He'd enjoyed every second of her company. And he hadn't wanted to go—an unusual situation for a man who generally preferred to be alone.

"What's up?" he asked.

Marco shook his head. "Next time you might want to make sure the intercom is off."

Joe felt sucker punched. "You know?"

"Everybody knows."

13

❧

*D*arcy sat propped up on her bed, several sketches scattered around her. She had a meeting in the morning with Grandpa Lorenzo and Brenna to finalize their choices for the wine labels, and she wanted to be able to offer them a variety of options.

Excitement made it difficult to concentrate on the designs. She wanted to dance around the room and scream her delight. Brenna had called earlier to say she was thrilled to finally have new label designs. Which meant Darcy had her first ever paying job.

Okay—she wasn't going to be able to make a career out of this one client, but at least she finally felt legitimate in her chosen profession.

As she worked, or tried to work, she hummed. She felt good all over. She loved this place, and she loved the Marcellis. Would they be willing to adopt her?

She grinned at the thought. Probably not a good idea, what with her and Joe having had sex. Not that they knew, but if she was adopted it would create, as Mia had said, a pretty serious ick factor.

Someone knocked on her closed bedroom door. Grandma Tessa to do a little more reconnaissance? "Come in."

The door opened, and Joe stepped into her room and closed the door behind him. Darcy instantly straightened. Her stomach tightened, her thighs heated, and she desperately wanted to pat the bed in invitation.

He was so gorgeous, she thought as she took in his tall, muscular build and the faint smile. Good enough to be both main course and dessert.

"Stop it," he said conversationally.

She blinked at him. "Stop what?"

"Whatever it is you're thinking. I can't help wanting you, and you're not making it any easier to say no."

He wanted her! Her emotions did a little soft-shoe. "Maybe you don't have to say no."

He groaned. "Yeah, I do."

"But it was so good." Perfect even.

He narrowed his gaze. "Darcy, I'm not kidding. There's a problem."

She refused to let go of her good mood. "You're not going to get weird on me, are you?"

"Not in the way you think. They know."

The last two words didn't quite make it to her brain. "They know." Huh. Who knew what? Who could possibly know. . . .

She collapsed onto her pillows. "Oh God. Your family?"

"That would be them."

Panic filled her. "No. They can't. I didn't say anything. I didn't even hint." She stared at him. "I know you didn't say anything. You wouldn't even under threat of torture."

"I wouldn't even with *actual* torture." He crossed to

the bed and sat down next to her. "We were in the storage room," he said.

"I actually know that. Did someone see us?"

"No, they heard. There's an intercom system."

She felt herself blush. "Who was it?" she asked, not sure who would be worse.

"Brenna, Grandma Tessa, and my mother."

She opened her mouth, then closed it. What exactly was she supposed to say?

Brenna she could handle, but. . . . "Your mother and Grandma Tessa?" The blush turned fiery.

"They spread the news to the rest of the family. Marco pulled me aside about an hour ago and tried to have the sex talk with me. It was humiliating."

"I'll bet." She covered her face with her hands. "They know. I can't believe it. I always thought the ongoing humiliation of my life was because I'm in the public eye, but I guess not. Maybe it's just me."

Joe reached for her hands and pulled them away. "Don't worry. No one's going to say anything."

"Not to my face, but they'll be talking about it. They know." She wanted to crawl under the bed and never come out. Then she thought of something. "Did they tell Paige or Alex? Alex really wouldn't like us doing that, and he might try to get you in trouble. You have your career to think about."

"I know. But the Marcellis are good at closing ranks. No one on the Secret Service team knows."

"Are you sure?"

He nodded. "If Alex had a clue, he'd rip me a new one. Trust me." He leaned close and gently kissed her. "Want to take it back?"

She didn't have to think about that. "Not even for a second."

"Me, either."

They stared at each other before Joe straightened and said he should get out of her room before there were even more rumors. Darcy nodded but couldn't speak. She couldn't do anything but stare at him. Because in that short period of time, somewhere between the light kiss and his walking out of her room, she felt a definite sort of tugging in the vicinity of her heart.

She wasn't sure what it meant, but she knew it couldn't be good. Not when her stay here was temporary, her track record with men was worse than dismal, and Joe was the kind of guy who didn't do relationships.

Paige hung up the phone and finished writing her notes. When Alex walked into the kitchen, she pushed the paper toward him.

"They've arrested two of the kidnappers," she said. "They have leads on the rest of them. I'm going to tell Darcy when I see her. She'll be thrilled."

Alex looked over the paper. "At least if the rest of them are on the run, they won't have time to plan another kidnapping."

"That should make our job easier," she said.

"I don't need my job easier."

Of course not, she thought. But he did need a sense of humor.

He walked to the refrigerator, opened it, and stared inside. Then he closed it and turned to her. "Would you have married me?"

Paige stared at him. "Excuse me?"

"If I'd asked. Before. Would you have married me?"

She had no idea what he was thinking or why he'd brought this up now. It didn't make sense.

"Alex, I don't understand why—"

"Yes or no," he said sharply. "It's a simple question."

"Not for me." Nothing about this was simple.

Would she have married him? She stared at his eyes. There'd been a time when she'd wanted to get lost in those eyes. When being with him had been so important.

"I don't know," she said after a while. "I don't believe you would have asked. And if you had and I'd said yes, then one of us would have had to leave the Secret Service. You would have expected me to be the one to leave."

He frowned. "Right."

She smiled. How typical of him. "Then no," she said gently. "I wouldn't have married you."

He folded his arms over his chest. "Why? Because I wasn't willing to give up my career for you? This is what I've always wanted."

"What about what I wanted? You'd have asked me to give up the one thing you wouldn't. It doesn't seem fair or a very healthy way to start a marriage. One criterion of a successful relationship is love makes each party stronger, giving them more of what they want. Love isn't supposed to take your dreams away."

"There was no way for us to win."

She considered the statement. "I guess not. Some relationships are like that."

"I don't accept that."

What was it about stubborn men? "You not accepting it doesn't change the truth."

He stared at her for another couple of seconds, then turned and walked out of the room.

Paige had no idea what all that had been about. She respected Alex a lot. She thought he was totally hot, and his being in the next room made some nights long and difficult. But there were times when his mind was a complete mystery to her.

She gathered her paperwork, but before she could stand up, he stalked back into the room, walked over to the table, bent down, and kissed her.

He cupped her face in his large hands and pressed his mouth to hers. The action was so unexpected, she didn't know what to think, and then she couldn't think because her brain had shut down in order to let her feel everything.

He held her gently. His lips rediscovered hers in a soft caress that took her breath away. She parted before he even asked, wanting him to claim her the way men had been claiming women since the beginning of time.

He swept into her mouth and circled her tongue with his. Then as quickly as it had begun, the kiss was over. He straightened, then walked away without saying a single word.

"I'll fix you a nice cuppa," Grammy M said to Joe as he walked into the kitchen the next morning.

He squinted at the time and saw it was barely after six. "You're here early."

"I like to start my day with the sun," she said cheerfully.

Tessa walked into the kitchen and scowled. "It's all that sinning. It keeps you from sleeping."

Grammy M glared at her. "You're very concerned about the state of my soul. All this talk of sinning. Could it be because your own man isn't making you happy in the bedroom?"

Joe winced and headed for the door. No way did he want to get in the middle of this.

Tessa might be elderly, but she was fast, spry, and she had that killer grip. She got him by the arm and steered him to the table.

"Sit," she ordered, and he sat.

"I'll make that tea," Grammy M said, smiling at him.

Tessa narrowed her gaze. "Joseph doesn't drink tea. He's a man. He drinks coffee."

Grammy M turned to him. "Didn't you say you'd be wantin' tea?"

"I, ah . . ."

Tessa speared him with a look that could stop a tank. "Joseph, you always have coffee."

"I, ah . . ."

They ignored him as they both raced to the stove. Joe figured he was about to get both and he'd better drink them equally. Maybe they could just pour them into a big mug and he could choke them down together.

"I'll fix you an omelet," Tessa announced.

"I have fresh scones to go with that," Grammy M said.

"Fruit," Tessa added.

Grammy M sniffed. "And some bacon. Maybe sausage."

"I'll be using the stove," Tessa told her.

"Oh, I see. And you'll be needin' all of the burners for

your omelet. Last time I made one, I only needed the one pan. But you were never very good in the—"

"Stop," Joe yelled. "I beg you. It's too early for this."

The Grands stared at him, at each other, then turned their backs and went to work.

Coffee arrived first. Joe sipped it until Grammy M plopped a cup of tea in front of him. Then he alternated. The women worked in silence, carefully stepping around each other, not getting too close.

He looked away as he remembered how it had been his first couple of visits. Before Grammy M had moved in with Gabriel and the old ladies had had a falling-out. He remembered their elegant dance in the kitchen, a rhythm honed from years of practice and working together. He'd never heard a harsh word exchanged.

"Will you be seein' Darcy later today?" Grammy M asked.

Joe held in a groan. So the news had been passed on to her, had it? No doubt Colleen had told her. Which meant Mia and the other sisters knew, too.

"She lives here," he said. "Hard to avoid her."

"Not that you want to," Tessa said with a wink. "She's a pretty girl."

"Not my type."

Tessa smacked him on the back of the head. "You say that now?"

Okay, poor strategy, he thought as he rubbed where she'd nailed him. "I mean she's not . . ." He closed his mouth and reached for the coffee. It would be better to endure whatever they had in mind, then make his escape.

"It's past time you were married," Grammy M said as she put bacon into a pan. "You're not getting any younger."

He nodded and reached for the tea.

"A man shouldn't be alone," Tessa said. "It's not good. What will happen when you're old, eh? You'll be living above the garage with a dog. What kind of life is that?"

"Is that my only option?" he asked before he could stop himself.

"What will become of you?" Grammy M wanted to know.

The only bright spot in this conversation was that they were finally on the same side of an argument.

"You need love in your life," Tessa said. "You need to love a woman and let her love you."

After getting smacked for saying Darcy wasn't his type, he didn't want to think about what would happen if he said he didn't love her.

Grammy M put a plate of scones in front of him. Tessa slid an omelet onto a plate and set it on the table. Bacon and fruit quickly followed.

"The president's daughter, Joseph," Grammy M said, her voice scolding. "You can't have your way with her then turn your back on her. You're a better man than that."

"She's right," Tessa said, looking as if she'd smelled something disgusting.

Joe felt the walls closing in. These were thicker and harder to climb.

"You don't have to live here, in this house," Tessa

said. "You could build something else. Close by. On the land."

Joe stared at the food, then at the Grands. He believed what Darcy had told him—that for these old women food was love. But right now he couldn't take any more. He stood, backed away, and when he was clear of the house, he turned and escaped.

14

❧

"*D*id you hear?" Lauren asked eagerly, her voice as clear as if she were in the same room, despite the distance and the secure line. "They've caught a couple of the kidnappers."

"Yes. Isn't it great?" Darcy asked, trying for as much enthusiasm as possible when in truth the news had made her heart sink.

"We'll be able to leave soon," Lauren said. "I can't wait. I'm getting so tired of my own company. The agents are nice, but they're not here to baby-sit me. The good news is I've caught up on my reading."

Darcy felt a twinge of guilt—her stay at the Marcelli house had been so perfect, she never wanted it to end.

"The downside," Lauren said, "is you're going to have to leave Joe. Or will you still be seeing him?"

Despite being upset at the thought of leaving, mention of Joe made her smile. "I don't know. Maybe." She wanted to. But in reality was that possible? Her smile faded. "He lives in San Diego. I'm in D.C. He's a naval officer, and I'm the daughter of the commander in chief. I think that makes us more star-crossed lovers than the happily-ever-after type."

"Lovers, huh?" Lauren teased. "I want to hear all about that."

Darcy wasn't willing to talk about it—not yet. "It's a figure of speech. Don't get too excited. Besides, this isn't going anywhere. He's not the relationship type."

"How do you know?"

"He resists his family."

"You're not trying to be his mother. Romantic love is different."

"He's been married." Darcy filled her in on the generalities, then sighed. "They say people who don't learn from history are destined to repeat it. In my case, that's true. Here I am, falling for a guy as inaccessible as my father."

As soon as the words came out, she wanted to call them back. She clutched the phone tighter and braced herself.

"Dad's not inaccessible," Lauren said softly.

"I know. I didn't mean it that way. I'm sorry. Please, let's not get into this long-distance."

"Okay." Lauren sighed. "Joe sounds so great, regardless of whatever issues the two of you may have. I want to meet him. I know. When this is all over, you stay there and I'll come by to pick you up. That way I can check out the military cutie and meet the family."

Darcy sat up. Her first thought was to scream out her protest. Not Lauren. Not here. This was the one place on the planet where everyone liked her for herself. There hadn't been any comparing, any disappointing second finishes. No one had rejected her. If Lauren came now, all that would change.

"Your enthusiasm is overwhelming," Lauren said, the hurt clear in her voice.

Darcy flopped back on the bed. "It's not that. Of course I want you to meet Joe and everyone."

"You might try saying that like you mean it. Don't worry. I'm not going to show up."

She felt like a worm. A selfish worm who had been living the good life while her sister had been stuck in a cornfield.

"Lauren, please. I'm sorry. It's just . . ." She drew in a deep breath. "I'm scared, okay? Joe is really special. I like him a lot. Maybe more than a lot. I haven't felt this way before, and it's scary and exciting and new and I don't want to lose him."

"Why would you?"

Darcy squeezed her eyes shut. "Have you looked in the mirror lately?"

"Oh, please. You're just as pretty and much more exotic looking. I'm just your basic blue-eyed blonde. With very common features. Besides . . ." She lowered her voice. "You have to know I'd never do anything to take Joe away. I'm not even saying I could. Just that I wouldn't. Ever. I love you. You're my sister. My family. That means everything to me."

Darcy went from feeling like a worm to feeling like slime. Slime was definitely worse. "I know. I'm sorry. I'm not worried about you trying anything, Lauren. You'd never do that." Had never done that. "It's not you. It's . . . them. Him. Everyone likes you better. Most of the time I don't care, but this time it would really hurt."

"But I never did anything wrong," Lauren whispered.

Darcy rolled onto her side and pulled her knees to

her chest. "I'm sorry. This is all about me. I'm the one who's insecure and stupid and acting like a child. I'm sorry."

"I'd never try to take Joe away from you. Or anybody. I don't want to love that much again. Ever."

"You're going to have to let him go eventually," Darcy said.

Lauren's breath caught. "I can't. I loved him so much. I could never love anyone else like that. I don't think my heart's big enough."

"You could date. That would be fun."

"I'm okay by myself. I have my memories, and that's enough."

Darcy thought about pointing out that Lauren was only twenty-seven. A little young to be settling for mere memories.

"Anyway, how did this get to be about me and my lack of love life?" Lauren asked. "We were talking about you."

"Right. How stupid and jealous I am. Not my favorite topic."

"You're not the only one," Lauren said. "You think I don't get jealous of your life and your freedom?"

Darcy rolled onto her back and opened her eyes. "What? You're jealous of me?"

"Sure. You have a lot more privacy than me. No one expects you to be a saint, so you're not always getting judged. I love how you can tell the world to piss off if you're not in the mood."

Darcy couldn't believe it. Lauren wanted to tell the world to piss off? "A lot of that's just a facade," she said cautiously.

"Who cares. You can do it. All I can do is cut ribbons

at opening ceremonies and raise money. The money-raising part is good, but the rest of it? Sometimes I just want to curl up with a good book or watch *Oprah*."

Darcy realized she was free to do that and a lot more. Funny how she'd never seen herself as the lucky one before.

"I can TiVo *Oprah* for you if you'd like," she offered.

Lauren started to laugh. "That would be great. Although I'm catching up on reruns while I'm here. It's really fun."

"I miss you," Darcy said.

"I miss you, too."

She cleared her throat. "I think you should come visit me here. When it's safe for us to travel."

Lauren sighed. "No, it's okay."

The slime feeling returned. "I mean it, Lauren. Please. Come visit. It will be great."

"I'll think about it."

They talked a few more minutes, then hung up. Darcy sat up and thought about what her sister had said. That she thought Darcy had the better life. Impossible. But it was good to know she wasn't the only one who got jealous and crazy about her world.

As for Lauren coming here, maybe it was a good idea. It would force Darcy to face her demons. If the Marcellis liked Lauren better, well, Darcy would just get over it. And if Joe wanted her . . . Darcy grinned. Then she would just have to beat the crap out of him.

Joe left the guesthouse after the daily security briefing. Progress had been made—kidnappers caught. Not all of them, but a couple. And if they talked, he would soon be out of here and back where he belonged. Assuming the admiral had cooled down.

"Joseph. Joe."

He looked up and saw Lorenzo limping toward him. The old man leaned heavily on his cane.

"Come," he said. "Walk with me."

"No, thanks," Joe told him. "I'm not interested in more conversations about changing my name, learning about the wine, or accepting this as my destiny."

Lorenzo nodded. "All right. Walk with me anyway."

"Why?"

"Can't a grandfather want to spend time with his grandson?"

Joe swore under his breath, then fell into step with the old man as they headed toward the vineyards.

"We have good weather," Lorenzo said. "It makes for good grapes. Brenna wants to be a part of all of it this year, but I think her baby has other plans."

"I hope so," Joe said, remembering how huge she'd been the last time he'd seen her. "It looks painful."

Lorenzo grinned. "Women are strong. Never tell them, but I would not want to give birth. With Tessa, it was only twice. First Marco, then a little girl. She died."

Joe glanced at him. "I didn't know. I'm sorry."

He shrugged. "God gives and then he takes. It is always that way." He raised his cane and pointed toward the horizon. "I can remember when there were no vines up there. When we needed only one crew to pick the grapes. Now I can't even walk the land, there is so much." He winked. "But not too much, eh? There can never be too much."

"Land is wealth," Joe agreed.

"But it is more than money. It's about who we are. When I was a boy, I dreamed of when I would run Marcelli. My father was a stern man. Difficult to please. But I knew I would and one day this would all be mine. I have lived a long time, long enough to see my great-grandchildren born. Tessa speaks of blessings, and she is right."

Joe didn't know what to say so he nodded. "You have a good family."

"More to come. Brenna and Nic's baby will have wine in his veins. He'll be strong."

"He might be a she."

Lorenzo shrugged. "If God wishes. But there will be sons, too. And more children. The families will join. We will grow. I wanted that for you."

Joe didn't know if he meant children, family, or what. He'd meant what he said about not wanting to argue anymore so he kept quiet.

"I wanted so many things," Lorenzo said as they stopped by a row of grapes. The old man bent down and fingered a leaf. "All those years ago, when Marco told me he'd gotten a girl pregnant, I was angry. I thought he'd thrown his future away. She's Irish, you know."

"I'd heard," Joe said dryly.

"I wanted Marco to marry a nice Italian girl. But he loved Colleen, and I couldn't make him stop. But I could force them to send the baby away." Lorenzo looked at him. "I was stubborn and a fool and I've paid every day since. You've paid. So much lost. I'm sorry."

Joe had expected a lot of screaming but not an apology. He started to speak and found his throat had gotten tight and the words wouldn't come. Before he could make them, Lorenzo spoke again.

"Now I give you advice. I know you think I'm an old man who doesn't know much, but I've lived a long time. Get married. Not because of the family or because I've told you to but because it will make you happy. It's not good for a man to be alone so much."

"I already tried that and it didn't work," Joe told him. He wouldn't go through it again. Not the caring, the wanting more, the hope that maybe it could work only to come home and find a letter and an empty house.

"You didn't love her," Grandpa Lorenzo said flatly. "When a Marcelli man loves, it's forever."

"I don't think—"

"I know!" Lorenzo yelled as he thumped his cane. "Love like that never dies. It is who we are—like the land."

"All the more reason to avoid it," Joe told him. "I'm fine. I have what I need."

"Ah, yes. Your navy. There are things a woman can do to a man your navy will never do to you."

"Agreed, but I don't have to be married to get laid."

Lorenzo's expression hardened. "You think I'm talking about sex? Marriage is about the soul and the heart. It's about one person who knows everything and still reaches for you in the night. Love like that is a gift." He paused and the anger faded. "Joseph, don't have regrets. I've lived with them for thirty-three years and they're a heavy burden. I want so much for you. I want you to be happy. I want—"

"There you are!"

They both turned and saw Katie hurrying toward them, a red-haired toddler in her arms.

Katie Marcelli Stryker was the oldest of the Marcelli

daughters. She and her husband, Zach, lived in Los Angeles, where he was a big-time lawyer and she ran a party-planning business.

"Look," Lorenzo said pointing. "Two beautiful women want to talk to us. We are lucky men."

Joe smiled. "I agree."

Katie stopped in front of them and laughed. "Look what she can do," she said proudly, then turned to her daughter. "Come on, honey. What did you want to say?"

The green-eyed beauty held out her arms to Lorenzo and said, "Gram."

The old man pulled her close and hugged her. "How are you? Such a little princess. Have you been practicing my name?"

Valerie nodded shyly and wrapped her arms around his neck. Katie turned to Joe.

"Where's my hug, big guy?"

He gathered her close. "Good to see you."

Katie squeezed him hard. "I heard we've got famous company."

"That's right."

She straightened and smiled. "Gee, Joe, did you have to have sex with the president's daughter on her very first visit?"

Darcy had been through enough Marcelli meals to expect insanity, but this beat all records. Leaves had been added to the already massive table in the dining room so that the whole family could sit together.

She'd been introduced to Katie and her family. Francesca, Sam, and the twins had arrived, along with Brenna and Nic. Only Mia was missing, and as Colleen had whispered in the kitchen, the blessing behind that was no Ian.

"Katie, you take that end," Colleen said. "We'll put Valerie in her high chair next to you. Francesca, I'll take one of the twins by me."

"I'll take the other," Brenna said. "I might as well practice. Unless you think *being* a twin and sitting next to another twin might make me have twins."

Nic leaned over and kissed her cheek. "It doesn't work that way. Whatever you've got, you've got."

Brenna patted her huge stomach. "I'm thinking a really big baby and a beach ball."

Everyone took their seats. Darcy found herself in the middle of the table, next to Grammy M and across from Joe. High chairs were slid into place and toddlers settled. Most of the food was already on the table, although Tessa carried in the last few dishes.

Lorenzo passed open bottles of cabernet down both sides of the table.

"It's good to have family here," he said. "We eat, we drink."

"We talk," Tessa said. "What did I forget?"

"The bread," Grammy M told her.

The two old women scowled at each other before Tessa returned to the kitchen.

Darcy took the wine Marco passed to her. She poured a glass, then filled Grammy M's. Gabriel took the bottle from her and winked.

Lorenzo pushed to his feet. "To my family," he said, raising his glass.

Darcy instantly looked at Joe, who hesitated before picking up his glass. Darcy picked up hers as well, knowing that while she wasn't part of the Marcellis, she was happy to wish them the best. They had been more than kind to her.

As soon as the toast was over, Tessa ordered everyone to "Eat. Eat before it gets cold."

Serving dishes circled the table. Darcy took small portions of everything. Despite her working out, she'd managed to put on enough weight to make half her wardrobe too tight to wear. But it was hard to care about that when she was having such a good time. Funny how just a few short weeks ago she'd arrived feeling scared and angry. It was as if she'd been nothing but sharp edges, and now she was all rounded corners and curves.

"What do you think of life on a winery, Darcy?" Katie asked. "It must be different for you."

"It is. I really like it."

"Did you see her designs?" Tessa asked. "So beautiful."

"I'm thrilled to finally have new wine labels," Brenna said. "So please accept my heartfelt thanks."

"I enjoyed working on the labels. And it was my first paying job in the graphic design business."

"Good for you," Katie said. "Is that what you studied at college?"

"Actually I was an art major. Painting—oils mostly. Then I discovered I wasn't very good and switched to graphic design and marketing."

Grammy M patted her hand. "I'm sure your pictures were delightful."

"Thank you. I tried, but I didn't have the talent."

"You have plenty of talent," Lorenzo intoned. "You should have seen the labels Brenna has brought me over the years. Goats. Who puts goats on wine bottles?"

Brenna shook her head. "They weren't goats."

"Animals then."

"Stop it, you two," Katie said mildly. "They're always like that, but I'm sure you're used to it by now."

"Pretty much," Darcy said with a laugh.

"It was worse before," Francesca said. "When Brenna moved back here, before she and Nic got together, wow, did she and Grandpa Lorenzo go at it."

"I had to be sure," the old man said. "Sure that she wanted to devote herself to the winery. Now she has, and all will be well."

"We're a living, breathing soap opera," Colleen said. "We should be on daytime television."

"But you hate daytime TV," Marco said.

"Oh, I wouldn't watch," Colleen told him. "I'd like the money though."

She laughed and everyone joined in. Darcy glanced around the table, then spotted Katie watching her.

"Sorry," Katie said. "I know everyone else is used to you being here, but I'm still getting over the strangeness of the president's daughter sitting in the dining room of the house where I grew up. Until now the closest I've ever come to seeing you is in magazines."

"Occupational hazard," Darcy said.

"I guess. It would be so strange. People thinking they know you when they don't. Of course I think I know you because of what everyone has told me."

Darcy instantly glanced at Joe, then away. Katie grinned. "Oh, yeah, I know about that, too."

"Katie!" Colleen said, scolding her daughter. "Leave Darcy alone."

"It's okay," Darcy said, fighting a blush and having a bad feeling she was losing.

"It's not her fault," Francesca said. "Please don't take this the wrong way, Darcy, but we're all much more interested in Joe's part in this than yours. We assume you're normal, but to the best of our knowledge, our big brother has never dated. No one knew about his ex-wife until recently. Intellectually we know there must be dozens of women, but we've never *seen* him with one before. So we're all curious about how this is working."

"I'm not a freak of nature," Joe growled. "I've had girlfriends before."

Conversation ceased. Darcy didn't mind, because she didn't have anything to say either. Girlfriends? As in women in relationships? As in, she was one of them? She was his *girlfriend?*

Her insides got all warm and squishy. Was it true? And if it was, did it matter? Joe wasn't exactly a commitment-type guy. He handed out crumbs when she wanted a banquet. Had she somehow gotten past his emotional wall, or was she just fooling herself?

Joe shifted uncomfortably in the silence. Brenna opened her mouth, no doubt to say something funny but potentially embarrassing. Fortunately just then Valerie spilled her milk and Eric threw carrots at his sister. Shrieks and tears erupted and Colleen, Francesca, and Katie all jumped to their feet and grabbed for extra napkins. The conversation was forgotten by everyone except Darcy, who found herself staring at Joe. And in a quirk of fate she couldn't explain, he was staring back. Just looking at her in a way that made her wonder about possibilities and romance and hope and if maybe, just this once, she was going to get it right.

After lunch there was discussion about going for a walk. In the end only Darcy, Grandpa Lorenzo, Brenna, and Nic started out into the vineyards.

"I'll accept the back pain, being unable to sleep, and the soccer games played in my belly, but why do I have to swell up like a toad?" Brenna asked as they strolled along a shady lane. "My shoes barely fit, I haven't been able to wear my wedding ring in three months, and we won't even discuss clothes."

"It will be worth it," Nic assured her as he helped her along.

"Ha. Want to trade?"

"Not really."

Brenna turned to Darcy. "A piece of advice—pass on the whole pregnancy thing. It's so much more disgusting than anyone tells you. There are things going on in my body that make it feel as if it's been taken over by aliens."

"So much talking," Lorenzo scolded mildly.

"You try carrying around a watermelon in your stomach for nine months." She came to a stop and rubbed her back. "Okay. This is as far as I go. You two have a nice walk."

Darcy glanced at Lorenzo. "Do you want to go back?"

He stared out at the horizon, then shook his head. "No. Let's see how far we can go."

"I hope you feel better," Darcy told Brenna.

"Not as much as I do." Brenna waved, then leaned heavily on Nic, who led the way back to the house.

Darcy moved next to Lorenzo. The old man surprised her by taking her hand and squeezing it.

"We'll be happy to have you in the family," he said.

She winced. "I appreciate that, but Joe and I aren't . . . That is to say we haven't . . . I'm not sure what's going on with him."

"I think my grandson is thinking about giving his heart."

Darcy wasn't sure about that, although it sounded nice.

"Do you love him?" Lorenzo asked.

Darcy stepped back and smiled. "Okay, I can't answer that, and maybe we should change the subject."

"You think I'm an old man who asks too many questions."

"Pretty much."

Lorenzo chuckled. They started walking again. The afternoon was still and clear. There were only the calls of birds to break the silence. After another ten or fifteen minutes, Lorenzo stopped, then looked around.

"I must sit down," he said.

They were in the middle of a row of grapes.

"Right here?" Darcy asked, then gasped as Lorenzo sank to the ground. She rushed over to him and crouched beside him. "Lorenzo?"

He didn't say anything, but something was very wrong. She could tell by his rapid, shallow breathing and lack of color in his skin.

Oh God. What should she do? She stood and looked around. Where was her Secret Service agent?

But no matter how she scanned the horizon, no one appeared.

She bent down and touched Lorenzo's hand. "I'll go get help," she said. "I'll be back as soon as I can."

"No." He gripped her fingers. "Don't go. It's too late."

Panic became fear. She felt for his pulse but couldn't find it. Tears filled her eyes and made it impossible to see.

She knelt on the dirt and looked around. "Help!" she yelled. "Someone help us."

"Shh." Lorenzo gave her a slight smile. "Don't worry, Darcy. It's all right."

It wasn't all right, but she didn't know what to do. She sat on the ground and lifted his head onto her lap. She held his hand until she realized the only breathing she heard was her own.

"Help," she called again, knowing it was too late. Over and over she called, but no one answered. For the first time in as long as she could remember, she was well and truly alone.

15

❧

*J*oe put down the phone and reviewed the list in front of him. Even though several things had been checked off, the pile of things to do was getting longer, not shorter. He knew part of the problem was that no one could concentrate. Even he was having trouble staying mentally on task.

It had been two days. Only forty-eight hours since the Marcelli world as he knew it had changed forever. He couldn't think of this place existing without Lorenzo running things. The old man's gruff pronouncements were as integral as the house or the vines. How could he be gone?

Everyone had the same question. Everyone wanted to know what to do next. While it made sense for Marco to be in charge, Lorenzo's only child had turned to Joe when he'd heard the news. The shock in Marco's eyes had told Joe he was in no shape to make any decisions.

There was a knock at the open library door. Darcy entered and handed him a list.

"The rest of the phone calls have been made," she

told him. "Everyone has been notified. The funeral home will take the body as soon as it's released, and the church has been arranged for the services Friday morning."

Joe ignored the list and looked at her. The shadows that had finally started to fade had returned. She looked thin and pale and unbearably sad.

"You shouldn't be making calls," he said. "What if someone recognized your voice?"

"I had to help." She moved into the room and sat down across from his desk. "I didn't call any friends or family members. Then I would have had to explain who I was. But I took care of the church and the catering. Tessa is saying she wants to cook, but I spoke to Colleen and Marco and they agree it's just too much for her. They're expecting nearly five hundred people at the funeral and nearly that many back here. Katie told me who to call, and they're going to be ready on time. I'm working on getting tents set up in the backyard, along with tables. I should have confirmation before five."

"You're good at this," he said, appreciative of the help. What did he know about putting together a funeral for a man who had been a part of the community for nearly eighty years?

"I grew up in politics," she said with a shrug. "I know how to organize parties. I know Katie was the more logical choice, but she's pretty broken up. They all are. Oh, and Mia just got here."

The youngest Marcelli sister had been missing for the past two days. "Where was she?" he asked.

"She and Ian went down to Mexico and didn't tell

anyone. She got to her hotel in San Diego this morning and got the message. They drove right back. I'm sure she'll be in to see you in a second."

He leaned back in his chair and rubbed his eyes. "There's too much to do."

There wasn't. He'd organized tactical assignments for entire SEAL teams. This was nothing, in the logistics department. But emotionally—it was hell.

"It'll get done," Darcy said. "There are plenty of hands to lighten the load."

"When did you get philosophical?"

"When Lorenzo Marcelli died in my arms."

"I want to talk to you about that."

She looked away. "I'm okay."

He doubted that, but before he could say anything, Mia ran into the room. Tears poured down her cheeks as she headed directly for Joe. He pushed back from the desk in time for her to drop into his lap and rest her face against his shoulder.

"I can't believe he's gone," she cried. "I loved him so much and I never told him."

"He knew," Joe told her as he awkwardly put his arms around her.

She cried until he felt the moisture seep through his shirt. He patted her back and looked at Darcy, desperate to know what to do next.

"It was very quick," Darcy said. "He was at peace."

Mia straightened and looked at her. "You swear? He wasn't in pain."

"Not at all."

"I'm glad." The tears made her face all blotchy.

Ian walked into the room, and Mia left Joe to hurry

into his arms. "I can't believe it," she said. "He was fine when we left. Just fine."

For once Ian didn't seem to have anything to say. He gave them a sympathetic smile and ushered a sobbing Mia out of the library.

"Too much emotion," Joe said when she'd left.

"Mia leads with her heart," Darcy told him. "I'm going to guess she'll keep doing that until someone breaks it."

He didn't want to think about that happening. Honestly, he didn't want to think about anything. Right now he would sell his left nut for a military crisis calling him back to duty. He didn't care where, just so long as it was away from here.

But the phone didn't ring and Tessa entered the room with a tray of sandwiches and a pot of coffee.

"You've been in here so long," she said quietly. "You missed lunch."

She seemed smaller and more frail. As if the essence of who she was had been lost. As she set the tray down, she began to tremble. Joe stood, then looked helplessly at Darcy.

"Hold her," she mouthed.

Joe stared at the tiny woman, then opened his arms to her. Tessa stepped into his embrace and began to cry. He pulled her close and stroked her back. She barely came to the center of his chest, and he was afraid if he held her too tightly, she would snap in two.

Darcy stood and moved to the bookcase, where she grabbed a box of tissues and passed them to him. He offered a couple to Tessa, who took them and wiped her face.

"I'm a foolish old woman," she murmured.

Darcy hugged her. "You're wonderful and you miss your husband. Of course there are tears. We're all sad. Lorenzo would probably tell us we were being foolish, crying over what we can't change. Then he'd want to know if anyone is checking on the grapes."

Tessa looked at her. A slight smiled pulled at the corners of her mouth. "Yes, you are right. That is what he would have said. But he would have been happy, too, to know how much we miss him."

She touched the large, carved desk. "He would sit here sometimes in the evening. He would do the books and I would read to Marco, or knit. In the winter we'd have a fire." Tears filled her eyes again. She opened her mouth, closed it, then quickly left.

Joe sank back onto his chair. "I've reached my limit. When is this going to be over?"

"Not for a long time."

He didn't like the sound of that. "Marco should be running things. Everyone's looking to me."

"Because you're the strong one. Those with natural leadership ability always rise to a position of authority."

"It's *his* family."

She walked around the desk and crouched in front of him. After taking both his hands in hers, she looked at him. Just looked.

He knew what she wanted—for him to admit it was his family, too. But he couldn't. Accepting the Marcellis as his own changed too much.

"I'm not one of them," he said stubbornly. "I know that makes me a real bastard, but I'm okay with that."

"Denial doesn't change reality."

"This isn't my reality."

She rose and, still holding his hands, leaned forward and lightly kissed him.

"Don't keep pushing them away. Learn from your past."

He jerked free. "You don't know what the hell you're talking about."

He hadn't pushed Alicia away. She'd gone on her own.

Darcy shrugged. "Have it your way." She left.

Alone in the silence, he thought. It was all he wanted. All he'd ever wanted.

Thursday morning Darcy reported for kitchen duty. Grandma Tessa had found out about the caterers and had a fit. She'd called in all the Marcelli women and Darcy to prepare everything. A menu had been posted on the refrigerator, Mia, Colleen, and Ian had been sent out for supplies, and now Grandma Tessa assigned tasks.

"Brenna, you'll need to stay off your feet," she said. "You can sit at the table and chop. Nothing more."

Brenna nodded. "Anything you want. You know that."

Her grandmother glared at her. "Stop being so nice to me. It makes me want to cry. No tears today. Today we cook. Tomorrow all those people will come to pay their respects to Lorenzo. They'll drink Marcelli wine and they'll eat Marcelli food. Nothing else." Her gaze narrowed as she turned her attention to Katie.

"I was only trying to help," her granddaughter said. "I thought I was helping."

"No. Helping is washing all the chickens when Mia brings them back."

The back door opened and Grammy M walked into the

kitchen. Tessa stared at her for a long moment, then held open her arms. The two old ladies rushed together and hugged tightly.

"I'm sorry," Grammy M murmured. "Oh, Tessa, your pain. I would have come sooner, but I was thinkin' . . ." She gave a little sob. "I don't know what I was thinkin'. I can't believe he's gone. I've barely seen him these past three years. I regret that. And not seein' you."

They rocked back and forth.

"No," Tessa said. "I'm sorry. My harsh words."

Grammy M straightened and looked at her friend. "'Tis no matter. I'll be moving back in. Gabriel's packin' my things. It'll be like it was before."

Tessa stared at her. "What did you say?"

"I'm movin' back in. Oh, Tessa, you need me now. I feel so horrible about what I did. You made me mad with your talk of the good Lord punishin' me, so I vowed not to come back until you apologized. Now I see I was an old fool. We're not gettin' any younger. We need to take advantage of the time we have left."

"Do you love him?" Tessa asked fiercely.

"Gabriel? Of course I love him."

Tessa marched to the phone and picked it up. "Then you call him right now and tell him to stop packing. You're staying there. If you love him, Mary, then hold on to him for as long as you have together. I don't care if you're married or not. I was mad because you seemed to leave so easily. As if I didn't matter."

"You matter," Grammy M said, throwing herself at her friend. "You matter more than anyone."

Brenna was already weeping. The Grands cried, Katie cried, Francesca had put aside the flour she was measuring and searched for tissues. Darcy felt her own emotions give way.

Brenna pushed herself to her feet and waddled over to the Grands. "Group girl hug," she said, motioning Darcy in. Katie and Francesca joined them.

For Darcy, the pain of loss combined with the sweetness of feeling as if she belonged. In this time of family tragedy, the Marcellis reached out to include her.

Later, when the groceries had arrived and the tasks were assigned, she went with Grandma Tessa to collect the family silver from a pantry under the main staircase.

"We'll need all the serving pieces," Grandma Tessa said. "Bowls, chafing dishes."

She stepped aside so Darcy could duck into the small room. Shelves filled the space, and each shelf was crowded with beautiful pieces in silver, silver and glass, and crystal.

"This is all so incredible," Darcy breathed. "I've been to the White House, and I have to tell you, this is just as lovely."

Tessa smiled. "You're kind to say so. Bring everything to the dining room table. Don't worry, I won't put you to work washing it all. You're helpful in the kitchen. Francesca will be in charge of washing and polishing. She never was very handy with a knife."

Darcy nodded. She would have to put the leaves in the table first, or there wouldn't be room. But then five hundred was a lot of people to feed, especially on three days' notice.

Tessa turned to leave. Darcy hesitated, then stopped her. "I know I probably shouldn't say anything, but I . . ." She cleared her throat. "I'm sorry I didn't come get you or anyone. I wanted to, but then he said he didn't want to be alone. I screamed for help, but no one heard me. I just . . ." She had to swallow against the tightness and the tears. "I'm sorry he wasn't with family. At the end, I mean."

Tessa looked at her for a long time, then patted her arm. "Lorenzo died with someone he cared about very much, Darcy. That makes you family. I'm glad you were with him. So very glad."

Darcy nodded, but she couldn't see or speak. There were too many tears and no way to stop them.

Paige was prepared to go to the mat on this one. "Darcy's request isn't unreasonable," she said, striving for patience, when she really wanted to hit Alex over the head and tie him up in the closet for a couple of days.

"No one is supposed to know the president's daughter is here. You don't think one of the five hundred people at the funeral will notice?" Alex demanded in a tone that told her he thought she was an idiot.

"She's hardly going to be parading herself around. She'll be in a hat with a heavy veil. We'll walk her in at the end and she'll duck out a side door right before the services end. She's not asking to go to the graveside and she's going to stay in her room with the door locked until the wake is over. That's more than reasonable."

"What's reasonable is not going out at all. We're talking five hundred people, Paige. Do you know what kind of security nightmare this is? We should move her to a secure location until all this mess is over. Typical Darcy, she's refusing to leave."

Paige took a step toward him and raised her chin.

"Typical Darcy? What does that mean? How has she even once been difficult? How has she made your job harder? The only goddamn time she was left on her own was because of a shift change and the fact that you forgot to schedule overlap. Which happened to be the exact moment Lorenzo Marcelli died." She poked him in the chest with her index finger. "Darcy was on her own with a dying man and no one around her. Did she come to you and point out the screwup? Did she threaten you? Not even close. So don't you dare tell me that she's been difficult."

Temper flared in his dark blue eyes. He carefully pushed her finger away. "Why is this so important?"

"Because she cares about these people. Because they mean something to her. An emotion you've probably never experienced, but it's there for the rest of the world."

Alex glared at her. "We do things by the book on my watch."

"Right. And sometimes mistakes get made."

He didn't respond. Paige knew it had to be killing him that he'd messed up. Such a minor thing, not assigning any overlap. It could have happened to anyone. But it had happened to Alex, and she was more than willing to press that point home.

"She will be completely covered and unrecognizable," Paige said more calmly. "I will be with her every second. You can have agents in the church. But she's going to that funeral."

"Fine," he said curtly. "Straight to the church and straight back. Nothing graveside, and I'll post agents on the stairs so no one gets up to her floor during the wake."

The victory surprised Paige. What had caused Alex to give in? She'd thought they'd have to fight a lot longer and she would have to threaten him with Darcy calling her father.

As it was, she was all charged up for a fight that had ended too soon. Lucky for her—there was still one more thing.

She moved in close again and glared at him. "Just so we're all clear on this—don't start something with me unless you intend to finish it. I'm not a toy, and this is not a game."

Under other circumstances his bewilderment would have been amusing. Right now it just pissed her off.

"What on earth are you talking about?" he asked.

"Figure it out," she told him, then stalked away.

The Catholic church closest to the Marcelli vineyards usually held three hundred. On a foggy, cool, Friday morning, nearly twice that many squeezed inside. Colleen had given Joe an idea of whom to expect. Even so, he was surprised to see so many unfamiliar faces.

Some were old—contemporaries of Lorenzo's. Others were much younger. Distant relatives, employees, fellow vintners. A half a dozen politicians sat in the pews.

There had been over two hundred requests to speak at the funeral. Last night Colleen and her daughters had gone through them and picked thirty. Twenty would speak in the church, the other ten by the graveside.

Joe listened to the religious service, then to the first few mourners. He heard stories about a Lorenzo he had never known. In some ways the tales made the old man seem alive again.

Tessa sat next to him, with Marco beside her. She cried through the service, seeming to shrink with every minute that passed. Unable to stand her quiet tears, he put an arm around her and pulled her close.

She looked up at him. "Your grandfather was so proud of you," she whispered from beneath her veil. "So proud."

His grandfather. He'd never claimed that relationship with Lorenzo. Joe had been careful to avoid calling him by name, much as he did with Marco and Colleen and Tessa. Grammy M had escaped the name stigma because her title didn't seem to be about any familial relationship.

There were too many people, Joe thought, wanting to bolt. He forced himself to stay in place, trying to think about other things. He felt Darcy's presence in the church. She sat in the back, on the side, where she would be whisked away before the service ended. She'd insisted on coming, saying she wanted to be there for the family and for herself.

He knew in his head funerals were supposed to help. That the ceremony clarified the moment of death and allowed those still living to move on. It had never worked that way for Joe. He'd been to funerals of guys he'd worked with, and the pomp and circumstance had only pissed him off, as it did now.

Nic stood and walked to the front of the church. He nodded at Tessa and Marco, then introduced himself.

"I first met Lorenzo when I was ten. I'd walked over from Wild Sea to taste some of his grapes. I was a kid—what did I know?" Nic smiled sadly. "Lorenzo found me snooping and took me back to the winery, where we did some barrel tasting. He listened to my opinion and told me his. I was terrified, of course. He was a Marcelli and we weren't supposed to get along, but he was kind that day and made me wish I could be a part of his family."

Nic paused and stared into the crowded church. "Years later, I met and fell in love with his granddaughter Brenna. After a little complaining because I was a Giovanni, Lorenzo welcomed me into the family. And there I've stayed, grateful to have known him. He was a man bound by tradition, yet farsighted enough to see what the future would require of those around him. He has given us all room to succeed, while offering us a haven of support and caring."

Joe let the words wash over him. Speaker after speaker spoke of a man Joe had barely allowed himself to know. He thought of all the times Lorenzo had pressed him to be part of the family, and of all the times Joe had refused. Lorenzo had wanted little more than a chance to get to know his grandson, but Joe had been determined to make sure that never happened.

Why? What was the point of disappointing an old man? What had he gained by resisting?

And now it was too late. He couldn't go to Lorenzo and say he understood why he, Joe, had been sent away all those years ago. He couldn't acknowledge that whatever his last name might be, Marcelli blood flowed in his veins. He couldn't stop rejecting what had been offered because the man who refused to give up was finally gone.

Several hours later Joe moved through the crowded kitchen. The guests were being kept outside by a combination of family and Secret Service agents gently ushering them in that direction. Tessa held court over the stove, accepting the condolences of those who stopped by to see her and share stories. Colleen and Grammy M stayed close, while Marco, Francesca, Katie, and Mia circulated with the guests. Nic had taken Brenna home. She'd been inconsolable after the funeral, and with her due date so close, everyone had agreed she needed to rest.

For the first time, Joe felt out of place. He didn't know where to go or what to do. Several family friends had spoken with him about his grandfather, but he hadn't known what he should say in return. He had no stories to share, no fond memories. He'd spent the last three years resisting.

Finally he made his way to the back of the house and went upstairs. The agent on the landing nodded, then stepped aside to let Joe pass. He walked to Darcy's room, knocked once, and entered when she called for him to come in.

She sat on her bed. The plain black dress was still in place, but she'd kicked off her shoes and removed the veil. Her skin was pale, her eyes large and filled with pain.

"How are you holding up?" he asked.

"That's my question for you," she told him as she stood and stepped toward him. "Are you okay?"

She wasn't mad. Typical Darcy. She liked to act tough, but she was all heart.

"I'm getting through it."

She studied his face, then touched her fingers to his cheeks. "I don't think so."

He swallowed. "I never told him it was okay. A couple of days before he died, he apologized to me for forcing

Colleen and Marco to give me up for adoption. I never said I forgave him. He thinks I'm still mad at him for that."

She pressed herself against him. "No, he doesn't. He knows what's in your heart, Joe."

If only that were true. But in his book, it was a bunch of crap. "I never said I cared. I never admitted that I was one of them. A Marcelli. I wouldn't say it. I wouldn't even call him my grandfather."

Tears filled her eyes and spilled down her cheeks. He touched the moisture. "Hey, I'm the one who screwed up. Why are you crying?"

"Because you can't."

16

❧

*J*oe couldn't remember anyone ever crying *for* him. He didn't know what to say, so instead of trying to speak, he bent down and kissed her.

The gesture was supposed to offer comfort and thanks, but the second his mouth brushed hers, heat exploded inside of him. The wanting was as instant as it was powerful. Need took over, making him grab her and pull her close.

Darcy responded by clinging to him, urging him on. She parted her lips, and when he slipped his tongue inside, she welcomed him.

Blood raced south, making him hard in a heartbeat. He reached for the zipper at the back of her dress. One long pull had it free. A quick tug at her shoulders and it fell down her arms, exposing her black lacy bra.

He pulled back enough to get a good look. Soft, pale skin, black lace, tight nipples. If he'd had thoughts about turning back, one eyeful took care of that. Still, there was enough sanity left for him to remember where he was and what was happening.

"What the hell am I thinking?" he asked, more of himself than of her.

"Don't think," she said. She lowered her arms and stepped out of the dress. Underneath she wore a pair of tiny, black panties, her bra, and nothing else. How was he supposed to resist that?

As he watched, she crossed to the door and turned the old-fashioned lock. Then she drew the curtains so the room was in semidarkness. She moved back in front of him and gently pushed his suit jacket off his shoulders.

"Allow me," she whispered.

"Darcy," he began, but she shook her head.

"No talking," she told him. "No thinking. No analyzing. Just feel my touch. What I'm doing to you. Nothing else. Clear your mind."

She loosened his tie and pulled it off, then went to work on his shirt buttons. He stood there, feeling strange and awkward, not sure what was going on. Oh, he understood they were both about to be naked, but this was different from his usual lovemaking, although he couldn't say why.

There was something in her eyes, something in the way she seemed so solemn, yet determined. Something in her touch that kept him quiet and immobile.

When she'd tossed his shirt on the chair, she walked behind him and pressed her mouth to his back. He felt her tongue slip across an old scar.

"What happened?" she asked.

"Knife fight. I rolled when I should have ducked."

She nipped the area, sending a jolt of fire right down to his crotch. She moved her hands to his waist, then to his chest, where she stroked him from shoulder to belly, getting close to his erection, but never touching him.

"And this one?" she asked before tonguing another spot on his back.

"Not a clue." He picked up one of her hands and brought it to his mouth, where he bit down on the swell of flesh below her thumb and licked her palm.

"You can't remember?" she asked, her voice breathless.

"I have a lot of scars."

"So I see. Sit down and take off your shoes and socks."

He stepped away and did as she requested. Then he stood again and removed his slacks and briefs. When he was naked, he turned toward her, waiting for more instructions.

Her gaze swept his body, pausing on his erection.

"Nice," she said with a smile. "Lie down on your stomach."

He did and watched as she slipped off her bra and panties. He had about two seconds to enjoy the view before she moved onto the bed, then straddled him just below his butt.

She leaned forward so the very tips of her breasts brushed across his back. The light touch drove him crazy, especially as she rocked her hips slightly, grinding his dick into the bed. It was just enough friction to be dangerous.

But he didn't tell her to stop. Not when she kissed and nibbled her way across his shoulders.

"You're so strong," she whispered. "You carry so much weight and worry. You can let it go, just for a few minutes. Just for now."

Under any other circumstances, he probably would have told her to keep her emotional mumbo jumbo to herself, but right then, the words made sense. He did want to give up the burden for a little while. To not think about anything except how she made him feel. But kisses on his shoulders and back weren't going to get it done, despite how nice they were.

In one quick move, he flipped over. He grabbed her around the waist, keeping her in place. Only now her hot, wet center was directly on his.

She sighed. "That's what I get for playing with an expert, huh?"

"Exactly."

He could have pushed inside of her. A large part of his body wanted just that. To bury himself inside and let the feelings take him away. But not just yet, he thought, thinking about things he could do to her and how good they would feel.

So he stayed in place, and when she moved up his body so she could kiss him, he didn't stop her.

Instead he claimed her with a deep kiss. He traced her tongue with his, to explore the soft sweetness of her mouth. He slid his hands to her breasts and cupped them. When he teased her tight nipples, she groaned.

That throaty, hungry sound was his undoing. Suddenly he had to have all of her. He had to touch her and taste her everywhere, except he didn't want to stop kissing her. Not yet.

He ignored the throbbing between his legs and concentrated on her pleasure. When she raised her head to catch her breath, he drew her up so that he could suck on her breasts.

First one and then the other. Her breathing increased and he felt her body tremble. He urged her up onto her knees as he slid down a little. For the first time, she hesitated.

"No, that's okay."

Joe looked at the beautiful naked woman straddling his chest and knew he needed her more than he'd ever needed anyone before.

"I want to," he told her.

She made a vague motion with her hands. "It's um . . . just . . . I don't know. I'm fine."

He didn't want her fine. He wanted her writhing and panting and completely out of control. Had some guy refused, saying it wasn't his thing? Had some bastard hurt her by going down on her? Or was this her first time?

He had a fantasy of her straddling his face, hanging on to the headboard and riding him to heaven. But that would have to wait for another time. In one quick series of grabs, shifts, and drops, he had her on her back with him between her legs.

"Jeez, how do you do that?" she asked. "I need more self-defense lessons if I'm going to keep up with you."

He thought about telling her she couldn't possibly keep up, but that it was okay because he had no intention of leaving her behind. He opened his mouth to say just that, but instead he realized he was inches above her belly and that any conversation could be had another time. Right now he had important erotic work to do.

He kissed her stomach, then along the top of her thighs. She squirmed, but it wasn't in a good way. Her hands pushed at him.

"Please," she said.

He braced himself on one elbow and looked at her. "What's wrong?" he asked.

Color stained her cheeks. "Nothing. It's not important."

"It is to me."

She closed her eyes. "I've only slept with a couple of guys. I was always afraid of who would talk and what they'd say. Maybe to the press or something."

"Makes sense."

"Well, the first one was someone from college. I thought he was really special. I thought I was in love with him." She opened her eyes and looked at him. "I wasn't. But before I found that out, I suggested we try, you know, oral sex. He got all disgusted and said it was gross and he couldn't believe I'd asked."

"Which made you embarrassed."

"Among other things. It was a couple of days before Christmas and I was taking him home to meet my family. On Christmas afternoon I overheard him coming on to my sister. He said that he and I were only friends, that he had a real thing for her, and that he wanted to make love with her. Then he detailed exactly what he wanted to do with her, including that."

Joe wanted to go find the bastard and pound him into a bloodstain on the sand. Instead he kissed her thigh and asked, "What did Lauren do?"

"Slapped him as hard as she could, called him a sex-crazed asshole, and told him to get out of the house."

He thought about saying he liked Lauren, but he figured Darcy would misunderstand his words.

"I've been a little sensitive about the whole thing ever since," she said.

"Makes sense. Give me five minutes."

"Joe, don't."

He moved between her thighs. "Five minutes and if you hate it, I'll stop."

She twisted away. "But you don't have to—"

"I got that. I want to, and I took this correspondence class on some real interesting techniques. You might like them."

Her eyes widened, then she started to laugh. "You did not," she said.

"I can show you my certificate. I graduated at the top of my class."

Then while she was still laughing, he used his fingers to part her and lightly stroke his tongue against her swollen center.

Darcy had big plans to endure the five minutes, then push him away. Sure she'd heard that some men liked that sort of thing and she was curious, but Greg's reaction had scarred her in a way she'd never forgotten. The look of absolute disgust and horror on his face had pretty much shattered her tiny burst of confidence.

With her second lover, she'd been passive, not daring to ask for anything in case he reacted the same way. Joe had been her third foray into sexuality, and their passionate encounter hadn't left any time for doubts.

But now she could think, and once she started, it was impossible to stop her brain.

The first brush of his tongue felt good. Really good. The second set nerve endings to humming in a way she'd never felt before. Her legs fell open, her hips tilted toward him, and suddenly breathing didn't seem all that important.

He licked her over and over. It was different from being touched by his fingers. More intimate. Softer, but more direct. She could feel his breath. His shoulders pushed against her thighs. She was torn, wanting him inside of her and never, ever wanting this to stop.

Which, of course, it did.

She opened her eyes and stared at him. Fear swept through her. He hadn't liked it. He hadn't liked doing it to her. He hadn't—

"Relax," he said. "Give me your hands. Hold yourself open."

He positioned her fingers so she parted herself for him. She felt exposed and stupid, but before she could ask what he was doing, he returned his mouth to her body and rational thought fled.

The licking, gentle sucking, circling, breathing all continued. Tension moved through her body, starting at her toes and working its way up. At one point she thought she might have felt his teeth lightly graze that one most sensitive spot, but then there was his tongue again and a slight pressure at the opening.

Then she was caught up in a whirlwind of sensation. Even as he continued to use his mouth on her, he slipped in first one finger, then another. He filled her in a slow, steady rhythm designed to make her scream and beg.

She drew her legs back and dug her heels into the mattress. She rocked her hips and tried to catch her breath. Need swept through her. It was hot and thick and too powerful to ignore. Closer, she thought as pleasure tightened and grew. She was so close.

His fingers moved faster, sliding in and out of her. His tongue kept pace. Suddenly her body was out of her control. She shuddered into her release as incredible sensations washed through her. She bucked against him, desperate to keep him there, touching her everywhere.

He read her mind, slowing but not stopping. Again and again she came until the climaxes slowed and her body relaxed.

She opened her eyes and saw him smiling at her.

"Not bad for a rookie," he told her, then he pushed into a kneeling position and shifted closer. He thrust into her, filling her completely.

Understanding dawned.

"You're still hard," she whispered.

"Very hard. I liked doing that. A lot."

Difficult not to believe him when the proof pushed in deep enough to make her clench around him.

Gratitude made her ache. Not only because he'd pleasured her, but also because he'd replaced a horrible memory with one that bordered on spectacular.

In a matter of seconds, the steady rhythm had her on the edge again. She wrapped her legs around him, drawing him closer, then quickly lost herself in more waves of release. Two thrusts later, he followed, groaning her name and hanging on as if he would never let go.

When they'd recovered enough to speak, Joe rolled off her and pulled her against him. He settled her head on his shoulder and wrapped his arm around her.

"Thank you," he said.

Darcy snuggled close. "I believe that's my line," she whispered. "You were great." With more than just sex, she thought. In all of it.

"I needed to be with you."

His words did a funny thing to her heart. It sort of stuttered a beat, before returning to the regular pace.

Danger, she told herself. This was the wrong man. She needed someone to love her back, not run for the emotional hills.

Oh but she wanted him to be different. She wanted him to care. But Joe had pushed away one wife and the entire Marcelli family. Why would she be any different?

"You need to get back," she said, giving him a little shove, knowing that if he stayed with her much longer, she was at risk of saying something that could embarrass them both.

"I don't want to."

"Perfectly understandable, but I'm not excited at the thought of someone in your family coming looking for you and finding you here. They already know about the last time."

"Good point." He kissed her, then sat up and reached for his clothes. "I wish you could come."

"Me, too. But Paige and Alex are right. Better for me to stay securely hidden away."

He dressed quickly and left. When she was alone again, Darcy dressed in shorts and a T-shirt, then stretched out on the bed. Now what? Everything had changed, and she didn't know how to make it go back. Falling in love with Joe was a huge mistake. Was it too late to protect herself? And even if she could stop herself from caring about him, however was she going to get over falling for his whole family?

Three days after the funeral Darcy walked into the kitchen and found Grandma Tessa sitting alone at the kitchen table. It was so strange to see the tiny woman simply sitting. Grandma Tessa was always on the move— carrying, chopping, stirring, serving.

When she saw Darcy, she stood up. "It's nearly lunchtime," she said briskly. "I'll fix you something."

Darcy knew the whole "food is love" talk. She'd given it to Joe more than once. But just this once she couldn't listen to her own advice.

"No," she said gently, pushing Tessa back in her chair. "Let me bring *you* something."

Tears filled Tessa's eyes, although she did her best to blink them away. "You're a good girl, Darcy. It's been a blessing to have you here." She fingered the rosary beads on the table in front of her. "Honestly, I'm not hungry. I know I have to eat, but not yet. I miss him too much."

Darcy sank down next to her and took her free hand. "I know. You've loved him a whole lifetime. It's only been a few days. You're allowed to grieve."

Tessa nodded and squeezed her fingers. "I keep expecting to see him walk into the room. I can't sleep. The bed, it's so big. When did it get so big?"

Not knowing what else to do, Darcy hugged her. Tessa held on tight.

"I'm glad you're here," she said. "With the girls all gone, the house is so quiet. You bring us life again."

Darcy thought that might be an exaggeration, but she knew having people around gave Tessa something to think about other than her sadness. She wished she had something to say, something that would help ease the other woman's pain. But there weren't any words.

So they sat together, hugging and rocking, not speaking. Darcy breathed in the scent of spices and rose soap and did her best to be strong.

The back door opened. She glanced up, hoping to see Joe. He'd been busy with family stuff for the past couple of days, and they hadn't had any time alone. But instead of him, Paige walked into the kitchen.

"I have news," she said.

Tessa straightened and turned. "Paige. Are you hungry?"

Paige walked to the older woman and crouched in front of her. "You've got to stop feeding me," she teased. "I've gained twenty pounds."

Tessa cupped her face. "Maybe, but on you they're beautiful pounds."

"That's not what my supervisor's going to say after my next physical." She straightened and glanced at Darcy. "They've caught the last of the kidnappers. Your father will be calling in the next minute or so. The call will be put through here."

Darcy wondered if she looked as surprised as she felt. Caught? "Already?"

Paige smiled. "It's been nearly four weeks. But the ringleaders had gone pretty far underground."

Tessa stood and patted her hair. "The president?" she asked, sounding stunned. "Phoning here?"

"You look fine," Paige said with a grin.

Darcy tried to enjoy the humor of Tessa worried about her appearance for a phone call that wasn't for her, but she could only deal with her rising panic.

No! It couldn't be true. If the men were caught then she was free to leave. Actually, she *had* to leave. The Marcellis would want their house back.

But she wasn't ready. She and Brenna hadn't finalized the label designs, and the family was still in mourning, and what about Joe? They had to talk and she had to tell him that she. . . .

The phone rang. Paige reached for it.

"Agent Newberry," she said crisply, then nodded at Darcy. "Yes. She's right here." She held out the phone.

Darcy took it. "Hello?"

"Please hold for the president," a female voice said as Paige left the kitchen.

Darcy waited a second, then heard, "Darcy?"

"Hi, Dad."

"You've been told?"

"Uh-huh."

"Good news all-around. The last of them was rounded up this morning." He laughed gruffly. "I'll sleep better at night knowing my girls are safe now."

Two months ago Darcy would have dismissed the statement or at least reinterpreted it to mean he was glad Lauren was safe. Now she wasn't so sure. Maybe he meant it. Maybe she did matter to him.

"I've been talking to your sister," he continued. "She mentioned you'd like to get more involved with things here at the White House."

Darcy winced. That wasn't *exactly* what she'd said. "I thought it would be nice to do more."

"I'm glad," he said, sounding as if he meant it. "I always knew your space was important to you." He hesitated. "Do you young people still talk about having your own space?"

She smiled. "Not really. But I know what you mean."

"Good. When you come home, we can talk. I'd like to

have you around more, Darcy. You're very important to me."

"Thanks." She shifted awkwardly. "Um, you, too," she mumbled.

"All right. I have to run. Let me know your travel plans. I can have a plane pick you up whenever you'd like. Maybe in the morning?"

So soon? She wasn't ready to go. "I'll let you know, Dad. Thanks."

"All right. Talk to you soon."

The line went dead. Darcy handed the phone back to Paige. "He's ready to have me home."

Grandma Tessa stared at her. "Of course you want to go be with your family," she said. "If you're safe now."

Darcy nodded. Tears burned, but she refused to give in to them. It wasn't right. "You've all been very kind."

"Kind." Tessa dismissed the word. "We like having you here."

"I've liked being here."

"You have things to do, yes? A life?" Tessa asked.

Darcy shrugged. "I guess."

The old woman took her hand. "If you don't have anything special waiting, you could stay a few days. Maybe a couple of weeks."

Darcy wanted to so much it hurt. "But I'm an intrusion. I have a Secret Service team. Less now, but at least two agents."

"Two. It's nothing." Tessa squeezed her fingers. "Say you'll stay. We want you here."

"But Marco and Colleen may not be happy about—"

"Of course they'll be happy," Tessa said. "I know my own children."

Just then Joe walked into the kitchen. Tessa turned to him. "Tell her to stay."

He frowned. "You're leaving?"

"They've found the rest of the kidnappers," Darcy told him. "Your assignment is over."

The second she said the words, horror washed over her. Of course. Joe was only here because of her. Now he was free to return to the naval base and continue his regular life. The one that didn't include her.

"But she should stay," Tessa said. "Tell her. A few weeks. For the harvest and the first pressing. To bring life to this house. For you, Joe. She can stay for you."

Darcy braced herself to hear that he was leaving as well. Emotions crossed his face, but they went so quickly, she couldn't read them.

Tessa's eyes widened. "You're not going, are you?" she asked, sounding frightened. "Joseph, your family needs you."

Time stood still until Joe nodded. "I know. I'll ask for compassionate leave and I'll stay a few more weeks." He looked at Darcy. "You should stay, too. Unless you have something else you should be doing."

That would mean having an actual life, which she didn't.

"Not really."

"Then we'll both stay."

Four simple words. They shouldn't have given her heart wings, and yet they had.

17

❦

"You'll be leaving soon," Paige said. "That must make you happy."

Alex shrugged. "I didn't mind the assignment."

"But it's not very high profile. When you get back to D.C. maybe you can get assigned to the president."

He had the feeling she was talking about something other than the topic at hand, but then conversations with Paige were always filled with undercurrents.

"I enjoyed the opportunity to protect Darcy," he said carefully, wondering why he cared about Paige's opinion on anything. She was the one who'd pointed out the unfairness of his attitude—that if they got married, she would be the one to give up her job, not him. While he understood her intellectual argument, he resented the implication that he was the jerk in all this. Even if maybe he was.

Not that he gave a damn. Whatever they'd had was long over. They'd each gone their separate ways, and they would again.

"Hey, guys."

Alex turned and saw Darcy standing at the entrance to the guesthouse. "You heard the good news?" he asked.

"About the kidnappers? Yes, Paige told me." Darcy smiled at her. "I wanted to let you know, I'm not leaving here. Not just yet. There's so much going on, and well, Tessa asked me to stay and I said yes. I'm thinking for maybe two weeks. I don't know who my regular detail will be, so that's why I'm telling you."

"Not a problem," Paige told her. "I'll make the arrangements."

"Thanks."

Darcy waved and left.

Paige watched her go. "She's changed," she said, more to herself than him. "She used to be distant and sarcastic. Now she is warmer. Happier. I'm not sure how much of it is Joe and how much of it is the family, but I'm thrilled for her." She turned to Alex. "I'd like to stay."

"Here?"

"Yes, here. With Darcy. I'd like to be assigned to her. With the threat gone, she'll go back to a normal-size team. I want to be a part of that."

He'd thought they would both return to Washington. He'd thought they would have a long plane ride to discuss what she'd said to him about this not being a game.

"So that's it?" he asked, angry but not sure why.

"What else is there?" she asked. "You want your high-powered career. You want to be the best agent ever, to be alone. I don't want that anymore. Oh, I want to do a good job, but I want a life, too. I want people around me I love."

Not him. She didn't want him. Which was fine. The hell with her.

*   *   *

Joe had claimed the library as his office. He didn't want to work in the winery, and there weren't any other rooms that had desks and file cabinets.

Over the past couple of weeks, he'd settled into a rhythm of dealing with winery business in the morning and Lorenzo's personal papers in the afternoon. The will reading was at the end of the week. That was his cutoff date, he told himself. The Monday after the will was read, he was out of here.

He hadn't told anyone yet, although he didn't know why he was putting it off. No one would be surprised. The family understood his stay was only temporary.

Only they weren't acting like it. Assumptions had been made, and he needed to make sure they got unmade.

Darcy walked into the office, took one look at him, and collapsed into a chair. "Okay, you're looking fierce about something. Are you planning a revolt?"

As always, the sight of her eased the band of tension around his chest. Her easy smile welcomed him, and the sway of her body made him think of hot nights—an excellent distraction. She was the one person here who didn't want something from him.

"Not a revolt, an escape."

"Going anywhere interesting?"

"I haven't decided. You want to pick?"

She wore a short black and white skirt and a black sleeveless top. Her time here had added color to her skin and while she was still too skinny by far, there was a bit more meat on her bones.

He liked the changes. He liked her—which confused him, but in a good way.

"I've never been to Hawaii," she said. "Living on the East Coast, our escape for sun and sand is usually Florida or the Caribbean. But Hawaii sounds really nice."

"I know a couple of places. Quiet. Secluded. You could go naked."

"Joe!" She glanced over her shoulder toward the closed library door. "You have a family of lurkers. I love them to pieces, but they don't grasp the concept of privacy."

She was cute when she blushed, cuter still in his bed. They hadn't had much opportunity to make love. Not with so many people in and out of the house. But soon, he promised himself. Soon.

"How's it going?" she asked in an obvious attempt to change the subject.

He decided to go along with it. "Not bad. Running a winery is a lot of work. Sometimes I can feel the walls closing in."

Her concern turned sympathetic. "Your family is dependent on you in a way they've never been before."

He nodded.

"That makes you feel funny," she said. "You thought it would be different. That they were strong on their own. But things aren't always as they seem."

He looked at her. There was something in his voice. "We're not talking about the Marcellis, are we?"

She shook her head. "I was thinking about my situation."

"Lauren?"

"No. My father. He's . . ." She looked out the window. "I haven't felt a part of his life for a long time. I thought he didn't care about me, but now I wonder if that was just an excuse for me to stay mad and not try."

He didn't know what they were talking about but knew Darcy would explain further if she wanted him to know.

She returned her attention to him. "As a naval officer, are you legally and morally obligated to keep the president's secrets?"

He hadn't seen that coming. "Yes. I have top secret clearance. I'm a good security risk."

"You have to be better than good," she said. "You have to be. . . ." She swallowed. "You can't tell anyone."

She was serious. Joe leaned forward. "I give you my word, Darcy. But if you're not sure, don't tell me."

She smiled. "I appreciate that. But I want to talk about it. I never have. Not even with Lauren. Oh, I know she knows, but we never discuss it. It's our elephant on the table. The one we all carefully ignore."

"All right."

He stood and crossed the library, where he carefully locked the door. Then he returned to the desk, but this time he sat on her side of it, in the chair closest to hers. He took her hand and laced their fingers together.

She glanced from the door to him. "Gee, no pressure."

"I told you—don't tell me if you don't want to."

"I do. It's just, I don't even know where to begin."

"How about with 'It was a dark and stormy night.'"

She burst out laughing, then leaned toward him and kissed him.

"Thank you. I feel better now." She laughed again. "Okay, it was a dark and stormy night. My mom was dying. She'd come home from the hospital because she wanted to die at home. I was sixteen, Lauren was seventeen. We were scared and waiting to hear she was gone.

Lauren fell asleep, but I couldn't. I went downstairs—
a hospital room had been set up in the study of our
house—and I sat in the hallway. I don't know how long.
It felt like hours. I remember it was so cold, but I didn't
want to leave to go get a blanket or a sweater."

Joe had known that Darcy had lost her mother at an
early age, but he hadn't known the details.

"Didn't you have anyone to sit with you?" he asked.
"Other family members?"

"I don't remember. That night it was just me. Finally
my dad came out. I could tell from the look on his face
she was gone. I started to cry and go to him. He . . ." She
paused, then continued. "He pushed me away. I tried to
cling to him, and he told me not to touch him. That I
wasn't his daughter. He never wanted to see me again."

Joe hadn't had any idea what she'd been going to tell
him, but he hadn't expected this. Horror filled him, but
nothing he felt could match the pain in her eyes.

"I didn't know what to do," she said in a whisper.
"What to think. I ran to my room. I was crying too hard
to speak. Lauren woke up and she got that Mom was
gone. We cried together." Darcy tightened her grip on his
hand. "Later my dad came to me. He said he was sorry
about what he'd done, what he'd said. He told me it
wasn't about me."

Joe moved his chair closer and wrapped his arm
around her. "You don't have to talk about this."

She blinked away tears. "I'm kind of into it now, so
you're going to have to hear the rest."

He kissed her forehead and rubbed her back. "Sure
thing."

She drew in a deep breath. "He told me that my mom

had had an affair. She'd met this bright young lawyer at some campaign event, and they'd had a torrid affair. She'd gotten pregnant and had been prepared to leave her husband and baby daughter, only the guy died. So she stayed and they patched up the marriage."

Darcy looked at him. "I'm the baby. The child of her lover. No one ever told me until that night. I never guessed. My dad—the man who raised me, not my biological father—never let on. Until the night she died, he loved Lauren and me exactly the same. Or at least he acted that way. But when my mom was dying, she called out for her lover. She died speaking his name. So that's what upset my dad—so much. When I went to him, he was thinking of her and what she'd done. That's why he was angry."

She brushed away tears. "He told me he was sorry and that I was still his daughter. He did everything he could to make it up to me. But I didn't believe him. I wasn't angry, exactly, but I was scared and hurt. I shut down. For weeks I wouldn't talk to him. At some point he told Lauren, but we never discussed it either. He kept reaching out to me, and I kept turning away. One day he stopped trying and when I was ready, I didn't know how to reach out to him. We sort of reached an impasse, which is where we've stayed. And in the middle of that is Lauren."

"All this family crap. Now you know why I want out of here."

She clutched his hand tighter. "No, I don't. You have wonderful people here who love you. There is nothing more important than that in the world."

He didn't want to have this conversation with her, but

he knew she was vulnerable, and he didn't want to lash out at her.

"You don't understand," he said, determined not to get angry. "It's not forever. It's never forever. Why should I walk away from the work I do, the career I love, for this?"

She stared at him. "What are you saying? The Marcellis will change their mind? They'll wake up one morning and decide they don't want you in the family?"

He pulled free of her and stared out the window. "They already did that once."

Her breath caught. "The circumstances were completely different. You were a baby."

"Yeah, and now I can fight back."

He felt her gaze on him. When he finally looked at her, pain darkened her eyes.

"This isn't about them, as much as it is about her," Darcy murmured. "Your ex-wife. The one who left."

"That was years ago."

"What happened?"

He shrugged. There was no point in rehashing that old news, yet he found himself starting to speak. "I'd been gone nearly five months. I'd shipped out without warning. I couldn't get in touch with her while I was away. I got back after midnight. When I walked in the house, it was dark. It took me a minute to figure out it was mostly empty. She'd gone a few weeks before. Moved out, took the kids. She left a note and the divorce papers on the kitchen counter."

Darcy made a noise low in her throat. He saw tears fill her eyes.

"Don't sweat it," he told her. "I'd told her the life

was rough. She didn't believe me until she lived it herself."

"Did you talk to her?" Darcy asked, her voice thick.

"I called to let her know I'd signed the papers and sent them back to the lawyer." He'd wanted to ask about seeing the kids but had figured it would only make things harder for them. Still, he wished he could have let them know he missed them.

"You didn't ask her to come back?"

"No. If she'd wanted to be with me, she would have stayed."

Darcy wiped her cheeks. "Maybe she wanted to know she mattered. Maybe she was trying to get your attention."

He looked at her. "I'd married her with the idea I'd spend the rest of my life with her. How much more attention did she need?"

His heart, Darcy thought, trying not to give in to the sobs rising inside of her. Joe told the story so casually, as if it had all happened to someone else. But she didn't believe that. She believed he'd been blindsided. Oh, sure, he had a part in the divorce. It took two to screw up a marriage, but for him, this blow would wound deeper than most. Yet one more person had shown him that love wasn't something to be counted on.

He was trapped—unable to give emotionally because he believed there was no point, and unable to learn otherwise because he wouldn't give.

She wanted to hold him and somehow convince him everything could be different. All he needed was a step of faith. But he was a powerful, capable man. What did he need with faith?

Which left her where? Falling in love with a man who could never love her back?

"Are you sure you're okay with this?" Lauren asked. "I don't have to come visit."

Darcy rolled onto her back and stared at the ceiling. "It will be great to have you here," she said and nearly meant it.

"It's just you've made everyone sound so wonderful, and I'm dying to meet Joe." She lowered her voice. "You know I'm not going to do anything to get in the way of your relationship, right?"

"Of course. So not your style."

Besides, Joe was avoiding everyone and since their conversation the previous day, they didn't seem to have much of a relationship.

"I'll let Grandma Tessa know that it's for sure. She'll be beside herself. The president's daughters. She'll be cooking up a storm."

"Okay. See you Friday afternoon."

"I'll be here."

She hung up, walked out of her room, and headed for the kitchen. Although she'd already asked the Marcellis about Lauren coming for a couple of days, she wanted to let them know that it was for sure. And someone was always in the kitchen.

Grandma Tessa stood by the stove. She smiled when she saw Darcy. "There you are. Are you hungry?"

Darcy laughed. "I can't wear most of my pants and shorts. I'm barely squeezing into skirts I brought."

"You're too skinny."

Darcy patted her stomach. "Not for long." She

cheered at the thought of Lauren packing on a few pounds. That was the one place where her sister had more of a problem. Then she scolded herself for being so shallow.

"I talked to my sister. She'll be here Friday afternoon, after the reading of the will."

Tessa clapped her hands. "Good. Good. We'll plan a special dinner, eh? I'll call Mary and have her come help. You can help with the menu. We'll have wine. Such fun. We can . . ." She frowned. "You're not happy, Darcy. Why?"

"It's nothing. Really. This is great."

The tiny woman walked over and put her hands on her hips. "I've had children in this house nearly all my life and I know when something's wrong."

Darcy figured she might be too old to be considered a child, but she was certainly acting like one. She sighed. "It's just . . ." She shifted her feet. "This is really stupid." Even more stupid when the first tear slipped down her cheek.

Tessa led her to the table and motioned to a chair. "Tell me."

Darcy sank into the seat, then covered her face with her hands. "I love it here," she said as the tears really let loose. "You've all been so good to me, and I really love this family so much. But Lauren is really a much better person. She's nicer and prettier and more fun to be with. You're all going to like her better and Joe isn't talking to me and I'm not going to have anyone and I found you guys first. Which makes me sound like a three-year-old. Plus, you're still mourning Lorenzo and me talking about something so selfish and stupid is really bad."

She braced herself for the scolding or at least a disapproving silence. Instead she heard a soft laugh. She looked at Tessa, who grinned at her.

"Is that all?" the elderly woman asked.

"All? It's a ton."

"I know. Poor Darcy." Tessa wiped her tears. "You're a good girl. You try hard and you give with your whole heart. Of course we'll like you best. You're one of us now. Who is this Lauren anyway?"

Darcy sniffed. "She's really great. Trust me. Everyone adores her."

"Maybe, but she's not you, eh?"

Because her life was one entertainment after the other, Joe chose that moment to walk into the kitchen. He took one look at her tear-stained face and started to back out. Tessa stopped him with a glance.

"Joseph. Come here. Darcy is worried about her sister visiting. Tell her that she'll always be first in our hearts. And you should make up with her. She's a good girl. You're lucky to have her. But do you tell her? No."

Darcy winced. This was so not the way to win Joe's affections.

"I'm okay," she said quickly.

Not surprisingly, Joe ducked out without speaking.

"He's been doing a lot of that lately," she murmured.

"He'll come around," Tessa assured her.

Darcy wanted to believe it was true, but she had her doubts. So far he'd been doing a fabulous imitation of a man doing his best to bolt for freedom.

Paige considered the contents of the refrigerator, but it was really tough to get worked up about cooking when all she had to do was walk up to the main house and collect some of the best leftovers on the planet. She didn't know the secret ingredient Grandma Tessa and Grammy M put into their meals, but it was worth millions. Paige was willing to give up a large percent of her pension to get daily access to Grammy M's scones alone. And Tessa's marinara sauce was worthy of stardom.

There was, however, the calorie issue. She was already five pounds over her normal weight. So a salad for dinner made sense. The fact that there was an entire platter of chicken marsala with a side of grilled potatoes less than a hundred yards away was meaningless. Salad was the far healthier choice.

She closed the refrigerator and looked longingly at the door. Okay, principle over self-indulgence. Which would win? Alex walked into the kitchen. "I'm not leaving," he announced.

The unexpected statement left her blinking. She banished thoughts of flavorful chicken and considered his words.

"Not leaving here?" she asked.

"Right. I'm on the team. With you."

"Okay. That begs the question of why. Isn't there something more important for you to be doing with your day?"

"I'm not always interested in the high-profile cases," he told her. "I'm not in this for the glory."

"Agreed, but nobody even knows Darcy's here. The odds of something happening to her are pretty close to zero. So you're setting yourself up for some long days when nothing is going to happen. That isn't exactly your style."

"Maybe my style is changing."

Funny how she wanted to believe that. Being around Alex had a way of making her remember the past—their past. But to what end?

"I'm thinking of leaving," she said.

"This job?"

"The agency. When Darcy returns to D.C. I'm going to resign."

Nothing about his expression changed. She'd thought he might be disappointed, but she was wrong. He wasn't anything.

"Why?" he asked, although she wasn't sure why he bothered.

"We've discussed this before. I want a life. I want to belong to something other than my job. I want a personal worldview that doesn't include daily concerns that someone I care about is going to be shot or kidnapped."

"So you're leaving me again?"

She stared at him. "This has nothing to do with you."

"It has everything to do with me," he said. "You told me not to play games, or start something I wasn't prepared to finish. I'm going to tell you the same thing."

He left. Paige gave in to the inevitable and headed for the main house, where she would drown her confusion in sweet sauce and perfectly cooked chicken.

She and Alex seemed to have mastered the art of the cryptic conversation, which made for an entertaining afternoon but didn't really get them anywhere.

Did she want to change that? Did she want to talk to him about what was in her heart? Did she know what was in her heart? All those years ago, life had been both harder and easier. With her late husband, she'd learned what loving someone really meant. She wanted that again. But did she want it with Alex, and if she did, was he willing to make the sacrifices love required?

The reading of the will took place in the living room. The family lawyer was a young woman of thirty or so, which surprised Joe. He'd expected some old and dusty family retainer. Good to know that Lorenzo still had the power to shock him, even after he was gone.

The entire family gathered on sofas and chairs. As this was the Marcellis, there was plenty of food, although wine was noticeably absent.

Joe listened to the lawyer, who explained the nature of the will. There were several provisions for charities, a significant trust fund for Marco and Colleen and the great-grandchildren. But the biggie, the winery itself, was left for last.

The lawyer flipped the page and cleared her throat.

"Marcelli Wines," she read, "is my pride and joy. Four generations have worked the land. Soon that will be five. It is my dearest wish that the winery go on forever. To ensure that, I leave it in capable hands. Hands I trust. I leave each of my granddaughters fifteen percent of the winery and to my grandson, Joseph Larson, I leave forty percent. The majority share."

18

❧

After the reading of the will, Joe sat in the library until the lawyer and most of the family had filed out. Marco and Brenna stayed behind.

Joe took one look at their calm faces and said, "You knew."

Marco sat on the sofa across from Joe's chair and nodded. "My father told me what he wanted to do about a year ago. We discussed it and agreed it was a good idea."

Joe didn't know who the "we" was in the conversation, nor did he care. "It's not a good idea for me."

"He wanted you to be a part of the family," Marco said. "He wanted you to belong."

"You can't force me to do this," Joe told him. "What was he thinking of, leaving me the majority share?"

"It's what he wanted. What we all want," Brenna said from her seat at the opposite end of the sofa. "Partners, Joe. Remember?"

"You run the winery," Joe told her. "You have for years. You should be in charge."

"I will be." Brenna rubbed her stomach. "But Four Sisters winery is growing. That's going to take more and more of my time. Plus, honest to God, some of the choices Nic wants to make at Wild Sea. He needs me. You don't have to panic, Joe. We're going to hire a manager to run Marcelli until you learn what you need to and get your feet under you."

"You're deciding for me? In case you've forgotten, I have a career. One I've worked for. One I want. Not here."

He stood and glared at them both. "You think you can finish what he started?" he asked, furious with the change of events. "It's not going to happen. I'm leaving on Monday, and right now I have no plans to come back."

Brenna paled. Marco looked as if he'd been shot. Before either could react, Darcy stepped into the library.

"Sorry to interrupt," she said.

"This is not the time," Joe told her, his voice cold.

She narrowed her gaze. "Amazingly enough, everything isn't about you, Joe. As requested, I'm letting Brenna and Marco know that my sister is due to arrive any second. And just in case it's of interest to you, your captain left a message to say he would be delighted to join us for dinner tonight and it's formal. So you'll need your dress whites."

He felt like a jerk. "Darcy," he said as he reached for her.

She sidestepped him. "I have to go see my sister."

Darcy headed for the kitchen. She appreciated that Joe was under a lot of strain, but she wanted to walk back to the library and smack him upside the head.

Katie had already told her what had happened when the will was read, so she knew he couldn't be happy about that. While she was willing to offer friendly support, she didn't appreciate him turning on her as though she was the enemy.

Mia and Ian were in the kitchen, while Grandma Tessa was nowhere to be seen. Had the ever chatty Ian driven away the matriarch of the family?

"I can't wait to meet your sister," Ian said. "I've seen lots of pictures of her. She's really pretty. Is she that pretty in person? I've heard she's really nice. Is she nice? I sent money to that children's charity she supports. Only a few dollars because I'm a student, right? It's not like I have a ton of cash. But still, it was something."

Darcy walked to the coffeepot and tried to block out Ian's incessant conversation. Mia joined her.

"I know he's a little hard to take," she whispered. "I'm going to dump him as soon as we get back to D.C. He's starting to get on my nerves, too. It's just been nice to have him around, especially after Grandpa Lorenzo died, you know?"

Darcy nodded. She heard a car pull up outside and hurried to the back door.

She walked out onto the back porch just as the rear door of the SUV opened. Lauren stepped out into the early afternoon light. Sunlight brightened her hair to the color of spun gold and made her features seem as if they'd been touched with starlight. Her tailored cotton blouse topped a trim khaki skirt that showed off her voluptuous curves to perfection. Darcy tugged at her black dress and suddenly felt like a grandmother in mourning.

Lauren spotted her and grinned. Darcy smiled in return. As she took a step forward, she had a moment of complete clarity. It was what Oprah always called a light-bulb moment.

She didn't want to *be* Lauren. She'd never actually envied her sister. She'd envied what her sister had—a life she adored, a great love, a close family. Darcy didn't want to be blond, she wanted connections. A sense of belonging.

The downside was falling for a man incapable of committing, but whose life was perfect?

Grandma Tessa hovered. There was no other word to describe the older woman's anxious, quivering movement as she motioned to the room in question.

"If we'd had more time," she murmured, gesturing to the floral wallpaper and fifteen-year-old rock star posters, "we could have decorated."

Lauren hugged the tiny woman. "It's lovely. Just like my room back in high school. You're so sweet to take me in on a moment's notice. I could have stayed at a hotel. This is such an inconvenience and I apologize. It's just I've missed Darcy so much, and she's made all of you sound so wonderful that I couldn't resist the opportunity to crash the party. Is that horribly rude?"

As Darcy watched, Tessa, Grammy M, and Colleen were completely charmed by Lauren.

"We're delighted to have you here," Colleen said.

"'Tis no trouble a'tall," Grammy M assured her.

"Stay as long as you like," Grandma Tessa requested.

Lauren laughed. "You might want to be careful with invitations like that. What if I never want to leave?"

Being who they were, and Lauren who she was, the Marcelli women only looked delighted at the prospect.

Her sister was gracious, Darcy thought. She wasn't sure if she'd been born that way or had developed the skill over time, but it was something she was going to have to cultivate. It seemed to smooth over rough patches. There were other changes she could make, she thought. She could get more involved in her father's life. Go to the White House more. Her stubbornness was costing her a once-in-a-lifetime opportunity.

That decided, she completed the tour of the amenities, showing Lauren the bathroom across the hall.

"At least we won't be sharing," Mia said as she raced up the stairs with one of Lauren's small suitcases. "Good thing. I'm not too bad, but Ian hogs the mirror for hours."

Lauren looked at her and smiled. "Mia, right? All these names. I'll never get them straight."

Mia set down the suitcase. "Oh, I'm easy to remember. I'm the fun sister. And the only one who isn't married." She frowned. "How on earth did that happen? Oh, yeah. Right. Didn't want to be tied down."

She grinned, and Lauren laughed. Colleen welcomed her again, then ushered the Grands away.

"We'll let you girls help Lauren unpack. Don't forget dinner tonight is formal. Mia, you know what that means."

Mia rolled her eyes. "Yes, Mom. I'll tone down the

makeup and wear something nice. And I'll be polite to Joe's captain." She watched as her mother went down the stairs with the Grands, then leaned in close.

"She's afraid I'll ask about the sexy SEALs. I tease Joe about it all the time and it makes him crazy."

"How do you tease him?" Lauren asked.

"Pretending I want to sleep with them all."

Darcy eyed her. "I don't think it's much of a pretense."

Mia grinned. "Sometimes it's not."

They returned to Lauren's temporary quarters. Lauren closed the door, put her hands on her hips, and shook her head. "Do you have to always wear black?" she asked.

Darcy laughed, then hugged her. "I missed you, too."

Mia looked between them. "You're right. Darcy *is* always in black. I never noticed before. It's very city chic."

"You hear that?" Darcy asked. "I'm chic, and you're an Easter egg."

Mia flopped down on one of the beds. "Hey, don't pull me into a family argument. Lauren looks fabulous, too. But in a different way."

"I'm much more wholesome," Lauren said primly. She picked up one of her suitcases and put it on the other bed. "And I wear colors."

Mia looked at the pile of luggage. "Do you have a maid or something to take care of your clothes?"

"No. Just me. Well, back home there is a full laundry and dry cleaning service, so I don't have to worry about that."

Mia sat up. "You mean back home at the White House."

Darcy sat next to her. "I can't believe you're star-struck. I figured you were too cool for that."

Mia laughed. "I only pretend to be cool. I've never known anyone who's been related to a president before I met you two." She leaned toward Lauren. "So tell me everything."

"Hey." Darcy bumped her shoulder against Mia's. "You didn't ask me questions about the White House."

"I know." Mia looked at her. "I guess I just think of you as one of us."

Darcy felt her whole body relax as Mia's words sank in. It was about the nicest thing anyone had ever said to her.

Mia squinted at Lauren. "I see the resemblance a little, but you guys are pretty different."

"Lauren's the beauty," Darcy said easily.

Lauren threw a pair of socks at her. "You're very attractive."

Mia glanced between them. "Lauren's the classic beauty," she said thoughtfully, "but Darcy has the face you can't look away from. At least my brother can't."

Darcy rolled her eyes. "Don't you start with me."

"I can if I want to." She leaned toward Lauren. "They're having sex. We all know about it, but we're pretending we don't."

Darcy groaned. "You weren't supposed to say anything."

"Why not?" Lauren asked. "I already know you have sex with him. Although she won't give me details. I hate that. I want specifics."

Mia shook her head. "Normally I would, too, but he's

my brother. He's going to look gorgeous tonight," she added. "You'll both have to control yourselves."

Lauren hung up yet another pastel-colored skirt. "Because of the formal dinner?"

"Dress whites," Darcy said. "He'll be impressive."

"Then we'll all have to look nice," Lauren said. "So he can be impressed, too."

19

❧

*J*oe was downstairs fifteen minutes before his captain was due to arrive. As per his custom, Owen Phillips was ten minutes early. Joe stood at attention by the house and waited until Phillips stepped out of his fully restored '68 Mustang and closed the door.

"Sir," Joe said, saluting.

Phillips returned the salute, then said, "Good to see you, Joe. Sorry about your grandfather."

"Thank you, sir."

His captain smiled. "It's a family dinner. I think we should ease off on the formalities."

Joe nodded, thinking if they weren't standing on ceremony then why were they both wearing ice cream suits.

"Great place," Phillips said as he looked around at the vineyard. "I've always enjoyed this part of the state. Very pretty."

"Yes, ah, it is. The vineyards do well. We'll be having Marcelli wine with dinner."

Phillips looked at him. "You told me you'll be back on

base on Monday. It's only been a couple of weeks since your grandfather died. You're welcome to take more leave."

"I appreciate that, but I'm ready to get back to work. My team needs me."

"The admiral has cooled down enough that you should be safe to return to duty, but I have to tell you. If I had a home like this, I don't think I'd be so quick to leave it. A man could search all over the world and never find anything quite like this."

Before Joe could respond, the back door opened and the Grands hurried down the stairs. For two old ladies, they sure moved fast.

"We heard the car," Grammy M said, beaming at the captain. "We were thinkin' it was your friend."

Joe winced. "Captain Phillips, may I present the matriarchs of my family? This is Tessa Marcelli and Mary-Margaret O'Shea. Better known as Grandma Tessa and Grammy M."

Phillips nodded at them both, then took Tessa's small hand in his. "I'm so sorry about your loss," he said quietly. "I hope I'm not imposing too soon."

"Not at all," Tessa told him. "We invited you so we could meet you. Besides, I like the company." Then, before Joe could warn the other man or stop her, Tessa reached up and pinched Phillips's cheek. "You're a handsome one. Married, I suppose?"

Phillips looked stunned. "Yes, ma'am. Nearly twenty years now."

"It's all right. You're too old for Mia."

Grammy M stepped forward and managed something that looked suspiciously like a curtsey. "We're all so happy to be havin' a friend of Joe's here. You work with him, do you?"

"Ah, yes." The captain still seemed shell-shocked.

Colleen and Marco came out next. "We heard you were here," Colleen said as she smoothed the front of her silk dress. "Welcome."

"So much for trying to get you in the door before you meet everyone," Joe told his commanding officer. "I did warn you."

"Yes, you did." Phillips grinned. "I'm liking them."

Joe looked at the couple and opened his mouth to introduce them. "Marco and Colleen Marcelli," he said. Then without planning the words in advance, he added, "My parents."

There was a moment of silence. The Grands, Colleen, and Marco turned to stare at him. Colleen recovered first.

"It's a long drive, Captain. Thank you so much for making it."

"My pleasure, ma'am."

"Please, call me Colleen."

He shook her hand. "And you must call me Owen. All of you." He glanced at Joe. "Not you."

Joe grinned. "Yes, sir. Understood."

Joe finally got everyone in the house. Katie, Zach, and Valerie were in Los Angeles, but the rest of the family had come for dinner. He made introductions, then realized not everyone was there.

"Where's Darcy?" he asked.

"With her sister," Mia said smugly. "They were trying to figure out what to wear. It could be hours."

"Not likely," Colleen said, chiding her youngest. "Darcy is always on time." She smiled at Owen. "Very polite and simply charming. I'll admit we were a little nervous about hosting a daughter of the president."

"Too much like royalty," Mia joked.

"Actually, that's true," Colleen said. "But she's been a delight. We'll all be sorry to see her go."

Mia jabbed Joe in the ribs. "You could do something about that."

Before he could tell her to shut up, he heard something on the stairs and glanced up. Darcy and the sister he'd yet to meet started down the stairs. He had a vague impression of long blond hair and curves, but neither interested him. Instead he couldn't stop staring at Darcy.

She wore a long, silky-looking dress in a pale peach color. The cut or style or something emphasized her slender body in a way that got his blood boiling. Thin straps were all that held it up, he thought, knowing he could make quick work of them.

Her large eyes seemed to glow and her mouth was soft and pouty-looking. Pearl earrings hung nearly to her bare shoulders, while a twisted strand hugged her neck.

She was beautiful. More than beautiful—she was spectacular. Feminine, sexy as hell, and if he remembered correctly, he'd spent the last few days acting like a complete idiot around her.

Colleen moved toward the two women. "You're both so lovely," she said with a smile. "Allow me to present our dinner guest. Captain Owen Phillips. Captain, this is Darcy Jensen and Lauren Jensen-Smith."

"Nice to meet you," Darcy said as she shook his hand.

Lauren did the same and pleasantries were exchanged. Colleen ushered everyone into the living room for a predinner drink, but Joe lingered in the hallway. He touched Darcy's arm before she could follow the family.

"You look great," he said, when they were alone.

She gave him a once-over, then shrugged. "Not bad, yourself. I always did like dress whites."

Emotions swelled up inside him. The sensations were unfamiliar and uncomfortable and all unnamed. But they made him want to say something, do something.

"Darcy, I—"

"Comin' through," Grammy M said as she walked toward them with a tray of appetizers. "Hot food here."

Joe moved to one side and let his grandmother pass. He tried to think of what to say when Marco came out of the living room.

"Your captain wants to start with our wines." He grinned. "It's going to be a long night. Good thing we booked him a room at the hotel down the road."

When Marco had passed, Darcy touched his hand. "It's okay," she told him. "I understand."

An interesting concept, when he didn't understand himself.

"Now will you believe me?" Lauren asked sometime close to midnight as she sprawled across Darcy's bed. "I swear, Joe looked like something out of a cartoon the way his mouth dropped open when he saw you. I thought he was going to dislocate his jaw or something."

Darcy curled up in a chair in the corner of the room. She'd traded in the dress she'd borrowed from her sister for shorts and a T-shirt, but she could still remember the sensual feel of the silk on her body and the stunned appreciation in Joe's eyes.

"He was pretty surprised."

Lauren grinned. "Color is our friend. When we go home, I want to go shopping with you and you're not allowed to buy anything black."

"Except for lingerie."

"Okay. Yeah, that can be black, but nothing else." Lauren sat up and faced her. "He's really great. I can see the appeal. And when you look at him, there are stars in your eyes."

"Not stars."

"Something. You're in love with him."

Darcy nodded. "Which doesn't mean anything."

"Of course it does. You've never been in love before."

"My track record with men isn't the greatest, and I don't think this time is going to work out any better."

Lauren shook her head. "You're wrong. Joe couldn't stop looking at you all through dinner."

"I know, and it was really cool, but how much does that mean? He finds me attractive, and okay, the sex is hot, but that's not a real relationship."

"It's not a bad start."

Darcy wished that were true. "He's not like other guys. He holds back. No one touches his heart. He let his wife go without a word. It's been three years and he's still resisting the Marcellis. How long will he resist me?"

"Maybe he won't. Maybe he's starting to get it."

Darcy wished that were true, but she didn't have any evidence to back it up. "He's a good man. Strong and loyal. I'd trust him with my life and even my heart, but I don't think he's interested in either. I've learned so much being here. About myself and life and people. I'll be okay when it's time to leave. I'll . . ."

"Survive?" Lauren asked, her face serious, but her eyes bright with humor.

"Don't you dare disco me. Yes. I'll survive. Better than that. I want to get closer to you and Dad. I want to come to the White House and find a charity I can support and get involved in."

"What about Joe?"

"What do you mean?"

"Are you going to tell him how you feel?" Lauren asked. "Before you leave."

"I can't decide. It's not that I want to keep the truth from him, it's that I'm not sure letting him know how I feel is very kind. I don't think he can take one more person wanting him to love her back."

"I don't agree. He seems like a pretty tough guy."

Someone knocked on the door.

"I'll get it," Lauren said as she stood and crossed the room.

She pulled open the door, and Darcy saw Joe standing there. He looked between the women.

Before he could speak, Lauren grinned and stepped into the hallway. "I was just leaving. You kids have a good time. Don't stay up too late."

With that, she was gone.

Joe hovered awkwardly in the hallway. "She didn't have to leave," he said.

Darcy laughed. "Okay. That could make things interesting."

He stepped into the room and closed the door behind him. "I meant I didn't want to run her off."

He stood in the center of the room and stared at her.

There was a sadness in his eyes she hadn't seen before. She rose and faced him.

"What's wrong?" she asked.

"Hell if I know." He took a step toward her. "I'm sorry. I've been difficult and a jerk. Whatever I have going on isn't your fault. I've always been good at moving on. At taking the next assignment. I don't know what to do. But I do know that this is the only place where I can draw a breath."

"My room?" she asked, surprised it was anything close to a haven for him. "It's not as if your family won't think to look for you here."

He reached for her and pulled her close. "Not your room. Being with you. It doesn't matter where."

Alex paced outside the guesthouse. The night was clear and cool. There was a forecast of rain, but he didn't believe it. Not that it mattered one way or the other. Rain, snow, sleet, weather wasn't his problem. Paige was.

He didn't understand her. He'd stayed because . . . because. He swore. He didn't know why. Because leaving hadn't felt right. Because they'd had unfinished business. Or so he'd thought. But in the past couple of days, she'd acted as if he didn't exist. Or matter. If he lived to be a thousand he would never understand women. Why did they have to be so damn complicated?

He turned and stared at the front door. He could talk to her. That was something women really seemed to like. Talking. Endless talking.

But about what? She was going to want to ask a bunch of questions, and he didn't have the answers. She was like that. Tricky. Sly. Beautiful.

He stared up at the stars and thought about how she moved and the sound of her laughter. That in all the years they'd been apart, he'd never forgotten her or wanted anyone the way he'd wanted her.

Alex swore under his breath and walked into the guesthouse. He headed directly for Paige's bedroom and opened the door without knocking.

She lay on her bed, reading. Her hair was mussed, her face free of makeup. The tank top she wore over pj bottoms looked thin and worn. Not the least bit sexy—but that didn't stop him from wanting her.

They stared at each other. Neither spoke. Paige put down her book, then slid down on the bed and smiled.

That's all it took. One smile.

Even as he jerked off his T-shirt, he moved toward her. He reached for her as she reached for him, and then he was in her arms. She felt soft and feminine and so familiar that he ached inside. Their mouths locked in a deep, hungry kiss. It had been so long, he thought as need rocketed through him. Too long.

Even as their tongues tangled and brushed and circled, they tore at each other's clothes. He needed her naked—he had to touch her or die.

There were no gentle preliminaries, no murmured words, no light touches. Just reaching and getting naked and kissing. And then she was on her back and he was between her legs. She stared at him, her green eyes dark with passion.

"I want you," she breathed.

"I've missed you," he told her, right before he claimed her.

*   *   *

Tessa sat alone in the dark. Her room was quiet, even with the window open. Moonlight allowed her to see the vineyard and nearly to the ocean. Hints of salt air mingled with the heavy fragrance of the ripening grapes.

The chardonnay harvest had begun. Soon the machinery in the pressing room would clank to life, and the cycle would begin again.

Across from her chair stood the big, empty bed where she and Lorenzo had slept for so many years. She'd avoided it, spending her nights dozing in her chair. But tonight she felt differently. More at peace.

"Are you here?" she asked the quiet darkness. "Lorenzo?"

As she asked the question, she smiled. Even if her husband could reach her from the great beyond, he was just stubborn enough to refuse to speak to her.

"I miss you, Lorenzo," she whispered. "So much."

There was no response.

Tessa stood and made her way to the bed. As she lay down on the cool sheets, she waited for the knot of fear and panic that had driven her from this bed the first night after he died. It didn't come. Instead she felt somehow safe and comforted. And a slight dipping of the mattress, as if someone had joined her.

No one had, of course. When she turned to look, she was still alone. But not so lonely anymore.

Four hours later, Darcy was asleep, but Joe couldn't relax enough to stay in bed. He dressed and quietly left her room. Instead of returning to his own, he walked out of the house and into the night.

The sky was clear, the moon nearly full. He walked

into the vineyards, brushing against the heavy grapes.

The leaves were dry from lack of rain, but dry, warm conditions were supposed to be good for harvesting. Or was it less sun and no—

He shook his head. None of it mattered, he told himself. He was leaving on Monday and he wasn't coming back for a long time. He had SEAL teams to get ready. Plans had to be made, training implemented. There was a whole world outside of the vineyard, and he intended to be a part of it.

"Anywhere but here," he murmured into the night.

But even as he spoke the words, he felt a heavy weight on his shoulders. Brenna's baby was due anytime now. How would she hire a manager before she gave birth? What about Marco and Colleen? They were sticking around to help when they really wanted to be on the road, selling the wines. There was the harvest, the pressing, the bottling. So many responsibilities and he—

"No!" he roared, glaring up at the heavens. "I don't know where you are, Lorenzo, but you couldn't make me care before and you can't make me care now. I'm not staying. This isn't where I belong. I've never belonged here. I don't blame you for this—it's simply the truth. Not here."

His words drifted into the night. There was no response, and he felt a little foolish after his outburst. Yelling at ghosts wasn't going to accomplish anything.

He turned to walk back to the house, only to pause. There was something . . .

He inhaled deeply and realized what it was.

Smoke.

20

❧

Darcy woke to a loud shrieking sound she couldn't place. Joe wasn't in her bed and there was no way the alarm signaled good news.

She'd barely thrown back the covers when Mia burst into her room.

"It's a fire," Mia yelled. "There's a fire in the vineyards."

Fire? How could that happen? Sure it had been dry, but what on earth could start a fire in the middle of grapevines?

Rather than consider an answer, she grabbed clothes and pulled them on. Lauren ran into her room.

"What's going on?" her sister asked.

"A fire in the vineyard. Get dressed. We'll go downstairs and see if we can help."

In a matter of a couple of minutes, everyone had assembled in the kitchen. The emergency siren had been turned off, but there was still a sense of urgency.

Grandma Tessa was already making coffee. Joe paced back and forth, talking to Marco in a low voice and making notes on a pad of paper. Marco left the kitchen and Joe glanced at everyone else.

"There's a fire in the east field. I can't tell how big it is, but it's spreading fast. Everything is just dry enough to burn. The fire department is on its way. They're sending three companies, and at dawn we'll get air support."

"What about Brenna?" Darcy asked. "She'll want to know."

Joe nodded. "I've already spoken with Nic, and they're on their way."

"A fire," Ian said. "Wow. Do you know how it started? There hasn't been any lightning, has there? I didn't think you got a lot of lightning in this part of the country. Maybe some homeless guy smoking or something. Could a match have started the fire? Or a downed electrical wire. Only why would it be down. There are—"

Joe, Colleen, Marco, and Mia all turned to Ian.

"Shut up," they said together.

Ian took a step back. "Sorry. I was just trying to help."

"Help silently," Joe said.

The back door opened and Alex and Paige raced inside. "You know about the fire, right?" Alex asked.

Joe nodded. Marco returned. He had several rolled sheets of paper in his hands.

"Maps," Joe said. "We need to help the fire department find the best places to fight the fire."

Marco spread out the large maps on the kitchen table, anchoring the edges with salt and pepper shakers and a bowl of sugar.

"Here's the house," the elder Marcelli said. "Here's the east field."

Everyone gathered around the table.

"There's a service road," Joe said, tracing a dark line on the map. "Where are the water connections?"

Marco pointed to several triangular icons. "These show them. The trucks can hook up directly to our main water supply."

Joe straightened and counted heads. "We'll split up into teams and take maps with us. Tessa, I'll tell you where to send Nic when he arrives. You'll stay here with Brenna, Lauren, and Darcy."

"I'm not staying," Darcy told him. "And before you start arguing, I've spent the last five weeks walking all over this vineyard. I know it better than you do. I know what the water stations look like. I'm going to help."

His dark gaze locked with hers, then he nodded once. "Alex, you're with Darcy. Mia and Ian, as well. I want this fire stopped, but even more than that, I want Darcy kept safe."

"That goes for everyone," he added, before she could wonder if his concern was about her, Darcy, the woman he shared a bed with, or her, Darcy, the president's daughter.

"I know the vineyard is important, but it's just grapes. They can be replanted, but none of you can be. Stay safe and think before you do anything rash. Agreed?"

Everyone nodded.

Sirens could be heard in the distance. A car pulled up and squealed to a stop.

"Let's get ready," Joe said.

The next fifteen minutes passed in a blur. Brenna was helped inside where Grandma Tessa did her best to keep her calm. The various teams went out to join the firefighters, which was how Darcy found herself seated in a large truck, staring at a map by flashlight and calling out when she thought they were close to a water connection.

"It's here," she said, looking up and pointing.

The truck stopped on the service road. She waited for the firefighters to scramble out, then she eased to the ground and got her first good look at the fire.

It stretched across what looked like miles. Bright, hot flames consumed the vines much more quickly than she could have imagined. Every now and then a column rose to salute the sky, as if in victory.

"No, you don't," Darcy murmured, even as she inhaled the sharp scent of scorched grapes and burned leaves.

The firefighters went to work with their hoses. Darcy circled around the back of the truck and found Mia.

"We have to go locate the next water station," Darcy said. "For the next truck. It shouldn't be that far."

"Lead on," Mia told her. "Alex, we're going up to find the next water connection."

He nodded and joined them. In the distance Darcy saw another truck pull up. Several people climbed out. She thought she saw Joe, but in the swirling smoke, it was hard to be sure. Still, her heart jumped a little, as if it recognized its one true love.

And then she knew she had to tell him the truth. She couldn't leave without admitting she loved him. To do so would be to dishonor the connection she felt with him.

But first, there was a fire to fight and a vineyard to save.

*   *   *

For a Navy SEAL, water was a safe haven. Joe didn't like this new enemy that consumed without conscience. The flames grew and stretched and took. It didn't seem to matter how much water they sprayed, the fire lived on.

He stayed close to the fire chief, giving information when he could and helping with hoses. As he worked, he eyed the sky. How long until dawn? How long until the air support could join them?

Time seemed to stand still until the world was simply heat and flames and water. He sweated and coughed from the smoke and hoped everyone was staying safe.

Too many civilians, he thought. Too many people who didn't have the training. It wasn't supposed to be like this. The winery was supposed to be easy. *Not on my watch,* he thought. *Not on my watch.*

Frustration became anger. Lorenzo had left him the winery so he would stay. The old man had wanted him to care. Now, with the fire destroying all that four generations of Marcellis had built, Joe found himself cursing his own worry and concern.

"Good news," the fire chief said as he handed Joe a bottle of water. "The fog's coming in."

Joe unscrewed the top of the bottle and swallowed half the contents in one long drink. Then he turned to the west and saw the stars had disappeared behind a bank of heavy fog. The air was less dry, the flying ash and cinders less hot.

"Will this make a difference?" he asked.

"It'll help," the chief told him. "A heavy fog bank will combine with the smoke and make it a bitch to see, but there isn't any wind. If we can get the humidity high enough, we'll get a handle on this son of a bitch."

Joe finished the water. "I want to know how it started."

"You and me, both," the chief told him. "I have a feeling you're not going to like what we find."

"Arson?"

"Could be. You have cultivated vineyards up here. No power lines, no lightning strikes. The ground is dry, but not parched, and the heavy fruit doesn't burn easily."

Joe couldn't think of anyone who would want to burn down Marcelli Wines. They were successful, but not a major holding. Not like Wild Sea.

He reminded himself this wasn't the time or the way to find answers. Instead he went back to work on the fire. When the firefighters came and asked him to help pull up several rows of grapes to widen a fire break, he reached for a shovel and dug in.

Time passed. The moments were measured in sweat and sparks and smoke. The fog continued to roll in until some of it reached behind the fire, creating an eerie backdrop for the dancing flames.

He heard a horn honk and turned to look. Paige and Lauren drove up on a golf cart.

"We have food and water," Lauren yelled. "Take a break."

He joined the other men as the women handed out thick sandwiches and chilly bottles of water.

"How's it going?" he asked.

"Good." Paige tucked a bottle of water into his jeans pocket. "The other teams are making progress, too. The fog's helping. We're hoping for rain."

"I'm going to go check on them," he told the chief.

"You know where to find us."

Joe hopped on the back of the cart and directed Paige toward the other teams.

"Thanks for helping," he said. "You didn't have to."

She glanced at him over her shoulder. "I've put in my time here, too," she said. "I care about the Marcellis as much as you." She faced front and shrugged. "They're good people."

They *were* good people, he thought as he jumped out of the cart and walked over to another group of firefighters. Marco and Colleen were studying maps spread on the ground.

"Here," Marco said, pointing. "Above it is the steepest terrain we have. I wouldn't risk going any higher. If we make our stand there, we should be fine." He glanced up and saw Joe. "We're winning."

"You think?"

Marco motioned to the thickening fog. "Pop wouldn't have it any other way."

Joe wanted to point out that the fog was a weather phenomenon common to the area, not proof of ghostly interference, but he couldn't seem to say the words. Maybe because he'd felt Lorenzo's presence as well. Four generations of Marcellis had worked the line. There was no way the old man would let that be lost.

The smoke was less thick here. He could see the acres of grapes yet to be touched by the flames.

"If we can get a protective break around them," he said, thinking out loud.

"Exactly," Marco said. "We can save most of them. Still have a decent year."

There was, Joe realized, a point when a soldier knew to give up the battle. When the victory or the loss became inevitable. Casualties could still occur on both sides, but the outcome had been determined.

When had that happened to him? He'd been fighting long enough, but against what? His destiny? What was so bad about claiming this as his heritage? What did he resent about it?

He liked it here, he admitted to himself. He liked the family and the location. Darcy loved it and them. She was . . .

Colleen touched his arm. "What are you thinking about? You're smiling."

"Darcy," he admitted, wondering when exactly he'd let Darcy in.

"Really? I knew you two were getting along, but I didn't think things were that serious. She's the president's daughter."

"Yeah. I figured that out already."

"I only meant that there will be complications." She smiled. "We're here for you, Joe. You know that, right?"

He nodded. "Okay, back to the fire. I'm going to check on the other teams."

His mother hugged him. "On Darcy, you mean."

"That, too."

Suddenly he was eager to see her. This wasn't the time or place to discuss anything, but he needed to hear her voice and know she was all right.

Darcy had never fought a fire before, and she made a mental note to keep it off her to-do list. So far the fire-fighters had kept them back, relegating them to behind the truck activities. Even so, carting water and supplies, showing the way to the next hose hookup was hard, hot work. The smoke made it tough to breathe easily, and even with the fog rolling in there were still sparks flying everywhere.

But she wasn't going to give up, especially when it seemed as if they were making progress. The flames didn't seem to reach as high, and every now and then she thought she could see a little farther into the vineyard.

She walked back to the trucks and reached for one of the sandwiches Paige and Lauren had brought. She'd just taken her first bite when Ian came running up.

"Joe's looking for you," he said.

"Really? Is he all right?"

Ian grinned. "I think he wants to make sure that you are. Come on. This way."

He led her around the trucks and into the vineyard. They were heading away from the fire.

"Joe's out here?" she asked.

Just then someone called her name. She turned back and saw someone running after them, but she couldn't see who it was. A man, but who?

"Wait," Darcy told Ian. "Is that Joe?"

Ian moved beside her and took her arm in his left hand. Then, before she realized what was happening, he pulled a gun out of his jacket, took aim on the approaching man, and pulled the trigger.

The world slowed. Later, Darcy would swear that she could actually see the bullet burst out of the barrel. She saw the man stop in midstride. He twisted and then he was falling to the ground.

"Joe!" she screamed in horror. Not him. It couldn't be him.

She started to run but found she couldn't move. She turned to see what was holding her in place. Ian had a grip on her arm. Other men appeared out of the darkness. There were four of them. Just like before.

"No!" she screamed into the night.

The men didn't stop. One of them tackled her, and she found herself flat on her back. She couldn't breathe, and no matter how she squirmed and clawed and kicked, they didn't let go. Her arms were yanked behind her back, and ropes were fastened around her hands. More ties bound her ankles. She screamed again and one of them stuffed a handkerchief into her mouth. The dry, dirty cotton made her gag.

Joe! Joe! Was he shot? Bleeding? Dead?

Two of them half dragged, half carried her to a van. Past and present blended until she wasn't sure what was real and what was from before.

She bucked and twisted and lashed out as best she could. One of the men released her. She hit the ground on her side. Pain shot through her shoulder, but she didn't give in to it. Instead she rolled toward the vines, intent on hiding, on getting away.

Then the men were around her. They picked her up. One of them used bolt cutters to remove her security bracelet. Ian held a gun to her cheek.

"Try escaping again and I'll splatter your brains all over the place. Got me?"

Ian, she thought. How could it be him? He was harmless. He was Mia's annoying boyfriend. It couldn't be Ian.

But it was, and the gun in his hand told her he was deadly serious.

*   *   *

"They're right over here," Paige said as she stopped the cart. "We should be able to find them by following Ian's chatter."

Joe nodded as he got out of the cart. He looked around. The firefighters were clearly visible, but not anyone else.

Without warning, his gut clenched. There was no reason, but he'd learned to trust the sensation.

"Something's wrong," he told Paige. "Get backup."

"What?"

"Now," he ordered, even as he headed out into the vineyards. "Darcy," he yelled. "Darcy?"

It was hard to hear anything with the roar of the fire in the background, but he listened intently. A groan caught his attention.

He raced toward the sound only to find Mia on all fours. She'd just finished vomiting.

"My head," she said weakly. "That bastard hit me on the head."

"Who?" Joe asked, although he already knew.

"Ian. What the hell is wrong with him?" she demanded.

Joe felt her pulse, then touched the bump on her head. He stood and called for Lauren. "Mia's been hurt," he told her. "Get her to the cart."

"Where's Darcy?" Lauren asked frantically. "Where's my sister?"

Joe didn't know and thinking about the possibilities made his blood run cold. Who else had been part of the team? "Alex," he yelled. "Alex!"

Paige joined him. "Where are they? Where are Alex and Darcy?"

Rather than answer, Joe hurried to the edge of the vineyard. There he saw the broken vines, ripped leaves. A struggle. He reached down and picked up Darcy's security bracelet. Paige was behind him and to his left. She screamed.

"Alex's been shot. He's been shot."

21

Once again Darcy found herself tied up in the back of a van. There was just enough predawn light coming through the back window for her to see the filthy floor, complete with a hole about eight inches across.

What was it with kidnappers that they couldn't afford decent vehicles? she wondered, trying to be disgusted and angry instead of terrified. And if they had to buy some beat-up piece of crap, couldn't they at least keep it clean?

The van took a corner at high speed. Darcy went sliding, along with candy wrappers, sheets of paper, and who knows what else. She didn't want to think about things like rats and bugs, nor did she want to remember the easy way Ian had shot someone.

Not Joe, she prayed. Not anyone, but especially not Joe.

Ian! A kidnapper! It wasn't possible. How had he ever shut up enough to plan anything? Oh God. Joe. Be alive.

She didn't want to consider any other possibility, so she forced herself to think about something else. Like how she was gagging on the handkerchief. She pushed her tongue against the cloth and worked her mouth until she was able to spit it out. The cloth hit the floor, rolled, and fell out the hole in the bottom of the van.

As she watched it go, she wished she were small enough to simply fall out the bottom of the van. Any bumps and bruises from hitting the road would be better than what Ian had in mind for her.

Oh God. Fear exploded inside of her. She turned and twisted on the dirty floor as she tried to free herself. She screamed and screamed but knew no one could hear her. It was five or six in the morning on a narrow road in the middle of nowhere. Who was going to be around to listen?

Worse, did anyone even know she was gone? With the fire and everyone busy with that, it could be hours before they noticed she was missing.

Tears burned her eyes but she refused to give in to them. Be strong, she told herself. Tough. She'd already survived one kidnapping. Of course those kidnappers hadn't wanted her, they'd wanted Lauren and—

Darcy sat up. Lauren had been right there at the winery. Ian could have taken her just as easily, but he hadn't.

"This is not how I wanted to be the special daughter," she screamed, kicking at the side of the van. "I was thinking more of an award or something."

A few candy wrappers fluttered out the hole. Great. Now she was littering.

"Wait a minute."

She stared at the hole, then at all the garbage in the back of the van. Could she use it to signal where they were going, or at least where they'd been?

She scooted so her back was against one of the walls

of the van, and kicked a candy wrapper toward the hole. After counting to sixty, she pushed it out. Another minute later, she pushed out a rag.

Would anyone realize it wasn't just trash? she wondered. Would the trash get blown away? She needed something bigger. Something more significant.

She looked around at the back of the van. Nothing came to mind until she looked at her feet. Her shoes.

While she didn't like the thought of being barefoot, she liked the thought of being dead even less. She toed off one of her shoes and nudged it toward the opening. It slipped through and fell to the road. She would continue with the trash, then put out the other shoe in another ten minutes or so.

If only she knew how long they would be driving, she thought. Should she wait longer than ten minutes? What would happen when they got wherever they were going?

"Don't think about it," she told herself. "Don't think about it."

But there was little else to occupy her mind. Fearing and wondering if Joe were alive. After dumping out more trash, she debated removing her other shoe. Before she could decide, the van came to a stop. The fear returned and with it a certain sense of dread.

"Towels," Joe yelled. "Thick towels."

"They're not sterile," Tessa told him as she and Grammy M hurried around the kitchen.

"It's fine. We need pressure." He took the towel Tessa handed him and held it over the wound in Alex's side.

The Secret Service agent looked up at him. "I didn't see it coming. Should have."

His color was nonexistent, his breathing labored. From what Joe could tell, the bullet had gone in and out cleanly. But what it had done while passing through remained to be seen.

He looked around at the frantic faces in the kitchen. Paige was on the phone, detailing what had happened. He felt a burning need to hunt down Ian and kill him. But until Paige was done, he was the only one in the house with the training to keep Alex alive.

"What should we do?" Colleen asked, her expression both worried and grim. "I can't believe Ian took Darcy. Should we start searching the buildings?"

"No point. They're gone. I saw tracks heading west."

"Toward the interstate," Marco said. "They could be anywhere."

Goddamn son of a bitch, when he got his hands on Ian, he was going to rip him apart and watch him bleed to death.

Mia crouched in a chair. She was still woozy from being hit on the head and needed to be checked out. There was too much to do, he thought grimly.

Paige hung up the phone. "Okay, the team's coming. Local, state, and federal law enforcement have been notified. Road blocks will be up within the half hour. We'll have full tactical support in less time. The president has been notified."

Joe didn't want to think about that phone call or what the other man must be feeling. Joe had enough trouble battling his own worry, and he was a trained professional.

"I should have known," he muttered.

Paige hurried to the kitchen table where she stared down at Alex. "We all should have known."

"He checked out clean," Alex said, his voice heavy with pain.

"Too clean," Joe said. "I never liked him."

Someone began to cry. He turned and saw Lauren. Grammy M and Colleen hurried to her. Lauren looked at him.

"She'll be all right, won't she? You'll get Darcy back."

He didn't have an answer to that, but he nodded. "Of course we will." He turned to Paige. "Get her team back here."

The extra Secret Service agents had been at the hotel in town, the same one Captain Phillips had retired to the previous evening.

"I've already called them. The rest of Darcy's team will be assigned to Lauren until we can get her out of here."

"No," Lauren said. "I'm not leaving. I want to know what's going on."

Paige shook her head. "You'll be safer somewhere else."

"No. You can protect me here. I want to know what's happening."

"We'll all be here to protect her," Marco said. "Anyone trying to kidnap Lauren will have to come through us."

Joe appreciated the sentiment, but it wasn't going to be much help against trained experts.

He replaced the blood-soaked towel with a fresh one. "We don't have time to argue," he told Paige. "She's staying until the team arrives. Then let them deal with her."

"I'm not leaving," Lauren said stubbornly.

Joe glanced at her. It was the first time she'd reminded him of Darcy.

Darcy. Fear crashed in on him. He'd never felt anything like it before. Sure, he'd worried about his team, but he'd never felt this icy, crushing sensation in his chest. If something happened to her . . .

Brenna limped into the kitchen. She cradled her belly with one hand and leaned against Nic. "So, ah, how is Alex getting to the hospital?"

"Helicopter," Paige said, pressing on the bleeding wound from the underside.

"Is it big enough for two?"

Joe turned to look at her. Really looked. It was only then he noticed the dark stain down the front of her maternity dress.

"My water broke," she said. "I guess I'm in labor."

In the second between when the van stopped and Ian opened one of the doors, Darcy heard an odd sound. It was familiar, but she couldn't place it. Something rhythmic and swooshy. Then the door swung open and she saw they were parked on the beach. The thick fog added a sense of the macabre to the otherwise perfect view.

Why here? Why not some airport or a freeway?

"Come on, Darcy," Ian said. "Let's get going."

Her instinct was to fight them. There were only two of them. Then Ian pulled out his gun and smiled.

"I'd prefer you didn't make trouble, but if you do, I'll shoot you. Not to kill, you understand. Just enough to slow you down. I've never been shot, but I'd think it really hurts. Especially if I mess up and it goes through bone. So you don't want to be a problem, right?"

She looked at him and nodded slowly.

"Then get out of the van."

She did as he said, sliding forward on her butt until she reached the open door. The other man, tall, with dark hair and cold eyes, grabbed her arm and pulled her to her feet.

Darcy looked between them as a horrifying thought occurred to her. She could see their faces. Which meant she could easily identify them. Which led to the logical conclusion that they didn't plan for that ever to happen. They weren't going to let her go.

She wasn't ready to die, she thought frantically. Not now. Not like this. Joe was . . .

Joe might be dead. No, she couldn't think like that. He was strong; she would be strong, too.

Instinctively, she twisted away from the man. She managed to get free, but with her feet tied, she couldn't run. She teetered, then fell to the sand. Seconds later, something hard slammed into her ribs as Ian kicked her. She screamed.

"That was a warning," Ian said coldly. "Next time I *will* shoot you."

She couldn't catch her breath. The pain was incredible. It was like fire along her rib cage. Had he broken something?

Ian stood over her. "Here's the thing, Darcy. You're our prisoner, and there's nothing you can do about it. If you cooperate, I promise to make your time with us as pleasant as possible. If you don't, I'll hurt you. Those are simple rules, right? You can understand them."

She nodded slowly. "What do you want?"

"To use you as a bargaining chip."

Not good, she thought as she sucked in air. Not good at all. "The president doesn't negotiate with terrorists."

"Yeah, I've heard that. I'm guessing I can change his

mind. See, it's a great policy right up until someone you love is kidnapped. We'll start with polite requests, and if that doesn't work, we'll send you back to him in pieces. I know that sounds scary and I'm sorry about that. We'll give you something for the pain, but it's probably still going to hurt. We can't help that. The point is when we send your finger or your ear or your hand to the press, your dad is going to be a whole lot more willing to give us what we want."

She was going to pass out. The good news was, she wouldn't have to listen to Ian anymore. He was speaking so calmly, she thought, unable to believe any of this was really happening. How could Ian be doing this? Ian, who had stayed at the Marcelli house. Ian, who had dated Mia and driven them all crazy with his talking.

"They'll find you," she said.

"I don't think so. They won't know where we are, and I've found a spot they'll never even look."

He nodded at the other man, who then pulled her to her feet, bent down, and shoved his shoulder into her midsection. When he stood, the pain of her bruised side nearly made her pass out. She thought she was going to throw up.

They started walking toward a small boat pulled up on the sand. She didn't like boats, especially small ones. She didn't like being kidnapped, either, she thought grimly.

"We're going to a cave," Ian said. "I found it years ago, when I went fishing around here with my grandfather. I used to think it was a really cool hideout, but I never thought I'd use it for a headquarters."

She slipped free of the man's shoulder and felt herself falling and falling. When she hit the boat, the impact was hard. Her head cracked against a wooden seat.

"Watch it, Jesse. We don't want to kill her."

Not yet, she thought as the world started to fold in at the corners and then fade to black. Not yet.

Joe stared at the maps spread out on the counter of the kitchen. Where would they take Darcy? They had an hour's head start, which gave them a lot of leeway. Still roadblocks were already up, and the heavy fog meant all regional airports were closed.

Would they try to get distance between themselves and the winery or were they holing up close by? What would he do?

Joe touched the largest map, but he couldn't think, couldn't figure out the plan. Ian had done this. He'd been the enemy all along, and no one had noticed.

Had he planned this from the beginning? Joe didn't think that was possible. No one had known Darcy was coming here more than forty-eight hours before it had happened. Which meant Ian had taken advantage of a lucky break.

Who was he? The name had to be false, along with the identity. He'd been completely clean. No one that clean pulled off something like this.

"The bleeding's slowed," Paige said, sounding relieved. "Hold on, Alex. The helicopter will be here soon. You, too, Brenna."

Brenna waved from her sprawled position on a kitchen chair. "Don't worry about me. I'm sure I'll be in labor for hours. I appreciate the ride, though. Right now the thought of a thirty-minute car trip is very disheartening."

Nic crouched next to her and held her hand. "Just breathe, okay."

She smiled at him. "I can breathe and scream. I'm good at both of those. It's the whole birthing process I'm worried about. And the fact that I swear I can feel more than two feet pressing against me."

Joe blocked out the conversation and concentrated on the maps. But before he could figure anything out, Mia walked over and touched his arm.

"I'm sorry," she whispered.

He took a second to give her a hug. "It's not your fault."

"Yes, it is. I'm the one who brought him here. I can't believe I didn't know who he really was. I traveled with him, I slept with him. I should have guessed."

"You can only see what you see. You can't read minds."

She shook her head. "I should have known. Somehow."

Joe led her into the dining room. "Did he ever say anything about his family? About friends? Do you have any names?"

Mia stared at him. "No. He talked about his grandfather all the time. The one who took him fishing. But not his parents. He was more interested in mine. I just . . ." She stifled a sob. "He was so excited about meeting Darcy. I thought he was starstruck. Then, later, he asked me all kinds of questions. I figured he had a crush on her or something. But it wasn't that. Now Alex is shot, and they have Darcy, and it's all my fault."

She began to cry. Joe pulled her close and kept his mouth shut. A part of him did want to blame Mia, but he was as guilty as she.

*   *   *

Darcy regained consciousness when she was carried from the small boat and put onto a canvas chair in the middle of a cave. Her hands and feet were still tied and her ribs ached, along with her head. If this kept up much longer, she was going to be one big bruise.

She waited until Ian and someone she hadn't seen before walked away, then she raised her head and looked around. The cave was larger than it looked from the outside, for which she was grateful. She'd grown to dislike small, dark spaces.

The boat had been tied up next to one just like it on the side of the cave, not that far from where she sat. On the other side were a couple of tables covered with electronic equipment. Bottled water and canned foods filled a pallet by the rock wall.

She could hear men talking, which made her nervous. She didn't want to know who they were. She wanted to be set free and not be able to identify them later so they wouldn't have to kill her.

The cave itself seemed to bend around, perhaps creating a second room. She wasn't sure, as she couldn't see it, but that's where the voices came from. Maybe the rest of them would stay there, she thought.

Ian reappeared. He walked toward her and held out a length of chain with bands at each end. "For your ankles," he said cheerfully. "So you can't get away. Oh, in case you're wondering, these are heavy. If you head for the water, you'll sink right to the bottom. No swimming for freedom, Darcy."

He was so calm, she thought. Calm to the point of pleasant, which just wasn't right.

When he bent at her feet, she thought about kicking

him but decided it wasn't the time for an escape. Not when she was tied up and didn't know how many other men were around. He secured the chains around her ankles, then unfastened the ropes. Finally he used a smaller chain to attach her left arm to the chair itself, leaving her right arm and hand free.

"Thirsty?" he asked, motioning to the bottles.

She nodded.

He brought her water and opened it, then crossed to the table of communication equipment. "I'm going to call your dad," he said as he put on a headset. "I don't mind you screaming, but you can't tell them where we are. And as I don't trust you . . ."

He motioned with his hands. Jesse appeared with a gag. Darcy tried pulling away, but she was weighed down by the chains and the chair. Jesse quickly secured the gag, effectively silencing her.

Ian hit a button on a console. Instantly the sound of a dial tone filled the cave. He punched in a phone number, then waited until a woman said, "This is the White House operator. How may I direct your call?"

"I need to speak to the man in charge," Ian told her. "President Jensen. I'm the guy who has his daughter. She's right here. I'd let you talk to her, but she's all tied up."

He laughed at his own joke.

"One minute, sir."

There was a moment of silence, then a man picked up. "This is Special Agent in Charge Allister. Who is this?"

"I'm Ian Welton, Allister, but you already knew that. I'm sure the folks back at the ranch, or winery in this case, have already told you all about me. And you're not who I want to speak with. I called for the president."

"He's not here right now."

Ian glanced at Darcy and raised his eyebrows. "Daddy's not home. Where do you think he is?"

Darcy didn't have a clue.

"I'm sure you can patch me through to him," Ian said, returning his attention to the call. "Which I want you to do. I have a list of demands. And before you tell me you don't negotiate with terrorists, I'll remind you I have his daughter here. He only has the two, so I think he'd miss this one if we had to return her in pieces."

Stay calm, Darcy told herself. Stay calm. People were looking for her and they would find her. She would be okay. She had to be. For Joe. Because if he'd been shot, he would need her. And if he hadn't, then he would come find her.

"Threats don't help your cause," Allister said. "What do you want?"

"Right now I'd like a really good burger, but instead I'll take the release of Jonathan Misner from prison. He is to be picked up by helicopter and taken to the county airport. There you will have a plane waiting, along with two million dollars in cash."

Misner, Misner. The name was familiar, but she couldn't place it at first.

"The domestic terrorist?" Allister asked.

Then she remembered. Jonathan Misner was responsible for the bombing of a large suburban Chicago mall nearly three years ago. Dozens of people had been killed and hundreds injured. He and his men had been opposed to money being sent abroad for foreign aid. They'd wanted the funds to stay home, along with jobs and technology. Their demands had been for the United States to isolate itself from the rest of the world.

Misner had been captured nearly a year after the bombing. It had been one of those quirks of fate—a routine traffic stop had brought him to the attention of a small-town deputy. Later, the deputy had followed him to a local motel and called in federal authorities. Several of Misner's men had gotten away, but the leader had been captured. He had been arrested and convicted, and was on death row in federal prison.

"We see him as a revolutionary," Ian said calmly. "Imagine what the king of England thought of the signers of the Declaration of Independence. Not an original argument, I'll grant you, but accurate. You have twelve hours. If I don't see Misner staring on CNN as he's led out of prison, I'll have to hurt Darcy."

Ian glanced at her and gave her an apologetic smile. "Funny thing is, I really don't want to do it. I like her a lot. But the cause is bigger, and I want Misner out of prison. If he's not released by"—Ian glanced at his watch—"seven-forty-three P.M. Pacific Time, I'll have to make my point. We'll start small. Her little finger from her left hand. She'll be gagged, so you won't hear her screaming, but trust me, she will be."

22

The task force arrived by air. Shortly after eight in the morning, three Sikorsky Superhawk helicopters descended from the sky and landed on the open grassy area by the long driveway leading up to the house.

Most of the personnel were navy, with a few Secret Service agents thrown in the mix. Joe knew that other members of the team would arrive as soon as they could be flown in from other parts of the country. Captain Phillips had driven from his hotel to act as a liaison.

Joe stood by the front of the house as the helicopters shut down. When the team was assembled, he stepped forward to lead them toward the winery. He'd already commandeered the conference room and had Marco call the office staff to tell them not to come in to work. The team could spread out into the various offices and have access to the phone lines if necessary, although it wouldn't take long for them to establish their own communications system.

"Through here," Joe said as they walked into the main building of the winery.

One of the team members, Admiral Grant, moved next to Joe. "The fire was started as a diversion?" he asked.

Joe nodded. "We have preliminary confirmation of arson. A final report will take some time, but there's enough evidence for our purposes."

"There were two Secret Service agents with Darcy?"

"No. Just Alex. Alex Vanmeter. The agent who was shot."

The admiral raised his eyebrows. Yes, Darcy should have been protected by two agents. She also shouldn't have been sent off with the very man trying to kidnap her. Joe had already beaten himself up about it a dozen times.

"Lauren was with Paige," Joe continued.

"No doubt the reason only Darcy was taken," the admiral said.

Joe wasn't so sure. Ian and his group had planned their kidnapping very well. If they'd wanted Lauren, he didn't doubt they could have taken her. The fire had put everyone in a panic.

"You've given your report to Captain Phillips?" the admiral asked.

Joe nodded. They'd reached the conference room. He pointed out the maps of the area and the contact list, which included local law enforcement officials, the fire chief, and the main number of the house.

Joe started to step into the room, but the admiral blocked his way.

"That will be all," the man told him.

Joe glared at him. "Sir, I know I screwed up. I know the kidnapping is my fault. But I'm still the best tactical officer you have."

The admiral shook his head. "A good tactical officer doesn't let his subject get kidnapped. You're relieved of duty, sailor."

The door closed in his face.

There was no lock. Joe could have stepped inside and forced them to listen, but to what end? He didn't have anything to say. Nothing useful, anyway. Telling them that he wanted to trade himself for Darcy was meaningless. Letting them know that he would give his life for hers a hundred times over would only get in the way.

He turned from the conference room and headed for Lorenzo's office. There he could stare at the maps on the wall and will them to reveal their secrets to him. Where had Ian taken her? What would the little shithead do with her?

An hour later, he was no closer to a solution. He slumped in Lorenzo's chair and endured the frustration of having no way to act. Nearly as bad as imagining what Darcy must be going through was the reality of knowing that he had had Ian within his grasp and had never considered him a danger. If he had, he would have cheerfully ripped him into a dozen pieces.

But he hadn't. Instead he'd listened to Ian talk on and on about everything from his opinion of the growing world economy to his seemingly endless anecdotal stories about his studies, his various roommates, and the time he spent locally with his—

Joe stared at the map. Ian had talked about his grandfather taking him fishing around here. He'd talked about caves.

He reached for the phone and called the main house. "Marco," he barked, when Tessa answered.

Marco came on the line.

"Meet me in the conference room right now," he ordered. "Hurry."

Joe slammed down the phone and raced to the conference room. He burst in without knocking. The fourteen people sitting around the table all looked at him.

Captain Phillips stood. "Joe, you're screwing up here," he began, his voice cold.

"I don't give a good goddamn about that," Joe told him. "I know where Ian's taken her."

Phillips stared at him. "What are you talking about?"

"You haven't caught him, have you? Not with any of the roadblocks. You're not going to. He's already off the road. He's taken her to a boat somewhere close. There are caves on the coast, some of them big enough to hide in. He'll wait until dark, then use a boat to get her away."

Phillips and the admiral exchanged a glance. The Secret Service agent in charge nodded.

"We've found the van," Phillips told him. "It was abandoned on the beach. Apparently there was a hole in the rear floor because we also found a trail of trash, rags, and one of Darcy's shoes."

Joe felt a flash of pride. As scared as she must have been, she hadn't lost her head. Good for her.

The conference room door opened and Marco stepped in. "My father," Joe said. "Marco Marcelli." He crossed to the maps pinned to the walls. "We think Ian took her by boat to a cave. Which ones are big enough to hold a dozen or so people and equipment?"

Marco joined him at the map. He studied it for a second, then pointed. "Here. There are three caves big enough. I used to play in them when I was a kid. A couple of these have several rooms."

Three was manageable, Joe thought. Three caves, three teams. "What's the deadline?" he asked.

Phillips shook his head. "Joe, this isn't your fight."

"Yes, it is. This happened on my watch. What are his demands and how long do we have?"

Phillips considered the question, then explained Ian's demands for Misner's release. "The first deadline is seven-forty-three tonight."

Not much time, Joe thought, calculating the travel time from San Diego to here. But enough. "We'll have three SEAL teams, one on each cave. They can be here by one, and we'll put together our plan."

Phillips looked at the admiral. "It's what he's best at."

Admiral Grant nodded. "All right, Joe. You take charge of your SEALs. Everything comes through me." He glanced at his watch. "The president will be landing in a couple of hours, and he'll want a full briefing."

"Can we make Ian think we're giving in to his demands?" Joe asked. "Having him monitor that will provide a distraction and keep Darcy safe."

The admiral picked up a phone. "Let me see what I can do."

Despite Ian removing the gag and offering Darcy more water, she still felt nauseated and faint. She wanted to cradle her left hand against her stomach and protect her suddenly vulnerable fingers. She wanted to run screaming out of the dark cave, into safety. She wanted to be back at the Marcelli house, with Grandma Tessa offering her food and Joe tempting her into his bed. She wanted to live, fingers and all.

Fear grabbed at her and refused to let go. The need to scream built until she had to press her hand to her mouth to hold it inside. Focus, she told herself. She had to focus. Be calm. Relax.

Tears burned, but she held them in. Eventually the need to scream faded to a whimper. She thought about Joe and how tough he was, how he would want her to be tough, too. She thought about Lauren and knew however much she loved her sister, Lauren couldn't possibly handle being kidnapped. She would be too scared.

Darcy nearly laughed. After all these years had she just realized she was the strong one, emotionally? What a time to have a self-actualization-type breakthrough.

Sometime around noon, Ian offered her a sandwich. She didn't want to eat, but she knew she needed to keep up her strength. Later, she was allowed to use the Porta Potti in the back of the cave. There was no escaping from that route, she thought as she glanced around at rock walls.

She returned to her chair, was chained in place, and waited to see what would happen. Ian kept the television turned to CNN, but there was no mention of her kidnapping at all. The first hint of news came a little before three when the phone rang.

Ian picked it up and flipped on the speaker. "Welton here," he said.

"Ian, how are you?"

Darcy watched as Ian grinned and waved toward the back of the cave. "Jonathan?"

"Yeah." The other man chuckled. "I don't know how you did it, but they're letting me out. Hell of a job, kid. Hell of a job."

Ian squared his shoulders. "I told you I wouldn't let you rot in jail. I'd planned on kidnapping the British prime minister when he came to San Francisco in three months, but then someone dumped a better idea in my lap."

"They won't tell me anything. What have you done?"

Ian glanced at Darcy and winked. "Kidnapped the president's daughter."

"Lauren?"

"No. Darcy. She's right here. Couldn't have been easier." He explained how he'd been dating Mia and had gone to meet her family, only to discover Darcy in residence.

"Luck like that doesn't happen every day," Ian said. "What could I do?"

Jonathan laughed. "Good for you, Ian. Now you know this could be a trick."

"Already got that covered."

Darcy didn't know what to think. There was no way she believed her father would agree to release a prisoner on death row. He couldn't. Which meant it *was* a trick, or someone was lying. She shivered from fear and cold, even though it was warm in the cave.

She stared at the lapping water only a few feet away. If not for the heavy chains, she would take her chances in the ocean. Maybe she could swim to shore.

Ian ended his call and disappeared into the other room of the cave. She heard the men cheering as they discussed the good news. A few minutes later he came back with something in his hands. Something that looked like a vest.

"You're going to have to wear this," he said, holding it out to her. "I know it looks scary, but it's perfectly safe. There isn't even a manual detonation. It has to be done by remote control, so you can't trigger it yourself by sneezing or something. See?"

The fear became tangible. She felt it deaden her arms and legs. She could barely breathe as she stared at the vest.

Strips of gray material had been sewn into rows of

pockets on the outside of the vest. She'd seen enough action movies to know the claylike substance was some kind of explosive.

Everything had been wired, with the colorful wires all meeting back at a common point that would be right above her left breast.

"Look. No boom." He smiled and shook it, then dropped it on the floor. As if that proved anything.

Hysterical laughter threatened. Right. Safe, right up until the minute someone pushed the little red button on the detonator and she exploded into a million pieces.

"I can't," she whispered.

"I know you don't want to, Darcy, but I'm not giving you a choice. I'd like to. You're really nice. Lauren's okay, but you're prettier, and I like you better, which is why I wanted to kidnap you. Although I'll be real sad if I have to kill you."

She wanted to point out he was probably going to anyway, but what was the point?

"The thing is, we have a greater good to think about," he continued. "That's why I'm doing this. The government has to understand we're not responsible for the world. We have our own problems to deal with. Charity begins at home, right? We're not being especially charitable right now. Do you know how many children go to bed hungry every night right here in this country? Shouldn't we be taking care of them? So you see why I have to do this, don't you?"

He held out the vest. She leaned back and shook her head.

Ian sighed. "Jesse," he yelled. "We've got to get the vest on her."

Jesse appeared from the rear of the cave and roughly pulled her out of the chair. She twisted and turned and wished her feet weren't manacled together so she could kick the crap out of him. But they were, and the heavy chains didn't allow for much mobility.

"No!" she cried as he put one of her arms through the vest.

Jesse raised his hand and slapped her hard across the face. The pain and shock immobilized her enough for them to unlock her hand and finish putting on the vest. Then they pushed her back into her seat and resecured her wrist to the chair.

The vest was thick and lighter than it looked. There was an odd smell that terrified her. Her heart beat so quickly she thought it might fly right out of her chest. This couldn't be happening to her. It couldn't. Her face throbbed from the slap, and she knew deep down in her heart she wasn't getting out of this alive. Not now. They were going to kill her, and there was no way anyone would ever find her in time.

Joe finished briefing the team, then picked up his diving gear and weapons. Everything felt good in his hands. Right.

He suited up, then climbed in the back of the truck for the short trip to the boats that would take them close to the caves. From there they would approach underwater.

At nearly five in the afternoon, he and his men waded out into the ocean and slipped onto the boats. Joe's headset crackled.

"Larson?"

"Yes, Captain."

"We just got word. They warned us not to try anything. They've wired her with an explosive. If anything happens they don't like, she's gone."

Joe heard the information but he refused to react to it. Now he was on a mission and it was all about doing the job. He wouldn't allow himself to think emotionally or feel. Darcy's life depended on his ability to disconnect from her.

"This changes everything," Phillips said. "You have to come back."

"No, sir," Joe told him. "We're still going forward. If they've got her wired, they're prepared to kill her. They'll probably do it anyway. We have to get her out."

"Larson?" Another man came on the line. "This is President Jensen."

Joe stiffened. "Yes, sir."

"That's my daughter we're talking about."

It was also the woman Joe loved. "I understand what she means to you, sir. I'll bring her back alive."

"You'd better."

"Sir, I will bring her back or die trying."

Jensen didn't respond. Phillips came on and gave a few last-minute instructions, then Joe motioned for the team to head out. As they moved north across the ocean, Joe breathed in the scent of salt air. The water had always been a haven, he thought. It was the one place a SEAL could feel safe, and where he performed best.

Three caves. He'd taken the team going into the largest one. His gut told him she was there. They had a plan and a willingness to do whatever it took to save her life. He loved her too much to let her die.

*   *   *

Darcy sat in her chair, shaking. She would have thought that over time the fear would lessen, but it hadn't. She held on by a thread.

Ian and Jesse stood in the rear of the cave, speaking in low voices. The acoustics were such that Darcy could hear them, and their words didn't make her feel any more comfortable.

"You think they're really going to release Jonathan?" Jesse asked.

"Sure. They don't want anything to happen to Darcy. We've got them. Once we get word he's released, we'll call the boat and get out of here."

Boat? They already had two. Darcy glanced at the small vessels in question and realized Ian was talking about something bigger. Of course. They were flying Jonathan to a rendezvous point and they would meet him there with a boat.

"Good," Jesse said. "When we've put this place behind us, we'll dump her overboard. No one will ever find her."

Darcy froze and waited for Ian to deny the statement. When he didn't, she knew she wasn't going to be able to hold it together much longer. A scream built up inside her.

Suddenly the television picture disappeared into snowy static. Ian ripped off his headset and yelled, "What the hell?" Cries of pain came from the back of the cave. Without warning, the water seemed to rise up and a shock wave blasted across the open space.

Darcy felt herself tossed around like a toy. She and the chair slammed into the wall and everything went black.

Joe and his men rushed out of the water. The jamming signal had rendered everything electronic inoperative, including the remote detonation for the bomb. He'd sent in the stun grenades such that Darcy received the least of the impact, but she'd still been blown back into the wall.

"No one gets out of the cave," Joe said into his headset.

The instruction was unnecessary—his team knew what to do, but he couldn't help it. There was too much at stake.

He ran to Darcy's side and checked her for injuries. No blood, although her head might have hit the wall. He saw the chains and cursed, then reached for the vest.

"Joe?"

"Hey, Darcy." She was awake. Thank God. He fingered the various wires, then reached for his small tool kit.

"You're not dead. I thought he shot you." Tears trickled from the corners of her eyes.

"That was Alex," he told her. "I'm okay and so are you."

"Alex?"

"He's in surgery."

"It was horrible. I was so scared." She touched the vest. "It's a bomb."

"I know. Trust me. I know what I'm doing." He managed a smile. "I've taught the class."

"I always knew you were a great guy to have around in a crisis."

He sorted through the wires, then cut three. "How do you feel?" he asked as he pulled off the vest and tossed it away.

"Like I was hit on the head with a hammer. You know, he could have detonated that remotely."

Joe wrapped his arms around her and pulled her close. She was still attached to the chair, but he didn't care.

"We jammed the signal."

"So that's why the TV went out."

"Yeah. Signals from the cavalry. You okay?"

She clung to him. As soon as he felt her hands on his back, he allowed himself to relax a little.

"Never better."

"You must have been scared."

She pulled back enough to look at him. "You can't imagine. Remember how last time you said I had to talk to someone?"

He nodded and touched the bruise on her cheek. "I have some names."

"I think I'm going to need them." Tears filled her eyes. "Oh, Joe. You're here."

"Yes, Darcy. I'm here."

"Don't let go."

"I won't. Not ever."

"You can't take me," Ian screamed as he ran out from the back of the cave and drew a gun.

Joe pushed Darcy behind him and, in one quick move, pulled out his gun. One of the guys on his team got there first. After a terse order to "freeze," three shots rang out in the cave. Ian stumbled then collapsed.

Joe ignored the bleeding body. "The rest?"

"All captured, sir."

"Call it in. Tell them to send the boat in for Darcy."

He turned back to her. She had her eyes closed. "I don't want to look," she whispered.

"You don't have to."

One of his men brought over a key for the chains. Joe released her and pulled her onto his lap. She huddled against him and started to cry.

"Hey," he said gently, smoothing her hair and kissing her face. "Don't do that. You'll want to look good for your dad."

She sniffed. "He's here?"

"Of course. The entire military is here. Lauren, too. The Marcellis are really worried about you. Oh, Brenna's in labor."

"You're kidding. Now?"

"Yeah. She's at the hospital. Last I heard, there's no baby, but plenty of screaming."

She chuckled. "I don't blame her. Nothing about the actual process of giving birth seems pleasant."

He cupped her face. "There's one more thing."

"What's that?"

He stared into her brown eyes and knew he'd finally found the one thing that had been missing his whole life.

"I love you."

She stared at him. "Excuse me?"

"I love you, Darcy."

She opened her mouth, but before she could say anything, Joe felt a tap on his shoulder.

"The boat is here, sir."

Joe shifted Darcy onto the ground, then stood and swept her into his arms. She grabbed him around his neck.

"What are you doing?" she asked.

"Saving you."

"You've already done that once today."

"I plan on doing it for a long time to come."

23

◆

*T*hey were escorted out of the cave and back to shore by the Coast Guard. Darcy had expected a Secret Service agent or two to be waiting, but what she saw instead was something closer to the staging area for a space shuttle launch. There were five or six ships cruising the immediate area. At least two dozen cars were parked along the sand. Three helicopters sat on the road, and two trucks filled with military personnel stood watch a hundred or so feet away.

Joe took her arm and helped her step onto the sand. She looked from the staring crowd back to him. "All this for me?" she asked, not able to believe it.

"Of course."

"Wow."

The fear had faded, but in its place was a shaky feeling. Too much emotion in too short a time, she told herself. She clung to Joe, her only stable point in a spinning world, and promised herself that as soon as she caught her breath she would deal with his amazing and unexpected declaration of love. She would have guessed he cared, but not that he could admit he actually loved her.

The crowd parted and her father hurried toward her. "Darcy!"

He held out his arms.

The unexpected gesture made her hesitate at first, then she rushed forward to hug him. He pulled her close and squeezed so hard, she could barely breathe.

"I was scared to death," he murmured in her ear. "When I heard what had happened, I couldn't believe it."

"Me, either," she said.

He cupped her face in his hands. "I don't want anything to happen to you. I'd be lost without you."

She read the truth in his eyes and felt sadness for all the time they'd wasted.

"I love you, Daddy," she whispered.

He kissed her forehead. "I love you, too, Darcy. You're my daughter. You know that, right?"

She nodded, too close to crying to speak. Her father put his arm around her and led her to the waiting SUV. Before she climbed in, she looked back for Joe, but he was gone.

"Where is he?" she asked. "Joe Larson."

"Debriefing," her father told her. "Don't worry. You'll see him later, and you can thank him for rescuing you."

She planned to do a whole lot more than that but doubted her father wanted to hear about the details.

"Is Alex all right?" she asked as she slid onto the leather seat.

"Yes. He's already out of surgery."

"I'd like to go see him."

"Of course. We'll stop by the hospital on our way back to the Marcelli house."

The Marcellis. She'd nearly forgotten. "The fire. Is everyone all right? Did they get it out?"

"Yes. Just as you were kidnapped, it started to rain. That put out the rest of it. A few acres were burned, but I was told they can be replanted."

"Ian did that," she said. "He started the fire as a diversion."

"The authorities know."

"You're not letting that Jonathan person out of prison, are you?"

Her father pulled her close and put his arm around her. "Stop worrying, Darcy. I'm doing a good job of running the country. Just think about yourself and the fact that you're safe now."

She hadn't been held by her father in more years than she could count, but the sensation was still familiar and comforting. Funny how she'd spent so much time looking for a place to belong and it had been waiting for her all along.

Mia sat alone in the house. She couldn't remember the last occasion when she'd been the only person there. Usually Grandma Tessa or Grammy M were puttering around, but not this evening. Everyone had gone to the hospital to check on either Alex or Brenna. Mia had promised to come as soon as she could. But she'd needed to be alone. To think. To recover from the horror of what had happened.

Ian had betrayed her. He'd used her to do something horrific, and she'd never had a clue.

She'd trusted him, both in and out of her bed. She'd thought he was funny and smart, if a little too talkative.

She'd been friends with him for nearly two years, lovers for three months, and she'd never guessed.

Paige had pointed out that she, Mia, was a civilian. She couldn't be expected to know. But Mia was used to being smarter than that. No one had ever fooled her so completely.

She reached for her backpack and pulled out her wallet. Tucked inside was a plain white business card. There was no name on it—just a phone number. She'd been given the card one of the many times someone had approached her about becoming a clandestine operative for the government.

She stared at the number for a long time before dialing it.

It rang twice.

"Yes?"

"Hi. I'm, ah, Mia Marcelli. I was given this card a few months ago."

"One moment, please."

Mia heard the man typing on a keyboard. "Yes, Mia. I have your file. How can I help you?"

File? She had a file? "I'm interested in what you do. In being, you know, a spy."

Paige sat by Alex and held his hand. He was still pretty out of it, but she wasn't going to let go. Not until he told her to go away, which, based on how out of it he was, wouldn't be happening anytime soon.

He stirred slightly. She rose and leaned over him.

"Hey, big guy. How are you feeling?"

His eyelids fluttered. "Paige?"

"I'm right here. You had surgery. They poked around

and made sure you're going to be okay. Apparently you got lucky. The bullet didn't damage anything you couldn't live without."

"Good to know." He stared into her eyes. "Where will you go?"

"After I leave the service?"

"Yeah."

"Texas. There's a little house I've been looking at outside of Austin. I'm thinking of getting my credentials and teaching."

"You'd be good at that." He opened his eyes and drew in a breath. "How small is the house?"

"About twelve hundred square feet."

"Not much room for anyone else."

Her heart stopped. She felt it stutter, then still completely. "I didn't think there would be anyone interested. I haven't bought the house yet. I could get something bigger, if you wanted."

He squeezed her hand. "I remember when you told me you didn't regret losing me. I want to be someone you'd regret losing."

She bent down and kissed him. "I was mad," she whispered. "I did regret losing you."

One corner of his mouth turned up. "I doubt that, but it's nice of you to say it. I want to change, Paige. I want to matter to you."

Emotions flooded her. They came on so quickly, she didn't know which one to experience first.

"You do matter. I love you, Alex."

The curve turned into a smile. "I love you more. Because you're a pain in the ass."

"You act like you've got a stick up yours."

"You're too emotional."

"You're too by the book."

He gazed at her. "Don't ever change," he said. "Promise."

"I won't, except I think I want to love you a little more each day. Are you all right with that?"

"Never better."

Joe wasn't sure what the other patients in the small hospital thought about the invasion. There were Marcellis everywhere, Secret Service agents, military personnel, the president, and his two daughters.

He'd been excused from his debriefing to visit Brenna, who'd just given birth. As he left her room, a marine stopped him and said the president would like to see him. Joe followed the man to a busy office on the ground floor of the building. But instead of hospital staff manning the phones7, there were agents and military officers.

Joe walked up to the president and saluted.

Ryan Jensen looked him over. "You're the man who rescued my daughter."

"Yes, sir."

"Well, done. Now, what exactly are your intentions toward her?"

The room went silent. For a split second, no one spoke, no one pretended not to be listening. Then a phone rang and the various staff members returned to their work, although Joe had a good idea they were all still waiting to hear his answer.

Joe squared his shoulders, looked his commander in chief in the eye, and said, "I love her and I intend to ask her to marry me, sir. I don't know if she'll have me."

Jensen didn't blink. "I see. And if she were to agree, where would you live? On base?"

"No, sir. I'll be leaving the navy to help run the Marcelli winery. I thought we could build a house near the hacienda. Darcy likes it there, sir. She likes my family. It's a good place to raise children."

Jensen's gaze narrowed. "My daughter is an extremely special young woman. You'd better take damn good care of her."

"Yes, sir. I will."

"Oh, Daddy."

Joe turned and saw Darcy standing in the doorway. She looked from him to her father and sighed.

"Stop interrogating Joe. What if he doesn't want to marry me? You can't make him."

"Want to bet?" the president asked.

"I doubt it's an executive order any of us would be proud of," she told him, then turned to Joe. "Don't worry. I'll get my father off your back."

He crossed to her and took her hands in his. "I don't want him off my back," he said, staring into her eyes and knowing he would never get tired of looking at her. "I want him monitoring everything I do because then he can see how happy I'm going to make you. And because you deserve that. I love you, Darcy. I want to marry you. I want you to have the wedding of your dreams and a life so filled with happiness, you can't stop telling people how lucky you are."

A single tear trickled down her cheek. He brushed it away with his thumb. "Why are you crying?"

"Because I'm already so happy." She threw herself at him. "I love you, Joe. I want to marry you. I want to get married in the gazebo on the winery grounds and have a dress made by the Marcelli women. I want to be a part of your family, and I want you to be a part of mine. I want to have kids and dogs and learn about wine and live with you until we're older than Grammy M and Gabriel."

He kissed her. "That's a pretty big list."

"You up to the task?"

"Absolutely. I can't wait to get started."

They kissed again and went on kissing until the sound of someone clearing his throat interrupted. Joe pulled back. "Think I should ask your dad's blessing?" he asked with a grin.

Darcy nodded. "He'll say yes, but it would be a nice gesture."

He turned to the president, who eyed him with two parts suspicion and one part acceptance.

"Oh, did you hear about Brenna?" Darcy asked.

Joe chuckled. "Oh, yeah. Twins. Brace yourself. They run in the family."

"We can handle it. We can handle anything."

The MARCELLI PRINCESS

1

❧

Mia Marcelli was used to sleeping alone so it came as something of a shock to wake up with a strange man in her bed. She did what any other self-actualized, self-defense-trained woman would do—she screamed and jumped to her feet.

"Big mistake," she yelled as she backed toward the door. "You shouldn't have broken in here. I have access to weapons, and grandmothers who don't like this sort of thing. My brother's a former Navy SEAL."

The man sat up and smiled at her. "I see you still talk too much, Mia. When an unknown man appears in your bed, you should run."

He knew her name. That startled her nearly as much as the fact that he was giving her advice. It didn't seem like normal behavior for a guy intent on raping and pillaging. Assuming anyone really pillaged these days.

She paused by the door and pushed her bangs out of her face. There was something familiar about the man. The hair and eye color were all wrong, but the shape of his face reminded her of someone. And that mouth—she would remember it until she died.

"Diego?" she breathed, knowing this stranger *couldn't* be him. Diego was dead. She'd seen the bullets hit his body, had watched him fall to the ground. There'd been so much blood.

"Am I that different?" the man asked as he stood and smiled at her. "Has so much changed?"

It *was* him, she thought, too stunned to do much more than gasp. "H-how is this possible? Why aren't you dead? I saw you die. Dead people don't have conversations."

"It is a long story. Perhaps one I could tell you over breakfast."

That voice. She would know it anywhere. It had haunted her dreams for the past five years.

Dead people also don't eat. "Get back," she said, feeling both shocked and angry. When in doubt, get pissed off. It was a philosophy she'd learned worked for her. "I don't know what this game is, but I'm not playing it."

"Mia, it is I. You must recognize me."

"Must I?"

Right now she didn't have to do anything but keep from having a heart attack from the shock, and wish she kept a weapon in her room. Something big and scary.

The bedroom door flew open and her two grandmothers burst inside. Grandma Tessa had a fire poker in one hand, and Grammy M threatened Diego with a rolling pin.

"Call Joe," Tessa ordered Mia. "He'll take care of this scumbag."

Scumbag? Someone had been watching just a little too many police dramas.

"I'm not sure he's a scumbag," Mia said, still finding it difficult to believe her own eyes. "I might know this guy."

"You do know me," he said, his voice washing over her like a familiar and welcome memory. "Mia, it is I."

Diego? Was it possible? Conflicting emotions raced through her. She wanted to run into his arms and have him hold her forever. At the same time she wanted to grab the poker and beat him over the head with it.

"You're supposed to be dead," she said, still confused and angry, and maybe just a little scared. Because if this guy really *was* Diego, she was going to have a lot of explaining to do.

"So you keep saying," he told her, sounding more amused than anything else. "Would you be more happy if I were?"

"It would make more sense. I don't believe in ghosts . . . or vampires."

He actually smiled. "Good, because I am neither. Mia,"—he took a step toward her—"trust your eyes and your heart. I am the man you knew as Diego."

"We don't trust people who pretend to be someone else," Grandma Tessa said with surprising force despite her small stature and advanced years. "Who do you think you are now?"

"I know I am Rafael, Crown Prince of Calandria."

Mia rolled her eyes. Great—a crazy man in her bedroom, and she hadn't even had coffee yet. "Right, and I'm the Sleeping Beauty."

This had gone on long enough. Mia took the poker from her grandmother and held it out in front of her. "That's it. I don't know who you are or what you want, but you're in big trouble. Grammy M, call Joe." She shook the poker at the intruder. "As for you, big guy, you stay right there or I'll take you out. Don't think I can't. I've had professional training."

The man who looked amazingly like Diego had the balls to smile at her again. "I'm not going anywhere, Mia. I came to see you. I've waited five years to be with you again. I can certainly wait until you're willing to listen to reason."

Reason? "Not my strong suit. I'm more into react now, say 'Oops' later. If you're who you say you are, you should know that."

"I know many things, including the fact that you once wore a silver ring bought in a market. It was a foolish trinket, yet oddly valuable to us both."

Mia's gaze involuntarily darted to the bottom drawer of her dresser. She remembered the ring and the man who bought it for her.

He took a step closer. "I know other things," he said, his voice low and seductive. "I know how you like to be kissed and touched and where you like to—"

"Hey," she said loudly, doing her best to both shut him up and break the spell he attempted to weave. "Grandmothers present. Let's avoid too much information."

Slowly she lowered the poker and looked at him. He was the right height and physical type. His voice was the same, as was his arrogance. His smile made her thighs go up in flames, which hadn't happened even once in the past five years. She wanted to believe because once she'd loved him so much, she'd thought knowing he was dead was going to kill her, too.

But what about the other changes? The color of his eyes, the hair, the scar? Then she remembered her brief time in a world of deception and secrecy, where people could easily be made to look different. Contact lenses, a quick dye job, and little glue—voilá, a new man.

"I assume you have some ID on you," she said, trying to hold on to her anger, because it was safe. Only she was feeling more confused than anything else. Shouldn't she get coffee before an event like this? And maybe a cinnamon roll?

"Walk to the window," he said.

She raised the poker again and shook it at him. "You walk to the window."

He sighed. "I see you are still stubborn. Very well, Mia, we will walk together."

She eyed him warily as he moved to the window and pulled open the drapes. Keeping him at arm's-plus-poker length, she glanced down and saw a very shiny black car complete with what looked like flags flying from the front. Flags amazingly similar to the royal coat of arms of Calandria.

"So you have access to a limo, and an active imagination. That proves nothing." Actually, it kind of proved something, but she wasn't going to admit that.

He raised both hands. "As you wish. May I show you my passport?"

Her throat tightened and her mouth went dry. Man, she really wanted to brush her teeth and take a shower and get some coffee. Because after all those normal activities, none of this would be real anymore.

"Sure," she muttered. "Whatever."

But her heart began to beat faster. She didn't know if she accepted the premise that he was Diego, back from the dead, but she was halfway to being convinced. Which made no sense and gave her a stomachache.

If Diego wasn't dead, then where the hell had he been for the past five years and why hadn't he found her and told her the truth? She'd mourned him and ached for him, and what, he'd been off being some prince?

Because that's what scared her the most. That he really was Diego and Diego was in fact the prince of Calandria. The knowledge would rock her world and she didn't know how she was going to recover. Because having the child of a bad boy turned art thief was one thing, but having the child of an heir to a throne was quite another.

He pulled his passport out of his suit jacket and handed it to her. She glanced at the cover, then nodded at Grandma Tessa. "Let her read it."

Mia told herself she didn't want to look at it because she needed to keep her attention on Diego . . . or possibly Prince Rafael of Calandria. But in truth, she didn't want to see the words printed there.

Tessa opened the passport. Grammy M moved in close and stared over her shoulder.

"A very flattering picture," Grammy M said, smiling at him.

"Thank you."

He was all graciousness and confidence, and he didn't seem the least bit intimidated by the poker in Mia's hand, which made her want to bonk him with it.

Grandma Tessa stared at the print on the page, then looked at Mia. "It says he's the prince. Crown Prince Rafael of Calandria. *Prince* is even listed as his occupation."

Oh God. This couldn't be good.

"Of course it could be a fake," Tessa said cheerfully. "People do it all the time. A couple of hundred bucks and you have a new passport."

Definitely too much TV, Mia thought.

"A prince," Grammy M said, eyeing Rafael. "There'll be a castle, then, with the title?"

He nodded. "Of course. We're also very rich."

Grammy M beamed at Mia. "So, maybe you'll be inviting your friend the prince to breakfast?"

Mia wanted to scream. "He broke in to my *bedroom*. We don't know who he really is. The last time I saw him, he was dead, and you want to invite him to breakfast?"

Grammy M slipped her arm through Diego's . . . or Rafael's . . . and walked him to the door. "So, how will you be taking your coffee?"

Mia watched them go, then dropped the poker to the floor. "Somebody shoot me now. I know matchmaking is a time-honored Marcelli tradition, but could we please first find out the man in question isn't an ax murderer?"

Grandma Tessa handed her the passport. "You're the one who'd know that. Is he who he says he is?"

Mia stared at the picture. So much the same and yet so much different, she thought. Was it possible Diego hadn't died that night? That he was really the Crown Prince of Calandria?

"I don't know," she admitted. "I don't know anything."

Grandma Tessa moved to the door. "He was supposed to have been killed five years ago?"

Mia nodded.

"So he's Danny's father."

She nodded again.

"Then this is going to be interesting."

Twenty minutes later Mia walked into the kitchen. She'd showered and dressed in record time. She would have been down sooner, but she'd debated both putting on makeup and blow-drying her hair. On a normal summer morning she wouldn't have bothered with either, but this was hardly normal. Besides, if Rafael was really who he said he was, a little mascara and lip gloss were probably a good thing.

She found the man who claimed to be Diego sitting at the kitchen table, being force-fed coffee and toast. Judging from the yummy smell coming from both ovens, fresh scones and cinnamon rolls were already on the way.

"Morning," she said as she approached the table.

Rafael immediately stood and smiled. "Mia."

He sounded so pleased to see her, as if he'd been waiting for this moment forever. But he couldn't have been. They'd been apart for years, and he hadn't once gotten in touch with her. She had a feeling she was only a simple Google away from being found, so why hadn't he looked before? And why was he here now?

"Your prince is very charming," Grandma Tessa said as she held out a cup of coffee. "Too charming, if you ask me."

"No one did," Grammy M said tartly. "You're always looking for the bruise on the apple. Sometimes there isn't one."

Grandma Tessa sniffed. "How can you be as old as you are and still so foolish about the world?" She narrowed her gaze as she looked at Rafael. "Crown prince or not, what do we really know about him?"

At that moment, Rafael's lineage was the least of Mia's problems.

"This has been fun," she said, and grabbed Rafael's coffee cup along with one for herself. "Let's go for a walk."

"Stay close to the house," Grandma Tessa told her. "I've called Joe. He'll be keeping an eye on you."

"Joe?" Rafael asked as they left the kitchen and stepped into the sunny late June morning. There was still dew on the flowers, and the scent of grapes from the acres of vineyards filled the air.

"The ex-Navy SEAL brother I mentioned before."

"He lives nearby?"

She handed him his coffee and nodded toward a large house on a hill, less than a quarter mile away. "He lives there."

"A very close family," Rafael said.

"You have no idea." She clutched her coffee in both hands and turned to the man walking next to her. "Who are you and why are you here?"

"I told you. I am the man you knew as Diego."

"As simple as that?" She tried to laugh, but the effort fell flat. Her mind wouldn't accept what was happening. She didn't know what to think, what to feel. Her anger had faded, leaving behind confusion and a sense of loss. As if seeing Diego after so long made her miss him all over again. "Nothing makes sense. You're supposed to be dead."

"You have mentioned that before. Are you disappointed to find otherwise?"

"I haven't decided." A lie. There were a thousand emotions swirling through her right now, but disappointment wasn't one of them. "I saw you die."

"You saw me shot and fall to the ground. There is a difference."

Not to her. That night was forever etched in her brain. The roar of the helicopter, the way the wind whipped up by the blades slapped her. She'd been crying, screaming, afraid. And then the gunshots. Diego had staggered back before falling. The world had slowed to just that moment, as he hit the ground and the blood poured out of him.

She'd yelled for the pilot to take her back. She'd tried to jump out of the helicopter, but someone had held her in place. She'd strained and clawed but hadn't been able to break free. They'd flown over Calandria. She remembered staring down at the bright lights, blurry through her tears, knowing that the hole his death had left in her heart would never heal.

"Mia?" He touched her arm.

His voice jerked her back to the present. She pressed her hand on his shoulder and shoved him back. "Dammit, Diego, you lied about dying? You lied and let me suffer all this time and never once thought maybe you should drop me a note saying 'Hey, not as dead as you'd think'? I *mourned* you. I didn't think I was ever going to recover."

She wanted to hurt him the way she'd been hurt. She could handle anything but betrayal and being played for a fool. She wanted to demand to know why he hadn't come after her, but she couldn't seem to ask that. Maybe because his sudden return from the dead illustrated the possibility that he hadn't loved her as much as she'd loved him.

Or maybe he hadn't loved her at all.

"Was this just a game?" she demanded. "Let's jerk around the American girl. It will be so much fun."

"It wasn't like that," he said, staring into her eyes. "I swear. I wanted to tell you the truth. I left Calandria to find you. It took me some time to learn your real name and then to convince your government to give me any information about you."

Right. Because he wasn't the only one keeping secrets.

She hadn't been the ditzy American tourist she'd led him to believe when they'd met. She'd been a newly trained operative, working for the United States government on her first assignment. In the words of James Bond, she had been a spy.

Not a very good one, she could admit now. She'd botched the assignment from the beginning. Fortunately, the only items of value on the line had been Calandrian artifacts, not lives. Not until she'd thought she'd seen her lover die.

"Allow me to start at the beginning," he said, his voice low and slightly accented.

She was willing to admit she remembered that voice. If she closed her eyes and simply listened to the words, it would be easy to believe, to get lost in a confusing mist of past and present. She almost wanted to—because back then her choices had been the relatively simple right and wrong. Now everything was complicated.

"My cousin Diego never accepted the fact that due to an ancient rule and a quirk of birth order, he would not rule Calandria. As he grew older, he vowed his revenge, on whom I do not know. Perhaps on the country herself. No one could reason with him, not even me, but we were, until our early twenties, close."

"But if you're the heir"—a fact she wanted confirmed by a reliable outside source, because thinking about it was just too crazy—"wouldn't he have resented you the most?"

"In a way he did. Yet we were friends. No matter how I tried to make Diego feel welcome, to give him something to do in our government, he remained bitter. He turned his energy to researching our ancient past and discovered a treasure trove of antiquities just beyond the waves. That discovery itself could have made him a very famous and wealthy man, but for Diego, it wasn't enough. Instead of announcing his find, he kept the knowledge secret and sold the jewels and artifacts on the black market."

"I know that part," Mia said. "That's why I was sent there—to help uncover the ring of thieves." She'd been thrilled to get an undercover assignment so quickly after finishing her training. "But *you* were Diego."

"Not at first. After he was killed, the director of intelligence came to see me."

Tiny Calandria had a director of intelligence? The island was barely the size of Manhattan.

"He and his men had decided the best way to trap all the would-be thieves was for me to go in and pretend to be Diego. We told no one. Not even the Americans who were assisting us. As no one knew Diego had died in a car accident outside of Paris, it was easy for me to step into his place."

She walked to the wooden railing at the edge of the vegetable garden and rested her arms on top. Her head hurt from trying to get all this straight. "You were a plant?"

"Yes."

"Then you were never the bad guy."

"Not in the traditional sense."

Mia would deal with that later. When she was alone, she would pick apart his story, piece by piece, and try to get her mind around the fact that Diego hadn't been bad at all.

She looked at him, then wished she hadn't. Listening was safe, but seeing the differences in his appearance startled her. Not that he wasn't good-looking now, but everything was wrong.

"You set me up. You wanted me to see you die so I would report that little tidbit back to my government. You used me."

"I didn't want to, but there wasn't another way. Per the plan, the authorities arrived to arrest everyone. You escaped, Diego's people watched Diego die, and the heritage of my country was restored."

All very tidy, Mia thought, except for the fact that she'd been in love with Diego. She'd gone against all her training and her beliefs when she'd found herself falling for the man she thought was the enemy. Torn between what her head told her was right and what her heart begged her to claim, she'd barely been able to function.

Anger returned. She glared at him. "You must have been so delighted that I conveniently fell in with your plans. Imagine how difficult things would have been if I hadn't fallen for you."

"Mia, no. I never meant to hurt you or use you. I wanted to tell you the truth."

"I know, but you were just so busy. There wasn't any time." She took a step back. "I suppose the moment you were pushing me onto the helicopter wasn't convenient enough? Or what about afterward, when I was falling apart? I thought I loved you. I thought you were special, and you walked away and let me think you were dead for five years?"

"I wanted to come after you," he said. "I needed to tell you the truth. You must believe me."

"Not a chance. How hard would I have been to find?"

He set his coffee on the fence post. "Your government

was not exactly forthcoming. You were an operative and they insisted on protecting your identity. In desperation, I went through diplomatic channels. I used every power of my office to find you. At last I received word from a source I trusted that you had been killed only a few weeks after you had left Calandria."

"Bullshit."

He reached for her again, but this time she stayed back.

"I'm not lying," he said. "I was devastated. I could not imagine a world without your laughter." He shook his head, then looked away. "I know what I felt and I will not explain myself further."

If he'd tried to convince her, she wouldn't have believed him, but the arrogant tilt of his head, the lack of concern for her feelings, sort of made her wonder if he was telling the truth.

Rafael was right—the United States government didn't give out personal information on intelligence personnel to foreign governments. Even intelligence personnel who quit after their first job.

He stared at the vineyard. "If they hadn't told me you'd died, I never would have stopped looking. I believe that's why they made up the story. The source was someone I trusted. I had no reason to question the information."

"So you knew who I was," she said.

"I knew you were with the American intelligence community. I knew you were there to get information on the thefts. I knew we were both on the same side."

"Wish *I'd* had that information," she murmured. "So what happened next? You returned to your life?" She shook her head. "Are you really the crown prince?"

He smiled. "You have seen my identification. Speaking of which, I will need my passport returned to me."

"Sure thing." She glanced at the driveway and saw the front of the large, long limo with flags fluttering. "You'd better not be lying about that being your car. Even as we speak, my brother is running the plates."

"Then he will be able to confirm the truth of my statement." His smile deepened. "Would I really lie about being a prince? Something so easy to prove or disprove?"

He had a point. She sipped her coffee and wished she could take a couple of days to absorb all this.

"Why now?" she asked. "Why did you come back?"

"I found out you were still alive. I came right away, Mia. I came for you."

Not quite as good as Kyle Reese coming across time for Sarah Connor in the first *Terminator* movie, but when spoken in Rafael's soft accented voice, it was a close second.

"There was a picture in the newspaper," he said. "President Jensen's sixtieth birthday, I believe. You know the president of the United States?"

Mia knew exactly what picture he was talking about. It had been taken at a private party for the president. President Jensen had picked up Mia's son and tossed the boy in the air. The photo showed him as he caught the boy. They were both laughing, with Mia standing just behind them, clapping at their fun.

The picture had been on the front page of *USA Today*, with a line about the president enjoying a family outing on his birthday. Who knew the newspaper's distribution went all the way to Calandria?

"Yes, well, that just sort of happened. The president's daughter was threatened and she came here to hide out.

She and Joe fell in love. When they got married, we all became relatives."

She shook her head. If Rafael had seen that picture, he'd also seen Danny.

"What have you been doing?" he asked. "I know you left the agency. You would not have had your picture in the paper if you had not."

"What? Oh, right. No press photos of operatives. I quit as soon as I got back to the States. After you died, after I thought you died, I couldn't do it anymore. I came home and tried to make peace with everything."

"Did you?"

No. She'd fallen apart—a new experience for her. She'd grown up confident and ready to rule the world. But something had happened in the short weeks she'd spent pretending to be an American looking for adventure.

"I thought you were the bad guy," she told him, still furious that she'd been lied to. "I thought I was betraying my country by falling for you."

He stepped toward her. "Mia, do not distress yourself."

What was she supposed to do? Be happy? "If I can't believe who you were, how can I believe who you are?"

"Perhaps you don't have to. Perhaps we could start at the beginning. Meet now." He held out his right hand. "Good morning. I am Rafael, Crown Prince of Calandria. And you are?"

She sighed. "Sorry, no. That isn't going to work. We can't just start over. There's too much messy past between us. Too many years."

"So I should not have come? You are not happy to see me?"

"I'm . . ." Annoyed, confused, furious, shocked. "I'm not really a morning person."

"Of course. You want me to leave."

He turned, as if prepared to walk to his limo and disappear from her life. Only she wasn't ready for that. Not yet.

"Wait," she said. "I . . . What do I call you? Prince Rafael? Your highness?"

"Rafael is fine."

"All right. Rafael. This is happening so quickly. I don't know what to think or believe. I need a little time. We have to talk. I'm still not clear on why you're here."

"To see you."

Was that all? "If you saw the picture, then you saw Danny."

He frowned slightly. "The boy? The child of one of your sisters."

Mia clutched her coffee. It was true that the caption hadn't identified the child in the picture, or her for that matter.

She didn't know if Rafael was telling the truth. She'd long since learned to be wary of the men she brought into her life. They were usually snakes. Diego had been no exception, but was Rafael different?

Did it matter? Either way, she had to tell him. He deserved to know.

"Danny is my son," she said, doing her best to keep her voice even. "And yours."

Rafael timed his reaction carefully. To show too much shock would be to put Mia on her guard. To show not enough would mark him as an indifferent father.

"My son?" he asked as he took a step back. "What are you saying?"

"I was pregnant when I left Calandria. Only a week or so along. I didn't know, obviously. When I came home, I was pretty broken up about everything. Finding out I was pregnant saved me."

He saw the pain in her eyes as she spoke and knew he had no reason not to believe her. Besides, he and Mia hadn't been lovers for more than a couple of weeks before the sting had ended.

"I had no idea," he said, willing his expression toward disbelief. "You had a child? Your government kept that from me as well?"

"I'm not sure they knew," she told him. "I quit and came home. That was the end of my relationship with the agency. Unlike in the movies, they didn't spend a lot of time begging me to return to my old job."

"Someone should have told me," he growled, not having to fake the anger he felt. What Mia didn't know was that it was directed at himself. He'd been the one who hadn't bothered to follow up with her. To make sure there were no consequences of their time together. For the past four years his son, his *heir*, had existed and he hadn't known.

"I would have, except I thought you were dead," she said sharply, then sighed. "Sorry. I don't mean to be crabby. This is all so much. Too much. I don't know what Danny's going to think. All his life, I told him his father died before he was born." She looked at him. "You're not questioning your paternity. I'm not lying, but you'll probably want to check this all out. It would be a big deal for any guy, but I'm guessing an even bigger one for a prince."

She was telling the truth. Before sneaking into Mia's room, he'd visited the boy. The child had slept soundly and it had been easy to check the small of his back. There, just to the left of his spine, was the small star-shaped birthmark all the men in his family possessed. The child was his, but better to play along and pretend to not be sure.

"I have never doubted your integrity," he said. "But under the circumstances proof will be necessary. I'm sure we can arrange for a DNA test of some kind."

"Circumstances?" she repeated. "You mean the one where you're a prince and heir to a throne and I'm just some commoner from California?"

"I would not describe you thus," he said, moving close and taking her hand in his. Her skin was warm and he enjoyed the contact.

Five years ago he'd claimed Mia as his own because it had pleased him to do so. Now he would claim her for other reasons, but the task would still be most pleasant.

"Great," she murmured, then took a sip of her coffee as she carefully pulled free of his touch. "Let me recap. You might be Diego, and hey, an heir to the Calandria throne. You're also not dead. In the short time we were together five years ago, I managed to get pregnant, because that's just how my luck goes. Now you're back and we're parents together. Did I miss anything?"

He remembered the first time he'd met her. Even then he'd been unable to decide which he admired more—her spirit or her beauty. His dilemma had not changed.

"Those seem to be the salient points," he said.

"Great. I need more coffee."

She took a step and stumbled on the uneven ground. He reached for her, grabbing her arm and holding her upright. She reached for him with her free hand—to steady herself, he was sure—which left them standing very close.

He found himself staring into her brown eyes. He could feel the warmth and enticing curves of her body. Her mouth called to him. Whatever else might or might not have happened with Mia, he had always wanted her. Apparently time apart hadn't changed that fact. How convenient.

"Mia," he whispered.

"Don't even think about it," she told him, but she didn't move away.

"Why would I think when action is so much more pleasurable?" he asked as he lowered his mouth to hers.

Her breath caught. She stiffened but stayed in his arms.

Then a loud voice cut through the morning and broke the mood completely.

"Step away from my sister. Do it slowly and I probably won't shoot you in the back."

2

Rafael straightened but didn't move away. Mia took advantage of his momentary distraction and stepped back so she could look at Joe.

Sure enough, her former Navy SEAL brother held a mean-looking handgun inches from Rafael's back. While she appreciated Joe's concern about her safety and that he was willing to be all macho and protective, she wasn't sure shooting the father of her son was an especially good idea. Not yet, anyway. Although she kind of liked seeing Rafael at the business end of a gun.

"I don't think he's dangerous," she said, only to gasp in surprise as two large and burly men in dark suits rounded the side of the house. Each of them had an equally impressive-looking handgun. They shouted in Italian, then in French, for Joe to drop his weapon.

In a move too fast for her to see, Joe grabbed Rafael and held his gun to the base of his neck.

"Get behind me," Joe told her. "Who the hell are you?" he asked the other two. "What do you want?"

Okay, this was quickly getting out of hand. Mia looked

at Rafael. "Let me guess—the bodyguards?" Traveling with protection certainly helped his credibility on the whole "I'm a prince" thing.

"Yes. Umberto. Oliver. There is no need to attack anyone so early in the morning. This is only a misunderstanding." Rafael, apparently unconcerned about the gun pressing into his neck, smiled at Joe. "Is it not?"

He sounded calm, which Mia respected.

The bodyguards, however, were not moved. They kept their weapons trained on Joe.

Just then the back door to the kitchen opened. Grandma Tessa walked out and planted her hands on her hips. "If you boys are finished playing, breakfast is ready." Her eyes narrowed. "It's getting cold."

Mia glanced at the men and realized this could take a minute. Rather than deal with the diplomatic disarming, she stepped around Joe and hurried toward the house. Maybe running away wasn't her preferred method of dealing with problems, but Rafael wasn't a normal problem. Besides, she had to be somewhere.

"Mia?" Rafael called after her. "Perhaps you could ask your brother to release me."

"You used to be a dangerous outlaw," she told him as she passed Grandma Tessa on the stairs. "You figure it out."

Once she was inside, she made her way to the second story. She'd grown up here—lived her life surrounded by these walls. At sixteen she'd gone to college but had still considered the hacienda home. At twenty-three she'd returned pregnant, emotionally devastated. Her family had taken her in and made her feel welcome.

In time she would leave again and take her son with

her. They would start a new life, but they would both always remember their time here.

When she reached the bedroom on the end, right across from her own, she paused in front of the closed door and pressed her hand against the painted wood.

Everything was about to change. She didn't know where they would end up, but as of this minute, her world had been tilted on its axis. Until this morning she'd wondered if her son would be interested in inheriting Marcelli Wine and the acres of vineyards around the house. Now, apparently, he might be next in line to inherit a whole country.

She opened the door and stepped into the colorful, toy-filled bedroom and smiled as her son sat up.

"Good morning, sleepyhead. Did you sleep well?"

"Mommy!" Danny held out his arms.

When she plopped down on the mattress, he climbed into her lap and leaned his head against her chest. Automatically she picked up his treasured stuffed tiger and handed it to him. He held it close while she wrapped her arms around him and rocked him back and forth.

"We have a busy day," she said softly. "So many things to do. Grammy M and Grandma Tessa have finished your costume."

He looked up at her and grinned. "For my play?"

"Uh-huh. I think maybe later we should practice your lines again."

"I know 'em."

She smiled. He knew his three lines about as well as any other child in his preschool class. Which meant the play would consist of a lot of parental prompting and giggles from the kids.

Danny snuggled close. She breathed in the scent of him,

knowing she could find him in the dark by smell alone. He was her child and her world. From the moment she'd found out she was pregnant, she'd known it would always just be the two of them. Well, as much as it *could* be the two of them, given her extended and loving family and the fact that she lived in the same house as her parents and both grandmothers.

"I want chocolate cake," he said.

She laughed. "Hmm, yesterday it was peanut butter."

"Grammy M said a peanut butter cake would stick to the roof of my mouth. So chocolate."

His fourth birthday was still nearly a month away, but Danny took the cake decision very seriously. As this was the first year he'd actually had an opinion, Mia was more than willing to let him pick.

"Chocolate it is," she said as she kissed the top of his head then set him on the floor. "Okay, big guy. Let's get you dressed."

Danny rubbed his eyes, set down his tiger, and tugged at his PJ shirt. He got it over his head, where it got stuck. Mia pulled until he popped free and grinned at her.

She pulled open a drawer and called out colors. "Blue, green, red, or yellow?"

Danny closed his mouth and blew through pursed lips. "Yellow."

She removed a bright yellow T-shirt with trucks on the front, a pair of dark gray shorts, and cartoon character–covered underwear.

He stepped out of his bottoms and underwear, then reached for the clean pair of little boy briefs. Next were the shorts, which he could pull on himself. She helped him with the T-shirt.

The familiarity of the morning routine allowed her to

momentarily forget the sudden appearance of Danny's father, but she couldn't ignore Diego . . . Rafael . . . any longer.

She tossed the dirty clothes into the hamper and grabbed the hairbrush from the dresser. Danny stood patiently while she smoothed his dark hair. When she'd finished, she looked at the familiar little face and knew he was very much his father's son.

The shape of their eyes was the same and they had similar smiles. Not that there was any doubt. Mia hadn't been in a relationship in months when she met Rafael. She'd fallen hard, even though she'd known it was the wrong thing to do.

Rafael might insist on a DNA test, but she already knew the truth.

"What, Mommy?" Danny asked, his face scrunching up in a frown. "Are you sad?"

"Not sad. I have to tell you something."

"I've been good."

She smiled. "Yes, you have. You're usually very good and I think that's great." She took the boy's hands in her own. "Do you remember me telling you how your daddy died before you were born?"

Danny nodded solemnly. "You were very sad for a long, long time."

"I was. But what I didn't know was he was playing a game. Not with me, but with some other people. He only pretended to die, but I didn't know. I thought he was gone."

Danny stared at her and she could see he wasn't getting it. Who could blame him? He was three weeks shy of turning four. She was twenty-seven and she was having trouble taking it all in.

She started over. "I thought your daddy was dead, but he wasn't. He was fine. But some people wanted to protect me and they told him . . ."

She sighed. Okay, this was getting worse by the minute. How to explain that while she'd thought Rafael was dead and he wasn't, he'd thought the same about her and . . .

"Your daddy isn't dead. He's here. Downstairs. He didn't know about you until today and he's very excited to find out he has a little boy."

Danny's face lit up as he pulled his hands free and clapped them together. "I have a *daddy?*" he asked with a reverence usually reserved for ice cream and puppies.

"Yes, you do. Would you like to meet him?"

Her son nodded vigorously.

"You sure you want to go there?" Joe asked from the doorway to Danny's room. "What about the DNA test and checking this guy out?"

"Uncle Joe!" Danny flew toward his favorite male in the whole world.

Joe grabbed him and tossed him in the air. "Whoa there. You grew in the night. I can tell."

Danny shrieked with delight as his uncle caught him. "I got a daddy."

"So I heard."

Mia stood. "So the four of you worked out your personal issues?"

Joe shifted the boy so that Danny sat on his shoulders. "Grandma Tessa bullied them into putting theirs away first. Then I was willing to play nice."

"Always the protector."

"I try. Aren't you being a little premature on the d-a-d-d-y front? What do you know about this guy?"

Mia couldn't answer that. Diego had been a notorious outlaw. Apparently Rafael was a prince. "I know what happened and I know Danny is his son. I'm not going to keep them apart."

"I want to check out the guy," her brother told her.

"I encourage that. Check away." But prince or not, Diego/Rafael had fathered her child. Although as Rafael had pointed out, why lie about being a prince?

"What's he doing here?" Joe asked her. "Why now?"

"It was that picture with the president. *USA Today* picked it up and apparently flashed it around the world."

"Yeah, them," Joe muttered.

"At least the Grands will be excited if he turns out to be a prince," she told him. "First you marry the president's daughter then I . . ." She glanced at her son. "Then I meet someone famous."

"Meet, huh? That's one way to put it." Joe grabbed Danny's ankles. "Ready to go downstairs?" he asked.

"Go fast," Danny yelled. "As fastest as you can!"

Joe obliged by racing down the stairs. Mia followed, wondering how it was possible that her perfectly ordinary life had just taken a turn for the incredible.

Rafael did his best to hide his amusement. Oliver and Umberto were highly trained bodyguards who were used to controlling every situation. Now they were held at bay by a tiny woman with a rolling pin. It wasn't that the two men couldn't take Grandma Tessa, as Mia had called her, but that their own sense of family, not to mention his orders to stand down, put them in an uncomfortable situation.

"Tessa, please," the other grandmother—Grammy M—said with a sigh. "You'll be frightenin' our guests."

"They're not guests. They have guns." Tessa's eyes narrowed as if she wanted to whack them both on the back of the head to teach them a lesson. "There will be no guns in this house."

"Joe had a gun," Grammy M pointed out.

"He's family. That's different."

Rafael enjoyed the blend of Tessa's slight Italian accent and Grammy M's lilting Irish voice.

"They're here to protect me," he said, hoping to smooth over the situation.

"I can see why you'd want protection from two old women," Tessa chided.

Grammy M sighed. "You'll have to be forgivin' her, your highness. Tessa's not one to deal well with change."

"I suppose you expect us to feed them, too," Tessa grumbled as she put the rolling pin on the counter and ignored the other woman's comment. "You show up without warning, claiming to be . . ." She shook her head. "I, for one, don't believe a word of it."

He'd spent the past couple of days researching Mia's family. His time working with the Calandrian intelligence department had taught him to know his enemies better than he knew any of his friends. Not that Mia or her relatives were necessarily enemies. Perhaps wild cards would be a better description.

He'd studied the names and faces, along with facts provided by the director of intelligence. But seeing a two-dimensional picture was very different from meeting the person in question.

He liked that Tessa mistrusted him. Her wariness showed a sensibility that would do well for his son. While Grammy M's soft and accepting heart was slightly less useful when it came to ruling a country, it might serve Daniel well in romantic matters.

"How can I convince you of my true identity?" he asked. "You have already seen my passport. Unfortunately, princes are not issued identification cards at birth."

"Too bad," Tessa said with a sniff. "But not to worry. Darcy has put a call in to her father. We'll soon know everything about you."

He pretended a confusion he didn't feel. "Darcy?" he asked, knowing exactly who she and her father were.

"The daughter of the president of the United States," Tessa said sharply. "She's married to Joe. My very sensible grandson. Good thing he takes after me and not some flighty people I could name who are won over by a couple of flags on a long black car and a title that may or may not be real."

Rafael bowed his head slightly and tried not to smile. "I have nothing to hide," he said. At least nothing they would find out by calling the president.

Grammy M walked to the table and poured him more coffee. "Don't let her be botherin' you. She's always been a bit of a crab."

Tessa ignored them and retreated to the stove. Rafael decided to use the moment to cement Grammy M's support.

"When did you leave Ireland?" he asked.

Grammy M glanced at the two bodyguards standing by the back door, then took the seat across from his at the large table.

"When I was a girl. I married young and my husband, God rest his soul, moved us here."

"A change from the beauty of those green hills," he said.

"'Tis true, but this is home now. It has been for a long time. My family is here. My husband died here, as did

Gabriel, a man I knew. He passed on a couple of years ago. Now Tessa and I are two old women waiting till the end of our days."

"Speak for yourself," Tessa snapped. "I'm waiting on Joe to throw that man out. All your smooth talking isn't going to convince me of anything."

Rafael knew he would have to charm Tessa into neutrality, if nothing else, but before he could start, Mia walked into the kitchen.

He stood and smiled at her. She acknowledged him with a nod of her head but nothing else. Instantly, both grandmothers were at her side, offering tangible support.

Five years ago Mia had come to his country to help rout out the thieves who were stealing Calandria's history. Her assignment had been to pose as a foolish but rich American tourist looking for adventure while collecting information on those who plotted against his country.

She'd been smart, irreverent, and determined. She'd also been a beauty, with streaked hair and big brown eyes. While the hair color was now darker, the eyes were the same. She hadn't lost her curves, but the air of joyous exuberance seemed to be missing.

"You'll want to meet Danny," she said.

He nodded, then felt an unexpected quickening of his heart. His son. His heir. Blood from dozens of kings and princes pumped in the boy's veins. Daniel . . . Rafael sighed—the boy's name would have to be changed to something more royal. Daniel was the hope of his country's future.

Mia retreated into the hallway, then returned leading a small boy by the hand. Although Rafael had seen him sleeping only an hour or two before, he hadn't taken the time to study the child's features.

Even without the telltale birthmark, the truth was there in the features, the shape of the body. Danny reminded him of Diego and Quentin when they had been young.

Still holding the boy's hand, Mia crouched next to the child and smiled. "Danny, do you want to say hello?"

Danny stuck his forefinger in his mouth and regarded Rafael thoughtfully. "Are you really my daddy?" he asked softly.

"Yes, I am. I am Crown Prince Rafael of Calandria and you are my heir."

Danny frowned. "I'm not air. I'm a little boy."

Mia smiled. "He means you're going to be like him when you grow up."

Danny turned and buried his face in her shoulder. Mia wrapped her arms around him. "Sorry," she told Rafael over the boy's head. "He's not usually shy, but this is a big deal."

"Of course. Anyone would be confused by the situation."

"You'd think a boy would know his own father," Tessa said, glaring at him.

"Rafael *is* his father," Mia said. "I don't have any doubts."

"We should have breakfast," Grammy M said. "Come on, Danny. I've made hot chocolate."

The boy let go of his mother and went with Grammy M to the table. He glanced at Rafael several times, as if trying to figure out what having a father meant.

Mia stood. "It's going to take time for all of us to adjust," she said.

He was close enough to inhale the scent of her skin. Something floral with the hint of a woman's heat. Instantly he could remember what it had been like to be with her. They'd come together in a fiery passion that had defied logic and some of the laws of physics.

Did that fire still exist between them? He would not mind if it did. Seducing Mia would not only be pleasurable, it would aid his plan.

"I do not mean to rush anyone," he said. "We will—what is the phrase?—make it up as we go along."

She smiled. "I'd like that."

"Good."

She had known him as Diego as well as anyone, he thought. But she didn't know him as Rafael. If she did, she would realize that he never allowed himself to simply go along with circumstances. He always had a goal and he always achieved it.

Danny's eyes were wide, but he didn't squirm.

Mia crouched in front of her son and took both his hands in hers. "Remember when you had to get a shot and I told you it would hurt?" she asked.

Danny nodded.

"And when we went to the dentist for a cleaning and I said it wouldn't hurt and it didn't?"

He nodded again.

"This won't hurt at all. Okay?"

He looked from her to Umberto, then opened his mouth and closed his eyes. The tall, burly bodyguard stuck the swab into the boy's mouth and rubbed it against his cheek.

"I am finished," he said in thickly accented English.

Danny blinked. "That's it?"

Mia grinned. "Uh-huh. Did I say it wouldn't hurt? Did you believe me?"

As she spoke, she tickled Danny's sides. He laughed and pretended to push her away, while cuddling closer.

"It was okay," he said between bursts of laughter.

Umberto nodded and left with the swab. Joe stepped out of the corner.

"They'll rush it through," he told her. "It should only be a few days."

Mia pulled Danny onto her lap and glanced at her brother. "Still having doubts?"

"More like false hopes," he admitted. "I don't like this."

"I don't know how I feel," she admitted. Too much had happened too quickly. Four hours ago she'd been asleep in her own bed and now a man she thought dead and buried had strolled back into her life. And not just any man.

"Is he really a prince?" she asked.

"Pretty much."

Impossible, she thought. "I've never been very good at reverence."

"You'd better learn to curtsy."

She couldn't imagine *that* ever happening. "It's a new century. Royalty isn't like it was before."

Joe smiled. "They've let go of their love of a good beheading." His smile faded. "I don't know what to hope for," he admitted. "Danny needs a father, but this guy?"

"I do have interesting taste in men," she said, still unable to get her mind around all that had happened.

Grammy M walked into the dining room. "He's leaving," she announced. "Just like that. Prince Rafael is leaving."

"Going back to Calandria?" Mia asked, wanting him gone and not gone in equal measure.

"Worse. A hotel. Tessa says he's not staying here, which is just ridiculous. I've never seen her like this before.

She was always difficult and stubborn, but not like this. Imagine takin' an instant dislike to little Danny's father."

Danny looked up at Mia. "Daddy stays here."

She wasn't sure if it was a question or a request. She turned to Joe. "What does your military training say?"

"We can keep an eye on him in either place."

There weren't that many hotels around the hacienda. Santa Barbara was the closest town, and as it was summer, the main tourist season was in full swing. Would he even be able to find a room nearby? Did she care?

"He could stay in the house," Grammy M said eagerly, "and those other two can use the guest cottage. That will get them out of the house. We shouldn't have guns in the house. Not with little fingers about."

Or even the whole boy, Mia thought. Technically there was room. Her parents were gone for a few months and the hacienda was big. "All right. Sure. Invite Rafael to stay." Assuming royalty was willing to bunk with the common man.

Grammy M held out her hand to Danny. "Come on, then. Let's go see if we can be convincin' your father to grace us with his presence."

Mia let the older woman lead Danny away.

"I'm not excited about the 'gracing us with his presence' attitude," she admitted when she and Joe were alone. "The situation is already difficult enough."

Joe moved close and put his arm around her. "We'll be fine."

"You sure about that?"

"Almost."

"Great. What can we do to move you to be completely sure? Because I'd like that better."

"You scared?"

Scared? Sure. And nauseous and apprehensive and a whole lot of other things.

"I saw him die, Joe. I've spent the past five years feeling guilty about the fact that he saved my life only to lose his own. Now he shows up and tells me he's not who I thought, he's not dead, and hey, 'I rushed to your side as soon as I found out you were still alive yourself.' There should be a limit on surprises in a twenty-four-hour period."

"Agreed. I'm going to call in a few favors and get extra security around the house."

Mia didn't like the sound of that. "Is there a problem?" Her body tightened with sudden cold. "Do you think once the DNA test is back he'll try to kidnap Danny?"

"Don't go there. We don't know enough, Mia. I want to be cautious."

"Cautious is good. Be the king of caution. You're good at that. In the meantime, I'll try to muddle through. This is all good, right? Like you said, Danny needs a father and who better than his biological one."

"You don't sound convinced."

"I'm not. I should be, but I'm not. I feel like I'm overreacting by expecting the worst. I don't know. It's all crazy."

He pulled her close and kissed the top of her head. "Don't worry. I'll keep you safe."

"Promise?"

"You bet. Nobody screws with my family."

3

❧

"You don't like him," Mia said.

Grandma Tessa slammed the side of her knife against several cloves of garlic. "Liking or not liking isn't an issue. If he's Danny's father, then he's part of the family."

"There's no 'if,'" she told her grandmother. "The DNA test will prove that."

Mia half expected the older woman to reach for her rosary. It usually took a lot less than this to get her to take a trip around the beads. But her small hands continued to chop the garlic.

"I know you're disappointed," Mia said, feeling young and awkward. "That we . . . That I . . . About Danny." Which was a polite way of saying she was sure her grandmother was disappointed that Mia had not only had sex with a man she wasn't married to, but that she'd gotten pregnant.

Tessa glanced at her. "Why are you saying that now? You never cared what I thought when you brought your boyfriends around before."

Mia winced. "Things are different," she admitted. "I'm not that wild child anymore. I'm Danny's mother." She no longer brought home boyfriends to share her room. Shocking her family had ceased to be entertaining, even if she couldn't seem to stop doing it.

Her grandmother smiled. "You're a good girl, Mia. You're smart and independent and sometimes you act before you think. At least you used to. Since you had Danny, you've settled down."

"Become boring," she muttered. Her life was her son, her family, and law school. Or it had been. "Of course now I know a prince. That's going to change things."

Tessa's smile faded. "I don't like him."

"Really? I hadn't noticed."

Her grandmother narrowed her gaze. "You're not to be taking that tone with me, young lady."

Mia leaned down and kissed her cheek. "You don't scare me."

A floorboard creaked overhead. Mia glanced up. "I guess Rafael is settling in."

"I'm not sure his highness will like living in a real home with regular people. This isn't a palace, and if he thinks he's going to have us at his beck and call, he can think again."

Mia found herself torn between defending Rafael, who, technically, had not been unreasonable, and siding with Grandma Tessa.

"The bodyguards are in the guest house," she said. "That's something."

Tessa scooped the garlic into the heated pan and stirred the garlic and olive oil mixture. Mia had no idea what she was making. Practically every Italian dish began with garlic and olive oil.

"That was Joe," Tessa said curtly. "He's looking out for his family. Imagine those gorillas wanting to stay in this house with a little boy around. What if one of us got up in the night? They'd think we were after their precious prince and shoot us all in our sleep."

Mia thought about pointing out that anyone walking around was unlikely to be sleeping, but she liked that Grandma Tessa was on her side.

"Why don't you like him?" Mia asked.

Her grandmother went to work on a bowl of tomatoes, chopping them quickly and efficiently. "I don't know the man. It's for the Lord to judge him. That's not to say I'm willing to ignore my good sense just because he has a title, like some people I could name."

Mia knew the dig was aimed at Grammy M, who seemed happy to accept Rafael at face value.

Tessa nodded at the refrigerator. "There's corn in there. It won't be shucking itself."

Mia collected the bag and went to work. "I don't know what to think about all this," she admitted. "I know who he was, but I don't know who he is." She brushed corn silk into the trash can, then put the clean ear on the counter.

"Have you called Marco and Colleen?"

"No. I will. I want to tell them; it's just they've been looking forward to this trip for years and it took so long to arrange." Her parents, in charge of the overseas sales of Marcelli Wines, had just left for China three days ago. They were supposed to be gone two months. "I'm going to wait until they're in Beijing, then phone them at the hotel. I don't want them to come home early just for me. It's not as if Rafael is going anywhere."

Nor did she know if she wanted him to. While it would make her life easier, what about Danny? She wanted him to know his father.

"What about the girls?" Tessa asked, referring to Mia's sisters.

"I left a message for each of them already." There would be plenty of shrieking when they found out. "Brenna's out of town until tomorrow night, so Francesca and Katie will come over with her."

"They'll want to be with you," Tessa said. "They'll understand."

"I know." Sometimes her family made her crazy, but in situations like this, she appreciated the support. She wouldn't want to be going through this on her own.

Not that she even knew what "this" was.

The back door opened and Danny raced inside. Grammy M followed a bit more slowly.

"We picked berries," Danny said proudly as he showed off his red and purple fingers. "For dessert. Grammy M said I could help make it."

"I thought a berry shortcake would be nice for tonight," Grammy M said as she carried a basket to the sink. "I'm sure Rafael will appreciate some fine home cooking."

Tessa snorted. "I'm sure he's been longing for a little homemade dessert to chase away the flavor of all those five-star meals he's been forced to eat."

The two old women glared at each other. Mia took Danny by the hand. "Let's get you washed up," she said, more than willing to let them fight it out themselves.

"Is that man really my daddy?" Danny asked as they climbed the stairs.

"Yes, he is."

Her son looked at her, his eyes large and filled with questions. "Does he like me?"

Mia stopped and dropped to her knees. She took Danny's hands in hers and smiled. "Of course he does. You're a wonderful boy. Smart and funny and kind. You always help the Grands in the kitchen and you know your letters."

"I can write my name," he reminded her.

"Yes, you can. But even if you couldn't do all those things your daddy would like you because of who you are inside. Because you're his son."

At least she hoped that was the case. Honestly, how much did she really know about Rafael? Diego's background had been carefully spelled out during her briefings, but the crown prince had only been mentioned in passing. Who was the man inside?

After washing Danny's hands in the hall bathroom, Mia debated whether to return to the relative safety of the kitchen or to face Rafael. While the former had more appeal, the latter somehow felt right, so she smiled at her son and asked, "Want to go see your daddy?"

Danny nodded eagerly, but as they left the bathroom, he clutched her hand tightly.

They walked the few steps to the main guest room, the one with its own bathroom. The door stood open. She reached up to knock anyway when she saw Rafael placing what looked like socks in a dresser drawer.

He might be a prince now, but when she first knew him he was a big, bad thief with a reputation for killing the competition. She couldn't imagine either man putting away his own socks.

"I guess this is really different from living in a palace," she said.

He smiled. "In some ways, but if you are curious, I assure you I will survive without my butler."

"Good to know." The man had a butler? Sure. It probably came with the prince thing. Someone had to be responsible for his formal wear.

"I'm sure you have dry cleaning nearby," he said.

"Yes. I can show you. Or will the bodyguards take care of that?"

"They will. And my laundry."

"How nice. Proficiency with handguns and knowledge of the delicate cycle. They truly are the contemporary version of the Renaissance man."

Rafael raised his right eyebrow in a gesture that was so familiar, her breath caught. In that moment she was transported back to her days with Diego after they had become lovers. She remembered sitting through a long planning meeting, barely able to stay awake because they'd been up all night making love. He'd caught her yawning and had raised his right eyebrow. The gesture, so unlikely in a dark and dangerous man, had caused her to giggle. Then he had smiled. The meeting had ended suddenly and he had ushered her back to his room.

She shook off the memory and her body's visceral reaction to it. Ignoring Rafael, she glanced at Danny.

"What do you think?" she asked.

The boy didn't speak.

His father crouched down in front of him. "This is a very unusual situation. It isn't every day that a man finds out that he's a father. We're going to have to take some time and get to know each other."

Danny's eyes widened slightly, but again he didn't speak.

"I am very fortunate," Rafael continued. "Some fathers never find their children. I'm glad that didn't happen to us."

"Do I look like you?" Danny asked.

Mia wanted to answer but sensed this was a moment when it was better to keep quiet.

Rafael looked Danny over, then smiled. "I think you do."

"Charlie looks like his daddy. So does Brandon. Billy looks like his mom." He glanced at Mia, as if wondering if she understood why that was a bad thing.

She smiled. "You have the same eyes and smile. The hair color could have come from either of us."

"You are my son," Rafael told the boy. "You are a prince and one day you will rule Calandria."

Mia didn't want to think of things in those terms. Right now she would be thrilled to get Danny to eat more vegetables.

"A prince?" Danny laughed.

"It's true," his father told him.

From the moment Mia had found out she was pregnant, she'd thought of her child as a Marcelli. But he wasn't anymore.

Danny lunged at his father, arms open, body quivering. Rafael pulled him close and they hugged.

She stood a little distance away, watching the moment, equally happy and sad. Of course she wanted her son to have a father, but at the same time, she realized that nothing would ever be the same again. It was no longer just the two of them against the world. They were no longer a pair—in a matter of seconds, they had become a family.

"It is very beautiful here," Rafael said later that afternoon as he and Mia walked through the vineyards by the house.

"Things are about to get crazy," Mia told him. "The grapes are ripening and soon Brenna will begin compulsively checking to see which are ready to harvest. From that moment on, it's a rush to get everything picked and pressed and put into barrels."

She forced herself to stop talking. It was one thing to

be nervous around Rafael, it was another to let him know. But jeez, Rafael here? Nothing felt real.

"We don't make wine in Calandria. There is not enough land. That which is used for agriculture is used to grow our olives."

"Ah, yes. The famous Calandrian olives. Worth their weight in gold."

He smiled at her. "Almost. If the price of gold is down that week." He stopped and looked at her. "How are you—what is the phrase?—holding up?"

"I'm good. A little shell-shocked but recovering." Give her six or eight weeks and she'd be an old pro at dealing with him.

"Me too," he admitted with a shrug. "A short time ago, I was a carefree bachelor."

"You're still that."

"Not so much. I have a family."

Exactly how she'd thought of them earlier. Why did it make her uncomfortable coming from him? "We have Danny in common," she told him. "But nothing else."

His mouth curved into a smile. "Once you would not have said that."

"It's been a long time. We're different people now. You more than me."

"Because I am not the dark and dangerous Diego?"

"That's part of it."

He reached for her hand. "Perhaps we should get to know each other again. We have a child together, Mia. That is a bond that will never be broken."

She was as mesmerized by his low, seductive voice as by the gentle pressure of his hand holding hers. He laced their fingers together.

There *was* Danny to think about, she reminded herself. Parents who got along were better than parents who didn't. Did she want that? To get to know him? Did she have a choice? She was drawn to Rafael but couldn't figure out how much of it was him as he was today and how much was the past.

"I agree that becoming friends is a good idea," she said carefully.

"Excellent. Then let us begin. Tell me about your family."

"Did you find out about them before you came here?"

"I have some basic information, but I want to hear about them from you. One can read a guidebook about a city, but until one has talked to a native, one cannot understand the flavor."

Interesting point. "Okay. This land has belonged to the Marcellis for nearly ninety years. Not impressive by European standards, but it's a big deal for us. My father is the third generation, and Danny the fifth. Obviously we're Marcelli Wines. Our neighbors are Wild Sea. That's the Giovanni family. Brenna, one of my sisters, married Nic Giovanni. The businesses are kept separate, but Brenna's the wine queen and pretty bossy, so things are changing at Wild Sea."

Rafael kept hold of her hand and began walking again. "Wild Sea is a much bigger company."

"They're huge. Brenna complains Nic is more into volume than quality, while he complains she's morally opposed to making a profit. Neither is totally true. But it's their passion and they argue all the time. They have five-year-old twins, Amy and Parker. Brenna's a twin herself. The other half of that is Francesca, who's married to Sam."

She paused to draw in a breath. "You really want to know all this?"

"Absolutely. Brenna and Francesca are twins. Go on."

"Okay. Francesca's a psychologist. Sam's a security expert. He has a daughter from a previous marriage—Kelly. She's a dancer and I adore her. They also have twins. Eric and Haley are seven. Then there's Katie, who's my oldest sister. She's a party planner in Los Angeles and is married to Zach. He has a son from a previous marriage, David, and they have two kids of their own. Valerie's six and Liana is three."

Rafael laughed. "Four girls. Your brother Joe was either very much in charge or tormented."

Mia wrinkled her nose. "You'd think, but Joe didn't grow up with us. It's complicated, but my mom got pregnant while still in high school and she gave up the baby. Then she and my dad got married and had us and finally realized they had to find their son. But he's a Marcelli now. He works in the winery. Darcy, his wife, is the president's daughter, which is how I was in that picture and you saw me."

"What if I hadn't?" he asked, sounding as if the thought distressed him. "I could have missed finding you."

There was an intensity that both drew her in and made her uncomfortable. In truth, she liked being with Rafael more than she should. But Grandma Tessa was right—what did she really know about the man? Still, there was enough of Diego in him to weaken her defenses. She couldn't be with him and not remember how much she had once loved him. Or at least the man he had pretended to be. Strong, intelligent, difficult.

"Where are your parents?" he asked. "Still alive?"

"Very much so. They've just left for China. It's a special trip for them and I hate to call them back. I'm sure you'll meet them, though."

"I want to." He looked around the vineyard. "I like this place. It is quiet and peaceful."

"Not much nightlife, though."

"Do you like that sort of thing?"

"Sometimes. The past few years, I haven't had the time or the energy. Even with all the help I have, Danny keeps me busy. And I've been going to law school. I have one year left."

"A lawyer. I wouldn't have guessed that."

"The spy business turned out not to be for me."

He squeezed her hand. "Mia . . ."

"I don't want to talk about what happened, Rafael. Not yet."

"As you wish. Then we will change the subject. What would you like to know about me?"

She had a thousand questions, but at that moment, she could only think of one. "Are you married?"

He stopped and faced her. "Mia, you do not have to ask me that. I would not have joined you in your bed if I had been."

"Oh. Right. That would have been tacky, huh?"

He smiled and touched her face. "You are different, and yet so much the same. I remember the first time I saw you in the plaza. You wore a very short dress and you were laughing. That is what I remember most, the sound of your laughter."

She felt herself getting lost in his eyes. Blue, she thought hazily. How could they be blue? She remembered how dark they had been. Contacts, of course. She'd never guessed.

He moved closer. She had a fleeting thought that he was going to kiss her, which immediately inspired panic.

Getting along with Diego in bed had never been a problem. She doubted she would have a difficult transition with Rafael. But she wasn't the same impulsive young woman she'd been back then. Now she had responsibilities.

"Tell me about your family," she said as she took a step back. Her body trembled slightly as heat filled her. Why was doing the right thing always such a bitch?

"I am an only child. My mother died when I was three and my father never remarried."

"How horrible."

He shrugged. "It is the world I know. I was raised with my two cousins. Diego and Quentin."

Like Chanel and Versace, Quentin didn't need a second name. "We all love his clothes," she admitted. "I can't afford them, but I love them."

"I will be sure to let him know."

"Absolutely. And if he ever has any couture overstocks, he should feel free to send them my way."

Rafael laughed. "As you wish."

They turned back toward the house.

"You have made a good life for Danny here," he said.

"I can't take all the credit. My family has been great. My mom and the Grands helped with everything from midnight feedings to babysitting. Now he's in preschool, which he loves. In fact, he insisted I sign him up for the summer program so he wouldn't miss anything. Not that he lacked for company before. With so many cousins around his age, he's had plenty of kids to play with."

"Do you enjoy law school?"

"It's interesting. I'm looking at international corporate law. My ability with languages could really be a plus."

"That's right. You are the language expert. How many do you speak now?"

"I'm fluent in about eight and I can get by in another five or six. I don't have the time to study new languages the way I used to."

"When we met you were studying Russian. I was most impressed."

"The language was nothing. It was that damn alphabet that really did me in."

As they approached the house, Mia saw a red BMW 3 series pull up. Instantly Umberto and Oliver appeared, guns drawn and shouting at the driver to show his hands.

Mia rolled her eyes. "Those guys desperately need a hobby," she said as she hurried forward.

"Relax, guys," she yelled. "He's family."

A rush of longing filled her. Another familiar face. Why did she suddenly feel the need to surround herself with people she could trust?

Rafael instructed the men to step back. They moved away from the car but kept their guns in plain sight. The driver's door opened and David Stryker stepped out.

"It's never boring here," he said, glancing from the guns to Mia. "I'm sure there's a perfectly logical explanation."

"There is," she said as she flew into his arms and clung to him.

"Hey, you're happy to see me." He hugged her back, then stared into her face. "Everything okay?"

"Fine."

He looked from her to the bodyguards, then at Rafael. "Why don't I believe that?"

"Not a clue." Mia bent down and waved at the slender blonde sitting in the passenger seat. "Hi, Amber."

David's fiancée gave a halfhearted wave back.

"It's the guns," David murmured in Mia's ear.

"Sure. They'd put anyone off." She turned to Rafael. "Want to call off the goon squad?"

Rafael winced. "They do not like to be called that," he said in English, followed by instructions in Italian. Umberto and Oliver reluctantly complied.

Rafael waited while Mia helped the blond woman from the car, then nodded politely as they were introduced. There was something about the younger man . . . a familiarity he had with Mia that Rafael did not like.

"Complications," Mia said brightly.

"You said they were family." His gaze narrowed. "Family by blood?"

"Not exactly. David is my sister Katie's stepson. In fact, David and I are responsible for bringing Zach and Katie together."

Rafael had a feeling that David sensed his mild annoyance. The other man slipped an arm around Mia and grinned.

"We were engaged. My dad thought we were too young and vowed to break us up. Katie took the other side of the argument. It was love at first sight for the two of them."

Mia shook her head. "If love means a lot of arguing. Although the sex was hot. At least that's what she implied."

David took a big step back. "No details, Mia. We have a deal. Parental unit sex is an unacceptable topic for discussion."

"Sorry. I keep forgetting. Katie's just a sister, so I don't have the same ick factor." Mia smiled at Amber. "Are we scaring you again?"

The pretty blonde smiled. "Of course not. I love all of David's family."

Rafael would not have been willing to bet on that fact.

Mia turned to him. "Rafael, this is Amber. She and David are going to be married in a couple of months. The Grands are going crazy, wanting to plan everything. Actually, they get along great with Amber's mom, which helps a lot."

"The wedding is to be held here?" he asked.

"David thought it would be beautiful and, of course, I agree," Amber said.

Rafael wondered if her concerns ended with Mia or did Amber dislike all the Marcellis?

"The Grands made two different kinds of cake for you to sample," Mia said. "I hope you're hungry."

Before Amber could protest, Mia led her inside. David chose not to follow. Rafael turned to the younger man and held out his hand.

"I'm Crown Prince Rafael of Calandria."

David raised his eyebrows. "That's a mouthful. It also explains the guys with guns. Interesting. You know Mia?"

"I am Daniel's father."

"Since when?"

"Since the night he was conceived."

David didn't look surprised or intimidated, which annoyed Rafael.

"You've been away a long time," David said.

"I was not aware that Mia or the child lived."

"Interesting story. I'll get the details later." David's gaze was steady. "You and Mia getting back together?"

"That is the plan."

"Does she know?"

Rafael resented the implication that Mia was not delighted to be once again in his presence.

"Is it your concern?" Rafael asked.

"Only as a brother. Mia and I are still close."

"A fact that must delight your fiancée."

David stiffened. "Met Joe yet? He's a pretty tough guy." He glanced at Umberto and Oliver. "If it came down to a fight, I'd bet on Joe."

With that, David turned and walked into the house. Rafael stared after him, then reached in his pocket for his cell phone. He dialed a number by heart, then walked away from the house as the call was answered.

"My father, please."

Seconds later, the king came on the line. "Do you have the boy?"

"Not yet," he said. "The situation is more complicated than we had realized."

"But you are there."

"Yes. I've seen the child. He is mine."

"An heir. You must bring him home at once."

"I will, Father. However, buying off the family is out of the question. They are wealthy in their own right, and they are not the kind to let the boy go easily."

"That is unacceptable. The heir to Calandria must be raised here. He must understand his duties."

Rafael knew all about those duties. He'd been raised with them as ever-present ghosts.

"They are a powerful family with close ties to the president. But do not concern yourself. I have a plan."

"Which is?"

"I will marry Mia."

4

❧

*B*renna Marcelli Giovanni checked the coffee table. "Cookies, chocolate, wine, glasses. I think that's everything."

Mia had been patient while her sisters met Rafael. Then the four of them drove over to Brenna's house for an afternoon of girl talk and wine.

"Well?" she demanded. "What do you think?"

"We need more wine," Brenna said. "Definitely another bottle."

Mia threw herself on the sofa and covered her face with a pillow. "Somebody kill me now."

"Don't say that," Katie told her as she settled next to her and put an arm around her. "Why would you want to be dead just when things are getting interesting?"

"She has a point," Francesca said. "Besides, death really isn't your style. Maybe you should start streaking your hair again. That would be a statement."

"A tacky one," Brenna said, returning with another bottle of Four Sisters pinot noir. "Everyone have what they need?"

There were murmurs of assent. Brenna sank into a club chair and motioned for Francesca to open the first bottle.

Francesca did the honors, poured them each a glass and passed them around. When everyone had appreciated the aroma, the color, and the subtle blend to Brenna's satisfaction, Francesca took her seat, then turned to Mia.

"So, you slept with a prince. That's new."

Mia threw the pillow at her. "Not helpful. Aren't you the one with the degree in psychology? Shouldn't you be making the situation better?"

"That seems like a natural assumption, but in this case, not so much."

Brenna and her twin grinned at each other. Katie tugged on Mia's hair. "Don't let them get to you. They're just having a little fun. You have to admit, this isn't normal, even for you. You haven't been on a date since you found out you were pregnant with Danny. You'd told us his father had died. Suddenly he's back and he's a prince. I think a little humor is in order."

"I know, it's just that I don't know what I'm thinking or supposed to think. Or feel, or any of that. He was dead. I saw him die. Only none of it was real and now he's here and I don't know what I'm supposed to do." Mia looked at Katie. "What did you think of him?"

"He was pleasant. Not pretentious."

"Good-looking," Brenna added, "which is always a plus. I mean if you have to look at them every day, why not get one who's pretty?"

"That is shallow, even for you," Francesca told her. "He said all the right things, Mia. What we have to figure out is if he means them."

Katie looked at Mia. "How are you handling this, aside from the death wish?"

"I don't know. It's been two days and I'm in confusion mode. The whole situation doesn't seem possible, but he's here and it's happening. He's Danny's father. Whatever else happens, I have to deal with that."

"Yes, there is the whole 'sperm meets egg' that changes things forever," Brenna said. "Why don't you start at the beginning and tell us how you met him. You were pretty vague when you got back from that assignment."

Mia knew her sister was being kind. She hadn't been vague, she'd been completely devastated. Because she'd been in the field as a covert operative—a reality she still had trouble grasping—she hadn't been able to tell her family anything. In theory, that truth hadn't changed. Except according to Rafael, nothing had been as it seemed.

"My first assignment was in Calandria," Mia said, figuring that was as good a place as any to start.

"Was it a dark and stormy night?" Brenna asked.

Mia grinned. "It was raining."

"You should always pay attention to atmosphere," her sister told her.

"I will now," Mia said, then wondered what it meant that it had been sunny the morning Rafael had shown up. Of course this was California. Where she lived, sunny was the norm.

"My job was to infiltrate a group of thieves who were taking newly discovered artifacts out of the country. I was supposed to play a bored, rich, ditzy American looking for trouble."

"Were you scared?" Katie asked.

"I don't think I knew enough to be scared," she admitted. "I thought it was a pretty easy assignment. I wasn't supposed to stop anyone, just get on the inside and then report back with what I knew. I flew into Calandria with the name of a contact. He was going to introduce me to a few key people in Diego's ring and then I was to take it from there."

"Diego's the bad guy, right?" Francesca asked. "Or the bad guy in disguise?"

"Right. The real Diego had been working this job for almost a year. He's the one who found the treasures and then got the divers to start bringing them to the surface. He had a reputation for being ruthless and dangerous."

"Your kind of guy?" Katie asked gently.

"I figured I was done with bad boys," Mia told her honestly. "After the disaster with Ian, I'd pretty much sworn off relationships period."

No one said anything, which Mia appreciated. She'd had six years to deal with the guilt of inadvertently bringing a domestic terrorist in close contact with the daughter of the president of the United States. She'd told herself there was no way she could guess that boring Ian, who had gone to grad school with her at Georgetown, was also secretly working to overthrow the government. Even the Secret Service had vetted him and come up with nothing. But she kept thinking she should have known her summer boyfriend was not a nice man.

"I spent a couple of days learning my way around town and sort of checking out Diego's people. He was too well known to come into town, so I didn't meet him at first. I did make contact with a couple of the women. As planned, a local policeman recognized one of them and began to arrest her. I started a fire in a trash can, which distracted him, and ran off with the women."

Brenna's eyes widened. "You were really a spy."

"Not a very good one. I lasted all of one assignment and fell in love with the bad guy. No one offered me a promotion."

"Don't be so hard on yourself," Katie said. "You weren't ready for what they asked you to do."

Mia agreed with that assessment. She should have been given a desk job for a while or at least a few low-level courier assignments. Instead, she'd been thrown into the middle of a gang of thieves, and their leader had mesmerized her from the start.

"They took me back to their hideout," Mia said. "Apparently that was considered a bad idea, because there was a lot of screaming. They discussed killing me as a way to keep me silent, which terrified me."

Her sisters stared at her. "They almost killed you? You never said anything."

"I wasn't supposed to. I probably shouldn't be telling you this now. But before anyone could shoot me or stab me, Diego came in and told them to let me go."

She still remembered everything about that moment. They'd been speaking in Italian, assuming she wouldn't understand them. Of course she had. Italian, Spanish, French. To her they were practically the same language.

Diego had asked how Mia had met the others, and when he heard about the fire, he crossed to her.

"Why did you help them?" he asked.

His voice had given her goose bumps. Her fear had faded in the heat generated by his nearness. To this day she couldn't say why she'd fallen for him in that second, but she had. She was sure there was some chemical explanation involving pheromones and the position of the moon or something, but it had happened. Hard, hot need had swept through her until all she could think about was giving herself to him. She would have been anything to him—lover, slave, sycophant. Anything, as long as he let her exist within the sphere of his world.

"They were nice to me," she'd said instead, proud that she'd been able to form words at all. "I'm loyal to my friends."

"What do you want with us?" he'd asked.

"Nothing. I don't even know who you are."

She'd lied, of course. She knew all about him from her briefing reports. Even more important, in that moment, staring into his dark eyes and willing him to take her right there, she understood the man.

He was darkness and she should be afraid of him, but she couldn't ignore the power of her need. If necessary, she would be in the darkness with him.

"I am Diego," he said, then watched sharply as if waiting for a reaction.

"Mia," she said with a shrug. "I'd offer to shake hands, but I'm kind of tied up."

He glanced at the handcuffs and smiled. "Do you travel alone?"

"I'm pretty independent. But don't get too comfy with the idea. If I don't check in with my dad every couple of days, he goes completely insane. We're talking about notifying four-star generals. Did I mention my father went to West Point?"

Diego had smiled then. "Release her," he told the others, speaking Italian. "She amuses me. She may stay. But make sure she doesn't go out by herself. And monitor her phone calls."

"I understood him, of course," Mia said to her sisters. "I thought he was the bad guy. I thought he was the one I was supposed to watch."

"Isn't the fact that he wasn't a good thing?" Katie asked. "Doesn't that make you feel better?"

"It should," Mia admitted. "It's just . . ." She drew in a breath. "I agonized over what was happening. I knew I was falling for him and that it would affect my judgment. I got in touch with my contact and begged him to get me out of there. I said I was at risk of compromising the assignment. But they left me in play. Every day he was there and every day I tried to resist. One day I couldn't."

"Okay, that's the part I want to hear about," Brenna said with a sigh. "In detail. Speak slowly."

Mia grinned. "It was another dark and stormy night. I remember sitting outside on a porch. Nearly everyone had gone into town. It was late and there were so many shadows. Suddenly, he was there."

He hadn't said anything—he hadn't had to. They'd looked at each other and then they were kissing and touching. He'd taken her without saying a word.

"The next morning I wondered if I'd dreamed the whole thing, but when I went to breakfast, he had me sit next to him. We were together from then on."

There were so many memories. So many times when she'd tried to walk away.

"I didn't want to do the wrong thing," she admitted. "If you knew how I tried to stay strong, to remember why I was there. I knew I was breaking every rule, I knew I was going to get fired. I told myself it wasn't so bad because no one's life was on the line. But I was wrong."

Two weeks after she and Diego became lovers, a rival gang attacked.

"I knew about it in advance from my handler. I was supposed to use the confusion to bring Diego in. If he resisted, I was supposed to shoot him. I wanted to warn him. For two days I nearly told him the truth." She laughed harshly. "For all I know, he arranged the whole damn thing."

"You think it was part of the plan to get him out of there?" Francesca asked.

"Maybe. I'm not sure. I do know that when the moment came, when I tried to take him with me, he wouldn't go. When I pulled a gun on him, he told me I wouldn't be able to shoot him. He was right."

"Did you try?" Katie asked.

"I knew it was the right thing to do, but I couldn't pull the trigger."

Mia had agonized over that. During her debriefing, she'd been grilled again and again about why she hadn't shot him when she'd had the chance. Now, knowing who he really was, she wondered if he'd replaced her bullets with blanks. It sure wouldn't surprise her.

"The fighting got closer," she continued, remembering the noise of that night. The sharp sound of gunfire, the cries of those who had been injured, then the roar of her helicopter.

"I didn't want to leave him, but I had to get out. I knew that. I begged him to come with me."

He'd smiled at her then, had kissed her hard and told

her to remember him. Because he'd known she was about to "see" him die?

"He literally tossed me onto the helicopter," she said. "I don't think I would have gone otherwise. As we lifted up, two men rushed him. I screamed, but it was too late. They fired and he fell and there was so much blood."

She would remember that for the rest of her life. The sound of the helicopter, her own screams, and the bright light that showed the rapidly widening pool of blood as Diego died.

Except he hadn't died. It had all been an elaborately staged event. Like a Broadway show.

Mia shook away the past and glanced at her sisters. "I thought he was gone. I went through my debriefing, then I quit and came here."

"And someone in the government told him *you* were dead?" Katie asked.

"That's what he said. I know they're not likely to give out information on operatives, even lousy ones."

"Mia, you were put in an impossible situation," Francesca told her. "Give yourself a break."

"I understand that in my head," Mia admitted. "But in my heart, I think about everything I did wrong. That's what's so hard for me. That I fell for the wrong guy again. You'd think Ian would have cured me of that."

"*Is* he the wrong guy?" Katie asked. "He's not the enemy anymore. He's a nice guy."

Brenna raised her eyebrows. "Nice? I don't think he's normal enough to be nice. He's royal, Katie. Does the man even know how to put toothpaste on his toothbrush?"

"He's doing it now," Mia said. "Unless Grammy M is sneaking into his bathroom every night to take care of that. When he was Diego, he had to act like everyone else. I know he's a prince and all, but he knows how to exist in the real world. At least he did."

"So *now* what?" Francesca asked.

"That would be my question," Mia said. "I'm trying to reconcile who he is with who he was and figure out where Danny fits in all this."

Brenna raised her glass. "I'll give you this—none of the Marcelli women are boring."

"Something we can cling to," Katie said. "I'm not sure that helps Mia, though."

Mia drank more wine. "I might be beyond help. Right now I'm dealing with crazy situations. Rafael is Danny's father. I can't change that, even if I wanted to, and I'm not sure I do. He's interested in his son, which is a plus, but what do I know about him?"

"You were once in love with him," Katie said. "Does that count for anything?"

Mia tried to laugh, but instead made a sound suspiciously close to a sob. "Not when you consider that the man I fell in love with was supposedly a notorious thief with a reputation for killing the competition."

"Maybe you sensed his goodness," Francesca said.

"I'm not that intuitive," Mia muttered.

"Are you attracted to him now?" Katie asked.

Brenna rolled her eyes. "Well, duh. Of course she is. Did you see the man? Did you think about him being naked?"

"Of course not! I'm a happily married woman." Katie sipped her wine. "I would never do that."

Mia looked at her, as did Brenna and Francesca. Katie sighed.

"Okay. Maybe. For a second. Yes, he's pretty amazing in the studly department, but that's no excuse to give in a second time."

"Ah, isn't knowing how good the sex was and could be again going to work against her?" Brenna asked.

Katie looked at Mia, who sighed. "It doesn't help," she admitted.

"Trouble," Francesca said. "All this is trouble. But you'll get through it."

"I don't see a way not to. I'm just glad Joe is around."

"Did you call Mom and Dad?" Katie asked.

"Yesterday. They're understandably shocked, but happy. I begged them to stay in China. Rafael will still be around when they get back."

"He's staying that long?" Brenna asked.

"I don't have exact dates, but I got the impression he would be parked here for a while. Even if he heads back to Calandria, there are going to be visits back and forth."

"So you have time," Katie said. "You can consider your options. Think with both your head and your heart."

"Don't make the same mistake twice," Mia said, and meant it.

"I have something for you, Danny," Rafael said as he entered the family room.

Mia sat on the floor with the boy on her lap. They both looked at him and smiled, Danny with more excitement than his mother.

"What is it?" Danny asked as he eyed the long, cloth-wrapped package. "A truck?"

"Better than a truck. I had it sent over from the palace." Rafael knelt on the floor and peeled back the quilted fabric. When he'd exposed the gold-and-jewel-covered scepter, he paused expectantly.

Danny stared at the scepter. "What's that?"

"The royal scepter of Calandria."

Danny looked at his mother. "What's that?"

Mia cleared her throat. "Well, it's a very important and beautiful part of your heritage. It symbolizes who you are."

"I'm Danny."

"Okay, yes, but you're also your father's son. Which makes you his heir."

"I'm the Crown Prince of Calandria," Rafael said, determined to be patient with the child. It was not his fault he didn't already know this. "I will rule as king and you will rule after me."

Danny considered that, then asked, "Where's Calandria?"

Rafael had come prepared. He pulled a European map out of his pocket and spread it on the floor. "Here is Italy and France. This is Spain. This is the Mediterranean and here is Calandria."

Danny stared at the island and wrinkled his nose. "It's small. Can I be the heir to a bigger place? What about Australia? Mommy and me read all about it in a book. There are kangaroos and crocodiles. I want to heir Australia."

As he spoke he reached for the scepter and slammed it against the floor. Rafael winced.

"Okay then," Mia said, grabbing it from him. "Maybe we should put this on a shelf until you're a little older. Why don't you go see Grammy M in the kitchen? I know she's making cookies. Maybe she'll let you help."

"Okay."

Danny scrambled to his feet and ran off to the kitchen. Mia turned to Rafael. "Sorry about that. He's still pretty young. I don't think he's grasping the whole 'heir' thing, which isn't a huge surprise as the rest of us are having trouble with it as well."

"He will have to learn," he told her, remembering how many responsibilities he had had when he had been little older than Danny was now. He needed to get the boy back to Calandria, where his real education would begin.

But that journey was a few weeks away. He had best remember not to rush his plan.

"You have done well with him," he told Mia. "A woman alone with a child, especially a boy."

"Hardly alone. Once I knew I was pregnant, I moved back here. It worked out well. I had help and I'm close to the campus for my studies."

"What happens when you graduate from law school?"

"I'll get a job and move to Los Angeles. By then Danny will be in kindergarten." She paused. "Well, that *was* the plan. I guess now I'll be discussing things like that with you."

"There is plenty of time for that," he said. In truth she would most likely still get a job in Los Angeles. The only difference was that her son would be in Calandria.

But that conversation was for much later. First he had to convince Mia to trust him . . . and seduce her into wanting him again.

He looked forward to both activities, especially the latter. He still found her most appealing, although he'd never been able to say exactly why. She was attractive, but great beauties populated his world. She was more intelligent than most women of his acquaintance, not that he set a great store by a woman's mind.

No, it was something else. He remembered the feel of her skin and how that had aroused him. Her scent, even when she was fresh from the shower, had lingered in his mind long after she had disappeared from his life. He had been with a great many women and most of those encounters blurred. Oddly, he remembered nearly everything about making love with Mia, and that remembering made him want to be with her again.

If she were someone else, someone with even minor titled connections or the daughter of a great leader, he would consider making their marriage a permanent connection. But she wasn't, and when it came to whom he would have more children with, he had to consider his obligation to the throne. Still, they were together for now and he planned to enjoy every minute of it.

He reached for her hand and rubbed his thumb against her knuckles. "You have been most patient and understanding."

She smiled. "Not much choice there. You're Danny's father. The prince thing is a bit of a shock, although it doesn't come close to the one about you not being dead."

He shifted closer and let his gaze drop to her mouth. "Are you glad I'm not dead?"

"Of course."

"I can say the same about you. I was most distressed when they told me you were gone. And later, when I thought you'd been killed . . ." He hesitated just enough to give the words a sincere ring. "Mia . . . I had just found you."

"*Found* is strong," she murmured. "I was sort of thrust upon you by the agency. I was there to do a job."

"As was I. Instead we found each other."

He spoke easily, mostly because it was all true. He had been delighted to find her. He'd known about the American operative and knew the wisdom of beginning an affair with her as a means to ending his time as Diego. He would have seduced her regardless, but with Mia what could have been effort had turned into true pleasure. For both of them.

He had even missed her when he'd returned to his life at the palace. Perhaps not as much as he indicated, but more than he usually did. Under other circumstances, he would tell her that and know she would be grateful.

"Let us not be parted again," he whispered.

Her eyes widened. "Rafael, I—"

He touched her mouth with his finger. "Shh. I think we are done talking." Then he lowered his head so that he could kiss her.

A heartbeat before he finally claimed her with his mouth, he heard footsteps in the hallway and a familiar and irritating voice saying, "I sure have a habit of showing up at the wrong time, don't I?"

"Do I need to lecture you?" Joe asked when Rafael had excused himself and Mia had scrambled onto the sofa.

She leaned back against the cushions and sighed. "Maybe. I know it's crazy to get involved with him and I can't tell you how grateful I am that you appeared when you did."

"But?" he prodded.

"But knowing I shouldn't get lost in the past and *not* getting lost in the past are two very different things. He knows how to push all my buttons."

"Don't take it personally. He's a professional playboy

by career and temperament, Mia. He's had plenty of practice."

Not exactly what she wanted to hear. Still, the information needed to sink into her brain. "Keep telling me he's the enemy," she said. "Apparently I need help not making a fool out of myself."

There was something about Rafael. His physical appearance might be different enough to make her nervous, but the chemical attraction between them didn't seem to care about things like scars and a change in eye color.

Joe slapped down a folder on the coffee table. "The preliminary report on Rafael."

She eyed the pages inside. "And?"

"He's who he said. Heir to the Calandrian throne. Not married. Not even a fiancée waiting in the wings. There have been rumors of various arranged marriages, but nothing seems to happen with them."

"Good to know." What with the almost kissing.

"He was educated in Europe. Graduated from Oxford. No career, of course, if you don't count the whole soon-to-be king gig. He partied hard when he was in his early twenties—nothing too kinky. He's a thrill seeker, but that's calmed down, too. No dead bodies, no bastard children."

Mia shook her head. "Oh, there's at least one we know of."

"Okay, but aside from Danny, he's clean. Which means Danny's the real heir."

"What if he marries and has legitimate children?" She shook her head. "I can't believe I'm actually discussing this. Legitimate children. Like we're in Elizabethan times."

"There's nothing like dealing with a royal family to bring up the past," Joe told her. "Per Calandria law, it's the acknowledged firstborn son of the crown prince/king. Whoever he is at the time. So if Rafael doesn't marry you or he doesn't officially acknowledge Danny, then there will be no Marcelli rule of Calandria."

"Gee, and we were all so anxious to expand our winery business. What's involved in officially acknowledging?"

"Paperwork mostly, and a presentation to the parliament. He's taken the DNA test, Mia. My guess is he's going to acknowledge Danny as his heir."

"Swell."

"Look on the bright side. If Danny's a prince, you have to be something too, right?"

"Screwed. I believe I'm mostly screwed."

"It's not as bad as that."

She leaned forward. "In all likelihood my son is going to one day rule Calandria. How long do you think he's going to be allowed to have a normal life?"

"Whatever happens, you're his mom. You'll be there to protect him."

"I know, but king. Jeez. I better get going on teaching him to tie his shoes."

5

❧

"What kind of a surprise?" Danny asked. "A big surprise? Is it a puppy? I'd like a puppy, Mommy. I'm big enough now."

Maybe he was, but she wasn't, Mia thought wryly, knowing that dealing with a puppy was exactly enough to push her over the edge.

"We talked about a puppy," she reminded him. "It will come under consideration when you're eight."

Danny sighed. "I know. But that's so far."

Twice his life. He was already growing so fast. He would be eight before she knew it.

"What surprise?" he asked again.

"I don't know," she told him. Rafael hadn't been clear. He'd only asked them to meet him at three-thirty and said there would be a surprise.

She knew he'd gone out. The huge limo was gone, as were the ever-present Oliver and Umberto. What a life— trailing after a crown prince, watching him have all the fun. Or did royal bodyguards have groupies who made things more interesting?

Just then the limo turned the corner. Danny squealed

and pointed. "I can see the flags, Mommy. Can we have flags on our car?"

She had a feeling that diplomatic flags were hard to come by but might be worth the effort, especially during tourist season in Santa Barbara when parking was impossible to find. No doubt with diplomatic immunity came freedom from parking tickets.

The vehicle pulled to a stop. Umberto climbed out of the front passenger seat and walked to the rear door. When he opened it, Rafael stepped out.

"How nice to see my family waiting," he said with a smile. "My very handsome son and his beautiful mother."

Mia reminded herself that it was his job to be smooth on command, but still, she liked the compliment and the way his gaze lingered on her.

"What did you bring me?" Danny demanded.

Mia winced. "How about some manners? You could say hello first."

"Hello. What did you bring me?"

Rafael walked to the trunk of the limo and opened it. Inside was a fully assembled three-wheeled bike with a horn and flags that matched those on the limo.

"Maybe they aren't so hard to get," Mia murmured, wondering if she could borrow them for her car when she went into town.

"Cool!" Danny cried as he raced to the bike. "Can I try it now?"

Mia cleared her throat. "Hmm, what do we say when someone gives us a gift?"

Danny wrenched his gaze from the bike and looked at his father. "Thank you very much." He turned back to his mother. "Now?"

She nodded.

Danny sat down and immediately started pedaling. The wide tires gave him plenty of traction on the driveway.

Rafael moved next to her. "I considered a real bike, but I knew he would have to learn to ride it. I wanted this to be fun for him."

"Making up for the scepter?"

He smiled. "You were right. He was a little young to grasp the significance."

"I'm not sure it's an age thing. *I'm* not clear on the significance. What does it do?"

"It is a symbol of the throne."

"You'd probably do better with an action figure."

"For Danny or for you?"

"Danny. I've outgrown action figures."

"And moved up to the real thing? Or do you prefer more adult toys?"

Tempting, she thought. Very tempting. But an intelligent woman wouldn't be sucked into the vortex of charm that was Rafael.

"Any other surprises for him in that trunk?" she asked.

His gaze sharpened, as if he acknowledged her attempt to change the subject and decided to let her. "No. I assume anything else will seem tame by comparison."

"He'll enjoy spending time with you. He's very excited to finally have a father."

"I am excited to know he is my son."

"You don't know that for sure. The DNA tests aren't in."

He stared into her eyes. "*You* are sure, Mia, and that is enough for me."

"Yes, well, I wasn't exactly sleeping around when me met. Or after. But you'll have proof soon enough."

He shrugged as if to say it didn't matter. "I wish I'd known sooner. I wish I could have been here with you."

"That would have been nice," she admitted. "I love Danny with all my heart, but I'm not all that maternal. Developing those instincts was difficult for me. If not for my family around me, I don't think I would have made it."

"Of course you would have. You are steel." He lightly stroked her cheek. "And silk. So many contradictions. I always liked that about you. How tough you were and yet so feminine. An ideal woman."

She took a step back. "Ideal is so not me. I'm totally filled with flaws. Flaw girl, that's me."

He chuckled. "I do not think so."

"Then you'd be wrong. And speaking of dinner, you do remember there's a whole big family thing tomorrow night. You've met my sisters. Now it's time to meet the husbands and kids. Brenna might even bring her dog, Max. You need to brace yourself."

"I have survived formal state dinners. I'm sure I'll survive your family."

"Ha. Formal state dinners have nothing on the Marcellis. You're gonna be scared. Trust me."

The next evening Rafael followed the sound of conversation from the stairs into the large formal living room in the Marcelli home. As Mia had promised, most of the family had assembled to meet him.

Although he'd dressed in a suit, he wasn't worried about making a good impression. He was, after all, Crown Prince Rafael of Calandria. How could they not approve of him?

He stood in the doorway, as yet unnoticed. He recognized Mia's three sisters and assumed the men standing near them were their husbands. Several young children ran around, including Danny. Rafael frowned. The boy should not be allowed to be so boisterous at events like these. He had to learn to understand protocol and respect ceremony.

The Grands were by the plates of appetizers, making sure all was well with the food. Grammy M saw him and waved. Grandma Tessa saw him and quickly turned her back. He still had not charmed the matriarch of the Marcelli clan, but he would. He had yet to meet a woman he could not win.

"Rafael," Mia said as she hurried toward him. "Are you braced?"

"More than that. I'm delighted to finally be meeting the rest of your family."

"Not the rest, actually. My parents are still in China, which you knew. Also Kelly isn't here. She lives in San Francisco. I left her a message, but I haven't heard back."

He didn't pay attention to her words; instead he concentrated on the woman speaking them. As always, Mia was pure energy. Life radiated from her eyes, her smile, the movement of her body. She was small, barely five three, and he was a man used to dating models. She had curves to their lean lines. Her face was pretty, and he often chose women for their classical beauty. Yet there was something about her, something that drew him. In a room full of strangers, she was the only person who mattered.

"You look especially lovely tonight," he murmured. "That color suits you."

She stopped in midsentence to brush the front of her green sleeveless dress. "Oh. Thanks. It's, um, not new or anything." She cleared her throat. "Okay, back to the family. Let's get you introduced." She took his hand and faced her family. "Hey, everyone. This is Rafael."

The room quieted and he found himself the center of attention. Danny raced toward him.

"He's my daddy and I'm the heir." Danny turned to one of his cousins. "That means I'm going to be a prince and you have to do what I say."

"Do not!" the older girl said as she stomped her foot. "Mo-om, I do not have to do what Danny says, do I?"

"No, Haley, you don't," Mia told her niece. "Danny, you're not in charge, okay?"

Rafael started to correct her. Daniel was in fact in charge. At least of the other children. The sooner he learned his importance, the better. But perhaps this wasn't the time.

"Everybody, pair up," Mia said. "Grab your kids and we'll go down the line. I think that will be easier."

"We should have name tags," Grammy M said. "Would you like that, Rafael?"

"I don't believe it's necessary, but it's very thoughtful of you to suggest it," he told the older woman.

Grandma Tessa shook her head. "I'm sure his shoes need polishing, Mary. Or you might want to ask how he's fixed for socks."

Grammy M ignored her. "Go ahead, Mia. Introduce the family to Rafael."

Mia worked her way through the names. Rafael had already met Mia's sisters. Now he had the chance to meet their husbands and children. Joe's wife, Darcy, greeted him enthusiastically.

"I'm so happy to have someone around more famous than me," she said with a laugh. "Now the press can follow you and make snide comments about *your* clothing choices."

"Does that happen often?" he asked politely.

"Joe keeps them off the property, but sometimes they tail me in town." She sighed. "I can't wait for my father's second term to be over. Once he's no longer president, no one will be interested in me."

"I'll still be interested," Joe told her.

Darcy smiled at him. Rafael watched the exchange and was surprised to realize the former SEAL was completely in love with his wife. He wouldn't have thought such a dark man would allow himself softer emotions.

"You've met Amber and David," Mia said, guiding him to the next group of people. "Amber and David are engaged. David is Zach's son and Zach is married to Katie, my oldest sister."

Katie winced. "I'm over thirty. You've got to stop introducing me as the oldest."

"How about the sexiest?" Zach asked. "Would that work?"

"Absolutely." Katie put her hands on the shoulders of two children. "These are my twins. Eric and Haley. They're seven."

Rafael nodded at the children and noted that Haley had been the one to protest Daniel's authority over her. He had a feeling she would grow up to be a most stubborn woman.

"That's everyone here," Mia said. "Are we ready to go in to eat?"

Grandma Tessa led the way. The large table in the

dining room had been set for the adults, while a smaller table by the window was for the children.

"There are so many kids now, we don't all fit," Mia told him. "It actually works out. We hire a sitter to keep the kids occupied. This way everyone has a good time. Of course on holidays, everyone manages to fit around the main table and it's complete chaos. But in a good way."

She handled herself effortlessly, with a natural grace he appreciated. He knew from past experience she could think on her feet. Once again he had the thought that under other circumstances, she would make a good match for him. At least their son would have had the opportunity to inherit her intelligence and style.

"You're over here, Rafael," Grammy M said. "Mia, you're next to him. Amber and David, right here."

Rafael glanced up and saw David's fiancée watching Mia. Amber noticed his observation and quickly looked away.

A few minutes later, everyone had been seated. Open bottles of Marcelli wine were passed around, and when the glasses were full, Joe stood.

"Before we begin our dinner, I would like to propose a toast to those who are no longer with us. To my grandfather, who is still missed every day."

"Grandpa Lorenzo died about five years ago," Mia whispered. "He was such a great man. Difficult and gruff, yet so loving. I wish Danny could have known him."

Before Rafael could say anything, Joe continued. "And to Gabriel Reese. You were a blessing to this family."

Mia raised her glass as she whispered, "That's Sam's grandfather. He and Grammy M fell in love. He died a couple of years ago. It's been hard on the Grands, but at least they have each other to grow old with. Like I'll have my sisters."

"Your sisters are married."

Mia shrugged. "Marcelli women live a really, really long time. We've already talked about it. When the men are dead, we're getting a house together by the vineyard. It will be great."

"I'm sure their husbands are delighted to know how you anticipate their demise."

She grinned. "They're used to it."

The toasts concluded with everyone drinking. Then the plates of food arrived, and Rafael was overwhelmed by delicious choices.

Katie leaned across the table and smiled at him. "This must all seem very different to you."

"I'm enjoying my time here. I am beginning to see where Mia inherited her charm."

Katie looked at her sister. "She wasn't always charming."

"That's true," Brenna added. "She was kinda bratty."

Mia hung her head. "Please, no. I beg you. Not the stories about what I was like when I was young."

"I would like to hear those stories," he told Katie.

"I'll just bet," Mia muttered. "I was very intelligent and precocious. I knew five different languages by the time I was eighteen."

"She was a good girl," Grandma Tessa said. "Very bright. She got all A's."

Rafael caught Amber rolling her eyes.

"But her fashion sense," Francesca said with a grin. "The constant streaking in her hair."

"It wasn't subtle," Brenna told him. "We're talking big chunks of bright blond. And the eye shadow. Katie was forever after her to blend, blend."

"I was finding myself," Mia said primly.

"I don't think so," Joe added. "You knew exactly what you were doing. Making trouble."

"Engaged at eighteen," Grammy M said. "That was exciting."

"Maybe we could avoid that story." David shrugged. "I don't do so well in that one."

"I'd like to hear all about that," Amber said. "David's never told me what really happened."

There was a moment of uncomfortable silence, followed by all the Marcelli sisters speaking at once. Rafael glanced from Mia to David and wondered what had caused the young couple to break their engagement. Even as he reminded himself that Mia's past had no value, save that with him, he was still curious.

Just then the dining room door opened and a tall, slender woman staggered inside.

"Am I late?" she asked as she leaned heavily against the door frame.

She was casually dressed, with long, curly red hair and pale skin that only emphasized the shadows under her eyes.

Francesca stood. "Kelly? What's wrong?"

"Wrong? Nothing. I'm here. Hooray." She took a step and almost lost her balance. An even taller, thinner man appeared behind her. He grabbed her around the waist and kept her on her feet.

"Hello," the man said, his voice faintly accented.

French, Rafael thought. Working class.

Francesca's husband stood. "Kelly, what the hell is going on?"

"I'm here for the party." Kelly looked at Rafael. "So you're the new guy. Cool. Mia, he's really, really cute. Is he rich, because rich is always such a plus."

"You're drunk," Francesca said, sounding stunned. "Kelly, tell me you're not drunk."

"I'm not drunk." Kelly took a step and found herself contained by the man's arm. "Oh, yeah. This is Etienne. We're lovers. But he's not rich. He's just a dancer, like me."

She turned in a slow, graceful move, then sank to the floor and passed out.

The dinner broke up early. Mia got Danny down for the night and then went looking for Rafael. She found him outside, leaning against the fence by the vegetable garden. Umberto and Oliver weren't around, but she saw lights in the guest house and figured they'd settled in for the night.

She paused at the bottom of the steps and stared at the large silhouette of the man who had once been her lover. She couldn't see his face, only the rough outline of his body, but it was enough to help her remember what she had felt when they had been together.

Between mourning his death, finding out she was pregnant, then dealing with a baby and law school, she hadn't been in a relationship since she'd been with him. For the past couple of years she'd wondered if that part of her was dead. But now, in the darkness, her body stirred back to life. Wanting filled her and she ached to feel his touch on her skin.

But it was more than that. She wanted to talk as well as

touch. They had different worldviews and had frequently argued. He'd never been intimidated by her intelligence.

He turned and saw her. "Mia."

There was pleasure in his voice, as if she were the one person he'd been waiting for.

"Daniel is asleep?" he asked.

"In theory. I read him two stories and then turned out the lights. After all the excitement at dinner, it may take him a while to zonk out."

"Ah, yes. The unexpected arrival. Very dramatic."

She moved toward him and stopped next to the fence. "I don't understand what's happening with Kelly. She's always been so together and mature. I'm not horrified that she drinks—she's on her own and most of her friends in the ballet company are a few years older—but that she would show up here drunk. She had to know everyone would be here."

"Perhaps she wasn't prepared to face the entire family. Responsibility can be daunting."

Mia rested her forearms on the fence railing. "Kelly's been a part of the family since she was a kid. No one scares her. She loves being here. She would come and spend long weekends here several times a year. I've never seen her like that. I wonder if it's the guy."

"Etienne?"

"Yeah. He's new."

"Would you like me to have Umberto, how do you say, check him out?"

She smiled. "That's really nice, but Joe's already on it. No one messes with his family." She thought about Kelly's boyfriend and shuddered. "He's too old, too dirty, too yuck. What does she see in him?"

"Few can see into the secrets of a woman's heart," he told her.

Kelly a woman? Was it possible? Mia still remembered her as the mouthy twelve-year-old who had been determined not to let everyone know how much she was hurting inside. Still, she was twenty and making her own way in the world.

"Sometimes I forget how complicated our family is," she said. "It's not usually this crazy."

"I suspect it is; however, that is part of the charm."

She laughed. "We're many things, but I'm not sure *charming* describes us."

"You are wrong. I am enchanted by the Grands, as you call them."

"Even Grandma Tessa?"

"Especially her." He smiled. "I like that she wants me to earn her respect. I prefer my women difficult. There is much love and concern, each of you for the other."

"That's true. We're excellent at meddling. I guess it's not like that in royal circles."

"No. My parents had an arranged marriage. My mother died when I was young and I do not remember much about her."

"Rafael." She touched his arm. "I know that was hard. I feel bad that I don't know that much about your life."

"You are not one to read gossip magazines, where my entire life has been detailed. I grew up prepared to one day rule Calandria. There are many responsibilities both then and now."

"Even when you were three?"

"Of course. I had to learn about my country's history,

the people. I had nannies and tutors. When I was eight, I was sent to England to begin my education."

Just like that. Sent away from all that was familiar. "Sounds barbaric."

He shrugged. "It was necessary."

"Because you can't get an education at home?"

"Because that is how things are done." He touched her chin, raising her head so that she looked at him. "You are too softhearted."

"Gee, no one's ever accused me of that before."

In the night, his eyes were dark, as she remembered them. Here in the shadows, the blurring of Diego into Rafael was more pronounced. The past seemed closer somehow.

"So now you're duty guy?" she asked, her voice low. "All for the crown and the people?"

"Something like that."

"Any arranged marriages in your future?"

"No."

"But you will be marrying a princess or duchess or some other kind of 'ess' woman."

"It is expected."

She really had to go check out those gossip magazines and learn a little bit more about Rafael, she thought, as he seemed to move closer.

"Since when do you do what is expected?" she asked.

"On occasion it has occurred."

"But an arranged marriage. What if you don't like her?"

"Then I will say no."

"You can do that?"

"Arranged is different from forced. I accept suggestions but the final choice is mine."

"And hers."

"Yes. Hers as well." He sighed. "Did you always talk this much? I remember more silence."

"Then you remember wrong. I've always—"

He cut her off with a kiss.

The moment his lips brushed hers, she felt her entire body begin to melt. He had been the last man to kiss her, to touch her, to make love with her. She had mourned him, knowing she would never want to give her heart again. Not when having it broken had nearly destroyed her.

Yet here he was, so familiar. In the darkness she could pretend he was Diego once again.

As he pulled her close, she went willingly, finding comfort and need in the familiar strength of his body. His scent aroused her nearly as much as the pressure of his mouth claiming hers.

He still kissed with a combination of imperiousness and passion that left her breathless. The light touch of his tongue on her lower lip had her parting instantly. Wanting had her clinging to him, desperate for more.

He plunged inside her mouth and claimed her. Waves of passion nearly brought her to her knees as she felt the familiar desire and tasted the man she remembered.

His hands were everywhere—down her back, on her arms, at her waist. She couldn't get close enough. She wanted to crawl inside of him and let the old emotional wounds of missing him finally heal.

"Mia," he breathed as he kissed her cheeks, her jaw, her neck. "How I have missed you."

It was too much. The need combined with that voice. The voice that had haunted her dreams for nearly five years.

Diego, she thought. Only not Diego. Rafael.

He raised his head. "So the fire still lives between us," he murmured. "Tell me you can feel it."

She drew in a slow breath. "You know I can."

He dropped his hand to the small of her back and drew her against him. Her belly brushed against his erection.

"This is what you do to me, what you have always done." He cupped her face and stared into her eyes. "My father has been parading all sorts of appropriate young women in front of me for years. Marry this one or the next one, he tells me. But I refuse. I know my duty to my people and yet I can't deny the hunger of my heart. I need more than an arranged marriage. From that comes only children. My father says to take a mistress along with my wife. But that is not for me."

He smiled. "Have you missed me?" he asked quietly.

"Every now and then."

"You tease me."

"A little. I was devastated when I thought you were dead. I didn't think I'd make it. Finding out I was pregnant saved me."

"I only had the memories of our love," he told her. "You did love me, didn't you? You said you did."

"More than I should have."

He kissed her. "So much lost. So much time wasted."

She felt as if she'd had too much wine, except she'd only had the one glass at dinner. Still, her head was spinning and she couldn't seem to think straight.

"What are you saying?" she asked.

"That we have been given a second chance, Mia. I have found you again. We have a son. Daniel will one day be king of Calandria. But to see him grow up as I did—

it cannot be. You would change that. You are strong enough to stand against tradition."

She took a step back. "Danny's not going to grow up like you."

"I know. You will not let him. We will not let him."

Sure, he was Danny's father, but Mia had trouble thinking of Rafael and her as a "we."

"It is you. It has always been you," he told her. He kissed her again, then took her hands in his. "Marry me, Mia. Marry me and be my princess."

An earthquake would have made sense. Hey, this was California and the earth moved all the time. Locusts might have even been okay because they were in the Bible and she had seen one once in a museum. But a proposal of marriage from Prince Rafael of Calandria? Not in this reality.

"You're crazy," she said as she jerked her hands free of his. "Marry you? I don't know you and you sure as hell don't know me. Rafael, it's been three days."

He laughed. "I know how many hours and minutes. Would you like to hear? I thought you were lost to me and now you are found. I cannot let you go."

He captured her hands again and kissed her knuckles. It was a pretty smooth move, but then he'd had prince lessons. What other guy stood a chance?

"Don't say no. Give me time to prove myself. We have another chance, Mia. How many people can say that? I don't want to lose you again."

She didn't know what to say. Marriage? Sure, he was the father of her child, but she'd been thinking along the lines of Danny's spending a couple of weeks each summer in Calandria.

"I have a life," she said. "School. Family."

Instead of responding, he stared into her eyes. She felt his presence as tangibly as if he'd thrown a blanket across her shoulders. There was warmth and protection. And the ever-present need.

She *had* loved him once, she reminded herself. Or at least the man he'd pretended to be. How much had been about playing Diego and how much had been real?

"Don't say no," he murmured. "Give us time. Is that too much to ask?"

It was crazy. Foolish. Impetuous.

It was irresistible.

"I won't say no, at least not right now," she told him. "But I don't want you to mention this to anyone."

"Of course not." He pulled her close and kissed the top of her head. "I will win you back, Mia. You will see. I will be all you have ever desired."

With anyone else, she would have had her doubts. But Rafael was a different kind of man. In this case, she wasn't sure she would be willing to bet against him.

6

❧

Mia was up early the next morning. The Grands hadn't even stirred, which meant it was her job to get the coffee going. After pouring in grounds and water, she flipped the switch, then checked out the plastic-covered cookie sheets sitting in the refrigerator.

"Cinnamon rolls," she moaned as she hurried to the oven and dialed in the correct temperature. Caffeine and sugar. Was there any better antidote for a sleepless night?

She hovered by the coffeemaker until the hot liquid began to pour into the carafe. When there was enough to fill her mug, she pulled it out and claimed it for herself.

The first sip tasted heavenly. As the warmth slid down her throat and settled in her belly, she felt the first stirring of consciousness. Unfortunately with that came too—clear memories of the previous evening.

Had Rafael really proposed? She told herself he couldn't have, then took another drink of coffee and realized he had.

Marriage? She wasn't sure she wanted to get married. Besides, they barely knew each other, and while she had many really fabulous qualities, she doubted she would make much of a princess. She could barely find Calandria on a map.

Marriage? No way. She and Rafael were intelligent adults. They could find a way to share their son without resorting to what would only turn out to be a disaster.

"Good morning."

She looked up and saw the man in question standing in the doorway. His hair was damp from his shower, his body casually clad in jeans and a long-sleeved shirt, and his mouth . . .

Suddenly she couldn't stop looking at his mouth. Because whatever was the same or different about him, his mouth and his voice were exactly as she remembered.

Then, without meaning to, she suddenly recalled another kind of kiss from him. An intimate one that had her screaming out her release as he licked and—

"Morning," she managed through suddenly dry lips. She took a gulp of coffee and motioned to the nearly full carafe. "Help yourself."

"Thank you."

He poured himself a mug and took a drink. "Did you sleep well?"

"Not really."

"Anything in particular keeping you up?"

"An unnatural concern about interest rates and the latest drought in Africa."

"Really? I had no idea you were so concerned about current events."

"Sarcasm, Rafael. That was sarcasm."

He smiled slightly. "Yes, I know." He took another drink. "I did not mean to distress you with my proposal."

"*Distress* really doesn't cover it. I was confused—a pretty continuous state of affairs since you showed up in my bed." She frowned. "You could have just knocked on the front door."

"Perhaps, but far less interesting an entrance. Besides, I have not missed being at your front door."

Good one, she thought. The implication being he missed her bed. Or, one dared to assume, her in his bed.

"I, too, did not sleep well. You kept me up, Mia. I could not stop thinking about you."

"Yes, well, how interesting." She moved to the far side of the kitchen just as the oven beeped. Damn. Now he stood between her and cinnamon rolls.

He glanced at the appliance. "Are you baking?"

"Grammy M made cinnamon rolls last night. They need to go in the oven. They're in there."

She jerked her head toward the refrigerator. He crossed the room and removed them, then slid them into the oven.

"Better?" he asked.

"I will be in about twenty minutes." She glanced from him to the oven. "You know your way around the kitchen."

He grinned. "Yes, even I, Prince Rafael of Calandria, can find an oven in a kitchen. If you promise to show the proper amount of awe, I'll cut up some fruit later."

"You're making fun of me."

"I tease a little. I might live in a palace, but I do know how to exist in the real world."

"Unlikely."

"Why do you doubt me? I was on my own all through university. When I pretended to be Diego, I took care of myself."

"Barely. You had an entire harem of women. I distinctly remember being stunned by the number of otherwise intelligent women so eager to do the smallest thing for you."

He moved closer. "You are correct, but the leader of the pack always has his choice of the females. Diego was no exception. But you were not so willing to be my slave. You insisted I serve you."

"I have a very high IQ," she said primly. Mostly she'd refused to trail around after him in an effort to stand out. It had worked, although not in the way she'd imagined.

"One of them noticed I had my eye on you," he said. "She came after you."

"With a knife." Mia still remembered her fear and outrage when a tall blonde from northern Italy had called her some very disgusting names and ordered her to leave. Mia hadn't noticed the knife until she'd already told off the other woman.

"Do you still have a scar?" he asked as he placed his hand on her side.

The warmth of his fingers made it difficult to think, but she managed to nod. "It's pretty faint but still there."

"The cut was not deep, but there was much blood. You were very brave."

She'd been stunned by the swift attack. Rafael—a.k.a. Diego—had reacted with fury. The other woman had been sent away and told she would be killed if she returned. He had then taken Mia to his private rooms and had carefully stitched the cut. That night, he'd claimed her as his own. She still remembered how gentle he'd been, how careful so that she wouldn't feel any pain from her wound.

She'd already been half in love with him. His tenderness had pushed her over the edge. Afterward she'd been unable to sleep as she'd wrestled with the moral dilemma of her situation. She'd fallen in love with the enemy—a classic, almost clichéd, mistake.

As soon as she'd been able to get away, she'd contacted the agent in charge and explained that she was afraid of compromising the mission. She'd asked to be removed. Instead her boss had told her to suck it up and stay in play.

"There were no other women after you, Mia. Do you remember?"

His words made her more uncomfortable than the memories of her horror at being torn between her mission and the man she loved.

"I remember," she said softly, not wanting to let him get to her. Not again. Not until she was sure. Which might be never.

But he was telling the truth. From the second the two of them had become lovers, he hadn't looked at another woman. How long had it taken him to get over her?

He moved to the table and took a seat across from her. "My guilty secret," he said with a shrug. "I made you promise not to tell."

"I never knew why it was such a big deal. So you don't cheat. Most women consider that a good thing."

"My father has kept mistresses all his life. Usually two or three at a time. They know about each other and on the surface all is well. I was never comfortable with that. I could see the pain in their eyes."

He looked away, as if embarrassed by the turn in the conversation. That surprised her, and in a good way. She liked knowing that the imperious crown prince had a weakness or two. Twenty would be better but she would take what she could get.

"Tell me about life in the palace," she said, taking pity on him and changing the subject.

"It is not so different from your world," he said.

She laughed. "Oh, please. Royalty. It has to be different. Do you have your own wing or county or something?"

"I live elsewhere, in a private house on the edge of the sea. I am close enough to be reached quickly if there is an emergency, but I do not still live at home."

"I wouldn't have thought living in the palace would count as living at home."

"I learned very quickly that it was difficult to take girls to my room when we had to tiptoe past my father's quarters. At twenty, such things mattered to me."

"They would matter at any age. Okay, so you get up and one of your several harem women prepares you for your shower."

"I am sorry to disappoint you, but I do not have harem women."

"Not a good crop this year?"

"I get myself ready in the morning."

"What? No servants?"

"A handful. They prepare my breakfast and take care of my clothes."

"Nice work if you can get it. Then what?"

"Then I drive to the palace for my morning meetings with my father and officials from our government."

"Do Umberto and Oliver tag along?"

"I have bodyguards in a car following me."

This was one of the strangest conversations Mia could remember having. To her, none of what Rafael talked about was real, yet every bit of it was his life.

"So what happens after a hard morning of governing the little people?"

"You mock me."

"It's something I'm really good at. The reverence thing has always been a problem. Fortunately I don't run into many people deserving of that kind of attitude."

He sighed. "You are going to be difficult, but I expected as much."

"Really?" The thought pleased her.

"Of course. You forget, I know you. You are too smart for your own good and intimidated by no one. A dangerous combination."

"Ooh, let me guess. For a woman."

"For anyone. And to answer your question, which you have probably already forgotten, I lunch with different heads of state or visiting dignitaries. Sometimes I meet with officials in parliament. I spend my afternoons with charity work—I deal with three international organizations—or events in the city. Once a week or so there is an official dinner or fund-raiser of some kind."

"Sounds boring," she said. "What do you do for fun?"

"Polo, sailing, skiing, mountain climbing. I keep busy."

Her idea of excitement was a twilight stroll around the vineyards, followed by an extra glass of wine with dinner. They were practically twins separated at birth.

"I am in the unique position of training for a job that I may not have for years," he said. "I do not wish my father to die, yet this is the expected way of succession."

"Would he abdicate?"

"We have talked about it. He does not want me to wait indefinitely."

"So you would be king sooner rather than later?"

He nodded.

She didn't like the sound of that. Not with a proposal still hanging between them. Bad enough to be a lousy princess, but it was so much worse to be a horrible queen.

"You would do well," he said, reading her mind.

"I have many, many doubts. I could put them into categories and have them spiral bound for you, if you'd like."

"Calandria is a small country. Your duties—"

She cut him off with a strangled cough. "See, that's the thing. Any sentence that begins with the words *your duties* isn't for me. I'm not the duty type."

"There would be compensations."

She wasn't sure if he was going to talk about the wealth and relative power or the thrill of being married to him. Right now she didn't want to think about either.

"What about Danny?" she asked. "What would his life be like?"

"He would have tutors."

"Now?"

"Of course. There's much he has to learn."

That didn't sound good. She remembered what Rafael had told her about his years growing up.

"Just so we're clear," she said flatly, "he's not being sent away to some European boarding school. He can go to a regular school with other Calandrian children."

Rafael stiffened as if she'd slapped him. "My son is the heir to the Calandrian throne."

"Funny, because my son is just a little boy. Are you saying Calandrian schools are substandard?"

"Of course not. They are the best in Europe."

"Then think of the money we'll save. Besides, if Danny is going to grow up to rule the people, doesn't it make sense that he get to know them from an early age?"

She could feel Rafael winding himself up for some kind of princely tirade, so she quickly asked, "Did you like being sent away when you were all of seven? Didn't you miss your friends and your family? Do you really want that for Danny?"

"There are traditions," he began.

"There's also reality. It's a new century, Rafael. How about pushing the monarchy into it? I'm not sending Danny away to school."

She also was fairly sure she wasn't going to be marrying Rafael anytime soon, although the idea was fun to think about.

"You are right," he said, stunning her into silence. "I did not enjoy being sent away. I was angry and resentful. I vowed it would be different for my son."

"You might want to remember that," she said, trying not to melt at the thought of a scared and lonely seven-year-old Rafael.

"Was it too horrible?" she asked.

"I survived. I had my uncle Vidal, who visited me frequently. My father's brother," he added. "We were close. Much closer than I ever was with my father."

She imagined it would be tough to get close to the king. "It's too bad your father didn't remarry. Having a woman around would have helped."

"Perhaps, but my father had done his duty and saw no reason to do it again."

Marriage as duty—an interesting concept. "What about marrying for love?" she asked.

Rafael took her hand and lightly kissed the tips of her fingers. "Such a thing would not occur to him."

"What are *your* thoughts on the concept?"

His blue eyes darkened with emotion. "I have turned down three acceptable arranged marriages and I have been unable to tell my father why. Each of the women was exactly what I said I wanted, and yet when the time came, I was not willing to marry for duty."

"What did you say you wanted?" she asked.

He smiled. "You know that is not important."

"I want to know how close a match I would be."

"You are Mia," he told her. "That is enough."

Great response, she thought. He was good at saying exactly the right thing. She really was going to have to go online and become more familiar with his past. Was he serious about the three potential princesses?

"You worry for nothing," he said as he stood and came around to her side of the table. He pulled her to her feet. "Remember what it was like between us. Think of how it could be again."

Dangerous territory. She knew she could easily get lost in the past, and that wasn't a smart place to hang out. She had a pretty big present to worry about, including an almost four-year-old son who would—amazingly enough—one day rule Calandria.

"Rafael, I've been thinking, and it's the reason I'm up so early this morning. What you proposed . . ." Bad choice of words. "Your suggestion is really flattering, but I can't see how we could ever make it work."

"I will show you." He moved in close and wrapped his arms around her.

She already had a good idea of where this was going.

Not her favorite thing before she finished her first cup of coffee, but based on how great his kiss had been last night, she just might make an exception.

But before his mouth could claim hers, she heard footsteps in the hallway.

"Okay, that would be a chaperone on demand," she murmured as she stepped back and did her best not to look flustered.

David walked into the kitchen, took one look at them, and started back out. "Sorry," he muttered. "Just came down for coffee. Didn't mean to interrupt."

"You didn't. Really." Mia lunged toward him and grabbed his arm. "Rafael and I were finished."

Rafael smiled. "I would not say 'finished,' but we can certainly pick this up again later. Go ahead, David. Have your coffee. I will go and wake my son."

"Danny will like that," Mia said, more grateful for the interruption than she could say. Things were messed up enough without her getting lost in a sensual fog with Rafael. Sexual chemistry had never been their issue.

David crossed to the coffeepot and poured himself a mug. When Rafael had left, he looked at Mia.

"You always did do things in a big way."

She sighed. "This time, I didn't mean to. It was just one of those things."

He grinned. "Having a baby with the crown prince of a European nation doesn't just happen."

"It did to me. A week ago my life was perfectly normal. I had my plan. Finish law school, get a good job, get Danny into a nice private school in L.A., buy a condo. Suddenly I'm worried about co-parenting with a future monarch. It's unnerving."

"If anyone can handle it, you're the one."

She didn't feel like the one. She felt inadequate to the task and uneasy about Rafael. He was too charming, too everything. How was she supposed to resist him?

"It's good to see you," she said.

"I always like coming up here. The fact that we're planning a wedding here only gives me more excuses."

She wrinkled her nose. "Dinner turned into a disaster."

"What's up with Kelly? She was wasted."

"I don't know. I thought Francesca was going to pop a blood vessel. And Etienne. Yuck. Why is it some men think avoiding regular hygiene makes them sexy?"

The timer on the oven dinged. She grabbed a hot pad and pulled out the cinnamon rolls.

"You were always a frequent bather," she said. "I appreciated that. I just want you to know."

"Not a very high standard."

"I have others."

David was good-looking, in an easy all-American kind of way. While he and Mia were exactly the same age, their lives were so different. He'd graduated from college, gotten a great job at an investment firm, and had the perfect life. He was engaged to someone Mia liked a lot, owned his own home, and knew exactly where he wanted to be in twenty years.

She was a single mother, still living at home, with another year left in law school. Okay, yes, she had a master's and had been a spy, but she still felt as if she were waiting for her grown-up life to start.

David leaned against the counter. "I need your help."

She perked up. "Is this a shopping thing, because I am in the mood to spend some serious cash and it's always better if it isn't mine."

"It's not a shopping thing."

Damn. David had taken her with him to pick out Amber's engagement ring. They'd found the perfect set, with a 1.6 carat cushion-cut center stone. Mia considered it one of her crowning achievements in spending other people's money.

"It's Amber."

"What about Amber? She's fabulous." Mia grabbed the ingredients for frosting and set them on the counter. "Don't you dare tell me you're having second thoughts."

"I'm not," he said quickly. "How could I? Amber is incredible. Pretty and gentle and kind, and she thinks I'm funny."

"It's a miracle," Mia told him.

"Gee, thanks. She adores me, and I can't imagine ever loving anyone as much as I love her. I want to have kids with her. I want to grow old with her. I want to buy an RV with her."

"RV buying means it *is* serious." She measured out powdered sugar and butter. "So what's the problem?"

"You."

Mia paused in the act of pouring milk. "Excuse me?"

"She doesn't understand how I could have been in love with you once and not still be in love with you."

"Oh, please. You had me and realized you didn't want me." He winced.

"I don't mean that in a bad way," she added quickly. "We were young and thought we were in love. We weren't. End of story."

"She doesn't see it that way. Every time we come here, she can't stop talking about you." He held up his free hand. "Before you say anything, I already thought about staying away, but we're supposed to get married here. It was Amber's idea. There are family holidays and gatherings. There's no way to avoid you."

"Kind of like flu season germs."

"You know what I mean."

"I do and I feel bad. Have you told her there's nothing between us? That we're like brother and sister—not that we were when we were having sex, because ick."

He grinned. "I've mentioned the brother/sister thing. And that you weren't very good in bed."

She glared at him. "Ha!"

"Mia, seriously. I need help."

"I'm not an expert," she told him. "Look, be honest with her. Tell her you don't want to lose her. Tell her no one else has ever mattered as much. That you'd be lost without her."

Sort of all the things she'd felt when she'd flown away in that helicopter after thinking she'd just watched Diego die. It had been the worst moment of her life.

"Tell her she's your world."

"You think?" he asked.

"I know. It'll work. Trust me."

"Thanks." He put down his coffee and held out his arms.

Mia abandoned her frosting and stepped into his embrace.

David felt good—solid and familiar. Like family.

"I mean this in a very nonromantic way," she said. "But I never stopped loving you."

"I know exactly how you feel."

Life being what it was, the short, friendly, comforting silence didn't last long. Mia distinctly heard a gasp. She turned just as David swore, and wasn't the least bit surprised to see a wide-eyed Amber quickly backing out of the kitchen.

David pushed Mia away with a speed that was almost comical. Mia watched him hurry after the woman of his dreams.

She finished with the frosting. Then, despite her earlier hunger for cinnamon rolls, she left them on the counter and climbed the stairs to her room. Once inside, she crossed to the dresser and pulled out the bottom drawer.

There were all kinds of mementos inside. Yearbooks, pictures from school, postcards from everywhere she'd traveled.

She wondered if she should help David explain, then shook her head. Nothing she could say would make a difference. The situation wasn't actually about her—it was Amber's inability to trust her fiancé and his feelings for her.

Funny how easy it was to see what was wrong with everyone else while she still wrestled with her own demons. Speaking of which . . .

She pulled out a small jewelry box from a corner of the drawer. Inside was a simple silver ring. Nothing fancy, no stones or engraving. But Diego had bought it for her one afternoon. He'd slipped it on her left ring finger and had kissed her.

"Now you are always mine," he told her. "For as long as the ring survives, so does our love."

She'd worn it nearly a year after she'd come back home. Then, after Danny had been born, she'd removed it and stored it away. The love that had been so precious to her was not destined to last.

Or was it? Diego was back, in a different form. The same man, a different person.

Could she trust him? Did he mean what he'd said? Did he want to marry her?

And if so, what did *she* want? Hadn't she just spent five years wishing for the impossible—the return of her one true love? Was she going to let him get away just because he happened to be the heir to a throne?

7

"*T* hat poor girl," Grandma Tessa said as she expertly stitched a bead into place on the piece of white satin she held in her hands.

Grammy M rolled her eyes. "She should be more trustin' of the man she's marryin', or she shouldn't be marryin' him a-tall."

"Trust is a tricky thing," Mia said, hoping to avoid an argument between her grandmothers. There was already enough tension between them about Rafael. "I see her point. I mean, hey, it's me."

Grammy M smiled. "You are a special one, Mia, but you're not all that."

Mia laughed. "Not all that? Where did you learn that expression."

"HBO," Tessa said with a grin. "We watch it all the time."

"Okay. Now I'm scared."

"Don't be," Tessa told her. "Amber is a sensible girl and she loves David. That's plain to see. But she's cautious."

"Why?" Grammy M asked. "David is a good man. She's lucky to be gettin' him."

"Sometimes a little caution is a good thing. A smart woman isn't taken in by a pretty face, fancy words, and an accent," said Tessa.

Grammy M put down her piece of white satin. "I suppose you'll be meanin' me when you make that remark. As if I could be taken in."

"You have been. What do we know about Rafael, eh? What he tells us. Charming manners are nice at dinner, but they don't say anything about his character. Mia is smart to hold back."

"Okay, I don't want to get in the middle of this," Mia said quickly. "Really. Let's change the subject. How about those grapes? Are they growing or what?"

"I don't think Mia should go running off with Rafael just because he smiles at her," Grammy M said, her voice clipped. "I'm saying she should give the man a chance to prove himself before she accepts his proposal."

There was a moment of perfect silence. Mia paused in the act of reaching for another bead. While her grandmothers sewed on the front of David's wedding vest, she'd been trusted with two tabs in the back.

She replayed that last sentence, lingering on the final word. How on earth did her grandmothers know about Rafael's proposal?

There was only one possible explanation. Damn the man. She'd *asked* him not to say anything. She hadn't wanted the pressure. She didn't know what she was going to do herself and she wasn't looking for advice.

"He told you?" She tossed the tabs onto the table and glared at them both. "He *told* you?"

"He might have mentioned it in passing," Grammy M said as she continued to calmly sew.

Mia couldn't believe it. "How, exactly, does that happen? You're discussing the weather and you ask if he's proposed recently, then he chuckles and says as a matter of fact he has?"

Her voice rose with each word until it ended on a shriek.

"Who else knows?" she demanded.

"No one," Grammy M said soothingly. "It was just the three of us in the kitchen. We were talking about you and how smart you are. Rafael seemed to like that. He mentioned you would be a beautiful and compassionate queen." She sighed. "Imagine. Our little girl a queen."

Right then Mia wanted to throw something, which didn't feel very royal to her. She turned to Grandma Tessa.

"What did *you* say? Do you think it's a good idea?"

"I think you should get to know the man before making any decisions that take you so far away."

"Okay, maybe. But doesn't it bother you that he told you?"

"Not as much as you *not* telling us," Tessa said.

Mia sank back into her chair. "I needed to think about it. No, I needed to find out a way to tell him no."

Grammy M dropped her needle. "No? But he's the father of your child, Mia. Danny'll be needin' a father as he grows up."

"He has Joe."

"An uncle isn't a father."

Mia looked at Grandma Tessa. "You can't want me to marry him."

"I want you to be happy. And sensible."

"He shouldn't have told you," Mia insisted. "It's not right."

"We're your family," Grammy M said, as if that explained everything.

But it didn't. Rafael went behind her back. What was up with that? Did he want to pressure her into saying yes?

Even as the thought occurred, she dismissed it. Hello, they were talking about royalty. Princes didn't need to push women into their lives. Women went willingly.

"I have to go talk to him," she muttered.

"He's outside playing with Danny," Grammy M offered.

Mia waved her thanks and stomped through the kitchen toward the back door. Something about this just didn't feel right. The word *manipulation* kept popping into her mind, which seemed both harsh and unfair.

She stepped out into the warm afternoon and immediately heard the sound of childish laughter.

"You're dead," Danny said gleefully as he poked at an action figure in Rafael's hand. "Dead, dead, dead."

They sat on a blanket in the shade. Around them were the remnants of what had obviously been a hard-fought war. Plastic soldiers lay discarded in heaps. Mia would bet that nearly every military toy had been hauled out for today's game.

"I die, I die," Rafael said in a high-pitched voice. "You shot me and I die."

Both he and his plastic soldier fell to the blanket. Danny doubled over with laughter, and Mia found herself smiling.

Interesting that the imperial prince had allowed himself to be defeated. So maybe Rafael was good with his son. That had to count for something, didn't it?

He looked up and saw her. "You are in time to attend my funeral. I am killed."

Danny grinned. "He's not a very good soldier."

Rafael pressed a hand to his chest. "How you wound me with your words. I am an excellent soldier. Perhaps you are simply better."

"I am!" Danny crowed. "I'm the best. I'm the heir."

Mia narrowed her gaze. "You are, huh? Maybe in Calandria but not here. Here you're just Danny Marcelli. Okay, kid. Why don't you head inside and ask the Grands to fix you a snack."

"Okay."

He scrambled to his feet and raced to her. She dropped to her knees for his kiss and hug, then stood as he ran into the house.

"He is the heir," Rafael told her from his place on the blanket. "Do not discourage him from knowing his own importance. He will one day be king."

"Not something I can readily imagine. Besides, he already has a very strong sense of self. Trust me, you don't want to make him feel any more important than he already does."

Rafael patted the blanket. "Join me," he said quietly. "It is very nice out here."

She glanced around. "Where are the boys with the guns?"

"Oliver and Umberto have taken a tour of the winery with Brenna."

"I'm surprised they were willing to let you out of their sight."

"I insisted. I wanted the time alone with my son. It is not good to always have bodyguards lurking."

"I agree." She sank onto the blanket.

He reached for her hand, but she slid away from him.

"Mia, what is wrong?"

"My grandmothers just informed me that you told them about asking me to marry you. That's not my definition of playing fair. I asked you not to say anything."

He nodded. "You are right. I should not have mentioned it. Believe me, I did not tell them in an effort to trap you or make you feel obligated. I don't want you to marry me because you think you have to."

He gave her a half smile that she found boyish and appealing, but she was careful not to respond in any way.

"Don't worry about forcing me into marriage. It won't happen."

"Good. As for what I said, the words slipped out. I was thinking about us being together and . . ." He shrugged. "I apologize."

Really? Rafael was many things, but he was not the type who apologized.

"I mean that," he said quietly. "I was wrong."

The W word. So rarely uttered by a male. The combination of his sincerity and his accent was difficult to resist.

"Okay," she muttered, not sure how to accept his apology without encouraging him. "I, ah, don't want you mentioning the proposal to anyone else."

"Agreed." He moved closer. "May I discuss it with you?"

"I'm not sure that's a good idea."

"But if I do not, how can I convince you that you belong with me in Calandria? I know you are not the type to be enticed by talk of jewels or riches, so instead I thought I would talk about my house at the edge of the island. Of the sound of the surf on the rocks and how beautiful your skin will be in the moonlight as we make love. I thought I would admit that I still dream about what it was like to be with you, of the feel of your body under mine and the way you clung so fiercely to me. As if you would never let go."

She remembered, too. The need to hold on to him had always overwhelmed her whenever they were intimate. Even now, after all this time, she recalled the weight of him as he plunged into her, taking her to the edge of the world and then jumping with her.

"I remember the passion in your eyes," he murmured as he moved closer still. "How sensually you touched me. Your fingers, your mouth."

He rubbed his thumb against her bottom lip. She couldn't help grabbing his wrist and holding him still while she gently bit down on his skin.

His breath caught as their eyes locked. Need filled her. Five years of missing this man exploded inside of her. Her breasts tightened, her thighs squeezed, and she reached for him just as he grabbed for her.

They fell onto the blanket, him on top, their legs tangled. He was heavy and strong and hard, so very hard as his erection rubbed against her belly. She slid her fingers through his hair and guided his mouth to hers.

She opened instantly, needing deep, dark, passionate kisses that would touch her soul. He read her mind, or perhaps he needed the same, because he thrust into her mouth and claimed her.

Her tongue circled his; then she closed her lips around him and sucked. He groaned, then shifted so his arousal pressed between her legs.

Her thighs fell open as she welcomed him home; then

she wrapped her legs around his hips and urged him to rub harder and faster.

"More," she gasped as she dropped her hands to his butt and squeezed the tight flesh.

He grabbed her, then shifted so that she was on top, her center resting on his erection. They were both panting, needy, and she couldn't seem to stop looking into his eyes.

Blue instead of brown, but she had grown used to that difference. The missing scars no longer mattered. On the surface, Rafael might look different from Diego, but her body recognized its most significant lover.

"Kiss me," he demanded even as he reached for her breasts.

She braced herself on the blanket and lowered her head. At the same time he cupped her curves and began to tease her tight nipples.

The combination of sensations—his tongue in her mouth, his hands on her breasts, her swollen wet center rubbing against his cock—was too much. Despite the fact that they were outside and fully dressed, she shuddered into orgasm.

The release stunned her, but she couldn't stop moving against him, couldn't stop kissing him, and would have killed him if he'd stopped touching her nipples.

But he didn't. As wave after wave of pleasure claimed her, he stroked her and kissed her and urged her on.

Somewhere in the house, a door slammed. Mia came back to reality with a thud. She wasn't a wild teenager anymore and she had a child to think about. Did she really want Danny running outside and seeing his mother acting like this?

Reluctantly, she straightened.

The reality of what had just happened slammed into her. How had a petting session gotten out of hand so quickly? And was she so damn needy that she was only seconds away from an orgasm, regardless of the circumstances or the fact that they hadn't even gotten naked?

"Second thoughts are not allowed," Rafael told her in a low voice, thick with passion. "I forbid them."

"You're not the boss of me."

"Very mature." He smiled. "Are you angry?"

She shook her head. "Just . . . embarrassed."

"No. Not that. Never that. You are so responsive. Each man likes to believe he is a master in the bedroom. I more so than most."

"All that practice," she said wryly.

"Perhaps. But with you, I know it to be true. However I touch you, you are pleasured."

As if to demonstrate, he slid his fingers between her legs and rubbed. He immediately found her swollen center and circled it. Another climax claimed her.

She sucked in a breath, then pushed his hand away. "Stop that," she said as she stood. "You've made your point."

He rose and grabbed her wrist. "I think not. You are fire, Mia, and there is no greater gift to a man than to burn for him." He brought her palm to his mouth and kissed it. "I have missed your flames. No one else burns as you do."

She still felt funny about what had happened. No one enjoyed being a living example of a life of celibacy. She doubted Rafael had done without for more than fifteen seconds.

"Whatever," she said as she walked away.

He grabbed her again. "Mia. Do not dismiss what we have together. It is magnificent."

She wanted to believe him. She very nearly did. For her part, he had been amazing. Not just because he knew how to arouse her and make her whimper, but because the chemistry between them was so powerful. That couldn't have gone away, she told herself. He had to have felt it, too.

So if he had then, did he now?

She stared into his eyes and willed herself to see the truth. There was need and desire and nothing else. No hint of secrets, no holding back. It was as if she could see down into his soul.

"All right," she said. "I won't do the regret dance, but we're not doing this again. It's a very powerful form of persuasion and I'm not interested in being coerced."

He smiled his agreement, then took her hand in his. "I will concede to your wishes on the condition you show me the regret dance. Do you perform it naked?"

She sighed. "It's a figure of speech."

"No. It must be real. I will it so."

She rolled her eyes. "Welcome to the new world, prince. Here we're all equal and no one cares about your will."

He leaned close and whispered in her ear. "Perhaps you ignore my will, but what will you do with my wants?"

A shiver of desire rippled through her. An excellent question, she thought, and one for which she had no answer.

That evening Rafael escaped the loud chaos that signaled the end of the Marcelli evening meal by stepping outside for a few moments. He crossed to the fence by the garden and stared up at the stars.

Usually he enjoyed the conversation and animation of the family, but not this evening. Tonight they had been an annoyance. He had wanted to command them all to leave so that he could be alone with Mia.

He had not bothered to express his will—no one would have listened. How he longed for Calandria, where his word was law and he could drag Mia into his bed without anyone interfering.

Their game this afternoon had started as a way for him to convince her to accept his proposal. He'd been sure if she felt the fire again, she would be unable to resist him. Unfortunately, the fire had burned both ways, and no matter how he tried, he could not forget the feel of her body against his.

He had been hard for hours. Every time he managed to get his desire under control, he remembered the taste of her kiss and the feel of her breasts, and blood rushed to his groin.

Nothing helped, he thought grimly. Not thoughts of sports or finance or discussing the particulars of growing tomatoes with Grandma Tessa. He simply had to hear Mia's voice or catch sight of her, and he ached to take her.

Ironic that in this one area he did not have to pretend. He meant what he said—she was spectacularly sexual and he was desperate to revisit their passion.

A sharp scent caught his attention. He turned and saw a cigarette tip glowing in the darkness. He moved toward it and recognized the smoker.

"Good evening," he said.

Kelly Reese glanced at him. "Are you going to rat me out?"

"Of course not. What you do with your life is your business."

She sighed and continued to lean against the side of the garage. "Whatever. Aren't you going to lecture me about the perils of smoking?"

He shrugged. "Do you want me to?"

"Not especially. I know it's not great for my endurance, but it helps me keep my weight down. Let me tell you, being this skinny isn't pleasant. I've been hungry since I was fifteen."

He looked her over. She had the typical dancer's build. Powerful, lean muscles without an ounce of body fat to soften the lines. She was tall with perfect posture and wild, curly red hair tumbling down her back.

"So you suffer for your art," he said.

"That's me. Cliché girl."

Her phrasing reminded him of Mia, which made him hard again. He swore silently.

"How long have you been dating Etienne?" he asked, knowing the shadows would keep his secret. He did not want this child to think he was interested in her.

"A couple of months. Everybody hates him. It's the Euro-trash thing. You'd think I'd know better. My mom married some guy who was supposed to be a count or something and he wasn't. But, hey, it's not my problem."

"Did Etienne tell you he came from a titled family?"

"No. His dad is a policeman and his mother works in a bakery."

Working class, which fit his accent. Etienne might not be much for personal grooming, but at least he wasn't a liar. Not that Rafael cared one way or the other.

"So you knew Mia from a long time ago," Kelly said.

"Obviously, what with you being Danny's father. It's weird. Why didn't you come after her before?"

"I was told she was dead."

Kelly stared at him. "Huh. So she thought you were dead and you thought she was dead. Interesting coincidence."

"More sad than interesting. I mourned Mia for a long time."

Kelly's green eyes seemed to see more than most. "At least it's a good story," she said at last.

"You do not believe me." How could she not?

"What I think doesn't matter. Mia has always known what she wanted and no one gets in the way of that. If she wants you, no one will be able to change her mind."

"You don't like me," he said.

Kelly inhaled on her cigarette, then dropped it to the ground and stepped on it. "I'm not real keen on the Eurotrash set."

He stiffened. "I am Crown Prince Rafael of Calandria."

"I know. I'm sure the housing is much nicer, but you're still the type. Playing on what you have to get what you want. Right now you want Mia."

The child saw too much. Old before her years, he thought, recognizing the symptoms. For him the reason had been his upbringing, for her it was her commitment to ballet. He could both admire and sympathize with her position.

She picked up the butt and slipped it into her pocket. "I'm going to give you some advice, I don't know why. Maybe in exchange for you not mentioning the smoking thing. Don't screw with her. Joe will kill you."

"That is not possible."

Kelly grinned. "You think those two bodyguards could

protect you? Not in this lifetime. Nobody gets to Joe's family, and Mia is one of his favorites."

Her total confidence surprised him. "He would be killed as well."

"Maybe, but you'd be dead first. This is a friendly warning, worth what you paid for it."

Kelly walked away. Rafael watched her go. The child's words did not frighten him—nor did the thought of facing an angry Joe Marcelli. But he was surprised to feel something like regret.

It was increasingly obvious that Mia could be hurt by his plan. He didn't want to wound but he did require his son. Was there perhaps another way?

He immediately shook off the question. Sacrifices would be made by all. If Mia's were greatest, so be it.

Mia sat curled up in an old leather chair in the library. She loved the room with its high arched ceilings and the tall bookshelves filled with everything from rare first editions to her old copies of *Seventeen* magazine. She loved the quiet and the fact that no one ever thought to look for her here, but mostly she loved that the room reminded her of her grandfather.

Lorenzo had been gone five years. He'd never known about Danny, hadn't lived to see Joe and Darcy marry. Right now she missed the old man and his gruff ways. She had a feeling he would cut right to the heart of the matter with Rafael.

But what would he say? Would he tell her to marry the father of her son and be a good wife or would he shake his head and say that in a world that runs by computers, who needs princes?

The door opened. Mia tensed slightly, not sure she

would welcome any interruption. Then Rafael stepped into the room and she felt her heart flutter in anticipation.

Great. She was falling for him again. Just what she needed, because her life wasn't complicated enough these days.

"I am interrupting?" he asked.

She shrugged. "Not really. I'm going over my classes for the fall term at law school. I'm getting down to the serious stuff for my specialty and it's . . ." She blinked at his look of surprise. "What?"

"You plan to continue to attend law school?"

She put the catalog on the desk and scrambled to her feet. "Did you think you would stop me?"

"Of course not, it is just if we are married, you will not be able to practice law. Not in the traditional sense," he added quickly, then smiled. "You are right. You should complete your education, so when you speak before our parliament, you know exactly what you want to say."

She wasn't totally buying the sudden transformation. "Why would I be speaking before parliament?"

"Because you will never be silent, Mia. It is, how do you say . . . Not your style? You are life and you must be a part of things. I think that if you were to come to my country, you would want to tax the casinos more to pay for education. Perhaps you would start a teaching hospital so our future doctors did not go away to France or England."

"So you're saying I could affect policy."

"Of course. As queen you can do anything."

Except live a normal life.

He motioned to the chair she'd been in and waited until she sat before claiming the one next to it.

"What troubles you?" he asked. "I know you are find-ing it difficult to resist my charms."

She laughed. "That pesky ego. Doesn't it ever get heavy, carrying it around all the time?"

"No. I am used to the weight." His smile faded. "Tell me, Mia. I wish to know."

She drew in a breath, not sure she could even articu-late her concerns. "Calandria is very far away."

"That is true. However, you will have access to several private jets to take you wherever you want. Your family is no more than eight or nine hours away. They would also be welcome to visit us whenever they wanted."

"I'm not really princess"—she couldn't bring herself to say *queen*—"material. I'm not royal or rich or any-thing special."

His gaze narrowed. "What more would you require to be special? You are uniquely yourself."

She sensed that he was going to reach for her hand and snatched it back just in time. He grasped air, then raised his eyebrows.

"I know you enjoy my touch," he began.

"Too much," she muttered. "There will be no more touching until I get things figured out."

He smiled with the contented confidence of a man who knows how to please women. "You are afraid I can seduce you."

"I'm not afraid, I'm prudent."

"A good quality in a wife."

"You could say the same thing about a dog." She shook her head. "You would have to let go of the hot-and-cold-running women at your house on the rocks."

"There have been women in my life. Of course, I'm a

man. But none at the house. I take no one there, Mia. You will be the first."

Whoa. "You're serious?"

"Why would I lie? You could easily check the truth. I have not brought a woman to my house."

Good to know. "It's just I . . ." She clutched the arms of the chair. "You're different. I knew Diego. I understood him. But Rafael is a mystery to me."

"We are not so different. Not the Diego you knew."

"What about the real one?"

He shrugged. "He was angry. By a fluke of birth, he lost the crown. His brother never cared, but Diego was angry from the time he understood what it meant to be king."

"Did it change you to pretend to be him?"

"I am already a man ready to take what I want," he said. "But Diego was a fool." He dismissed the other man with a flick of his fingers. "Now he is dead."

The ruthlessness didn't surprise her. She'd seen it in him before. Men only crossed Rafael once. Which made his sense of humor and flashes of tenderness more fascinating. Rafael could laugh at the world. More important, he could laugh at himself.

"Why me?" she asked.

He stared directly into her eyes. "Because in all the years we have been apart, I have never forgotten you. I am very good at forgetting women."

He rose. "I wish to return home, Mia, but my business there will wait. You are the most important part of my world. I will stay here until you are comfortable with me."

"And if it takes years?" she asked, not sure she believed him.

"I am a young man. Despite what you have heard, I am also a patient one. You are worth waiting for. Take your time. I will be here."

He left and she was alone. A normal person would have felt relief, but suddenly she was lonely and wanted to call him back.

He'd always been a smooth talker. She had to remember that. No one came into a situation like this without an agenda. But he had an answer for everything and she didn't know how to deal with that.

Worse, she didn't know how to stop herself from wanting to believe it was all true.

8

〜

"Y̶ou're trying to make me feel bad on purpose," Mia muttered as she flopped on her bed.

"Not at all. I dance in the corps and I live in San Francisco, which, as you know, is about the most expensive city next to New York, so it's not like I have a lot of extra cash."

Mia eyed Kelly as the tall, slender redhead pulled on a skinny-strapped sundress Mia hadn't been able to fit into since before Danny was born.

"So go to the mall."

"Your closet is closer." Kelly turned and studied herself in the mirror. "It's too short."

"And too loose. God, I hate you."

Kelly grinned. "I happen to know you adore me, despite my height and lack of body fat." She spun in the pale green dress, then pulled it over her head. "What's next?"

"Have at it," Mia said, pointing at the closet. "My old clothes are your old clothes."

Kelly flipped hangers. Mia studied her narrow back and the clearly visible bones of her shoulders and ribs.

"Not to get too maternal on you," Mia said lightly, "but are you sure you're eating enough?"

"Uh-huh."

"But you're so—"

"I'm a dancer, Mia. In my line of work, they don't like chunky. I'll eat when I retire."

"Most people just want to garden."

Kelly shrugged, then dove back in the closet. She emerged with a long dress in a muslin bag. "I know what's in here."

"Me too." Mia sat up. "I haven't looked at that in years."

Kelly unzipped the front and pulled out the handmade wedding gown all the women in the family had lovingly beaded when Mia had been planning on marrying David.

"That was what, more than eight years ago?" she asked more to herself than Kelly. "I can't believe it. Was I ever really that young and foolish?"

"You were in love," Kelly reminded her. "I think it's very romantic."

"We were babies. Just eighteen and still in college. What were we thinking?"

"That you wanted to be together."

Mia remembered the heated longing of her first real love. "We were worlds apart," she said as she fingered the stunning beadwork. "I'd started college at sixteen, so I was already a junior. He was a freshman and had no idea what he wanted to do with his life. I was going to get my master's in international relations and be a diplomat."

Kelly settled next to her on the bed. "What happened with David? Was it horrible?"

"No. We both realized we weren't as in love as we thought. Better to find out before the marriage than after."

"But it was very close to the actual date of the wedding," Kelly said.

Mia fingered the dress. "Obviously." She looked at Kelly.

"Don't try to make the situation romantic. We were kids pretending to be grown-up. We could have made a disaster of our lives. We got lucky."

"I suppose," Kelly said. "Do you have any regrets?"

"Ian," Mia told her. "I don't even have to think about the question. When I think about how he tricked me. Used me."

She didn't want to get angry, but she could feel her temper growing.

"He didn't plan to use you," Kelly said.

Mia looked at her. "You're defending him?"

"Of course not. I think it's awful that he tried to kidnap Darcy and hold her for ransom. I'm just saying when you met Ian, he was a regular guy."

"He was a domestic terrorist in disguise. That doesn't exactly fit my definition of normal."

"You know what I mean. It was only after he realized Darcy was here that he hatched his plot." Kelly flopped back on the bed. "Hatched his plot. That sounds so exciting."

"Darcy nearly died," Mia said flatly.

"Oh, I know. I didn't mean in her circumstances. Just in general. Besides, you can't regret Ian."

"Why not?"

"If he hadn't been a total dick, you wouldn't have become a spy and gone to Calandria. You wouldn't have met Diego, a.k.a. Danny's father, and you wouldn't have gotten pregnant. I know you, Mia. You would never regret Danny."

Kelly had her there, Mia thought as she smiled. "I can't regret him. He's my world. But the rest of it kind of blows."

Kelly rolled onto her stomach. "I have a secret that you're not going to like."

Considering how much Mia didn't like Etienne, she wasn't sure she wanted to hear. "What is it?"

"I don't like Rafael."

"You don't know him."

"I've spoken with him a few times. He's too . . . I don't know. I can't put my finger on it, but he's not a nice man."

Mia didn't think her niece by marriage was in a position to cast judgment in the man department. "And here I thought only Grandma Tessa and Joe didn't like him. Joe wouldn't like him on principle, because he's a sweetie who loves his sister. I'm not sure what's up with Grandma Tessa."

"Does it matter?" Kelly asked. "Isn't the important question whether you like him?"

"I like him," Mia said cautiously.

Kelly rolled her eyes. "I'm not talking about the mild affection one would have for an acquaintance. I mean like as in 'This guy is incredibly cool and I must have him.'"

"Is that how you feel about Etienne?"

"We're not discussing Etienne. I know Rafael proposed."

Mia groaned. "Did he take out an ad?"

"The Grands told me, which means they've told everyone. You know they believe the phrase 'Can you keep a secret?' actually means 'Tell everyone you know.'"

"He said the words," Mia told her. "I'm not sure he means them. He's a prince. I'm not sure he's able to simply marry whomever he wants."

"A prince. Sometimes I forget that." Kelly slid to the floor and began stretching. "I want to be you when I grow up. I want your life."

"No you don't," Mia said. "I'm not a good example, Kelly. I'm the cautionary tale. Trust me, you need a different role model."

Kelly stretched her legs in front of her and then bent

over until her forehead rested on her knees. When she sat up in a graceful, fluid movement Mia couldn't dream of replicating, she said, "But you're happy, right?"

"For the most part." When she didn't think too much about everything going on. "And you?"

"Delirious. I'm living my dream, dancing with the most amazing company on the planet. What's not to like?"

Mia wasn't sure, but she sensed something was off in Kelly's world.

"You have Etienne," she reminded her niece. "Does he play into this?"

"Most of the time. I don't want to settle down," Kelly said. "I take lovers. Usually the one who buys me the best presents gets to keep me until I'm bored."

It was something Mia would have said at Kelly's age, so why did it sound so wrong now?

"Kelly, I'm all for having fun, but you should also think about finding relationships that actually mean something."

"Like Ian?" Kelly asked innocently. "I distinctly recall you saying you were just using him for sex. And aren't you the one who constantly threatened to sleep with all Joe's Navy SEAL friends and let the others watch?"

Mia winced. "I didn't mean it."

"Maybe I don't mean it either. Maybe I'm just being outrageous. Jeez." She stood and walked to the door. "You used to be fun. What happened with that?"

Kelly stalked into the hall and disappeared. Mia stared after her, not sure exactly what had gone wrong. Apparently being confused about one's life was contagious and Kelly had just caught the bug.

•   •   •

"Look!" Danny demanded. "I'm tall."

He stood with his back to the wall, his hand at a sharp angle, pointing up so that the place he marked on the height chart was at least three inches higher than his head.

"You are growing," Mia said, feeling both proud and wistful. Her little baby wasn't a baby anymore.

Rafael lined up several small race cars on the floor. "The men in my family are tall," he said. "You will be tall, too."

"Did you hear that?" she asked Danny. "You are going to be tall."

Danny beamed. Mia didn't bother pointing out that she was barely five foot three, the runt of the Marcelli litter by several inches.

Danny stepped away from the wall and grabbed his scepter. No matter how many times Mia managed to put it on a top shelf, it found its way to the floor. She was beginning to think Rafael had a hand in that.

"Tell me about your birthday party," Rafael said.

Danny grinned. "I have cake and presents and everyone comes."

"I'm looking forward to your party and you turning four. It is a very great age."

Danny looked at Mia. His eyes widened as if he'd just that moment understood his father would be at his birthday party. His mouth stretched into a grin as big as the morning and he launched himself at his father.

Rafael caught him and stood. "What's all this?" he asked as he swung the boy in the air.

"I think Danny just figured out you're sticking around."

"Of course I am," he told the boy. "I'm your father."

"I want presents," Danny said.

"That will put you in your place," Mia told Rafael before reminding Danny, "It's not polite to ask people to give you presents."

"But I want 'em."

"Sometimes social niceties get lost on the post-toddler set."

"I want my daddy at my party."

"I will be there," Rafael said.

"Promise?"

"Of course."

Rafael set the boy on the ground. While he appreciated Mia's attempt to educate the child on ways to behave, he couldn't help being pleased with Danny's demanding personality. He would need that strength as he navigated his way through all the potential pitfalls of growing up royal.

"There will be presents," Rafael told his son. "Many presents."

Danny grinned. He grabbed the scepter and banged it on the bed. "I'm the heir. I'm the heir."

Mia took it from him. "Not a toy," she said. "How about that race we were going to have?"

Danny collapsed to the floor and began pushing the cars around.

"You do well with him," Rafael told her as he sat on the edge of the bed.

"Practice. My mom and the Grands have really helped."

"I look forward to meeting your parents."

"They were really excited to hear all about you. They wanted to come home, but I convinced them you would still be available for meet and greet when they returned from China."

"Of course," he said, knowing he would be back in Calandria. Most likely Mia would have returned home by then and they could hear her complaints in person.

He studied the boy, then Mia, noting Daniel had the same color eyes as his mother. The boy was also very close to her, perhaps a result of her being a single parent. There would be a period of adjustment, he thought. But in time Daniel would understand why things had to be that way.

As for Mia . . . Rafael took in her easy smile, then dropped his gaze to her full breasts. She would not be so forgiving. Her fury would stir the heavens, but there was nothing she could do to him.

He briefly wished for another option, one that did not alter her world so completely and hurt her, but the choice was clear. He would do what was best for Calandria and for his son. She laughed at something Daniel had said. The sound filled him with the need to hear it again. Unfortunately, that was not his only desire where she was concerned.

"What are you thinking?" she asked. "You have the strangest look on your face."

"Just that I have missed you," he said, the lie easy and smooth.

"Are you bored here, living in the real world?"

"I am enjoying myself. Normal is more interesting than I had realized."

"Sorry, but this isn't normal. Normal means holding down a job and struggling to pay the bills and trying to save for retirement and the kids' college while hoping your company doesn't get bought out and you don't get downsized. This is a really cool vacation."

"Then I am enjoying my vacation."

She grinned. "Because you would never make it in Normal Land."

"I could get a job."

"Doing what? You'd never last, Rafael. You're too imperious."

"You like that I'm imperious."

"Sometimes."

She lowered her lashes as she spoke and his gaze dropped to her mouth. He wanted her in his bed. Not only because he sensed that once they made love he will have won, but also because he ached for her.

Their time together when he had played at being Diego had shown him that they complemented each other extremely well. She argued with him and sometimes won. She spoke different languages, understood different cultures, liked to laugh, and treated him as if he were just a man. Just as intriguing, there was a passionate fire that never seemed to go out, and no matter how many times he had her, he always wanted more.

Their recent encounter had left him hungry and restless. She might not be the most beautiful woman he'd ever known, but she was the most sexually exciting. After she'd gone home, he'd tried to figure out what it was about her that got to him. Was it the sharpness of her mind? The sound of her laughter? The way she gave herself to him so completely?

He had never discovered the answer, and now that he was with her again, he ached to claim her.

Danny crashed two of his cars and giggled. Mia glanced at her watch. "Okay, my man, ten more minutes, then we need to run through your lines again."

Danny wrinkled his nose. "I know my lines."

"All of them?"

He smiled. "Miss Valdrake will whisper them to me. She does when we practice."

"Uh-huh. Wouldn't it be totally, incredibly fabulous if you knew all your lines by yourself?"

Danny nodded as he laughed.

"This is his play for school?" Rafael asked. "He is the lead?"

"He's a tree," Mia said. "Get over it."

A tree? "But he is the heir to—"

"Actually, everyone in this room is very clear on that."

"But the teacher is not. My son will not be a tree in a play." It was not acceptable.

"I want to be a tree," Danny said, his smile fading. "I'm a good tree."

"Yes, you are," Mia said, and patted him on the back. "Don't sweat it, honey. You're going to be a tree. The Grands have worked too hard on your costume for that to change now." She looked at Rafael. "Did I mention the imperious bit, because this would be an example. Besides, it's a production for preschoolers in a summer program. There is no lead. The play is about the forest, and the trees are the really cool parts."

He was not convinced but told himself it did not matter. No one would be seeing the play except other parents. "When is the play?"

"In a couple of weeks."

Rafael wasn't sure if they would still be here or not. "I will attend."

Danny scrambled to his feet and started jumping up and down. "My daddy's coming to my play! My daddy's coming to my play!" Then he threw himself at Rafael and wrapped his arms around his neck.

Danny straightened. "You're the best daddy ever," he announced, then kissed Rafael and then Mia. "I'm hungry," he announced.

"I heard that," Grammy M said as she stuck her head in the room. "Come along, little man. I'll be gettin' you a snack." She smiled at Rafael, then took the boy by the hand and led him away.

Rafael stared after them. He was still absorbing Daniel's reaction to his attending the play.

"He wanted me to be there," he murmured. "And at his birthday party."

"Of course he did. You're important to him. That was one of the things that stunned me about being a parent. I knew there would be responsibility, but I didn't expect to be his whole world. At least until he grows up a little."

His world. Rafael hadn't expected that either. Until arriving, he'd thought of Daniel in abstract terms. A child. His child. But now the boy was more than that. He was a separate person with thoughts and ideas and dreams.

"Kind of scary, huh?" she asked.

He shrugged. "It is different. He is different."

She leaned against the bed. "Let me guess. Less well mannered."

"He has not been raised in a palace."

"You're going to have to teach him to salute."

He narrowed his gaze. "Even the mother of the heir should take care not to mock the crown prince."

She grinned. "Oooh, will the big, bad prince punish me now?"

"No, because that is what you want." He picked up one of the race cars. "When I was his age, I could already recite the lineage of my family back to the twelfth century."

"There's a party trick."

"It is not a trick. It is who we are."

"It's who *you* are. And Danny's not you. He's not even four yet. Give him a break."

Rafael appreciated her concern, but he also resented it. How strange. Perhaps if his mother had lived she would have . . .

He shook off the thought. "Before I left for school in England, I was already attending meetings of state. I would visit with my father three times a week and listen while he explained what was going on in our country and in the world."

"Arranged meetings?" she asked. "What about just hanging out. Playing, having him read you a story?"

"He is the king. He does not read stories."

"Right. Because he has a staff to do that." She leaned over and put her hand on his arm. "I'm sorry."

He stiffened. "Your apology is not required."

"I wasn't apologizing. I was expressing sympathy and compassion. That's a tough life for any kid. It shouldn't have been like that."

He stood and glared down at her. "It was exactly as it should have been. I am crown prince—"

She rose, put her hands on his shoulders, and cut him off with a brief kiss. "Get defensive much?" she asked as she drew back. "I know who you are. You've lived a life of great privilege and that's wonderful, but you've also paid a price for that. Everyone has trade-offs. Yours were different from most, but they still existed. That's okay."

He hated what she was saying as much as his body wanted to respond to her nearness.

"I do not need you making excuses for me," he told her.

"I'm not. I'm saying that childhood is a tough gig, even for a prince. No kid should have to get dressed up and have an appointment to see a parent. Parents should be the safest place in the world, and so many times they're not."

He didn't want to think about that—about how his father had been a stranger. There had been other people he could depend on. His uncle Vidal had talked to him about life and been a trusted confidant.

Mia took his hand and tugged until he sat next to her on the bed. "I have a question."

"That is hardly unusual."

"True. What would you be or do if you weren't a prince?"

He stared at her. "I *am* a prince."

"Yes, we're all totally clear on that. The flashing neon sign over your head doesn't let anyone forget. But if you weren't, what would you be? How would you make a living?"

"I have never considered such a thing."

Except he had . . . once. Rafael had spent a month his summer before university on the private island of a friend of his father's. There had been no press, no parties, no public appearances. Just the large house and its staff, along with those people indigenous to the island.

None of them had cared who he was or where he came from. They lived their lives bound by the seasons, growing crops, marrying, having children, getting old, and then dying.

"A doctor," he said without thinking, then wished he hadn't spoken.

"Really? An actual medical doctor?"

He nodded stiffly. "I would take care of people. I would also do research to fight diseases."

"You mean help them?" She sounded both intrigued and disbelieving.

"This conversation has no purpose."

"It does for me," she told him. "I'm still trying to figure you out. I wouldn't have thought a doctor."

It was a moment to push his advantage. He should discuss this more and allow Mia to believe he was everything she wanted. Instead he asked, "And you? When you were a young girl, what did you want to be or do?"

She laughed. "I wanted to rule the world. Sort of the ultimate imperial queen. It's been a joke in my family for years. Instead I decided to become a diplomat and along the way ended up, very briefly, being a spy. You know the rest."

He touched her cheek. "You would make a very good imperial queen. But why did you become a spy?"

Her brown eyes darkened. "Someone fooled me. I didn't want that to ever happen again."

Rafael stayed where he was, right next to Mia, but a part of him wanted to pull away. He was there to fool her. Perhaps in the biggest way possible. If there was another way . . .

There wasn't, he reminded himself. This was for a greater good. There was no choice. Funny how early he'd learned that in his life. For him, there never was a choice.

9

❧

"**I**'m loving this," Katie said as she and Mia walked toward the gazebo behind the wine-tasting room. "I'm semi–mother of the groom. I get all the fun bits and none of the stress."

Mia laughed. "Sort of like being the grandparent? Loading the grandkids up on sugar, then sending them home to crash?"

"Exactly. Amber's mother is handling the majority of the details and only calls every now and then."

Mia raised her eyebrows. "You are so lying. You are desperate to run every minute of the wedding and it's killing you not to."

Katie sighed. "Maybe. Okay, yes. I mean I *am* a professional party planner. You'd think she'd be impressed by that. But noooo. Every conversation Amber and I have, she's very determined to make it clear she and her mother are in charge. It's David's wedding, too."

Mia wasn't used to hearing her oldest sister whine and was really enjoying the moment. "What does David say?"

"He's a typical man. Whatever Amber wants is fine with him."

"You say that like it's a bad thing."

"It's not, it's just . . ." Katie lowered her voice. "Do you know they actually considered *paper* napkins. This is a formal sit-down dinner for three hundred and they discussed paper napkins."

"Did you run screaming into the night?"

Katie sighed again. "No. I reminded them that the linens, along with the tables and chairs, were being provided by Marcelli Winery. We have weddings here all the time and like to use our own vendors. Paper napkins. Can you imagine?"

"You didn't tell them that we pay our vendor, did you?"

Katie tucked her hair behind her ears. "I didn't really see the point. *They're* not paying for it." She stopped and looked at Mia. "Am I being horrible? I know weddings are expensive, and saving money where you can makes sense. But this is for David. I adore him and I want his wedding to be perfect."

"It's okay," Mia told her, still enjoying the sight of her normally unflappable sister just a little . . . flapped. "David doesn't actually care one way or the other about the napkins, but you do. If you can make it happen without upsetting Amber and her mother, then go for it."

"I've probably put together a hundred and fifty weddings," Katie muttered. "Why can't they talk to me?"

"Because we are the Marcellis and just a little intimidating for regular folks. Plus there's the whole 'Amber worrying about David still being in love with me' thing. That's got to put a damper on events."

Katie laughed. "My God, when did you grow up?"

"A couple of years ago. It was a Thursday."

"Okay, you're right about all of it. I'm going to have to wait until Valerie and Liana are engaged to plan a wedding for my kids."

"You could betroth them now. That should be worthy of a big party."

"Gee, thanks."

They walked out from behind the tasting building and stared at the beautiful white gazebo standing in the middle of a couple of acres of grass and carefully manicured plants before stepping inside.

"Every time I come here I'm surprised by how beautiful it is," Katie said wistfully. "I'm glad David's getting married here where Marcellis have been tying the knot for eighty years."

"He's not a Marcelli," Mia pointed out. "If he had been, I wouldn't have wanted to marry him."

"He's a Marcelli by love," Katie said firmly. "Just like Kelly." There was a momentary pause; then she continued, "Was it just me or is Kelly—"

"Completely out of control?" Mia asked, finishing her sentence. "It's not just you. Kelly and I talked a couple of days ago, I guess just before she and Etienne headed out. She said she admires my life. I couldn't believe it. I'm so not doing anything right."

"You are with Danny."

"That's more luck and really great role models. I'm not an intuitive parent. I didn't think I'd survive that first year when he felt so breakable. Rafael is different. He seems to know exactly how to get right down on Danny's level and connect. Which is surprising, considering the whole royalty thing. And impressive. He's imperious about nearly everything but he'll play in the dirt with his kid. Danny is thrilled and Rafael seems taken with his son."

"Rafael is doing it right where it matters. Did you think it would be different?"

Mia sank onto the floor of the gazebo and rested her forearms on her lap. "I never thought about it. Until he showed up here, I figured he was dead. Now he's here and so friendly and romantic."

Katie sat next to her and bumped her shoulder. "Romantic, huh? Come on . . . tell your favorite big sister all the details."

"He says all the right things," she admitted. "I know there's no reason to doubt him. He's straightforward and affectionate. He's answered all my questions and he doesn't seem to be in a hurry to get back to Calandria."

"But?" Katie asked.

"I don't know. I'm jaded and cynical, I guess. He's a prince. How on earth can he marry me? Doesn't his bride need a pedigree and access to really old jewelry?"

"Maybe not. The world is different. It's a new century."

"I'd noticed the century part, but Calandria has a monarchy. How different can it be?"

"What are you afraid of? Why don't you trust him? Is this because you don't really know him? Are you getting some signal or warning from your gut? Or is this about your unproven belief that you have lousy taste in men?"

Mia turned to Katie. "Excuse me? An unproven belief?"

"You've made a couple of bad choices."

Mia shook her head. "A bad choice is a guy who cheats on you, not someone who kidnaps the president's daughter. Ian fooled me completely, and Darcy could have died because of that." She drew in a deep breath. "It's not just the bad choice thing. I don't know Rafael."

"But you're in love with him."

"What?"

Katie patted her arm. "Mia, you've been in love with him since you got back five years ago. Having Danny only cemented your feelings. Why else would you have avoided any kind of dating situation for so long?"

"I'm busy."

"Many busy women manage to date. It's more than that and you know it."

"I don't love him," Mia said flatly.

"Fine. You don't. But you're also not willing to let anyone else get close to you and there has to be a reason for that. You might want to figure out what it is."

Mia nodded. Her sister had a point. About the reason, not the love. No way had she loved Rafael all these years. How crazy was that?

Katie stood. "All right, we're here to measure the gazebo. Let's get to work."

Mia eyed her tailored linen slacks and elegant, sleeveless silk blouse, then glanced down at her own T-shirt and cut-offs. "Somehow I missed the 'dress well' gene in this family."

"It's summer, you're off from school. Why would you want to worry about what to wear?"

"I wouldn't. I'm just saying, I don't have a closet full of beautiful clothes like you and Mom and Francesca. Brenna and I are misfits."

"You're individuals."

"That's very polite. My point is, I'm not really princess material."

Katie frowned. "What? You'd marry him except you don't know what to wear? I'm going to guess that all princesses have a live-in stylist to worry about that sort of thing for them. Mia, this is a really big decision. Make it for the right reasons."

"I know. I will. Part of me wants it to be like it was before. When he was Diego." She bit her lower lip. "Well, not the illegal stuff, but how it was just us and we were nearly regular people."

"You'd like Rafael better if he wasn't a prince?"

"Something like that."

"Sorry. Princely comes with the guy. You're stuck." Katie pulled a tape measure out of her purse. "It's not exactly ruling the world, but it's being in charge of a small country. That should count."

Mia grinned. "That's true. I'll bet I could even ask Rafael to get my picture on money. Wouldn't that be thrilling?"

"My sister—the five-dollar bill. We'd all be so proud."

Mia reached for the tape measure. "So what kind of flowers are they talking about?"

Katie sighed heavily. "Daisies. Lots and lots of daisies."

Mia listened to the mantel clock chime midnight. The house was quiet and she guessed that everyone was asleep. As *she* should be. But no matter how tired she felt physically, she couldn't seem to shut down her mind.

It whirled and swirled and dipped, jumping from past to present, while completely ignoring the future because that was just too big to deal with right now. Which led her to one glaringly obvious conclusion.

The most logical solution to all her problems was to

refuse Rafael's proposal and work out an agreement whereby they had some kind of shared custody. Maybe Danny could summer in Calandria and learn all his princely duties while spending his school year here, living like a normal child.

Except she had a feeling that normal wasn't possible. Not after the world found out that little Danny Marcelli was really the heir to the Calandrian throne.

Security wasn't a problem. Sam, Francesca's husband, was an expert, and Joe had plenty of experience dealing with Darcy's welfare. But what about school? Could Danny really go to the elementary school down the road and be a regular child? Was Mia kidding herself? And if Danny really was going to rule Calandria someday, shouldn't he grow up there? Which meant what? That she would move there with him?

And if she did move there with him, what would she do with her life? She had a feeling she wouldn't be able to practice law. So then what? Being a stay-at-home mom wasn't really her style. Would she just live in the shadows while Danny became a prince and Rafael married an appropriate future queen?

Thinking about him marrying someone else gave her a tight feeling in her stomach, which she hated, because it was a definite tally in the yes column of Katie's theory.

"I don't love him," Mia said out loud. What kind of idiot stayed in love with a dead man for five years?

So if she didn't love him, wasn't not marrying him the right thing to do?

She heard footsteps in the hallway. The door pushed open and Rafael stepped into the quiet of the library.

"You hide here," he said as he approached.

"I think of it more as a retreat."

She curled up in a corner of the sofa. He settled in the middle and angled toward her.

"I have news," he said, handing her an envelope. "It arrived today, but I wished to deliver it to you privately. A most difficult thing in this household."

She took the paper. "We are a crowd," she said as she glanced at the return address and saw it was a medical lab. "The DNA results?"

He nodded.

She gave back the envelope. "I already know the results."

"As do I. Daniel is my son."

Hardly news to her, but still, hearing him say the words made her tense a little. As if the situation had just gotten more serious.

"You'll have to tell your father," she said. "I'm not sure he'll be pleased."

"He wants a grandchild and an heir for me. He will come around much quicker than Grandma Tessa. She still resists me."

Mia laughed. "You're winning her over. Tonight at dinner she offered you seconds without you having to ask. That's progress. I'm not sure your father will be as easy as you think. This can't be what he had planned for your future."

Rafael shrugged. "He will adjust. At least he'll stop parading potential brides in front of me."

"He really does that?"

"It is not a marriage mart, but yes, women are brought to different events and I meet them." He smiled at her. "So far I have found it very easy to resist their charms."

"I can relate. If my grandpa Lorenzo had thought he could have gotten away with arranging marriages for his granddaughters, he would have done it in a heartbeat."

"Would you have said yes?" he asked.

She drew her knees closer to her chest and wrapped her arms around her legs. "Not my style."

"Because you are too independent."

"It's more than that. I loved my grandfather, but he would have made the best match for the vineyard, not the best match for me. Isn't that what the king is doing to you? Parading around the grand duchess of Whosits because her father owns shipping rights to Finland or whatever? Does he actually care if you fall in love?"

"Is love so very important?"

"Hello? We're talking about living with someone the rest of your life. I suppose if the castle is big enough, you could have separate wings. Is that what you want? The right marriage for Calandria rather than the right marriage for you?"

"I think I can make them the same thing," he told her, his blue eyes claiming hers.

There was a not-so-subtle message there, she thought, not sure if she should lean in and say yes or bolt for freedom.

"I don't even know any good princess jokes," she said at last.

"You don't have to. The rules can be learned, Mia. But not the heart of a person. That is more complicated."

"What do you know about my heart?" she asked.

"That you do not give it easily. That you are loyal. That when you love, you do so without reservation."

"What happens when you love?" She lowered her feet to the floor. "Have you been in love before?"

"You mean aside from you?" he asked.

She felt herself flush. "I didn't want to pressure you."

"I loved you," he said easily. "I thought we loved each other."

His words stirred her, body and soul. Relief tasted sweet. It was as if she'd been starving for weeks and he'd finally offered her food.

He *had* loved her. All that had been real.

"Then have you been in love aside from me?" she asked.

"When I was very young," he admitted. "A long time ago. I was just eighteen. She was a few years older and very beautiful."

"Right, because in real life, the prince never falls for the ugly girl."

He smiled. "You consider me shallow."

"I consider you a typical male. Go on. You met a beautiful, older woman who seduced you with her worldly ways and seductive charms."

His humor faded. "You are right. It is a cliché, but I did not know that at the time. She could claim some minor nobility, which made her acceptable, but my father did not like her and said we were too young. Or at least I was."

Mia knew the story didn't end well. If it had, Rafael would currently be Mr. Minor Nobility and they wouldn't be having this conversation. "And?"

"And I bought a ring so I could propose, despite my father's disapproval. Then I discovered she was selling the intimate details of our private relationship to the press."

She winced. "How intimate?"

"Very. I had only been with a few other women. She

taught me how to please a woman and then she told the world about it."

"That would be horrible for anyone to have happen anywhere, but to have it play out in the tabloids . . . I'm sorry."

"As am I. But I learned an important lesson. Now I do not trust so easily."

Did he trust her? How would she know if he did? What did it take to gain his trust? Did she want to?

"It was a long time ago," he told her. "I assure you, I have recovered."

"It's still sucky that she did that. I'm sure you gave her jewelry. If she needed money, she should have sold that instead."

He chuckled. "My innocent Mia. Don't you know that to a woman like that secrets are far easier to part with than anything that sparkles?"

"No. I guess this is why I don't belong in your world."

"Don't you?"

He reached for her and she went willingly into his arms. He might think the humiliation of that young man was gone forever, but she knew some wounds never completely heal. Knowing he'd felt pain made him seem a little bit more like a regular person.

His mouth claimed hers in a kiss that demanded more than comfort. She met him as an equal, willing to do a little demanding of her own. He shifted her so that she stretched out beneath him on the sofa.

As she parted her lips and circled his tongue with her own, she rubbed her hands across his shoulders and back. He braced himself above her, his eyes closed, his beautiful, talented, sexy mouth teasing her, making her tremble.

Need rushed through her like a storm-driven tide. She melted and found herself wanting more than just a simple kiss. Her body remembered what it had been like the last time they had been so physically close. Heat filled her. Between her legs she felt herself swelling in anticipation. She knew if he touched her, she would be wet and ready and hungry.

He drew back slightly and kissed her cheeks, her forehead, her nose; then he nibbled along her jawline. She turned her head to give him more room and he licked the sensitive skin below her ear.

"Mia," he breathed before he bit down on her earlobe. "I want you."

Simple words, she thought hazily. Magic words.

"I want you," he repeated as he stared into her eyes and covered her breast with his hand.

His touch was exquisite. The weight of him, the way he moved so that his palm caressed her hard nipple. She had to bite her lip to hold in a whimper of desire. He cupped her curves in a gentle caress that loosened the last slender threads of her control.

"I want you, too," she breathed as she pushed him back. She raised herself up a few inches and tore off her T-shirt. Next she reached behind herself and unfastened her bra. That got tossed to the floor, too.

She leaned back on the cushions, feeling the cool leather on her bare skin. Above her, Rafael smiled with anticipation. It was an expression she recognized.

"So beautiful," he told her. He used a single finger to explore her breast. First the underside, then the top. Finally he slowly, oh so slowly, moved to her nipple. Once there, he lightly brushed the very tip.

Her breath caught. Need tightened every muscle in her body. She swore, then raised herself so that she was inches from his mouth.

"Stop playing."

"As you wish."

He lowered his head, then took her nipple in his mouth. The hot, wet pressure pushed her to the edge. She couldn't get enough, couldn't be close enough, couldn't feel enough. Wanting grew until it consumed her. Wanting and desire and the heavy thickness of her body slick with passion.

He sucked her nipple, then replaced tongue with fingers and moved to her other breast. She writhed beneath him, wanting it all, yet desperate to have him between her legs.

He read her mind, or understood what the frantic tugging of her hands on her shorts meant. He drew back.

"Sit up," he commanded as he pulled his shirt over his head.

She did as he requested, but first she unfastened her shorts and pushed them down, along with her panties. He stared at her nakedness for a moment, groaned, then removed the rest of his clothing. She parted her legs, desperate to have him inside.

But instead of accepting her invitation, he slid to his knees on the floor and moved between her thighs.

"Oh, God," she breathed as she remembered what he'd done to her before when he'd touched her with his mouth. It had been beyond exquisite, beyond sensation.

He cupped her hips and shifted her so she was at the very edge of the sofa, then he lowered his head toward her hot, swollen center.

At first there was only the puff of his breath. She tensed in anticipation. He parted her tenderly, then slowly, gently, lightly stroked her with the very tip of his tongue.

She felt the scream building up inside of her. She spread her legs as wide as they would go and wished she'd studied yoga more. If only she'd . . . He licked her again, this time with his tongue flat. From bottom to top, he covered every inch of her. Then he returned to that one special place and reintroduced himself.

He circled and teased and rubbed and sucked. He slipped two fingers inside of her and caressed her from the inside, the movements matching. She groaned, she begged, and did everything in her power not to come. Not yet.

She could feel herself getting wetter and wetter. She was swollen to the point of discomfort and still she held back because no one had ever gone down on her like that. But in the end, which was maybe three minutes, she had no choice. She covered her mouth with her hand and screamed her surrender.

The waves of pleasure swept her into another dimension. Muscles convulsed in rippling release, an orgasm that went on and on. Just when she thought she was surely finished, he reached up his free hand and lightly touched her left nipple. That sent her back into another release. Then he replaced tongue with fingers, keeping her going as he raised up, shifted, and thrust into her.

More, she thought, as she continued to come with each thrust. She wrapped her legs around his hips, holding him in place. More and deeper and forever.

He pumped and thrust, filling her over and over again. She felt herself begin to shatter as every cell of her body sighed in pleasure. Then he stiffened and came and they clung to each other as the aftershocks rippled through them.

She resurfaced on the sofa, his body pressing against her. They lay together, spent and satisfied. She looked at him, at the face that was familiar yet different, and in that moment she knew him.

"Just like before," she whispered.

He smiled. "Better. How I love to touch you, Mia. You are made for pleasure, and when I am with you, I am the most powerful man in the world."

Tears burned in her eyes. He had often said such things to her before, but now, knowing about his past and what his first love had done, she felt touched. She could easily use those words against him, humiliate him publicly. He trusted her to keep him safe.

"Katie was right," she said without thinking.

"Katie? Your sister? Right about what?"

Mia swallowed. It had been five years and she'd never stopped loving him. She'd never moved on. All this time she'd been waiting for the love of her life to return, and he finally had.

"I will marry you, Rafael. I'm proud to marry you."

His eyes widened slightly. "Are you serious? You are not just saying this in the heat of the moment?"

She grinned. "You're good, but you're not that good. This isn't about us making love, despite the fact that it was spectacular. It's about the fact that we belong together. I don't know how it's all going to work out, but we'll deal with that later."

"Mia." He wrapped his arms around her and kissed her hard. "Thank you. You are right. There are many things to discuss and much for you to learn, but you will see. All will be well." He grinned. "You're going to marry me."

"Apparently." She thought about the last royal wedding that had been broadcast on television. "It's going to be huge, isn't it?"

"A thousand or so guests, long ceremonies. Yes, it will be painful. Or we could elope."

She blinked at him. "Excuse me, but did you just say elope?"

He nodded. "Some formalities cannot be avoided. You must be made a princess of my country, which can happen through a different ceremony, but there is no need for us to have a big wedding if the thought of it makes you uncomfortable. Or if you don't want to wait."

"I don't want to wait," she admitted. "But more than that, I'm not ready to be the center of attention."

"Marrying me will make you such, Mia. You must be willing to accept that. You would one day rule as queen. You must not forget that."

His desire to make sure she knew what she was getting into just made her love him more.

"Are you sure a quickie wedding is legal?" she asked.

"Of course. You would officially be my wife."

"Even if we ran off to Las Vegas?"

He smiled. "Is that what you have in mind?"

"Well, any big formal thing is going to include my family. There's no way we'll be able to escape that. Which means it will take time and then the king will find out about it. So either we go for it or we stay traditional."

"Would you like to go for it?"

As he asked, he moved against her. He was already hard again. Her body tightened in response.

"All that for me?" she asked as she reached between them and took him in her hand.

"All that and much more," he murmured. "I give you my heart, my country, my history, my future. Marry me, Mia Marcelli."

He shifted so she was on top of him. She slid herself onto his erection and eased into another orgasm.

"Okay," she gasped as she tightened around him.

He reached up and teased her nipples. "Okay, what?"

"Danny's birthday is in a couple of days. We'll fly to Las Vegas after that."

He raised up and claimed her with a kiss. "As you wish, my love. As you wish."

10

ℬ

Rafael woke up alone in his bed. As much as he wanted Mia there with him, they had agreed it would be better for them to keep their relationship a secret until after they eloped.

As he walked into the bathroom attached to his room, he smiled. Last night had been most pleasurable, and not simply because Mia had finally agreed to marry him. Their lovemaking had been as exciting and sensual as he remembered. She had always been able to match him, desire for desire, and time had not eroded that connection.

Although her getting pregnant had been an unexpected complication, he could not regret Daniel's parentage. Mia brought great strength and heart to the boy.

He shaved, then stepped into the shower. As he reached for the soap, he remembered how she had asked if he had loved before. As if not sure he had loved her.

He had never allowed himself to examine his feelings for her. He had known they would only be together for a short time. But he had never forgotten her. Was that love?

Did it matter? Despite the brief marriage they would share, she was not an appropriate queen. He would let her go because it was the right thing to do. His responsibility demanded . . .

Everything, he thought, both angry and resigned. It always had. This time, Mia would pay the price for who he was. He stepped out of the shower. He did not want to hurt her. Before he had arrived, she had been an obstacle. Now she was uniquely herself.

When he had dried off, he dressed. Later he would call his father and tell him of his victory. They would need to begin to draw up the required paperwork. Rafael decided that he would be generous. He would allow Mia the right to visit her son as often as she would like. There was no need to keep them apart. Having his mother around would make the transition easier for the boy.

He heard a knock on the door, followed by a low, "Your highness?"

"Enter."

Oliver stepped into the room. "Your gift has arrived and is ready."

"Good," Rafael said, knowing how pleased Daniel would be. "I will get the boy and be right down."

Oliver nodded and left. Rafael finished dressing, then walked to Daniel's room.

Mia was already there. He paused in the doorway and watched her brush his son's hair while outlining their activities for the day. She worked quickly, with the easy grace of someone who has performed this particular task a thousand times before.

Rafael stepped into the room. "Good morning," he said.

Daniel looked up and grinned, then darted forward. "Daddy, Daddy!"

Rafael dropped to one knee and pulled the boy close. "It has only been one night. Did you miss me so much?"

He asked the question of his son, but his gaze was on Mia as he spoke. She stood by the dresser, wearing her usual shorts and a T-shirt. Her hair was damp from her recent shower, which made him think of her naked, which made him want her again.

"Did you sleep well?" he asked with a smile that only she could see.

"Better than I expected."

"Perhaps it was the exercise you had yesterday."

She blushed faintly. "Yes, well, maybe. And you?"

"I slept very well."

"Good. We're all rested. Danny, come on. I can smell breakfast."

Rafael ruffled the boy's hair. "Perhaps that could wait for a few minutes. I have a surprise for him."

Mia crossed to the door. "Let me guess. A crown?"

"You mock the scepter."

"It's fairly mockable."

"Your circumstances suggest you will want to understand all of my country's traditions."

Her smile faded as something very close to panic filled her eyes. "Good point. Danny, your dad got you an early birthday present. Do you want to go see it?"

The boy nodded eagerly and took his father's hand. Rafael frowned slightly. Was it appropriate for a male child this age to hold his father's hand? He could not remember ever having such contact with his own father.

He glanced at Mia, but she didn't act as if anything

was amiss. Perhaps his childhood should not be the measure of normal, he admitted. There would be time for Daniel to learn how to behave royally.

"Where is it?" Danny asked. "Is it big? Is it soldiers? Is it lots of soldiers?"

"It is not soldiers and it is not large." Rafael looked at the boy. "It may seem large to you. Come. You will see for yourself."

They walked down the stairs. The Grands were already in the kitchen, fixing breakfast.

"Mornin'" Grammy M said, beaming at him. "You're up early."

"I have a surprise for Daniel," Rafael told her.

Grandma Tessa narrowed her eyes. "He's barely four. Still a little boy."

Rafael paused to kiss her cheek. "And here I thought you had accepted me, Tessa."

She gave him a smile. "All right. I'll wait to see what it is before I complain."

"Thank you." He reached for Mia with his free hand. "You will be very impressed."

"I'm already having doubts."

"How can you not trust me?"

"Fascinating question. We'll have to explore that later."

Later he would have her in his bed again. Later he would make her forget everything but the pleasure she felt in his arms. Later she would make plans for their wedding and he would let her.

They walked outside just as Umberto led a small pony out of a horse carrier. The animal was pure white, with a long mane and tail. Ribbons and bells had been woven into both, so the pony fluttered and tinkled as it walked.

Danny gripped his hand tightly. "For me?" he asked with a gasp. "For my birthday?"

"Yes, Daniel. This is a Calandrian pony. They are specially bred and revered all over the world."

Mia came to a stop. "You bought him a pony?"

"As you can see."

"You bought him a pony and you didn't tell me?"

He frowned. "Why would I?"

"Gee, I don't know. Because I'm his mother? Because we don't exactly have a spare stable here on our vineyard?"

"You do not have to worry about details, Mia."

"Why not? Someone does."

"All will be taken care of." He turned to Daniel. "His name is Gaspare, which means bringer of gifts."

Danny stared wide-eyed. "He's really mine?"

"Of course."

"Can I ride him?"

"Right now."

Oliver appeared with a saddle and bridle.

"There is much work in owning a horse, or even a pony," Rafael told the boy. "You will have to be very responsible. Do you know what that means?"

Danny shook his head.

"It means you will have to take care of him. You will have to brush him and feed him."

"What? He doesn't get a groom with the horse?" Mia asked.

"Yes, of course there is a groom, but Daniel needs to learn to take care of things. To be responsible."

"All part of his once-and-future-king training?"

There was something in her voice, something that

made him watch her closely. "You are angry?" he asked, not sure how that was possible.

"*Anger* isn't the right word. *Shocked.* Rafael, a pony is a big deal. How could you not have discussed this with me?"

"You worry too much," he said, then kissed her on the mouth. "Help me saddle him so Daniel can ride him."

Five minutes later a very excited boy sat on top of his pony. Mia hovered, which Rafael allowed. It was a first ride, after all. But in time she would have to learn to let her son go. He needed to be a man.

"I'm riding, I'm riding!" Daniel crowed as they made a slow circle around the backyard. "Daddy, this is the bestest present ever."

"Socks are going to be a real letdown after this," Mia mumbled.

"You did not buy him socks."

"Not exactly." She tentatively patted the pony's neck. "He seems friendly enough."

"He is very gentle, but with enough of a spirit to be a challenge as Daniel learns to ride more. In a few months, he'll graduate to a horse, but Gaspare works for now."

"I love my pony," Daniel said as he leaned forward and hugged the animal's neck.

"Keep control of the reins," Rafael told him. "It is how you control your mount."

Daniel grinned. "He's a pretty pony. Can I take him to school to show my friends and Miss Valdrake?"

"His teacher," Mia said. "Honey, I'm thinking we're going to wait on pony show-and-tell. Just until we get this figured out." She looked at Rafael. "You haven't said what we're going to do about a stable."

"The weather is mild enough that the animal can stay out."

"And in winter?"

Daniel and his pony wouldn't be here, Rafael thought. But what he said was, "I have a staff to deal with details, Mia. Please, try not to worry. All will be well."

"I don't have a staff," she said. "I'm used to solving my own problems and you're not helping with that."

"Do we really need to discuss this now?"

She smiled at Daniel, who urged Gaspare to go faster.

"I guess not," she admitted. "It's just . . . Wow. A pony. The whole prince thing is still something I have to get used to."

"You will."

"I guess I have to. What with . . ." Her voice trailed off.

He knew she referred to her acceptance of his proposal. That she would have to get used to being royal herself. He wanted to reassure her that the job would be much less taxing than she imagined for she would be only have it a few weeks.

"He bought Danny a pony," Mia said as she paced around Brenna's office at the winery. "He never said a word. He just announced he had a surprise and then there it was. An honest-to-God pony."

"It wouldn't be my first choice," Brenna admitted, "but hey, he's royal. Maybe it's a big fourth birthday thing with his family."

"I guess. It's just . . . shouldn't he have talked to me about it? I'm Danny's mother."

"Rafael is his father." Brenna rolled her eyes. "I really hate taking the guy's side against a woman, especially my sister, but this time I think you're freaking over nothing. It's a pony. It's not like he bought him an island."

"Calandria is an island. As heir, I guess Danny already has that."

"Okay, then strippers. That would have been a gift to get crabby about. Families do odd things. Grandpa Lorenzo made all of us learn about wine even though I was the only one interested. It happens. Don't worry about it. Danny is a prince, which is just too weird. Don't all princes need to learn how to ride? Isn't it in the prince handbook?"

"Probably. I should Google him again."

"Rafael?" Brenna asked.

Mia walked to the desk and sat in the large chair across from Brenna's. "Yeah. I did it once and I was overwhelmed by pictures of him with beautiful young women. It got depressing."

"Mia, you're gorgeous and smart and a lot more interesting than any high-society rich bitch he might meet at some charity event."

"You don't actually know that."

"Of course I do. He fell for you years ago and now he wants to marry you. Doesn't that mean you win?"

Mia rubbed her temples. "I can't believe we're having this conversation. I can't believe Danny is a prince."

"It's a little too late to take back Rafael as his father. You should have thought of that before you did the wild thing."

"Who knew it would come to this?" She sighed. "Who knew Diego was really Crown Prince Rafael in disguise? My life is a soap opera."

Mia looked at her sister and drew in a breath. "I said yes."

Brenna stared at her. "To his proposal?"

Mia nodded. "Last night. I can't face anything huge or ceremonial right now. We're going to Las Vegas after Danny's birthday."

Brenna stood and clapped her hands together. "I don't know what to say. My baby sister, the queen."

Mia stood and they hugged. When Brenna released her, Mia asked, "Am I crazy to do this?"

"I don't know. Does it feel right? Are you happy?"

"I was until the pony."

Brenna laughed. "What is it about that damned horse that has you so freaked?"

"I don't know. I guess it's that he didn't discuss it with me. He made his own decision."

"I can understand that, but how many of your decisions have you discussed with him? Mia, it's been five years since you were last together. It's going to take a little time to figure out how this all fits."

"You're right. Which means running off to marry him isn't what I should be doing."

"I don't want to respond to that," Brenna admitted. "You have to do what feels right. Rafael is Danny's father. Whether or not you marry him, you're going to have to deal with him for the rest of your life."

"I've been thinking about that. How exactly does one work out a custody agreement with a prince?"

"Tell me that's not why you're marrying him. To make a custody agreement easier."

"It's not." Mia sank back into her chair. "I haven't been with anyone since him. I . . . Katie said I had never fallen out of love with him, which I violently disagreed with at the time, but I've been thinking maybe she was right. I have feelings for him. Strong feelings. And he's a really great guy. I like how he is with Danny and me. He's open and honest and I still get tingles."

"So what's not to like?" Brenna asked.

"That's what I keep thinking. So I said I'd marry him."

"You can change your mind. Or put it off. There's a lot to be said for getting to know the guy you're going to rule with."

Mia groaned. "When I think about being with Rafael I get butterflies, but when I think about actually ruling a country, I want to vomit. I look at what Darcy has to go through and I know I'd hate it. She's just the president's daughter."

Brenna sat on the edge of her desk. "If you're this unsure, then put things off for a while. No one is saying you have to marry him."

Mia smiled. "But I want to. Isn't that dumb? I want to marry him. I want to know that for the rest of our lives, we'll be together."

"So if Rafael were just a regular guy, you wouldn't have a problem with this."

Mia considered the statement. "Apparently not."

"In this case, the crown comes with the guy. Can you handle that?"

"I sort of have to. Otherwise, I let Rafael go, and I can't imagine doing that. When I thought he died, I didn't want to live myself. I ached for months. Being pregnant was the only thing that got me through. I can't imagine ever surviving that pain again. But the man I loved before was different."

"In good ways or bad ways?"

"Both. I liked that Diego wasn't a world-renowned sex object. Plus I have such lousy taste in men. Seriously, Brenna, do you know how badly I could be screwing this up?"

"He's a prince, Mia. How bad could it be?"

"That's what I keep telling myself." She winced. "I don't want to move away."

"I'm thinking you're going to have to live in Calandria. But there's good news. You could be on a stamp."

"I was hoping for money, but a stamp works. My God, I can't believe we're having this conversation. I guess if I do marry him we'll move to Calandria fairly quickly. We haven't talked about it, but it makes sense. I'm sure Rafael has responsibilities, and Danny and I need to start learning to be royal."

Mia stood and plucked at her T-shirt. "Who am I kidding? I bought this for five dollars at Wal-Mart. The only designer clothes I own are my mother's hand-me-downs. I don't do jewelry or know how to waltz."

Brenna stood and moved close. "You speak about four hundred languages, you're smart, you're capable, and you're in love. Are you ever going to meet another guy like Rafael? Because if you aren't sure there's another handsome prince waiting for you, I would say learning to waltz might be the way to go."

Mia smiled. "Kelly could probably teach me."

"I'm sure she'd be delighted to. Follow your heart, Mia. That's the best advice I can give you. If I'd followed mine, I would have married Nic when I was eighteen instead of wasting nearly a decade of our lives."

"Do you regret that?"

"I try not to, but sometimes, when I'm up late with the twins, I wonder what our lives would have been like if I hadn't been afraid to take the plunge."

"Don't you hate regrets?" Mia asked.

"More than anything. Follow your heart," Brenna said again. "Don't look back and think 'if only.' If you can't imagine life without him, then go for it. If you can, then don't. He's Danny's father and that's never going to change. The bottom line is you don't have to decide today."

"I know. I have two days until Danny's birthday."

"You don't have to elope. You can tell him you need more time."

Mia considered that. "I want to be with him," she said at last. "I love him."

"Then there's your answer."

The two women hugged again; then Mia headed back to the house. She was going to do it. She was going to elope with Rafael and then figure out what she'd gotten herself into.

As she walked across the lawn, she noticed the pony tethered under a tree. "I wonder what pony poop does to grass," she murmured as she climbed the steps and entered the house.

"It's me," she yelled as she walked into the empty kitchen.

A quick glance at the clock told her the Grands were probably resting before they started dinner. She stuck her head in the family room and saw Danny curled up on the sofa, watching a cartoon video.

"Doing okay?" she asked.

Danny smiled at her and nodded.

So if her son was occupied and the Grands were sleeping, that sort of left her at loose ends. Maybe she and Rafael had time for a quickie.

Anticipation propelled her upstairs. She walked down

the hallway toward his room. The door stood open and she could hear him talking on the phone.

At first the words didn't register. She wasn't trying to listen in. She caught a word or two in Italian and paused. Was he talking business? Should she wait?

As she considered her options, she took another step and the floorboards creaked. Instantly Rafael went silent. When he continued the conversation, he spoke Portuguese.

Mia froze. Why on earth would he change languages like that? The most obvious explanation was that he didn't want to be understood. Which made no sense.

Even so, she crept forward to listen.

"Not to worry," he said, his voice low. "Yes, all is well. As I told you, Mia has agreed to marry me. We are to fly to Las Vegas in a few days. No, she knows nothing. We will go after Danny's birthday. I have the paperwork all ready."

He was silent for a moment. "We will return to Calandria as soon as possible. I know. Once we are there, Calandrian laws apply. No, Mia would never think to study such a thing. She has no idea that once the heir arrives in Calandria, he can never be taken away without permission from the throne. Of course. I will have my son and heir."

He was silent again. "Yes. A divorce. I have those papers as well. It is unfortunate she is not more suitable, but I understand my responsibilities. I will keep Daniel with me and send Mia way."

11

❦

Mia found herself unable to breathe. White-hot fury poured through her until she felt sure she could melt steel simply by touching it. She stood as if nailed to the floor, unable to move as Rafael finished his conversation with his father. A conversation that revealed everything.

When he'd hung up, she forced herself to walk into her bedroom, where she picked up the phone and called Joe's cell.

"Get to the house now," she said, her voice low and thick. "Bring a gun."

She hung up before he could ask anything; then she stalked into Rafael's bedroom and wondered if she was truly capable of murder.

At that moment it seemed more than possible—it seemed likely. She wanted him dead. No, she wanted him in pain. She wanted to see blood and bone jutting through flesh. She wanted him writhing and begging, and she wanted to watch him disappear into a puddle of green slime.

He turned and smiled at her. "Mia. I was just speaking

with my father and we were—" He stared at her. "What is wrong?"

She could feel the scream building, but as it hadn't reached the surface yet, she spoke in a quiet voice, one laced with so much anger, it practically snapped.

"Did you think I was so fucking stupid that I didn't speak Portuguese?"

He paled slightly. "What do you mean?"

"Just what I said, you bastard. I heard and understood every damned word. Ironically, I wasn't paying attention when you were speaking Italian. I wasn't even listening. But you switched. I guess you thought I could be Grandma Tessa, who also speaks Italian. You sure as hell wouldn't want her hearing your little plan for my future."

She felt as angry about his assumption that she wouldn't understand him as she did about what he'd said. That bothered her for a second until she realized it was safe to be furious about the language he'd chosen. She wouldn't kill him over that.

"I heard you," she told him. "I heard every word. You lied. You deliberately lied. How dare you? You're not here to marry me, you're here to take my son."

The scream built and built until it finally burst free. She reached for the lamp on the dresser by the door and threw it at him.

"You fucking bastard. You tricked us all. You came here with your stories and your princely manners and the whole thing was a scam."

He'd sidestepped the lamp easily. Now he walked around the mess on the floor and moved toward her.

"Mia, calm down. You have misunderstood."

"Get away from me. I swear, if I had a gun I'd shoot you right now. Right in the gut. Or the balls. You didn't come here for me. You don't care about me or my family or anything. You want your son. You want to kidnap him."

"You're being ridiculous. Daniel is my heir. It is reasonable for me to—"

"Don't talk to me about reasonable," she screamed. "Don't you dare. You lied. It was all a lie."

"Daniel is my son."

"His name is Danny. He's a little boy. You want to take him away from me, but that will never happen. Never. Do you hear me?" She looked around for something else to throw at him and was frustrated by the lack of vases and lamps.

"He is my heir. My people have a right to—"

"Fuck your people and fuck you. Go to hell, Rafael. You're never getting him. Never. I don't care what I have to do. This is all bullshit. Why now? Why did you suddenly show up?"

She pressed a hand against her forehead as she remembered what he'd told her. "My God. The picture in the paper. That damn picture. You saw it and you recognized me and him. The age is right and he looks enough like you." She paused again and found herself unable to do more than gasp out. "The birthmark. Somehow you saw it."

"That first morning," he agreed. "The men in my family have carried it for generations."

"You didn't need the DNA test, did you?"

He shrugged. "I knew he was my son after I saw the birthmark."

"Of course. You saw the paper and knew, so you had to come here. Only you couldn't just show up. I would get really suspicious if after five years you suddenly appeared in my life. So you . . ."

She couldn't believe it. No. This wasn't happening. "You lied about everything. About being told I was dead, about missing me. You came up with that story as a way to make me trust you. You not coming after me had nothing to do with me being dead or not. You didn't care. You'd had your fling and then it was time to get back to your regular life. The prince one. You didn't give me another thought. Then you found out about Danny and suddenly you had an heir to worry about."

"Mia, you will make yourself sick."

"So what? I'll survive. You living through the day seems much less likely."

"Do not threaten me."

"Or what? You'll pretend you care about me so you can trick me into marriage and steal away my son?"

Her eyes began to burn, but she refused to give in to the tears. She couldn't think, couldn't believe this was happening.

"I was such a fool. How could you do it? How could you steal my child?"

"You are being melodramatic. Of course I would have allowed you to see Daniel. We would have made arrangements for—"

She heard footsteps on the stairs. "In here," she yelled.

Joe ran down the hallway and she was pleased to see he held a handgun.

"What the hell is going on?" he demanded.

Rafael stepped into the hallway. "Mia, you are taking this too far. Be reasonable."

"Reasonable?"

She lunged for Joe's gun, but he easily kept it out of reach.

"Shoot him!" she told her brother. "Shoot the goddamned prick right in the balls. He wants to steal Danny. He tricked me. He tricked us all. He pretended to care, but he doesn't. He wanted me to marry him so that when we got to Calandria he could take Danny away from me."

Joe grabbed her and shoved her behind him, then turned the gun on Rafael.

"Get out," he said quietly. "Get out of this house and take the bodyguards with you."

"I'm not finished here."

"Yes you are."

Rafael stared at the gun, then at Joe's face. He swore in Italian, then stalked out. As he passed Mia, he paused.

"This isn't over."

"It is," she told him. "More than you know."

And then he was gone. Mia stared into the empty room and saw the broken lamp. It was as if that shattered bit of ceramic represented all her hopes and dreams.

"Oh God," she breathed as her muscles began to shake and she felt herself go down.

Joe grabbed her and pulled her close. She went into his arms, feeling his strength and knowing nothing would ever be right again.

"I can't believe it," she whispered.

"I know."

"He lied. He tried to take Danny."

"But he didn't get him. We'll fix this, Mia. I swear."

She wanted to believe him, but she couldn't. It was too horrible.

"Danny," she said with a gasp. "Where is he? He was in the family room. What if Rafael took him?"

"Mommy?"

She turned and saw the Grands holding Danny's hands. Her son looked terrified and confused. She dropped to her knees and held out her arms. He rushed toward her and clung so tightly she couldn't catch her breath.

But that didn't matter. He was here and he was safe. She was going to make sure that never, ever changed.

They held a family meeting after Danny was in bed. Mia didn't want to attend. She didn't want to cry or breathe or eat ever again. Most of all, she didn't want to think. She didn't want to keep reliving those horrible moments when she'd found out the truth about Rafael, when she'd realized that everything he'd told her was a lie.

No, she thought as she stood at the top of the stairs and listened to the low voices coming from the family room. His lies weren't the worst of it. The true pit of her life was that she'd believed him.

Once again she'd trusted a man and he had betrayed her.

If Rafael had come after her, she could have handled it. If he'd wanted to hurt her or kidnap her or even kill her, she would have been able to cope. But he'd come after her child, and she would never forgive him for that.

She made herself walk downstairs. When she entered the family room, she saw everyone was already there. Katie and Zach, Francesca and Sam, Brenna and Nic, Joe and Darcy. The Grands were there, too, pressing food on everyone. Only her parents were missing. Since she hadn't called to tell them about marrying Rafael, she saw no reason to upset their vacation by admitting she'd almost lost her son.

Katie saw her first. "Oh, Mia." Katie held open her arms.

Mia moved into them and felt her other sisters closing ranks. They hugged her and whispered promises of revenge. The men stood a few feet back, looking angry and uncomfortable.

Mia absorbed their love and support. She'd promised herself she wouldn't cry over Rafael ever again, and she managed to get through the group hug without breaking down.

When everyone took a seat, Grammy M pressed a mug of tea into Mia's hands. She took the hot liquid but passed on food.

"I'm not very hungry," she admitted.

Grammy M started to say she had to eat something, but Tessa pulled her away.

"Mia will eat tomorrow," her paternal grandmother said quietly. "She's strong. You'll see."

Mia didn't feel very strong. She felt as if her heart had been run over by an eighteen-wheeler and left for roadkill.

"How's Danny?" Darcy asked.

"Confused. Apparently he didn't hear what I said to Rafael, but he knows we had a fight and his father has moved out. He kept asking for him tonight. He wanted Rafael to tuck him in."

Katie looked at Joe. "You should have shot him when you had the chance."

"It didn't seem the time. Besides, I can always do it later."

"We can arrest him," Grandma Tessa said to Joe. "He broke the law, didn't he?"

Joe stood by the fireplace. He shifted uncomfortably. "Technically, he didn't do anything wrong."

"All lying and cheating aside," Mia said with a lightness she didn't feel.

"Joe, there has to be something," Katie said. "He can't get away with this."

"He won't," Mia told her. "Danny is staying right here, with us. If I don't take him to Calandria, there's nothing Rafael can do. Right, Joe?"

He nodded. "I suppose he could petition the international courts, but that could take years. Appealing to the president won't help."

Darcy leaned toward Mia. "I already called my dad. Should the Calandrian ambassador try to see him, he won't be available. He also said to tell you that he would be happy to have Rafael thrown out of the country."

"I'm not sure I want this going public," Mia said. "Let's just keep it between us for now. We need a plan. We need to keep Danny safe and keep Rafael away from him."

"I don't know how this happened," Grammy M said with a sigh. "He seemed like such a *nice* man."

"He fooled us all," Grandma Tessa grumbled. "I thought I was too old and too crabby to be fooled."

"It wasn't exactly a fair fight," Katie told them. "We're basically honest people. We weren't looking for deception. Plus there's the whole prince angle. He had our attention there."

Brenna patted Mia's arm. "See? You're not the only one."

Mia appreciated the support, but it didn't help. She'd been the one who'd been willing to blindly commit her life to someone she barely knew. That impulsive decision could have cost her Danny.

"You're all forgetting something," Joe said. "Rafael is Danny's father. He might be an asshole, but he's still the father, and Mia can't keep him away forever."

"I don't want to hear that," Mia said flatly. She didn't want to be reminded of any connection to Rafael.

Francesca crossed to where Mia sat and crouched in front of her. "I understand you're beyond anger. We all are. Rafael came in here and treated us all like idiots. He tried to steal away one of our babies. I would like to spend a couple of days thinking up very special tortures for him."

Mia glanced at her sister and sighed. "You're going to be rational, aren't you?"

Francesca nodded. "You can't keep Danny from his father. Being an asshole isn't against the law."

"It should be."

"I agree, but it isn't. However much we all hate Rafael, Danny doesn't. He loves his father. He loves every minute they're together. He doesn't know what happened and none of us are going to tell him. In his world, nothing has changed. He's going to be four and he has a new daddy."

Mia understood the message. What her sister was trying to say in her calm, trained, psychologist way was that Mia didn't get to throw a tantrum. That whatever had happened between her and Prince Jerk, there was still Danny to consider, and her little boy deserved to have a father.

"I don't trust him for a minute," Mia said.

"You shouldn't," Francesca told her. "Rafael has proved he can't be trusted. Whatever you decide about custody or visitation or whatever, I'm here to remind you that you don't want to break Danny's heart."

Mia hated all of it. "You're saying I have to let him come to Danny's birthday party? That I have to let them hang out and trust him not to simply disappear with Danny?"

"I'm saying you can't refuse to let Rafael see his son. You can do things to keep Danny safe. You can make it difficult for Rafael and easy for us, but you can't stand in the way of father and son being together. As for his birthday, that's your call."

Mia heard the words and knew their truth, but she didn't want to listen. She didn't want to think about how much Danny wanted Rafael there. She turned to her brother. "Joe?"

"I hate that she's right, too," he said quietly. "I want to tell him to go to hell and maybe even help him along, but he's the kid's father and we can't undo that." He paused for a second. "Sam and I will make some calls. We'll talk to a few people and get more security here. I would like to think Rafael is smart enough not to try to take Danny, but I wouldn't bet on it."

"I can help, too," Zach said.

Mia turned to Katie's husband. "You mean legally?"

"Sure. There are laws in place to prevent a child from being taken out of the country. Danny being the heir to a throne might complicate things, but he's only four. That should be in our favor. Plus Rafael tried to trick you instead of seeking a straightforward custody agreement.

One of the lawyers in my office is an expert on child abduction. Let me get her working on this."

"Thank you," Mia told him. "That would be great."

"I can get my sister to call the attorney general," Darcy said. "Lauren's dating her son."

"Talk about friends in high places," Mia said, feeling her insides shake as a dozen emotions washed through her. "I really appreciate all of you rallying around. I would hate to go through this alone."

Katie joined Francesca, who pulled Mia to her feet. The sisters hugged.

"This is going to be fine," Katie told her. "You'll see. As you said, you're not alone. You have us, and hey, we're the Marcellis."

Brenna joined them. "You have to stay strong. Don't go beating yourself up about this. Whatever happens, it's never wrong to fall in love."

Mia appreciated the sentiment, even if she didn't believe it. "Falling in love might not be wrong," she said, "but sometimes it's pretty damned stupid."

The hotel was not to Rafael's liking. Despite the fact that Oliver and Umberto had paid off enough guests to claim an entire wing, Rafael still hated to be in such a public place. He disliked the location, on the edge of a busy highway, the flowering plants that seemed to overrun the place, and most of all he hated that he was here at all.

He paced the length of his suite, ignoring the floral wallpaper and matching drapes and bedspread. The owner had been delighted to show him all the amenities of the suite, but Rafael had not so politely closed the door in her face. What did he care about blow-dryers and heated towel racks when everything of importance had gone terribly wrong?

He had no one to blame but himself. He hated to admit that, but it was true. He'd grown complacent. He should never have called his father from the house. He knew better. Until that last call, he had been very careful.

He paused by the window and stared out at the distant view of the ocean. Mia's fury had burned with a fire so bright, he'd expected the house to ignite. He wasn't sure he'd ever seen her that angry before. In truth, he couldn't blame her for her feelings. A part of him disliked that he had hurt her. She was angry now, but later there would be tears and he would not be there to comfort her.

Comfort? What was he thinking? He had to remember his goal and how his plan had failed.

He had now shown his hand and she would be on guard against him. No doubt her entire family would be upset when she told them what she'd overheard.

He tightened his hands into fists and cursed himself for forgetting Mia's ability with languages. When he'd heard footsteps in the hallway, he'd reacted without thinking. Better to have ended the call, but no. He'd switched to a language he'd been sure Grandma Tessa would not understand. He had not suspected the footsteps were Mia's.

Oliver knocked on the open door. "Everything is taken care of, your highness. We have all the rooms on this floor. Umberto is running background checks on the other guests, but there is no reason to suspect any of them."

"Good."

"I have arranged for the menus of local restaurants to be delivered. When you are ready, one of us will order your meal and then go get it."

He nodded. "Thank you for your efficiency."

Oliver nodded. "Sir, I do not mean to presume, but perhaps it would be best to simply take the child. We could go tonight and be well on our way to Calandria before anyone knew he was gone."

"An excellent plan," Rafael said. "If we had used it that first night. Now it will not be possible. Mia's brother is more highly trained than you and Umberto. Her brother-in-law Sam is a security expert. We would not be successful."

Oliver's silence indicated he agreed with Rafael's assessment. "Perhaps a diplomatic solution," he offered. "If our ambassador spoke with the president."

"I doubt the president will be available anytime soon. You forget Joe's wife is the president's daughter. She already will have called her father. It is what I would have done. They are not fools, which is unfortunate for us."

He had been the only fool. He hated that he'd been caught. Damn Mia for being the kind of woman who would make this all difficult. He'd meant what he said— he would not have kept her from Daniel. The boy was the heir to Calandria. He belonged with his people. But would she ever see that? Would she ever be sensible?

Would she ever forgive him?

"I will come up with a plan," he said at last. "There is a way and I will find it. I always win."

12

∾

Mia sat on the back steps of the house and waited for the limo. Joe had offered to do it for her, but she wanted to look Rafael in the eyes while she explained the new rules in play. Not that she was alone. Thanks to Joe and Sam, there were at least a dozen security personnel around the house, and Joe hovered nearby.

Anger and hurt still defined her existence, but she was learning to live with the pain and regret, along with the constant ache in her heart. Knowing she had only herself to blame was both a blessing and curse. On the one hand, she could have very heated conversations with herself about what went wrong and vow never to be that stupid again. On the other hand, no one else really understood what she was going through.

She drew in a deep breath and was pleased to feel somewhat in control. No more tears—at least not in public—and no more outbursts. She was going to stay in charge and that meant keeping her emotions in check.

The trick was not to think too much. Not to remember how she'd given her heart to a man who had betrayed her.

The long black limo pulled into the driveway. Mia stood. Joe was at her side in an instant, along with six of the guards. As the car moved closer, Mia saw Umberto behind the wheel. Which meant Oliver was in back. Unless Rafael had brought in reinforcements.

"You made sure he wouldn't have other security, right?" she asked Joe.

He patted her back. "Of course. Everything has been negotiated, from the time he could arrive to how many of my men would be on his men. He knows what will happen if he steps out of line."

"You'll kill him?" she asked brightly.

"No, I'll beat the crap out of him and then I'll make him leave."

Not nearly good enough, she thought as the rear door of the limo opened and Oliver stepped out.

Joe motioned to one of his men. Oliver was searched. The same thing happened to Umberto when he exited the vehicle. Mia tensed as Rafael stepped into the afternoon sunlight.

Damn the man, he looked perfect. Well dressed, but casual, still handsome. She half expected to see horns or cloven feet, but there was only his brown hair and expensive leather loafers. His blue eyes seemed as compelling as always and very specific parts of her body were all too happy to have him in close proximity.

"Mia," he said with a slight bow of his head.

"Judas." She took a step toward him and squared her shoulders. "Just so we're all clear, you are being allowed onto this property because it is your son's fourth birthday and he wants you here. The reason he wants you here is because I didn't tell him what a lying weasel you are. As you can see, you are severely outnumbered. The guards have been ordered to shoot to kill if you try anything."

That last bit was a lie, but she didn't care. Let him be afraid.

"You wouldn't kill me," he said calmly. "My being dead doesn't solve your problem. Daniel is still the heir."

"True, but your death gets rid of you, and for now that's enough."

"You wouldn't risk the life of your son with flying bullets."

"You want to make this about logistics, I'm making a point. You are not welcome here. No one likes you or trusts you. One false move and you are gone."

Joe moved in. "A little FYI—there are more than a dozen security guards on duty."

Rafael shrugged. "As you wish. I didn't think I was as dangerous as all that. You are taking this very seriously, Mia."

His casual attitude made her wish for long nails and a decent shot at his eyes. "You tried to steal my son. It doesn't get more serious than that."

Rafael drew in a breath. "I am sorry you are so angry and I am sorry I hurt you. That was never my intent. I should have told you the truth from the beginning."

"Do you think any of that matters?" she asked, furious he would think an apology would make a difference.

"I was never going to keep you from him. You would have been able to see him whenever you liked."

"How very generous you are. Give me a moment to catch my breath from the wonderfulness of you."

His eyes narrowed. "You do not accept my apology?"

"Not even if it came with a couple of diamonds on a gold plate. The only thing you're sorry about is getting caught before you could put your plan into action. You used me and my family. We trusted you, we believed you, and you repaid us with deception."

Anger was good, she thought. Anger kept the pain at bay.

She moved right in front of him and poked him in the center of his chest. "I will never trust you again. There is nothing you can say or do that will make me believe a word you say. You played me for a fool. I'll give you points for originality and effort. You did a hell of a job and told a great story. But you had your chance and you blew it. I don't know what would have happened if you'd been honest. It's something we'll never know. I despise you and I hate that you're Danny's father. I will do what is right because I love my son. But you are never getting a piece of me again."

She turned on her heel and walked away. Rafael watched her go. Even as he resented the situation, he found himself admiring the power of her convictions and the grace in her movements.

She was, he admitted to himself, quite a woman. Also, she was much more angry than he had thought she would be. Daniel was his heir—what did she expect him to do? Allow his son to be raised here? Away from his people?

"Impossible," he muttered.

Joe smiled insincerely. "That's what we were saying about you. The party is this way."

Rafael followed him around to the side of the house, where several large tables had been set up in the shade.

There were a dozen or so children, most likely from Danny's school, a few parents, and much of the Marcelli clan. He recognized Brenna and her husband, Joe's wife, Francesca, and, of course, the Grands.

They were all watching him as if waiting for him to pull out a weapon and hold them all hostage. He saw the anger in their eyes and knew that he didn't have to deal with just Mia's rage.

"Daddy, Daddy!" Danny raced toward him.

Rafael crouched down and reached for the boy. Daniel crashed into him and wrapped his arms around Rafael's neck.

For a moment, Rafael hugged him just as tightly.

"I missed you," Danny said. "Why'd you go away?"

He didn't have an answer for that, and oddly, he found he couldn't speak. His throat felt tight and thick.

"Daddy?" Daniel stepped back and looked at him. "Why'd you have to go away?"

"Business," Rafael managed as he stared at the boy. Until that moment, he hadn't realized he was afraid he would never see him again. "Sometimes it is work to be a prince."

"I like being the heir."

"I'm sure you do. Are you having a good party?"

Daniel nodded. "I have so many presents, and there's cake." He reached for his father's hand. "Come see."

Rafael stood and allowed himself to be tugged toward the gathering. He saw Umberto and Oliver surrounded by several of Joe's guards. While the other parents smiled warmly at him, the Marcellis all looked as if they were picturing him dead.

Mia wasn't kidding about protecting her son. She said

she would use any means and he believed her. She was strong, but he was stronger. Somehow he would defeat them all.

"I love it, Daddy," Daniel said as he fingered the new leather saddle Rafael had given him. "There's a D and a A and a N . . ." He frowned, then grabbed his mother's arm. "It's not Danny. I thought it was Danny."

Mia glanced at the saddle, then narrowed her eyes. "You're right. It's not Danny. It's Daniel. I'm sorry your daddy got your name wrong."

"That's okay," Daniel told Rafael. "Sometimes I'm Daniel, but mostly when I've been bad."

"In Calandria, you'll be Daniel all the time," Rafael said easily. "As the heir, you will go by the more formal version of your name."

Daniel stared at him for a second, then shrugged and reached for the next present. It was a remote car from Joe. Daniel gasped with delight and raced over to his uncle.

"Can we play tonight? Will you play with me? Please."

Joe ruffled the boy's hair. "Sure thing, kid. We'll have a race."

Daniel hugged the other man. Rafael watched, uncomfortable with the boy's obvious affection for the larger man. He turned back to the table of presents and scowled when he realized *his* presents—the saddle, brushes for the pony, and an expensive set of leather-bound children's stories—had been whisked away. All the other presents were still scattered about, but his were gone.

He turned to Mia. "Will you keep my gifts from him? That seems very small of you. Whatever your complaints with me, they have nothing to do with my son."

"Our son," she said evenly. "The pony supplies are near to the pony, and Brenna and Nic took the books inside so they wouldn't be ruined in the sun. Danny's not used to leather-bound books. It will take him some time to learn how to read them responsibly. Or read at all."

He felt the censure in her words, as if he'd chosen inappropriately. "Those are stories for children."

"Perhaps on your planet. Here on earth, we don't read our kids literal translations of the Grimms' fairy tales. They're just a little too brutal."

"What are you talking about?" he demanded.

"Have you ever read them? Really read them? Children do not fare well. Although I do remember a particular favorite about an evil prince being eaten by a bear. Hmm, perhaps I'll read that to Danny tonight."

"Who wants cake?" Grandma Tessa asked before he could respond to Mia.

The two grandmothers carried out a large cake decorated with race cars. The children gathered around as the cake was placed in the center of the middle table. Four candles were lit.

Mia sat on the bench in front of the cake and put Daniel on her lap. "Okay, big guy. This is it. Your chance to make a wish. Now close your eyes and wish really hard. Then open your eyes and blow out the candles. Make sure you don't tell anyone your wish, okay?"

Daniel squirmed with delight. He'd long since abandoned his party hat, and there were several food stains on his striped T-shirt. While he screwed up his whole face as he considered his wish, Rafael thought of his childhood birthday parties.

There had been other children, of course, and their

parents. Everyone had dressed formally. There had been an orchestra and some kind of entertainment. The gifts had been left on a table for him to open later, with his nanny. He'd been required to write a thank-you note after opening each present, which had stretched out the process to several days.

After he'd gone off to boarding school, birthdays had been joint affairs, celebrated with the other boys having birthdays that month. The school had prided itself on treating even royal sons like everyone else, so there had been no special celebration for him.

Daniel opened his eyes and blew out the candles. Everyone cheered.

"All right, birthday boy," Grammy M said as she hovered over the cake. "You get the first piece. Which one do you want? A corner, with lots of frosting?"

Daniel nodded, then pointed to the corner he wanted. Rafael recalled having to wait for his cake until everyone else had been served.

Grammy M cut him an impossibly large piece. Daniel took it and began to eat. The other children were served next, then the parents. Grandma Tessa passed Rafael a plate with a mint on it.

He stared at the small piece of candy, then looked at the old woman, who glared right back.

"Daddy, don't you want cake?" Daniel asked.

"Your father doesn't like cake," Mia said easily. "Isn't that true, Rafael?"

The fire in her eyes told him she would be delighted to have him defy her. That way she'd have an excuse to take him on again. But he didn't want to fight with Mia anymore. Not when the more important task was to win her back.

"Your mother is right," he said gently. "Birthday cake does not agree with me."

"I guess we'll have to put the rat poison in something else," Grandma Tessa muttered as she moved away.

Conversation quieted as the cake was consumed. Rafael was aware of how the Marcelli family kept tabs on him. If he moved close to Daniel, one of them was right there. Umberto and Oliver were never left alone. The other parents noticed nothing, but Rafael saw it all. The family had closed ranks against him.

Like Mia, he fought anger, but for a different reason. They were all acting out of ignorance. They did not understand that Daniel had responsibilities and a place in the world. He could not learn how to be king in this backwater.

At last the party ended. Parents collected their children and left. Rafael spoke pleasantly with them and waited until he could be alone with Mia. Somehow he would make her understand. But when the last guest had left, Mia picked up Daniel and walked into the house. The rest of the family followed. When he moved to go with them, several of Joe's security guards formed a line in front of the door.

"I don't think you'll be joining us for the post-party wrap-up," Joe said with a smile. "Sorry about that, but we didn't negotiate for more than the party."

Which Joe had done deliberately. "You can't keep me from my son forever."

"Were you kept from Danny? Did you miss any part of his party?"

"I must see him. I must speak to Mia."

Joe shrugged. "She doesn't want to speak to you. When

you first arrived, I warned you not to hurt her, and you didn't listen."

"I'm not afraid of you," Rafael said contemptuously. "You are all talk and very little action."

"I can't tell you how much I want to prove you wrong right now, but I promised Mia I wouldn't turn you inside out, and I keep my word. You blew it, prince. Mia's reasonable and intelligent. She could have been on your side in this. She could have respected you. But you decided to trick her and she will never forgive you. None of us will. You may be Crown Prince Bla-de-bla from some fancy island, but right now you're on my land. Marcelli land. We make the rules and the current rules are, you're screwed."

"Where's my daddy?" Danny demanded, tears spilling down his cheeks. "I want my daddy. I'm the heir and you have to do what I say. Bring my daddy back right now!"

Mia did her best not to react to Danny's tantrum. He was exhausted from the long day of celebrating his birthday and strung out on way too much sugar. But what she knew in her head didn't prevent the helpless feeling in her heart.

"I want my daddy *now*!" Danny screamed. "Why did he go away? Why did he go aw-way."

Danny collapsed on the family room floor, sobs making his whole body shake. Mia crouched next to him. "You'll see your daddy soon," she said quietly. "He came to your birthday and gave you a lot of nice presents. That was fun."

"But he went away." Danny raised his head and stared at her. "Mommy, make him come back. Please? Make him come b-back."

The Grands swept into the room. "How's the big birthday boy?" Grammy M asked as she pulled Danny to his feet and cuddled him. "What a fun day you had. So many friends and presents and just a little too much cake."

Tessa crouched in front of him and smiled. "Imagine. You're four now. Practically all grown up. You'll be driving soon."

That made Danny smile. "I can't drive. I'm a little boy."

"You don't seem too little today," Grammy M said. "You seem very big. I'm not sure I can carry you upstairs myself anymore. 'Tis a shame, because I liked that part of my day. Tessa, I'll be needing your help."

Tessa straightened and shook her head. "No, he's too big for the both of us. We'll need a crane. One of those large construction types. We'll put it right there in the hallway and it can lift Danny up to the second floor."

"I like that," Grammy M said.

Danny giggled. "You don't need a crane."

"I'm thinking we do," Grammy M said as she led him toward the stairs. "They're yellow, which means it won't go at all with the decorations. We'll have to paint it. Maybe pink with flowers."

Tessa moved closer to Mia and lowered her voice. "We'll put him to bed tonight. He's tired. Don't take it personally."

Mia appreciated the support but wasn't sure she could take the advice. Danny had bonded with his father so quickly—how was she supposed to keep them apart now? She couldn't trust Rafael, yet didn't Danny deserve time with his father?

She waited until the trio was in Danny's bedroom, then made her way to her own. She closed the door and crossed to the window.

The night was clear and cool. She could see stars, and when she opened the windows the scent of the ripening grapes filled her room like a strong perfume.

She wanted to turn back time. She wanted to have things like they were before Rafael had shown up, because his arrival had changed everything. In a matter of a few short weeks, he'd altered her world and nothing could make it as it was.

She knelt on the floor and rested her arms on the windowsill. Anger filled her. So much anger, and with it the uncomfortable realization that she was still in love with him.

Oh, she hated him and didn't trust him, but none of that meant she didn't love him. Even knowing he was a snake, her heart continued to beat out a rhythm designed to be heard only by him.

She supposed that's what happened after being in love with the same man for over five years. She was going to need some time to get over him. Having to deal with him would make the process harder.

Danny would want to see his father. She'd made the mistake of talking about him to the boy long before Rafael had ever shown up. She'd said he was brave and strong and a wonderful man. There was no way she could now tell him the truth.

She felt trapped by circumstances. Trapped and alone and clueless about her next step. At least her family would help, she thought. The Marcellis would always be there for her.

She stood and crossed to her dresser. She pulled out the small box and looked at the silver ring Diego had bought her so long ago.

Purposefully, she went downstairs and into the kitchen. There she rummaged through the junk drawer until she found a hammer; then she walked out to the porch, put the ring on the railing, and crushed it with a single blow.

After returning the hammer to the drawer, she dropped the crushed piece of metal in the trash, but as she walked back to her room, she found she didn't feel the least bit better.

The next night Brenna showed up with a box of chocolates and a bottle of Four Sisters cabernet sauvignon.

"You don't get a vote," she told Mia as she pulled her from the family room and herded her upstairs. "We're going to curl up on your bed, get drunk, eat too much chocolate, and call everyone who's ever pissed us off really bad names. You get extra points for creativity."

Mia smiled as she plopped on her bed. "I'm in."

"Good." Brenna set the wine on the nightstand. "It was a great year. Just perfect weather and the sugar in the grapes couldn't have been more right. I remember—"

"Uh, Brenna?" Mia interrupted. "Don't really care about the process. Just the results."

Brenna pulled a corkscrew from her jeans back pocket. "All my sisters are completely worthless about the magic of winemaking. How is that possible? How can I be the only one who cares?"

"A mystery you'll have to take up with the Almighty."

"I guess." She expertly pulled out the cork, then poured them each a glass of wine.

Mia took a sip. "Not bad," she said, reaching for the chocolates.

Brenna winced. "Not bad? Do you know how many medals this wine has won? Do you know how those brilliant people at *Wine Spectator* scored my wine?"

"No, and hey, don't really care. But kudos to you." She held out the now-open box of chocolates. "Want one?"

"Please."

Brenna grabbed a truffle, her wine, and sank onto the bed. "I'm the only one with a soul. That's all there is to it."

"Then speaking for the soul-free contingent, thanks for stopping by."

Brenna leaned toward her. "How do you feel?"

"Like crap. It still hurts to breathe. Most of the time I can't believe how much I hurt and how hard it is to do anything. Danny is furious. He wants his father around. It was such a mistake to have Rafael live here. Now Danny has expectations and I can't meet them."

"Rafael was only here a few weeks. Danny will get over it."

"He hasn't yet."

"He knows something is up."

Mia shuddered as she thought of her son's pain. "I never wanted him to be hurt."

"Of course you didn't. But you didn't make Rafael an ass. He did that all on his own."

Mia nodded. "I can't believe what's happened. How could I have been such an idiot?"

"We were all fooled. Like Katie said before, he had the prince thing going for him. Why would we think he was a liar?"

Mia nodded, knowing it was true and wishing it could make her feel better. "I'm going to have to deal with him, I just don't know how to get past the anger." She sipped her wine. "Nic betrayed you, Brenna. How did you recover?"

A few years ago Nic and Brenna had secretly started a relationship. She'd thought it was true love while he'd been planning to buy Marcelli Wines out from under her.

Her sister grabbed another chocolate. "It wasn't easy. I was so in love with him and I thought he cared about me and the whole time he planned to screw my family. Wow—I guess it isn't that different. I felt like you do, honey. I felt broken and stupid and empty. The difference was, we didn't have a child together. I could tell myself I never wanted to see him again."

"At least Nic came crawling back," Mia muttered, remembering how her now brother-in-law had begged for forgiveness. "Rafael doesn't even think he's done anything wrong. I can't believe the weasel apology he gave me at Danny's birthday. 'I'm sorry you were distressed. I'm sorry I got caught,'" she mocked, her voice low. "He should have started with 'I'm sorry I'm a lying worm bastard and here's a knife so you can run me through.' Now *that* would have been an apology."

Brenna reached over and patted her arm. "I wish I had magic words."

"Me too. I wish I didn't love him." She sipped her wine. "I was going to marry him. Can you believe it? We were going to run off to Las Vegas the day after Danny's birthday. What if I had? What if I'd gone to Calandria with him? I would have lost Danny."

"But you didn't. You discovered the truth in time."

Mia hung on to that slim thought. "I just don't know how I'm supposed to protect him from his father. Obviously I can't keep Danny from Rafael and I can't let him go to Calandria."

"Deep breaths," Brenna told her. "There's no need to panic right now."

"Because I can always panic later?"

"Exactly." Her sister smiled. "Come on. We have this under control. Or we're getting there. Isn't the lawyer in Zach's office looking into this for you?"

Mia nodded. "Her name is Sandy and she's amazing. We've already talked a couple of times. She has some excellent ideas and ways we can use the law. Darcy's been talking to the attorney general, and how many people can say that in casual conversation? Joe is looking into some interesting security measures. When I next have to face Rafael, I'll be ready."

Brenna shook her head. "No you won't."

Mia swallowed. "No, I won't. I'll have plenty of armor, but I won't be ready for the war. How can I still love him? How can I have feelings for him? I hate him, Brenna. I loathe and despise him and I still miss him."

"You can't just turn your feelings off because he's a jerk. You're doing everything you can to protect your son. That's the most important thing. But you've loved him for years. Why would that go away overnight?"

"But he's a bastard," Mia said. "Shouldn't that change my feelings?"

"Wasn't Diego a bit of a ruthless guy? He was a villain and you fell for him. Has Rafael really acted so out of character?"

Mia shuddered. "Yuck. What does that say about me and my taste in men? I was right to give them up. I should think about becoming a lesbian."

Brenna laughed. "Oh, right. *That's* going to happen. You could never do it."

"I guess not. Once Danny's grown up, I'll become a nun or something. Use my life for good works. If I'm never having sex again, I'll have plenty of energy to spare."

"You'll have sex again."

"I don't think so," Mia said. "I don't really see a romantic happy ending for me, do you?"

"Not with Rafael."

Mia wasn't sure there was another man for her. Which really sucked the big one.

"I wish I—"

The bedroom door opened and Joe stuck his head in. "Sorry to break up the girlfest, but we have a problem downstairs."

Mia sprang to her feet. "Danny?"

"No. He's fine. The Grands put him to bed. I just checked and he's sound asleep. It's Kelly."

Mia and Brenna followed him down the stairs. Mia heard voices coming from the kitchen. She walked in and saw Kelly leaning against the counter.

"Mia," she said, her voice thick. "Hey, how's it going?" Her gaze locked on the glass still in Mia's hand. "Is that wine? Can I have some?"

As she spoke, her entire body swayed.

"She's drunk," Brenna muttered. "This is perfect. Just perfect."

"Just a little taste," Kelly said. "Want me to dance for it? 'Coz that's what I do. Dance for my supper." She giggled, then tried a pirouette.

She managed half a turn, then she grabbed for the counter, missed, and sank slowly to the floor. By the time Mia reached her, she'd already passed out.

13

❦

*F*rancesca closed the bedroom door. As she turned, Sam caught her in his arms and held her close.

"I don't know what's wrong," Francesca murmured. "Why is she doing this?"

"I have no idea," he admitted.

Mia shifted uncomfortably, feeling that she was intruding. But before she could leave, Francesca looked at her.

"Tell me this is the first time she's shown up like this."

Mia made an X over her heart. "Trust me. If Kelly had been showing up here drunk and passing out, I would have been on the phone to you in a heartbeat. I don't get it. She's always been a pretty decent kid. Happy, interested. It's awful."

"I know." Francesca took Sam's hand and led the way down the stairs. They went into the kitchen, where the Grands had prepared a late-night snack that could easily feed thirty.

"Brenna went home," Grammy M said. "She's going to call you in the morning."

Francesca nodded. "I know she will. I know everyone is worried. I just wish we had some answers. I want to say this is typical acting out, except Kelly is twenty and she's always been so mature for her age. Shouldn't this have happened a few years ago?"

Grandma Tessa ushered them to the large table where sandwiches, cold pasta dishes, and salads waited. There were pots of decaf and tea, along with a pitcher of ice water and two open bottles of Marcelli wine.

Francesca reached for one of the bottles. "She was drunk," she said, as if she couldn't believe it. "Kelly's been tasting wine for years. She's never been interested in drinking to excess. Last I heard, she didn't even like hard liquor and she had trouble getting through a glass of wine in an evening."

Sam put his arm around her. "She's always been complicated."

"I know and I even understand why," Francesca said. "She went through some tough times. But I thought we'd worked through all that. I thought she felt happy and loved and wanted. We still ask her to come home when she's on break from the company and I was sure she knew we meant it. We've kept her room as it was. The twins adore her."

Tessa nodded. "She's doing well with the ballet company, isn't she?"

"Absolutely," Sam said. "Everyone was very impressed with how she did last year, and this year, she was given several important parts." He frowned. "Or is it dances?"

Mia grabbed half a sandwich. "There's something going on," she said. "Kelly was hanging out with me about a week ago. She stayed here for the night. We did a whole clothes–girl talk thing."

Francesca and Sam both waited expectantly, which made Mia feel bad. "She just said she, ah, admired my life. That it was romantic." When she finished speaking, she braced herself for the groans and recriminations.

Sam looked at Francesca. "I could live with Kelly being like Mia."

Francesca smiled. "Me too. Thanks, Mia. You're making us feel better."

Mia blinked at her. "Excuse me? Kelly is talking about patterning her life after mine? I'm the queen of poor choices in the male department, I'm twenty-seven and still living at home, I have no job, and I'm a single mother. On what planet is that a success?"

"On this one," Sam told her. "You're very intelligent, you go after what you want. You're not afraid to work for your goals. You have a master's and now you're getting a law degree. You're raising a great kid."

"He's right," Francesca told her. "Besides, a lot of women make poor choices with men. Not all of us can get lucky." She smiled at Sam.

"I wouldn't describe what I've done as a poor choice. Disaster maybe." But she didn't speak with a whole lot of energy. Hearing Sam and Francesca talk about her in such glowing terms was the first positive thing to happen to her in nearly a week. She'd never thought her very successful, very happy older sister would consider her much more than a screwup.

Francesca sank down onto a chair. "I hope Kelly isn't acting this way because of Etienne. I don't know what she sees in the man, and it would break my heart to have her behaving this way because of him."

"She didn't seem especially interested in talking about

him," Mia said. "Not in a romantic way. Usually Kelly can't stop talking about a guy who interests her. So that's something."

Francesca looked at her. "So Kelly is sleeping with someone she doesn't actually care about?" She touched her stomach. "Oh, God, I feel sick."

"No, I didn't mean it that way," Mia said quickly.

Sam shook his head. "Mia, please. Don't worry about it. We both know what you're saying. It doesn't seem that Etienne is the love of her life. That's good news. The rest of it we'll figure out how to deal with."

Francesca stood. "You're right. Oh, Mia, we've been bothering you with this when you have so much going on already."

"I don't mind," Mia said, and meant it. "As soon as you're gone, I'll only have my own life to think about, and right now, that's not a thrilling prospect."

The small hotel seemed to have more in common with a B and B than a large chain, Mia thought as Joe parked in the nearly empty lot in front of the long building. She took in the ceramic animals in the garden, the seasonal flag over the front door, and a large plaque proclaiming "Our Guests Are Our Family" by the porch.

The whole place screamed *cute,* and she had a feeling Rafael would hate every second he was there. The thought cheered her as she climbed out of Joe's SUV and walked to the reception area.

"He bought out a whole wing," her brother said as he fell into step with her. "They have the second floor. It's ten rooms. They're using three of them and leaving the others empty."

"At least it will be quiet for him," she murmured. "He can catch up on his sleep."

There was a young woman sitting behind the counter. She had an open biology book next to the registration log. A student, Mia thought. Probably from UC Santa Barbara.

"Hi," Mia said with a smile. "We're here to see Prince Rafael."

The girl glanced around, as if looking for spies, then spoke in a low voice. "We're not supposed to tell anyone he's here. He's been very clear about that. Not that anyone has been asking." She flipped through several papers. "Are you Mia Marcelli?"

Mia nodded.

"You're allowed to go see him." She glanced doubtfully at Joe.

"I'm her brother," he said easily. "Rafael and I go way back."

The receptionist nodded. "Okay. They have the second floor of the beach wing. The stairs are right out there. He's in room twenty-three." She smiled again. "It's our biggest suite. A really pretty room. He said it reminded him of when he stayed in Paris. Can you believe it? I've never been anywhere. He's so gorgeous and a real prince. I Googled him." She giggled.

"All right, then," Mia said. "Thanks for your help."

She and Joe found the stairs and climbed them. Before they reached the top, Oliver had stepped out onto the landing.

"Morning," Joe said cheerfully. "Great place. Can you see the ocean from your rooms? I'll bet they serve a nice breakfast. I heard the chefs are all culinary arts students."

Oliver glared without speaking. Umberto joined him. Joe moved forward until he reached the landing. Mia followed.

"You're not allowed in," Umberto growled. "Only her."

"That would be almost-princess Mia to you," Mia said brightly. "And I'm not going anywhere without Joe. He's not armed, though. We figured you'd get fussy about that. But feel free to check him out yourself. I always thought you got a bit of a thrill patting the guys down."

Umberto growled, then motioned for Oliver to search Joe. The pat-down was quick and efficient. Oliver shook his head.

Mia wore a cropped tank top over a long cotton skirt. She'd left her purse in the car and held nothing in her hands.

She spun in a slow circle. "As you can see, I'm not armed, either. Don't worry, as much as I want him dead, I don't want to be obvious about killing him."

The men exchanged a glance, then waved Mia and Joe through. Mia checked the numbers on the doors and knocked on 23.

Rafael answered immediately. She ignored him as she stepped into the suite. Just being close to him was enough to send her into a fiery temper, and right now she wanted to avoid any strong emotion. Far better to just get through the conversation without feeling anything at all. Emotional neutrality would be a win for her.

She took a moment to absorb the floral wallpaper and how it carefully matched the drapes and the cushions on the sofa. There were silks and satins and laces. Plants, tiny tables crammed with pictures in frames, and tiny crystal vases and knickknacks. There wasn't an inch of clear tabletop or a foot empty of furniture. The rooms were crowded and fussy. She knew instantly he would despise them. How lovely.

She turned back to Rafael. "Interesting room."

He shrugged. "I wanted to be close."

"I'm sure you did. All the better to kidnap Danny."

"Mia, please. That was not what I had planned."

She held up a hand to stop him. "This is my meeting and I'm in charge. You're going to listen." She reached into her skirt pocket and drew out a piece of paper. After unfolding it, she handed it to him.

"We've been to a judge," she said. "This is a restraining order. I'll give you the highlights, although I'm sure you'll want to read it all yourself later. You're not allowed on Marcelli land without first making an appointment to see either Danny or me. You must notify me first, and telling someone else in the family doesn't count. You must speak directly to me."

"So you can avoid me for as long as you would like," he said bitterly.

"Actually, I can't, and I wouldn't, but I don't care if you believe me or not. You're not allowed to see Danny on your own. I will be with you at all times. If you try to see Danny on your own or without setting it up with me first, you will be deported."

He stiffened. "That is not possible."

She tapped the paper. "Read it and weep, big guy. It is possible. I will supervise your visits and if you try to take him or influence him or anything else I don't like, you will be deported."

She nodded at Joe. "Why don't you do the next part."

Joe smiled. "Happy to. Danny has been fitted with a

small wristband that constantly monitors his position. If he is removed from the property, an alarm will sound and an APB will go out. Local and federal law enforcement will be notified and all airports within a fifty-mile radius will instantly be closed. When you and Danny are found—"

Rafael raised a hand. "Let me guess. I will be deported."

"I think you'll be charged with some serious crimes," Mia said. "Then your government will get involved because they won't like that you've been arrested. That will be messy. And I'm pretty sure you'll be fined for the whole airport closure thing. *Then* you'll be deported."

"Should you try to remove the wristband," Joe continued. "An alarm will sound."

Mia glared at Rafael. "Unlike you, I won't try to keep you from Danny. I think it's important he have a relationship with his father, regardless of how ratty that man may be. I was willing to trust you and you blew that, so now we do this my way. You may see him, you may be a part of his life, but you may not take him to Calandria. Not until he's eighteen, and then only if he's willing."

Rafael's anger was a tangible creature in the room. "You cannot do this. Daniel is the heir to the Calandrian throne. He has much to learn about his country and his people."

"I guess he's going to have to take his classes over the Internet."

"This is unreasonable."

"Unreasonable?" She felt her own temper flaring. "Let's talk about unreasonable. Let's talk about a man who slinks into my life, telling lies at every turn. Let's talk about someone willing to deceive my entire family. I would have worked with you," she yelled. "That's what really bugs me. I would have *been* reasonable. I would have done the right thing. Because that's the kind of person I am. But you weren't willing to find that out. The very first thing you did was to lie to me. You used me in every way possible to get what you wanted."

She curled her fingers into fists and wished she were strong enough to hurt him if she hauled off and socked him. "Do you think I like having to do this? Oh, sure, there's the initial thrill of getting a little revenge, but then what? How do I explain this to Danny? How do I tell him that his father is a liar?"

"You do not understand," Rafael said between clenched teeth.

"Actually, I understand perfectly." She moved toward him. "Why didn't you even ask? Why didn't you try telling the truth?"

"If you said no, I would be left with nothing."

"Which is pretty much what you have now."

He grabbed her by the upper arms. "Mia, Daniel has a great future. He will one day be king. You have no right to keep him from his destiny. Do you think he will thank you when he learns the truth?"

Joe hovered close enough to rip Rafael away if he tried anything. Mia hated that Rafael's touch made her blood heat and parts of her ache. So much for fury burning away baser desires. She'd been so hopeful, too.

"How do you think Danny will feel when he finds out that you were planning to steal him away?"

His blue eyes darkened with emotion. "He will understand why I thought it necessary."

"As a rule, four-year-old little boys don't appreciate losing their moms."

He released her. She hated how she instantly felt about twenty degrees colder.

"You keep saying that," he growled. "I would not have kept you from him. I planned for you to see him whenever you wanted."

The last of her emotional restraints snapped. "*You* planned? Where the hell do you get off making statements like that? You planned. That's bullshit. You don't get to make those kinds of decisions without me. A person planning visitation talks about it. He doesn't try to trick his child's mother into a fake marriage for the sole purpose of divorcing her and stealing her son."

"I know," he said. "I am sorry."

The apology surprised her, but it wasn't nearly enough. "It's done," she said. "We deal with where we are now. Danny stays here until he's eighteen."

"He needs to be in Calandria."

"Sorry, he's not going to be. If you want to compromise, then get your law changed." She smiled tightly at his look of surprise. "Oh, yeah, we looked it up. The second Danny is on Calandrian soil, he cannot be taken away without his father's permission. It's an heir thing. Change the law and we'll talk. Until then, we play by my rules."

He glared at her. "I am Crown Prince Rafael of Calandria. You can't do this to me."

"Watch me."

Rafael arrived at the Marcelli house fifteen minutes before his first scheduled visit with Daniel. While he was furious with the fact that Mia was able to dictate all the terms of his seeing his son, he also admired her strength and tenacity.

She dared to stand up to him. More impressive, she managed to broker a legal deal that put him at her mercy. He would not have thought her capable of such machinations.

Unfortunately for him, her legal maneuverings were proving most difficult to escape. The top lawyers in Calandria were investigating ways around what she'd put in place, but they were not hopeful. An appeal could be made to an international court. The most likely outcome was that Daniel would live part of the year in both places. But that would satisfy neither of them. In addition, Rafael was not yet ready to go public with this complication. He did not relish being made a laughingstock in the tabloids for a second time.

Something Mia could have done, he thought as he climbed out of the limo and saw the four security guards standing by the house and in the yard. She could easily have taken her story and her plight to any one of several television news shows. But she had not, and he appreciated her restraint.

Not that his appreciation blinded him. He knew her decision had nothing to do with him and everything to do with keeping Daniel out of the limelight. Something else he appreciated.

He had handled everything badly from the first. In truth, he had never considered compromise because that was not his way. But he had also forgotten Mia's determination.

He missed her. A foolish waste of time, but there it was. He missed her and Daniel. He missed how they had laughed together. With the two of them, he could be himself.

If things had been different . . . , he thought, not for the first time. If she had been from another family with different lineage. Except then she would not be the Mia he knew, and he would not have her change. Despite everything, he wanted her exactly as she was.

His father would not agree, he thought as he walked up to the back door and knocked. His father wanted Mia punished and Daniel returned at any price.

Joe opened the door and motioned for him to come inside. Oliver came with him while Umberto stayed outside. Rafael wasn't sure what the other man expected to do— he was outnumbered and outgunned. Still, he appreciated the show of support.

"You have ninety minutes," Joe said, then walked out of the kitchen, leaving Rafael alone to face the Grands.

Both old women stared at him. He could read the anger and hurt in their eyes. Grandma Tessa held a butcher's knife in one hand and he sensed she very much wanted to use it on him. Grammy M chose a different tack.

"I'm very disappointed in you, Rafael," she said, her voice sounding low and frail. "You were to be a part of this family."

Her words cut him in a way he had not thought possible. "I did not . . ."

Did not what? Plan to hurt them? Expect to steal Daniel away?

Tears filled her eyes and she trembled slightly. "So much for being a prince," she said, then left the kitchen.

He stood there, feeling uncomfortable in a way he had not experienced before. People were supposed to do *his* bidding. *He* was the one who decided what was right and what was wrong.

Daniel ran into the kitchen. "Daddy, Daddy! You've been gone so long!"

The boy raced right up to him. Rafael bent down and instinctively caught him as he jumped. Then he pulled him close and smiled at him.

"I am here now," he said.

"I missed you."

He stared into familiar brown eyes. "I have missed you as well."

"Look what I got." Daniel held out his wrist and rubbed a small metal band. "Uncle Joe says real soldiers wear one just like this. Now I'm a real soldier."

The tracking device. Of course. "Very nice," he told his son.

"Come play with me," Daniel said. "We can play soldiers and then I want to ride my pony and then read a story. Five stories."

"That is much to accomplish. Do you know how many stories five is?"

"A lot."

Rafael chuckled. "It is indeed."

The boy felt good to hold, he thought. He'd been telling the truth when he'd said he'd missed Daniel. In a matter of weeks, the boy had become important to him. In time he, Rafael, would have to return to Calandria and then what would happen? Would he truly be forced to leave Daniel behind?

Mia walked into the kitchen. Rafael stared as need flooded him. Not just to have her in his bed, but to talk to her, be with her. Ridiculous. He would stop needing her this instant.

"It's a little hot for pony riding," she said from the doorway to the kitchen. "Let's leave that for next time. But you can play soldier in the family room. I cleared off a big space. You can have a whole war."

"Mommy, no!" Daniel protested. "I want to ride my pony. I'm the heir and I said."

"I think your mother is right," Rafael said. "It's not good to be out when it is so hot. Not good for you or Gaspare."

Daniel pouted for a moment, then squirmed to be let down. "I'll get more soldiers. I'll get them all."

"Sounds like fun," Mia said. She turned her back and returned to the family room.

Rafael followed her. All right, perhaps he *had* expected some acknowledgment of him for taking her side, but if she chose not to give it, he would survive.

He found pieces of white satin scattered on the coffee table. There were several bags of open beads nearby.

"I did not know you sewed," he said.

"I don't," Mia told him as she sat down and picked up a small piece of satin.

The Grands came in and took their seats across from Mia. Each of them went to work on a larger piece of satin without speaking to him.

"We're beading a vest for David," Grammy M said grudgingly into the silence. "It's a tradition in the Marcelli family. Generally we bead the bride's wedding dress. Actually, we make the whole thing by hand. Katie's in charge. She made all the girls' dresses, which was a lot of work, let me tell you."

"Mary!" Tessa snapped. "He doesn't need to know."

Mia set down her beadwork and looked at him. "Maybe he does. Maybe he needs to understand that a family doesn't have to be royal to have traditions. Maybe then he could start to understand how much we all matter to each other and know cutting off an arm or a leg would hurt a lot less than losing a member of that family."

There was another pause, but this one felt much more awkward. Three pairs of eyes glared at him. He felt their combined anger as it grew and moved closer to him.

For the first time, he understood that he hadn't just upset Mia—he'd alienated the entire Marcelli family and anyone remotely associated with them. If they had their way, he would disappear, never to be heard from again.

He'd faced adversity before. Many people resented who he was, pointedly reminding him that he was a prince only by an accident of birth. In school, other boys had wanted to be smarter or stronger or faster. They had taken great pleasure in defeating him in the classroom or on the playing field. There were women who wanted to be with him simply to say they had, and others who wanted to make him fall in love so that they could break his heart. Simply because he was Prince Rafael of Calandria.

But this was different. This was personal. The Marcellis hadn't especially cared he was a prince before, and that title certainly didn't influence them now. They hated him for what he had done. For his acts, not his title.

Which meant they could have liked him for the same reason.

Over the past few days, he had wrestled with his own temper and frustration. He resented having to come up with a new plan and take more time to achieve what he wanted. He'd never once considered what he might have lost.

Not just Daniel, but all of them. Mia and the rest of the Marcellis.

Did he care?

He couldn't answer the question. Shouldn't he be able to instantly say no? He was here for a single purpose. Nothing else could get in the way.

Yet sometime in the past few weeks Daniel and his family had become entwined. He wasn't sure he could have one without the other. He wasn't sure he wanted to.

If he lost, he would lose more than the heir, his son. He would lose his family and the woman he had never been able to forget.

14

❧

"*B*ack to the hotel?" Oliver asked as he and Rafael walked toward the limo.

It was the logical choice, Rafael thought. He had finished his visit with his son. It wasn't as if he had business in town or knew other people.

Perhaps that was the problem. He had too much time on his hands. At home there were matters of state and different organizations to occupy his day. But here, now that he was in exile at that ridiculous hotel, he had nothing.

"A computer store," he said. "I will purchase a laptop and work from the hotel."

Oliver nodded and opened the rear door of the limo. Rafael glanced back at the house. No one stood at a window watching him go. No doubt the women inside had carefully distracted his son so Daniel would not miss him. He had been in the boy's life for such a short time. Would he now be forced out of it?

He knew that technically Mia couldn't exclude him forever, but there were subtle ways to make him matter less. If he had always been in the boy's life, she would have a more difficult time, but he had not. He was new and exciting, but not permanent. Not yet.

The thought of not seeing Daniel, of not watching him grow from a small boy to an active teenager, made his chest ache. The sensation was unfamiliar and uncomfortable.

"Your highness?" Oliver prompted, still holding open the door.

Rafael took a step forward then stopped. He would not lose his son, nor would he lose Mia.

But how? How would he make things better with her? How could he . . .

A bit of information came into his brain. Before flying out to meet the Marcellis, he had asked his staff to research them thoroughly. If he recalled correctly, Brenna Marcelli had had a rocky start with her husband. Nicholas Giovanni had planned to secretly buy the Marcelli vineyard and strip the family of everything. His plan had been discovered in time to stop it.

Yet Brenna had still married him. So she had forgiven him.

"The winery," Rafael said as he stepped into the limo. "The main offices."

"Yes, your highness."

Brenna's office was large and cluttered, with a huge map of the winery filling one wall. The massive desk had a heavy masculine style, and when Rafael entered the room and saw it, he wondered if it had belonged to her grandfather.

She was on the phone. When she glanced up and recognized him, her entire body stiffened. Her expression closed, her mouth tightened, and she quickly ended the call.

"Get your slimy royal ass out of my office," she said as she came to her feet and pointed at the door. "I don't want to see you or talk to you. I hope you get some horrible wasting disease brought on by a congenital defect inherent in lying, selfish, bastard princes."

He closed the door behind him and crossed to her desk. "I see that Mia gets her verbal skills honestly. It is a fascinating trait in the Marcelli women. I wish to speak with you."

"I have no interest in listening." She reached for the phone. "I can call security. Actually, I can call my brother. The ex-SEAL. He doesn't like you much, and seeing as he's a man who could take you out with a Q-tip, I'd be a little worried if I were you."

Rafael held out both hands, palms up. "Am I so frightening as all that? You have to call in reinforcements because you are afraid that by listening to me you might change your mind?"

"You're manipulating me."

He smiled slightly. "I doubt it will work on you, but it is necessary to try." He stepped closer. "Hear me out, Brenna. What harm is there in that? We both know I'm unlikely to influence you in any way. Later, when I am gone, you can call Mia and mock me behind my back. Think how that will bring you both pleasure."

She sat back in her chair. "Fine. But only because of the mocking. I'm really going to do that."

"I'm sure you are." He claimed the seat opposite hers and wondered how to begin. "I wish to make amends with Mia."

"Why?"

"I did not plan for things to go this way."

"Right. You just wanted to steal Danny, then leave town. I'm sorry we got in the way of that. What a serious bummer."

"Brenna, you deliberately misunderstand me."

"Oh, no. I understand you perfectly. Mia's right. You're sorry about getting caught, but you're not the least bit sorry about what you tried to do. You don't care about anyone, not even Danny."

He narrowed his gaze. "Of course I care about my son."

"I don't think so. Oh, sure, Danny as heir is really important to you, but that's about your country and tradition. It's not as if Danny is a real person to you. It's not as if you care about his happiness."

He stood and glared at her. "How dare you speak to me this way?"

"I believe you came to me, not the other way around. So I can pretty much talk to you any way I'd like. You're free to leave." She pointed at the door.

He sank back into the chair. "I'm not leaving."

"Then you have a problem, because I'm going to continue to talk to you any way I want." She leaned toward him. "Rafael, no one who genuinely cares about a child could imagine ripping a four-year-old little boy away from his mother and the only family he's ever known. Do you have any idea how that would devastate him? Of what he would go through?"

"He is my heir," he said, but the words came automatically. Without meaning to, he remembered a time long ago. He had been about Daniel's age when his own mother had died. He recalled the activity around her room and then nothing but quiet. No one would speak with him. For days he only saw his nanny. Then one evening his father had appeared and announced his mother was dead. The

funeral was the next day and Rafael was expected to behave appropriately.

He'd understood nothing, except the fact that his father was obviously very angry with him. It wasn't until
nearly a week later that he'd begun to figure out his
mother was gone forever.

He remembered feeling lost and afraid. Sometimes he
would creep into her room and curl up on her bed, closing his eyes as tightly as he could, hoping that when he
opened them, she would be there.

"I had no intension of keeping Mia from her son," he
told Brenna. "I had very specifically planned for her to . . ."
He paused, not sure how to explain what he hadn't decided
yet for himself.

"To what?" she asked impatiently. "See him for fifteen
minutes every quarter? Don't give me that crap. You
didn't have a plan. You didn't think of anything but what
you wanted. You're like a kid who only discovers he's interested in a toy after someone else has taken it from him.
It's not as if you cared about Danny until now."

"I did not know about him until recently."

Brenna leaned forward and gave him a cold smile that
warned him she was about to trap him. "Did you bother
to find out if Mia might be pregnant? Did it occur to you
to send one of your minions to do a little reconnaissance
work? Six or seven months after the last time you two got
personal, it would have been really easy to tell. My God,
Rafael. You let her think you'd died. What kind of weasel
behavior is that?"

"It did not occur to me she *could* be pregnant."

"Why? Hadn't the little soldiers been potent until
then?"

"I used a condom."

"Which obviously failed. Still, you had a responsibility and you're avoiding the question about just letting her go. Not even a good-bye? Wouldn't that at least have showed good manners?"

He shifted in his seat and glanced out the window toward the vineyard. "There were reasons."

"Uh-huh. Let me guess. You didn't want her to know who you really were. You didn't want to risk an American groupie. How embarrassing. Plus she could have told the world how you'd been playing dress-up."

He swung back to her. "I was protecting the heritage of my country. That is hardly playing dress-up." Brenna was a most annoying woman. Nearly as difficult as her sister.

"Call it what you like," she said with a shrug. "What do I care?"

"We are getting off the subject at hand," he said between clenched teeth. "I would appreciate your assistance in finding a way to communicate with Mia."

"I don't think so. I mean, come on. To what end? You had an affair with her once and let her go. Now you tried to steal her kid. You're not a really good catch, despite the title."

His frustration flared into anger. "What did you expect?" he asked heatedly. "That I would marry her?"

"You're the one who proposed."

He stood again and paced the length of the office. "I had no choice. I had to secure Daniel for my people. You think because I have money and a title it is all so easy for me, but you are wrong. With great wealth and power comes responsibility. I must not only think of today, I must think of five hundred years from now. Each law, each pardon, each act has consequences. Like ripples in a pond, they continue endlessly."

He paused by the map on the wall and traced the outline of the Marcelli land. "There are times when I wish it could be different. That I were a man like any other. That my life was my own. But it is not."

Brenna leaned back in her chair. "I wish I had some tissue here so I could weep for your sad little life. Poor rich boy all alone." She straightened. "I don't actually give a rat's ass about you or your sob story. The bottom line is you lied. You lied and you're not even sorry. If you had come to Mia and explained the truth from the beginning, she would have worked with you. She's intelligent and reasonable. But that never occurred to you. I guess *compromise* isn't a word in the royal vocabulary. You didn't bother to find out anything about her when the two of you were together before or you would have known that number one, she's more than willing to do what's right, and number two, she will die before she lets you take her child away from her."

"You speak of compromise," he said slowly. "I have been thinking about the concept."

"A little too much after the fact. Welcome to the real world, where people actually negotiate things like child custody agreements and stealing is against the law."

He looked at her. "You do not like me."

"No one does, except maybe Danny, and that's because he doesn't know any better. But he will."

"You will turn him against me?"

"I won't have to. I'm guessing you'll do that all on your own."

Her statement insulted him. "You do not know me."

"I have a good idea about you. You've never had to work for anything in your life. You get what you want and people just get out of the way. That's not happening this time. We're a strong family, and when you screwed Mia, you screwed us all." She paused. "Figuratively, of course, because otherwise, to quote my baby sister, ick."

"I will win."

"I can't see that happening. From where I'm sitting, there is only one win. You really fall in love with Mia and then somehow convince her it's for real. But what are the odds of that? Oooh, you'd have to go against Daddy and marry a commoner. I don't think you have the balls for it."

His blood ran cold. "If you were a man, I would call you out."

"Swords at dawn? I'm all a-tremble."

"You will not speak to me this way."

"How, exactly, are you going to stop me? This isn't Calandria and you can't throw me in the tower. Or is it a dungeon? I can never keep that straight."

"I will win, Brenna. I will defeat you all."

"Not even in seven lifetimes." She stood and walked to the door. "The funny thing is, I'm kind of glad you stopped by."

As if he believed that. "Why?"

"Because I'm not angry with you anymore. I actually feel sorry for you. You're so busy chasing after the moon, which you'll never get, that you can't see the beauty in the moonlight. You hide behind duty and privilege. There's a real world out there, Rafael. You should try leaving the titanium credit card at home and experience how the rest of us live. You might find what you've been missing."

• • •

David was being force-fed by the Grands. Mia grinned when she saw him and rushed to his side.

"Do you need rescuing?" she asked as he stood and hugged her.

"Apparently. I'm in danger of exploding."

"A man on his own," Grandma Tessa said. "I know you don't eat right."

"You can't make up for it in one meal," he protested.

"We try," Grammy M told him.

He released Mia and patted his stomach. "I'm going to take Mia for a walk. When I get back, you can ply me with desserts."

"I made a tiramisu just yesterday," Tessa said.

"I have fresh blueberry cobbler," Grammy M offered.

David had spent enough time at the house to know the right answer.

"I look forward to both," he said, then grabbed Mia's hand. "Get me out of here," he whispered.

She laughed and led the way outside.

The afternoon was warm and sunny, as often happened in August. They strolled to a shady tree, then plopped down on the grass.

"Where's Danny?" David asked. "With his dad?"

"Not without me around to supervise. He's at school this afternoon. His preschool class is doing a play and this is their final practice. I almost stayed, but I get so nervous watching him." She smiled. "I don't know how I'll get through the performance."

"You and Rafael are still at odds?"

"What do you think?"

"That you're stubborn and you won't forgive him easily."

That surprised her. "You think I should?"

"You're going to have to eventually. He's Danny's father."

"He's an asshole."

"That doesn't change the whole father part."

She stared at him. "You don't think what he did was so horrible."

"I didn't say that."

"You don't have to. I can see it on your face. What is all this? Guys sticking together?" She couldn't believe it. This was David. She trusted him.

"Mia, I'm not on his side. What he did was inexcusable. I'm simply pointing out that he's Danny's father and nothing is going to change that. You can try to keep Danny from Calandria all you want, but eventually you're going to have to let him go for a visit."

"No way. There's a law that says once he's on Calandrian soil, only a royal parent can say if he's allowed to leave. I would have no rights at all."

"Laws can be changed. You can make that a condition of his visiting." David put his arm around her. "Don't shoot the messenger. You know I'm telling the truth. The reason you're going to have to give in sooner than you'd like has nothing to do with Rafael and everything to do with Danny."

She pouted. "You're saying he'll want to visit Calandria."

"If you were him, wouldn't you want to?"

She couldn't even imagine her reaction if her mother had come to her when she was ten or twelve and told her she was a princess of some country. There was nothing that would have kept her away from visiting. Not even her mother's tears.

"So I should talk to Rafael about changing the law," she muttered. "I did before, but sarcastically. You're saying I should do it for real."

"I would use it as leverage now, before Danny starts making decisions on his own." David touched her chin. "I agree. Rafael is an ass. He acted badly and you shouldn't trust him. But you also have to be realistic about the situation."

She stared into his eyes. "You're the only sensible male in my whole romantic life and we broke up. Why is that?"

"We realized we weren't in love."

"If I'd known how much I was going to screw up every other relationship, I would have tried harder."

"You don't mean that."

She sighed and leaned against him. "I want to, but I know we weren't destined to be each other's great love. Still, I can dream about what if . . ."

"We wouldn't have made it a year," he told her.

"Stop being so damn practical. Did I say the word *dream*? Can't you go with that?"

"Sure."

She closed her eyes, but instead of a pretend future with David, she saw Rafael's face and remembered what it had been like to make love with him.

Instantly her body began melting from the inside out, which really pissed her off. How could she still want the man? Did he have to become a serial killer before her hormonal self let go?

"I want to talk about you," she said. "I need the distraction."

"Not exactly the level of interest required to get me to spill my guts," he told her.

She smiled. "You know I'm interested. How are things with Amber?"

When he didn't answer, she glanced at him and was surprised to find him staring off into the distance.

"David?"

He leaned his head back against the tree. "I don't know. The same, I guess. Maybe worse."

"Worse? Worse as in Amber still isn't convinced we're not an item?"

"Something like that. Imagine if she could see us now."

Mia considered their position, sitting close together, David's arm around her. "Okay, it might look bad, but there's nothing between us. You won't even let me fantasize about what could have been."

She'd been hoping for a smile. Instead he shook his head. "What if she doesn't love me?"

There was stark pain in his voice. Mia shifted until she faced him.

"She loves you. She adores you. Women who don't care about guys generally don't marry them."

"What if it isn't enough? She has to get over this, Mia. We can't spend our entire married life fighting about you." He smiled. "You're not all that."

"You've been talking to Grandma Tessa, haven't you?" she muttered as she considered the problem. "How much of this is about me and how much of it is a manifestation of Amber's insecurities?"

"I'm a guy. I haven't a clue."

"Maybe we should ask Francesca."

"Maybe we should keep it between the two of us," he said. "I don't want this being talked about at dinner. That would humiliate Amber."

"Good point." Mia knew her sister would keep a secret, but she didn't want to stress David out any more than he was.

"I have to know if it's just nerves," he said, "or something more serious."

"I agree. So bring her out and we'll prove there's nothing romantic between us."

"How?"

"I'll come up with something. Then, if she still doesn't believe you, there's a bigger problem."

His eyes darkened. "I'm not sure I want to know that. I don't want to lose her."

"She loves you," Mia told him. "I'm sure of it. And she is, too. I don't think her fears about me are all that big. I think I'm just the object of all her prewedding jitters. But we'll find out for sure and then you two can live happily ever after."

"Promise?" he asked.

And because she wanted him to be happy and live a wonderful life, she said, "Yes."

Rafael drove onto the Marcelli property a little before two. Mia had insisted that they go to Daniel's play together, which was fine with him. He wanted time alone with her so that he could explain . . . Explain . . .

He swore, still not sure exactly what he was supposed to say. All she had accused him of was true. He could claim he was the prince and that he had a right to his son, both of which were accurate. Yet neither excused his behavior.

Of all the statements Brenna had thrown at him the other day, one continued to haunt him. "No one who genuinely cares about a child would consider ripping him away from his mother and the only family he has ever known."

Rafael had never viewed the situation from Daniel's point of view. He had not thought how a small child could be scarred by such an upheaval. He had only thought about what he wanted and what was best for Calandria.

He turned onto the Marcelli driveway and found humor in how closely the black sedan followed him. Umberto and Oliver had strongly resisted his decision to drive himself. Although he had assured them he was unlikely to be assassinated between the hotel and Mia's house, they had protested his autonomy. He had agreed to allow them to drive behind him in another vehicle, but had refused to let one of them sit with him.

He wanted to be alone with Mia. He sensed that the fewer reminders of his royalty, the better. She was not the type of woman to be easily won and his position was only a source of contention between them.

He parked next to the house and climbed out. Kelly stood by the fence, a cigarette in her fingers. She glanced at his new ride.

"I didn't know they made them that big."

Rafael nodded proudly at his new SUV. "It is a Hummer. Such things are not practical in Europe, but here, where the roads are wide and gas is plentiful, it is appealing."

"I guess." She inhaled on her cigarette. "The good news is I don't have to worry about you giving me away anymore. No one in the family would bother listening to you. They all hate you. It's kind of cool."

He frowned. "What is cool about it?"

"You were a real dick. I like that Mia is going to make you crawl and then refuse to give in to you."

He did not like her choice of words, nor did he appreciate her assessment of the situation. "Mia and I will reach a point of compromise."

Kelly laughed. "Oh yeah. I want to be there for *that* meeting. Are you clueless about all women or just Mia?"

"I am very successful with women."

"Right. We're all in awe of how you handled *this* situation. I mean, come on, Rafael. It was sneaky and really low. You're a prince. Aren't you supposed to be held to a higher standard than the average guy?"

"Why do all the women in your family feel so comfortable pointing out what I did wrong?"

"Because it's fun and we're all highly verbal. Besides, it's not like Mia screwed up. She was honest with you from the beginning. The way I heard it, she didn't even try to keep Danny from you. She told you about him within seconds of finding out you weren't dead. Face it. You're the skanky one here."

Were there any names they weren't going to call him? "I will not stand here and be insulted."

She inhaled again. "Then take a seat."

He glared at her. "As if your life is so perfect."

"I'm twenty. I'm allowed to make mistakes. What's your excuse?"

"What was the mistake? Etienne?"

She shrugged. "I don't know. Maybe."

"Have you told him?"

"No, I just broke up with him. No big."

He studied her. "You are not wounded by your parting?"

"Wounded by our parting? You might want to think about communicating in a way slightly more relevant to this century, your highness. As for Etienne, no, I'm not wounded. I wanted him gone and now he is."

Which sounded correct, but in Rafael's experience, young women did not heal so easily from relationships.

"You were sleeping together?"

She frowned. "Get personal much?"

"If you were sleeping with him, then you should miss him."

"Thanks for the news flash."

"Why don't you?"

"I never really liked him."

Kelly immediately looked as if she wanted to call back the words.

"Why would you sleep with someone you don't like?" he asked.

"Don't you have a grovel appointment with Mia?"

"I am early."

"Lucky me."

"You are avoiding the question." He folded his arms across his chest. "Why would you sleep with . . ." He nodded slowly. "Because your parents wouldn't approve of him."

She took a step back. "Whatever. I have to go."

He didn't take the hint. "So you *wanted* them to be upset. I have seen you with your parents. You have a good relationship with them, so you are not trying to upset them out of spite."

"I would never do that," she snapped. "Now just shut up."

"I will not and you can't make me."

"That's mature," she muttered as she crushed out her cigarette, then picked up the butt.

"How is your dancing?" he asked.

"What?"

"You are doing well with the company?"

"Of course. They like me. I'm a hard worker. I'm moving forward with my career."

There was something in the way she said the words. Something brittle and filled with pain. He felt he was close to the truth.

"Most girls your age are in college," he said.

"I'm not a girl, you sexist pig, and so what? Why would I want to spend my day studying in some stuffy classroom when I can be on the stage? Do you know what a rush that is? Do you know how many really cute guys send me flowers after every show?"

He could relate to nothing in her conversation and yet he knew exactly what she felt. Perhaps because he had lived his whole life in a state of duty—doing what was expected rather than what he wanted.

"You must have spent a lot of time working at your ballet," he said casually.

"Well, duh. Of course. Hours and hours. Francesca used to joke that we should get some kind of frequent flyer miles for all the times we went back and forth to the studio. She was great, staying with me through class and really encouraging me. My dad was just as proud. He . . ." She glared at him. "Why are we talking about this?"

"Because you feel guilty." He felt triumphant, knowing he had found the key. "You thought this was what you wanted and your entire family sacrificed to make it happen. Perhaps not with money, but in time and effort. Perhaps the younger children had to give up time with their mother. Now you have what you vowed you always wanted and you hate it. You're acting out in the hopes that you'll so anger your parents that they will insist you quit and come home. You might even want them to punish you by sending you to college."

Her eyes widened in shock. "You're wrong!" she yelled. "You're wrong and you're stupid and you're a liar."

With that she turned and ran away. Rafael watched her go and knew he was right.

"What on earth have you done now?" Mia asked from the entrance to the rear of the house. "Was Kelly crying? Were you mean to her? I swear, Rafael, you're really an amazingly useless human being."

He turned to her. "Kelly is upset because I discovered her secret."

Mia didn't look convinced. "You're not exactly someone any of us want to confide in."

He walked toward her. "You're right. She didn't think she had told me anything significant, but she did. I recognized the symptoms. She is bound by duty."

Mia rolled her eyes. "Oh, please."

"She isn't happy dancing. She regrets her career choice, but because of all the sacrifices her family made for her, she feels too guilty to tell them. She's acting out, hoping to shock her parents enough so that they will punish her by bringing her home. She may even want to go to college."

Mia moved back into the house and he followed her. "You know I'm right," he said.

"I do not."

"Think about it. How unusual is her behavior? Hasn't it come on fairly quickly? The drinking, Etienne. She admitted she doesn't even like him. What twenty-year-old sleeps with a man she doesn't like?"

Mia leaned against the kitchen counter. "Maybe," she admitted. "I don't know. I'll have to think about it."

"I have solved the problem of your niece, Mia. Admit it. That should be worth something."

She glared at him. "This isn't a barter economy."

He eased toward her, enjoying the fire in her eyes. "Of course it is. You have something I want and I have something you want."

"You have *nothing* I want."

He touched her arm. She wore a sleeveless summer dress and he brushed his fingers down her bare skin to her elbow. He was close enough to feel her shiver and see the goose bumps that erupted.

Interesting. All her fury had not burned away her desire for him. He was pleased, because he still wanted her as well, but that wasn't what he spoke of.

"I wish to have a relationship with my son," he said. "You wish that as well."

She opened her mouth, then closed it. He had suspected she wouldn't be comfortable saying she *didn't* want him to be close to Daniel. What mother stood in the way of a boy and his father bonding?

"You're still a pig," she said.

"So Kelly informed me. The women of your family are not afraid to speak their minds."

"We're good at it."

"I have noticed. Come. We will go see Daniel in his play and you will think about what I have said about Kelly. In time, you will admit I was right. I am not as insensitive as you think."

"Don't push it," she grumbled as she collected her purse.

"I will not." He held open the door. "I have a surprise. I bought a new car so that I would fit in with the other parents."

She stepped out and stared at the massive SUV. "That's the biggest thing I've ever seen. You think it's inconspicuous?"

"It does not have diplomatic flags. And see? Oliver and Umberto are driving in a different car. No one will notice them. We are just like everyone else."

"Oh, right," she muttered as she walked over to the SUV and eyed the high step. "We're the walking, breathing definition of *normal*."

15

❧

Although Mia had mocked Rafael about his new SUV, she was actually pretty grateful to arrive at Danny's preschool in it rather than in a limo with diplomatic flags. As promised, Oliver and Umberto stayed in the background and did their security guard best to blend in. Which left her the yet unsolved problem of how to explain Rafael.

While she wasn't close with the other mothers in the school, she did chat with them from time to time. She'd never mentioned a father for Danny. Not that anyone had asked. In today's world of single mothers, no one thought it was unusual to be manless. But showing up with a well-dressed, gorgeous man who looked like a fallen angel and spoke like Antonio Banderas was bound to create just a little too much interest.

She stopped at the edge of the parking lot and looked at him. "I don't know how to explain you," she admitted. "To the people here."

"Will they ask?"

"Danny's been enrolled just over a year and this is

your first time showing up. Not to mention the fact that you haven't exactly been a subject of conversation."

"All right. Tell them I am his father. We will smile pleasantly and keep moving. If you do not give them time to gather their thoughts, they will not be able to ask questions. Most people are too polite to pry in a setting such as this." He smiled. "You may get a few phone calls later."

She'd already figured that out. As for his plan, it was the only one they had.

"Let's go," she said, and led the way into the low, one-story building.

There were several small classrooms, three playrooms, and a big meeting room that currently had a stage at one end. Mia smiled at several of the mothers she knew and did her best to ignore their wide-eyed stares at Rafael. Oh yeah, there would be *plenty* of phone calls later.

The two of them took seats on the far side of the room, by a fire exit. There weren't any other parents sitting there yet. She had a feeling that spot had been pre-arranged and that Umberto and Oliver were hovering just outside. She subtly shifted her chair a bit farther away from Rafael's so there would be no accidental touching. Right now she didn't need the distraction.

"I hope no one recognizes you," she muttered. "I'm not a big tabloid reader, but lots of other people are. I wouldn't enjoy someone standing up and screaming out your identity."

"Nor would I." He glanced around. "We do not have a camera. I did not think to bring one. This is Daniel's first play. We must have pictures." He started to rise. "Instruct them not to begin the play until I have returned."

Mia put her hand on his arm. "Settle down. I have a camera." Then she realized they were touching and that the heat from his skin burned her in a way designed to make her rip off her clothes and beg to be taken right that second.

She casually removed her hand and reached into her bag for her digital camera.

Why did he still have to get to her? If only they hadn't made love. If she didn't have such incredible and recent memories, she would be able to ignore her physical attraction to him. She loathed the man with every fiber of her being and she absolutely hated suspecting that if they were alone and he started to seduce her, she wouldn't be able to say no.

In her head, she knew the opposite of love was apathy. That as long as she had energy in her feelings for Rafael, she was far from being over him. But in her heart, she wanted to slice her feelings away, like an unwanted disease. She wanted to forget how good he was with Danny, how he could be sensitive at the oddest times, how, until the Portuguese incident, he respected her intelligence.

Two months ago, her life had been relatively uncomplicated. Now it was fodder for a cable movie of the week.

"You told me Daniel is the star of the play," Rafael said.

"No I didn't. He's a tree. I told you he has three lines, just like every other child. This is preschool, not Broadway. There are no stars."

"But he is . . ." He lowered his voice. "He is the heir to the Calandrian throne."

"Gee, you know what? I didn't have that information when they were casting the play. What a shame, because if I'd told them I'm sure they would have made him the star."

Rafael stared at her. "Do you not believe your son is special?"

"Of course. But because of who he is on the inside. Not because of his relationship to you. I thought he was the most amazing child back when he was the son of an antiquities smuggler."

He frowned slightly. "I had not considered that. Were you angry when you discovered you were pregnant?"

"No. Not angry. Shocked. But I was going through a bad time, and finding out I was pregnant got me through it."

She really didn't want to talk about this. Why couldn't they be arguing about the light bill like the other parents?

"You mean because you thought I was dead," he told her.

"Whatever." She stared straight ahead.

"Mia." He leaned close until his mouth was almost touching her ear. "I did not mean to hurt you by letting you think I was dead. I did not consider that you would mourn me."

She turned to glare at him only to discover their faces were very, very close. "I told you I loved you. I don't say that to just anyone. I thought you were a real bad guy. I was violating every belief I had by being with you."

"I see that now. I am sorry for not understanding it then. Returning to my real life was traumatic. My father was very angry. I had neglected many duties. There were complications, but I should have considered your feelings."

It wasn't much of an apology, but considering the source, it wasn't bad. Unlike the last one, when he'd been whiny and had complained about being caught rather than being wrong.

"Fine," she muttered, and faced front again.

"This is nice," he said. "The preschool. The play."

"If you're going to launch into some sob story about how you never had a normal childhood with the hopes that I'll feel sorry for you, forget it."

"My childhood was fine," he told her. "One of great privilege. I had a series of very nice nannies and tutors until I was sent away to school."

He spoke so matter-of-factly that she couldn't tell if he was being casual or playing her.

"I'm glad Daniel will have more than that," he continued. "Different experiences."

"Which you wanted to take him away from."

"He would have carried the memories. They would have shaped him."

As if that was an excuse. "He's four. How much would he remember?"

"Enough." He glanced at her. "I did not mean to take him from you."

That got her attention. "Excuse me? That was your entire plan."

"Yes, I know. I am saying now, after considering what would have happened, I was wrong. I wanted my son in my life. I still want that. I want him to understand who he is. His history, his place in the world. But I see . . ."

When he paused she turned toward him. The urge to be sarcastic and cutting pressed in on her, but she resisted. Maybe, just maybe, she and Rafael were actually going to get to the truth for once.

"It would have been difficult for him," Rafael said

slowly. "He would have missed you and your family. I would not have known what to say to comfort him. My father would have insisted he act like a prince and a new nanny would have been hired. I'm sure neither would have helped a four-year-old boy heal from that kind of wound."

"You're right. No child should have his whole world ripped from him. Sometimes things happen and it can't be helped. But it shouldn't happen like this."

His blue eyes darkened. "You know you can't keep him from me forever. Some point of compromise will have to be reached."

"You're ruining a perfectly good moment," she muttered as she fought against anger. "You have no right to talk to me about compromise after what you did."

"I know, but that does not change the truth. I want things to be different for Daniel. Better. I do not know how to make that happen. I would need your help."

As he spoke, he reached for her hand. She snatched it away. Any touching would only muddle her brain. It was just her bad luck that the first sex she'd had in nearly five years turned out to be with a lying weaselly dog.

"You would need my help if you were taking him away, but you're not, so there isn't a problem."

He settled back in his chair. "You're a very stubborn woman."

"It's a Marcelli trait. Something I'm very proud of."

She stared at the stage and was grateful that no one had come to sit near them yet. Talk about a fascinating conversation to overhear.

"You think I walked away from you and never thought of you again," he said.

Unable to resist the bait, she spun to face him. "Don't

even go there. Don't try to convince me that you pined for me for even one second. We both know you didn't. If you had cared, you would have come after me. You would have told me you weren't dead. You would have done something. I was a way to pass the time while you were playing at being the bad guy."

"So much anger," he said as he touched her cheek.

She jerked her head back. "Stop touching me."

"As you wish."

He dropped his hand to his lap and she immediately wanted him to put it back on her.

"You've already done this dance, Rafael," she told him. "Stop lying. You can't sell me on believing in you again, so just let it go."

"I did not come after you," he said. "When I returned to the palace, my father was furious with me. He thought I had been studying abroad. When he found out I'd risked my life, he nearly locked me in the dungeon. I pointed out I was of age and free to live my life. He disagreed. I am, after all, the heir."

She rolled her eyes. "Is there an actual point?"

"I am the heir, Mia. I am expected to marry a particular kind of woman."

"I wasn't asking you to marry me, you egotistical creep. A postcard would have been nice. You let me think you were dead."

"I did not have a choice." He shook his head. "I chose not to have a choice. You were not someone I could have married. There was no point in caring about you anymore."

There were too many emotions, she thought, wishing she could simply leave. Anger and hurt and confusion and a deep, stupid desire to believe him.

"I did not know what to say to you," he told her. "I did not know how to explain we could not be together. To say why seemed . . ."

"Arrogant? Stuck up? Presumptuous?"

He shrugged. "All of those. So I took the easy way out. I said nothing. I let you walk away."

"Why are we having this conversation?" she asked, wishing the damn play would start or someone would come sit by them so he would stop talking.

"Because I want to apologize for that. I behaved badly."

He sounded sincere. She would swear that she could see the truth in his eyes. And she hated that. Hated that after everything they'd been through, she still wanted him to be one of the good guys.

"You can't honestly believe I'm going to trust you," she snapped. "You're an expert at playing my emotions. You came here with the express purpose of seducing me in order to steal Danny. Why is this any different?"

"Because it is. I do not know how else to explain myself to you."

"Then stop trying, because I'm done listening."

"Mia—"

But whatever he'd been about to say was cut off when a family moved into the row in front of them. Mia breathed a sigh of relief. It was a testament to his charm that even knowing what she knew, she still had trouble resisting him. The man was the devil.

Maybe that was problem. Women had been losing their souls to the devil's brand of temptation since the very beginning of time. Who was she to buck tradition?

•   •   •

Francesca hesitated outside the bedroom door. "I'm scared," she whispered.

Mia squeezed her hand. "You love her. That's what matters."

Francesca nodded, then knocked once and pushed open the door. "Hi, sweetie, how are you?"

Mia followed her sister into Kelly's room. Kelly lay on the bed reading a fashion magazine. She barely glanced at them.

"What are you doing here?"

"I wanted to see you," Francesca said. "Just to talk about how things are going."

Kelly threw down the magazine and pushed herself into a sitting position. Her gaze narrowed. "So why is Mia here? And why is your face all scrunchy? You're not just here to talk. What's going on?"

Francesca glanced at Mia. "She was always really bright."

"Beats the alternative," Mia told her. "Want the chair?"

Francesca nodded and pulled out the desk chair. Mia settled in the window seat. Kelly folded her arms over her chest in a position even a layperson like Mia recognized as defensive.

"What?" she demanded.

Francesca drew in a breath. "Kelly, your dad and I love you so much. I hope you know that. We only want you to be happy."

"I am happy. Perfectly happy. I have a great life. I'm a dancer with the San Francisco Ballet. It's a fabulous company and I'm working really hard. Everything is fine."

"I don't think so."

Kelly rolled her eyes. "Because you're going to believe Rafael's bullshit? Isn't he the liar prince?"

Mia admired her sister's patience. Francesca didn't lose her composure. She kept eye contact and spoke in a low voice. Obviously she wasn't a real Marcelli—she must have been spawned by aliens from a galaxy far, far away.

"I think what you do is amazing," Francesca said. "When you dance, you move with such grace and beauty, it's as if you're one with the music. You're right. You are working really hard. You've given up so much for your dance. Maybe it's too much. We were all so caught up in the dream of you being a ballerina, maybe we never considered the reality."

Kelly opened her mouth, then closed it. "This is stupid."

Francesca continued as if she hadn't heard. "So many women your age are in college. They're going to classes and frat parties and changing their minds about their majors. Sometimes their biggest problem is how to fit all the dirty laundry in the trunk of their car. But not you. You're living in the real world. You have an apartment, you pay your bills. You're a working woman. I can't imagine that at your age. Of course I was a student at twenty-eight."

Francesca smiled as she spoke. Kelly's lower lip quivered a little.

"We want you to be happy," Francesca told her. "Sometimes you have to try something to know if it's what you want. Sometimes you have to stumble and fall before you can fly."

Mia shifted on the window seat. "Francesca, you would try the patience of a saint. I swear, if you have any more analogies, I'm going to have to scream. Jeez. Just spit it out. Tell the kid you don't care if she doesn't want to be a dancer anymore. That it's fine. She can move home or go to college or whatever."

Francesca shot her a very clear "would you please shut up" look.

"I'm not a kid," Kelly said, then burst into tears.

Francesca moved onto the bed and pulled Kelly into her arms. Kelly clung to her.

"I'm s-sorry," she breathed between sobs. "I hate being a dancer. I know you guys g-gave up so much for me. I know it c-cost a lot. But I hate it." She raised her head and wiped her face with the back of her hand. "I hurt all the time. The physical work is grueling. I'm tired and I'm hungry. I don't have what it takes. I don't. Even if I do, I don't want to anymore."

Francesca hugged her close. "Then you can stop right now." She smiled at Mia over Kelly's curly red hair and mouthed "Thank you."

Mia didn't bother to point out that she wasn't the one to be thanking. Rafael had figured out the truth none of them had been able to see. She wouldn't have thought he had the sensitivity or awareness, but she'd been wrong.

Kelly continued to cry. "I'm sorry. I'm sorry."

"You don't have to be," Francesca said. "You're only twenty. How can you know what you want to do with your life? You're allowed to change your mind."

Kelly raised her head and wiped at her tears. "Really?"

Francesca nodded. "Of course."

"Then I want to go to college. Maybe community college at first. I want to be a physical therapist, get married, and have kids. I could teach ballet on the side or something. I don't want to let it go, but I can't make it my life anymore."

"Then you won't."

Kelly smiled. "Thanks for making me talk about this."

"Not a problem. I want you to know you can always come to me or your dad if you need to."

"I know, I just felt so stupid. I finally had what I'd always wanted and suddenly I didn't want it anymore. And . . ." She ducked her head. "I'm really sorry about Etienne. He was another mistake."

"You were trying to get our attention."

Kelly grinned at her. "Did it work?"

"Big-time."

Kelly hugged her, then slid off the bed. She crossed to Mia and caught her in a hug. "Thank Rafael for me, okay? Maybe he's not such a big butthead."

"I'll keep that in mind."

Kelly straightened. "I'm gonna go call Dad, then ask the Grands for some leftovers."

"Good. He'll want to talk to you, and you know how the Grands feel about feeding you. You'll make their day."

Kelly raced from the room. Francesca watched her go. "I'm so relieved," she said with a sigh. "I feel so much better about things. I know Kelly does, too. It's just . . . how could we not have figured it out before? She's been crying for help and no one noticed."

"We noticed," Mia told her. "We just weren't sure what was wrong. To quote your daughter, it took the butthead to see it."

"Which means he isn't as completely self-centered as we thought."

"Actually he is. He told me with the idea of getting points in return."

Francesca shrugged. "Still, it took a little emotional awareness for him to figure it out."

"You say that like it's a good thing."

"It's not bad. Mia, we're talking about Danny's father. You can't ignore him forever."

"Watch me try."

"Oh, that's mature."

Mia shook her head. "I know what you're saying, but I'm not prepared to be mature right now. I'm still angry and I don't trust him."

She thought about all they'd discussed while waiting for Danny's play to start. What bugged her wasn't what he said—it was her desire to believe it.

"Maybe he's learned his lesson," Francesca said.

"People don't change."

"Of course they do. Look at you. You're not the same person you were six years ago."

"We're talking about days, not years," Mia reminded her. "People change if motivated. Do you really think Rafael is? Right now he's pissed because he didn't win. He'll get tired and go home."

"Do you really believe he's going to walk away from Danny?"

Mia drew in a deep breath. "No," she said slowly, knowing anything else was wishful thinking on her part. "He'll come up with another plan. Maybe he already has. Whatever happens, I refuse to trust him."

Francesca winced. "Be careful about drawing a line in the sand. You don't want to get trapped by your own words."

"It's a risk I'm willing to take. There is nothing Rafael can say or do to make me ever believe him again. He knows it and I know it."

"I'm riding, I'm riding," Danny cried as he circled the lawn behind the house.

"You look great," Mia called to the boy.

"Excellent," Rafael said. "Just like that. Very good."

Mia watched her son on the pony and realized that with the trip to Calandria off, she was going to have to find a place for Gaspare. She couldn't keep him tied up by the garage under Joe's makeshift tent/stable.

"I need to find a stable," she murmured. "Are they listed in the phone book?"

Rafael stiffened, but didn't protest that Danny and his pony would soon be leaving.

"You have land here," he said instead. "You could build a small stable."

"In theory, but unless the plans came with a way to build a little someone to care for Gaspare then we'd still have a problem. Danny's too young to care for the pony and I'll be busy with school. Even if you're still here, you don't strike me as the type to muck out a stall." She glanced at him. "It is 'muck out,' isn't it?"

"That is the term."

His expression was tight, his eyes narrowed.

"You're all pinchy," she said, feeling suddenly cheerful. "Is it the thought of being forced to stay here or the knowledge that the little prince won't be returning with you?"

"I am enjoying my time here with you," he said, avoiding the question. "Daniel has an excellent seat."

Not exactly a smooth change of subject, but that was okay. She glanced at Danny and saw he really did seem to have an instinctive understanding of how to ride.

"He must get that from you," she said. "I don't think a Marcelli has been on a horse in eighty or ninety years."

"Then perhaps it is time. I could arrange for the three of us to go riding."

"No, thanks. I think the pony is dangerous enough. I don't want to see a real horse."

"You are afraid?" he asked, his voice taunting her.

She refused to be trapped by threat of being called chicken. "Sensible. Very sensible."

"I see. How is Kelly?"

She groaned. "You love that you were right, don't you?"

"I'm glad she was able to tell her parents the truth and now she's happy."

"Oh, please. You're desperate to do the happy dance," Mia said. "You think you're Mr. Sensitivity."

He smiled. "I assure you, that title never crossed my mind. I meant what I said. I like Kelly."

"You're not fooling me, Rafael. I know all this pleasant chitchat is just part of your master plan. You're trying to lull me into liking you again. It's not going to happen."

He glanced at her, then returned his attention to Danny. "Is it so impossible to believe I might regret what happened? That I now wish for a chance to make things right between us?"

"Yes. It is impossible."

"Because I am so horrible?"

"It's not about being horrible. It's about being used to getting your way. You're not used to regular rules. You don't believe in them. Why would you play by them now?"

"Because they are all that is left to me." He looked at her again. "You are right—I planned to steal your son from you. But in my mind, I didn't take the idea any further. I did not consider that Daniel would be devastated by the loss. I would have, and then I would have realized we needed to come up with another way."

"That's it?" she asked, incredulous. "That's all you got from this?"

"What is wrong with what I said? I have admitted I was wrong. I would have hurt Daniel and that was never my plan. I have also told you several times that I intended for you to be able to see Daniel, that I wasn't going to keep him from you, but you choose not to believe that. So why would I continue to repeat myself?"

"That's it?" she demanded again, even as she smiled and waved at Danny as he continued to circle the lawn. "That's the best you can do?"

"What more do you want from me? Blood?"

"It would at least be a start."

"Be reasonable, Mia. I cannot undo the past. What would make you feel better now?"

"There's nothing," she said between clenched teeth. How she loathed the man. How she wished he'd never seen that stupid picture, had never come here. If only—

"Change the law," she said suddenly. "I was kidding before, but I'm not now. Change the law that says once Danny is on Calandrian soil I have no rights. Make us equals in Calandria law."

"Will that be enough?" he asked, surprising her. She'd been so sure he would protest.

"It will be a start."

"I will call the leader of parliament in the morning," he said. "I give you my word."

He held out his hand as if they were supposed to shake on it.

She didn't want to shake hands with him. She didn't want to touch him at all. Whenever she did, she was reminded how weak and rebellious her body could be. But there was no polite way to avoid the contact, so she braced herself and slid her hand against his.

The sparks were instant. Need exploded like a firecracker trapped in a box. There was light and heat, which she hated almost as much as his knowing smile.

"It's just physical," she snapped as she pulled back and stepped away from him.

"The body and the spirit are not so easily separated," he said. "They influence each other."

"Not in this case. Don't go getting any ideas." She glanced at her watch. "Your time is up. You need to leave."

She expected him to protest. Instead he walked over to Danny and lifted him down from the pony. "You have done well," Rafael told him. "I'm very proud of you."

"I don't wanna stop," Danny said.

"It is time for me to leave."

Danny's lower lip thrust out. "No!" he yelled. "You stay. Mommy, tell Daddy to stay."

"Danny, it's time for Daddy to leave."

She tried to gather him in her arms, but he pushed away and ran to Rafael.

"Stay, Daddy," the boy cried. "I'm the heir and I say you stay."

"Danny . . . ," Mia started.

Her son turned on her. "Why did you make him go away? Why can't my daddy stay with me? I want him to stay. I want him to live with me. I'm the heir and I say so. I say so!"

The last sentence came out as a shrieking scream. Mia was stunned when her normally reasonable, rational, emotionally stable child threw himself on the ground and began kicking and yelling.

"Danny," she said quietly. "It's all right."

"It's not. It's not."

"Mia," Rafael murmured.

She looked at him. "Just go. I'll deal with this."

"I will not leave you alone while he is like this."

Which, in theory, was lovely. But in reality, the longer he stayed, the worse it would get. Still, she couldn't force him to go.

She sat next to Danny and Rafael sat next to her. Danny cried himself out of his tantrum in about three minutes, then crawled on her lap. He put one arm around her neck and one around his father's, forcing them to lean toward each other. Then he cried as if his heart were breaking.

Parts of words tumbled out. It took her a minute to figure out what he was saying, and when she did, her heart broke, too.

"I want a mommy and daddy at the same time."

16

❦

Mia stood by David in the hallway. He smiled at her and then said, "You look like hell."

She fingered her hair and realized she was in desperate need of a trim and maybe some highlights, but she didn't think that's what he meant. The stress wore on her until she had arguments with Rafael in her dreams.

"Things have been better," she admitted. "It could be worse. At least I don't have classes. I don't think I could deal with all this and tort law at the same time."

He patted her arm. "I wish I could help. Want me to beat up Rafael?"

"Thanks, but Joe already called that one and I haven't said yes to him yet."

"I don't want to stand in the way of Joe and a mission," David told her. "Is there anything else I can do?"

"Just being here with Amber helps," she said. "Watching the two of you gives me hope. Not every relationship is destined for disaster."

He smiled and she saw the love in his eyes. For a moment she felt a twinge—not because she wanted him to still be in love with her, but because just once she wanted a man to look like that when he talked about her.

"I got lucky when I met Amber," he admitted. "Even more lucky when she agreed to go out with me. I couldn't believe she didn't have a serious boyfriend or wasn't already married." He chuckled. "I nearly proposed on our first date. I knew she was the one, but I figured if I said so, she would think I was crazy and disappear into the night. So I waited and played the dating game, but all the time I knew."

Mia sighed. "Now you're getting married."

"I know some guys think of it as a loss of freedom, but why would I want time away from Amber? To do what? Meet other women and be disappointed? She's the one. I want to wake up next to her every morning. I want to plan a future and have kids and curl up in the dark just breathing in the scent of her body."

Mia listened to his words and felt another twinge. Sure, David was doing what they'd talked about, but he also meant every word. He spoke from the heart about the woman he loved.

"She's going to be a great mom," he continued. "She loves kids and she's patient. What?" he asked with a frown.

"I didn't say anything."

He touched her cheek. "You're crying."

"I'm not." She felt the dampness. "Okay, maybe, but just because it's so wonderful. I want you to be happy."

"I want you to find what I have," he told her. "Mia, you're great. You're smart and beautiful and I want you to find the right guy."

"I'm sure I will," she lied. "But until then, I have you two to inspire me."

"I've never been an inspiration before."

"You were never marrying Amber before." Mia hesitated. "David, I need you to talk to her for me."

"About?"

She drew in a breath. "The Grands. They really want to bead something. You know we have the tradition of making the bride's wedding dress. Obviously Amber has picked out a dress already. The wedding isn't that far away. The Grands have beaded your vest and they loved it, but it's not the same. The thing is, it's about more than just helping. It's their way of showing Amber they love her and really want her to be in the family. But they're afraid they'll say it wrong, or she'll think they're weird or pressuring her. They mentioned something about working on her veil, if that would be okay."

"I'll talk to her," he said as he leaned against the hallway wall. "She really likes the family, but sometimes they're a little much."

Mia laughed. "Of course we are. I get overwhelmed and I was born into this craziness. I hope you can explain how much we already love her and how happy we are that she's going to be one of us. Even if that does mean having to marry you."

"Hey!"

She grinned. "I've seen you at your worst."

"I could say the same."

"You could, but you're a gentleman and you won't." Her smile faded. "I love you and I'm incredibly glad we're not the ones getting married."

"Me too." His expression turned serious. "We were kids. What did we know about marriage and forever?"

"Plus you probably would have met Amber eventually and left me for her."

"I would have felt bad about it."

She laughed. "And that's supposed to make it all better?"

He shrugged. "What can I say? She's the love of my life."

"David?"

They both turned and saw Amber stepping out of the dining room where Grammy M had carefully sent her to polish the silver. The preplanned move had allowed Amber to hear every word while staying out of sight.

"Amber." David shifted uncomfortably. "We were, uh, just talking. Mia and I. It doesn't mean anything."

Amber's eyes were bright with affection and understanding. "I know." She turned to Mia. "I'm sorry I've been so foolish about so many things. It's just you're amazing and I'm just . . ."

"The woman David loves," Mia told her.

Amber stepped into his embrace. "I am, aren't I? Wow. How did I get so lucky?"

David hugged her tight. Over her head, he mouthed, "Thank you."

Mia nodded, then turned away to give them privacy. Not that they cared. As far as they were concerned, they were the only two people in the world.

Mia returned to her room, where she could have her breakdown in private. This was the Marcelli family, after all, and if anyone saw her crying they would all want to know what was wrong, then work as a committee to fix it. Right now, she just couldn't handle that.

She closed the door and then threw herself on the bed. But once there, the tears refused to come. She squeezed her eyes shut and tried not to think about everything going on, but it was impossible.

She hurt. Every bone, every hair, every inch of skin. She ached with disappointment and a strong sense of having lost something that could have been—should have been—wonderful. For a few days, a couple of weeks even, she'd been in love with a caring, smart, funny guy who'd pretended to love her back. She'd allowed herself to believe. To have hope. It had been a long time since she'd had hope in the romance department.

So many pretty words, she thought. So many lies and she'd fallen for them all. Apparently she only looked smart.

Now everything felt broken. She knew Rafael was trying, but so what? How could she ever believe him again? How could she trust him? Or was that not her problem? Did she have to trust him? If he changed the law, then they would have to negotiate some kind of visitation for Danny in Calandria.

She rolled onto her back. If . . . There was no if. Rafael was nothing if not determined. He wanted his son to grow up knowing about his people and his duty. He wanted Danny to understand that being the heir meant more than waving a scepter and making pronouncements. Rafael would get the law changed and then she would lose Danny.

Her eyes burned as the tears came at last. Perhaps it was dramatic to think she would lose her son, but everything would be different. He would probably summer with his father and go to school in Los Angeles with her. He would have major life experiences without her, learn things, be independent. She'd expected that when he was a teenager, but not before he was eight.

She wanted to hate Rafael for all this. She wanted to

blame him for everything, but she couldn't. In truth, Danny was his son and he had as much right to the boy as she.

She closed her eyes and felt the trickle of moisture run down her temples and into her hair. Her chest ached. How would she survive without Danny around? The summer would be too long. She could—

Eventually he would have to go to school in Europe.

Mia sat up. He would need exposure to a larger world. An international one. She had the sudden hope that he'd inherited her ability to learn languages. It would certainly make his life easier.

But what about her? Should *she* move to Europe? Would that help Danny? There had to be law firms that would want to hire her. And then what? Make a life for herself living quietly somewhere while her son trained to be king and Rafael married someone appropriate?

She picked up a pillow and threw it across the room. "Damn you, Rafael," she cried as more tears poured down her cheeks.

"Mommy."

Mia froze and looked at the now open door. She'd been so caught up in her thoughts, she hadn't heard it open.

Danny stood there, his eyes wide as he stared at her. "Mommy?"

She quickly wiped her face. "Hi, sweetie. I'm okay. What's going on?"

"I want to do a puzzle."

He still wasn't very good at them. Even the ones with the really big pieces.

"Sure. I can help. Let me go wash my face and we'll head downstairs."

He crossed the room and climbed up on the bed. "Are you mad at Daddy?" he asked.

Her first instinct was to deny that she was, but based on what Danny had just seen and heard, that seemed kind of stupid.

"I am, right now, but that's okay. Grown-ups get mad at each other and then we talk and make up."

"Does Daddy have to 'pologize?"

"He has."

"But you're still mad?"

She sighed. "I'm mad about a lot of things."

"You could make a list."

She laughed, then put her arms around him. He hugged her back, his body small and sturdy.

"I love you, big guy," she whispered. "So much. You're my whole world and the best thing in it."

"I love you, too, Mommy."

She couldn't let him go, she thought as she continued to hold on to him. Not even for a summer. She couldn't survive. Which meant she and Rafael had a whole lot of stuff to work out.

But how was she supposed to negotiate with a man she didn't trust?

She straightened. "Okay. Let's go find that puzzle."

"Okay."

He smiled and slid off the bed. She followed him. In the hallway, he reached for her hand. She held on to his small fingers and vowed that no matter what, she was never letting go.

Rafael walked toward the back door of the Marcelli house. He'd had two angry phone calls with his father that morning. The king was not a patient man and he expected his grandson in residence before the end of the summer. Rafael didn't see how that was possible. He was no longer willing to simply spirit Daniel away, as he had been before. Mia had worked legal magic to keep Daniel with her in any other circumstances. It was a problem without solution.

The door opened before he could knock. Daniel stood there.

"Good morning," Rafael said pleasantly. "I thought we could go into town today. There is a children's museum that is—"

"You made my mommy cry," Daniel told him. "You made Mommy cry and say a bad word. Go away."

With that, the door slammed shut, leaving Rafael standing alone outside.

Mia looked up when Grammy M walked into the library. "What's up?" she asked.

The older woman was twisting an old dish towel. "It's Danny," she said, then quickly added. "He's fine."

"Okay." Mia stood. "Did he do something wrong?"

"I'm not sure you'll think so. Rafael was here."

Mia glanced at the clock and swore. It was ten after two. Their appointment was for two.

"I was trying to figure out my class schedule," she said. "I wasn't watching the clock." Her heart froze in her chest. "Oh, God, Rafael didn't take him, did he?"

"What? Of course not. None of us would be lettin' that happen. It's nothin' like that. Danny answered the door and told his father that he'd made you cry and that he should go away. Then he slammed the door in Rafael's face and ran up to his room. He's there now."

Mia winced. "He walked in while I was having a personal pity party last night," she admitted. "I didn't think he would take it so hard. What did Rafael do?"

"He left."

Mia blinked. "You're kidding. I would have thought he would demand his son."

"I think Danny hurt his feelings."

Mia couldn't imagine a building falling on the man and causing pain, but stranger things had happened. "Okay, I'll take care of this."

Danny first, then Rafael, she thought.

"Rafael really left?" she asked again.

Grammy M nodded. "He got in his car and drove away."

"So not like him to walk away." She couldn't believe he'd given up on Danny, which left what? He'd been shocked, maybe? Because the hurt thing . . . so not happening.

Thirty minutes later she pulled into the hotel parking lot. She'd had a very productive talk with her four-year-old, explaining he didn't get to say who came and went in the house, and now she was here to . . . to . . .

She parked and stared at the small hotel as she tried to figure out what she was there to do. Telling Rafael he was welcome to come over was the sort of thing she could say on the phone. So why had she left Danny in the very capable hands of the Grands and driven here herself?

Oh, well, now that she *was* here, she might as well deliver her message.

She walked up to the second floor and was immediately stopped by Oliver.

"It's me," she said easily. "I'm not armed and I'm not

going to let you feel me up to confirm that, but you can check my purse if you want."

She held out the bag. He quickly went through it, then handed it back.

She walked to Rafael's room and knocked.

"It's open."

She stepped inside and found him sitting on the sofa, reading what looked like a very thick report.

"Hi," she said as she entered. "I came by to, ah, talk about what happened with Danny."

Rafael rose and pointed to the sofa. "Please, have a seat. Would you like something to drink?"

"No, I'm good."

He waited until she was seated before claiming his own chair again. She studied him, trying to figure out what he was feeling, but his dark blue eyes gave nothing away and the half smile hid all his secrets.

"I heard what happened," she began, again wondering why she hadn't just phoned it in. "I'm sorry Danny did that. I didn't coach him."

"I did not think you did. Two days ago he was furious with you because he thought you were the reason I no longer lived at the house. Today I am the villain."

Bad guy, she thought, but didn't correct him. "Okay. Well, I thought maybe you were upset."

"So you came to gloat?"

"Ouch. That's not fair. I said I'm sorry."

"So you did. You are sorry and I am sorry. Where do we go from here?"

He was asking her? "I haven't a clue," she admitted. "We'll have to find some middle ground."

"Difficult when you don't trust me."

Difficult, yes. But impossible?

"I want to trust you," she said slowly.

"You say that as if it's a horrible thing."

"It is. How many times do you get to fool me?"

"I'm not fooling, Mia. This is very real. We're talking about our son and his future and how best to be parents. What is more real than that?"

"You're still an arrogant prince who doesn't believe he has to play by the rules."

"Perhaps, but you didn't come here because of Daniel."

He was on his feet before she had a chance to absorb his words. Once she did, she stood and glared at him. "If you're saying what I think you're saying . . ."

"You're here because of me. Because of the connection that exists. You're here because there is a need and a hunger and because when you close your eyes at night, I'm the man you see."

She started to stalk out, but he grabbed her arm and spun her toward him. They were inches apart. She could feel the heat of his body and hear the soft rhythm of his breathing. His eyes were as dark as midnight and she recognized the passion burning there.

"Admit it," he commanded.

"Never."

"But you must, Mia. You were never a liar."

"Of all the arrogant, self-centered, egotistical—"

He cut off her rant with a kiss. She knew what he was going to do the second before his mouth touched hers and she braced herself for the assault.

Only it never came. Instead he released her arm and pressed his lips to hers in a gesture so tender, so soft and tentative, she felt herself strain toward him to deepen the contact.

All the anger and uncertainty drained away, leaving nothing in their wake but desire. Her body remembered what it had been like to be touched by this man, and every cell called out to him. Her breasts ached, her thighs tightened, and between her legs, she was already wet.

All this and they were still kissing like schoolchildren.

"Mia," he breathed against her mouth. "How I've wanted you. How I've thought about what it was like when we made love. We have always had the fire. When I touch you, I feel your pleasure."

She felt the same. As she ran her hands over his body, she knew his response as if it were her own. But she didn't say that. She might be foolish enough to sleep with him again, but she wasn't going to get sucked in emotionally.

This was just sex. Fantasy and friction. Nothing more.

Still, when he pressed against her mouth, she turned into him. And when his arms came around her waist, she raised hers to his shoulders. Then she tilted her head and parted her lips and surrendered.

His tongue swept inside her mouth. His heat and taste combined with incredible sensations of delight. She surged toward him, wanting to feel the hardness of his body against hers. Even as he explored her mouth, he rubbed his hands up and down her back. She did the same to him, then went lower, to cup his rear and squeeze.

He immediately pressed his hips toward her, driving his erection into her belly.

He was already hard, she thought happily. Hard to her wet. She closed her lips around his tongue and sucked as she remembered what it had been like last time, when he'd driven into her so deeply, she'd been forced to come over and over.

He reached for the hem of her T-shirt. She released him long enough to step back and hold her arms up over her head. He pulled the shirt free, then expertly unfastened her bra.

Then his mouth was on one breast with his fingers matching the movements on the other. As he stroked and sucked and licked, she ran her fingers through his hair and tried to remember how to breathe.

It was perfect, she thought, her head falling back. With each tug on her nipples, she felt an answering contraction between her thighs. Her shorts confined her. She needed to be naked, her legs spread, him between them. Going down on her or plunging inside of her, she didn't much care. Just *something.*

He straightened and claimed her mouth again. She didn't complain because he covered her breasts with both hands and continued to caress her. Even as he kissed her over and over again, he nudged her back. She allowed him to urge her into the bedroom where the high four-poster bed beckoned.

When she bumped into it, he lifted her onto the mattress. She scooted back, only to be stopped by him unfastening her shorts. Somewhere along the way, she'd kicked off her sandals.

When he released her, she continued to scoot while he held on to her shorts. Her panties came off with them. When she was naked, he grinned and went to work on his own shirt.

Minutes later, he was next to her, touching her everywhere. She traced the muscles of his chest and skinny line of hair that led to his arousal. He teased her belly button before moving lower and slipping his fingers into her wetness.

They lay on their sides, facing each other, eyes open as they pleasured each other. He kissed her cheeks, her forehead, then her nose.

"The difference is," he said quietly, "that I very much want to make you come, but you do not have the same goal."

She continued to stroke his hard length. "Are you sure about that?"

"Of course. If you make me come now, how will I slide deep inside you later? How will I part your legs and move faster and faster?"

"We'll have to wait, what? Ten minutes?" she asked with a smile.

"Any time would be too much."

He had a point, she thought as she reluctantly released him. He, however, kept touching her, rubbing back and forth, occasionally dipping his fingers inside of her. She had a leg over his hip and they were so close she could see the various colors that made up his irises.

Not that she could really focus on them. Instead her attention kept slipping to the building tension in her body.

This was just sex, she reminded herself. Really great sex. And she wanted more. She wanted more touching and rubbing and dipping. She wanted to come like this, then do it all again.

"You have always been difficult," he said conversationally.

"What? We're naked and you want to discuss that now?"

"I can think of no better time. You never do what you're told."

"I take great pride in that," she said, finding it difficult to speak, especially when he bent down and licked her nipple. She was close and getting closer. The rhythm of his fingers drove her crazy, but in the best way possible.

More, she thought. She just needed a little more.

"But sometimes instructions are a good thing. For example . . ."

He eased her onto her back, all the while continuing to touch her. He positioned himself between her legs. He had to be millimeters from entering her, but he didn't. She strained toward him.

"Rafael," she breathed.

He stared into her eyes. "Come for me, Mia. Come now."

The unexpected order shocked her. She felt him pushing slightly, but he didn't enter. He waited.

Suddenly she knew he would thrust inside of her the second she started to climax. She tightened in anticipation of his hardness filling her over and over again.

That was all it took to push her over. The first shudder of her release claimed her. She arched her body.

"Now," she breathed. "Do it hard, Rafael. Do it."

He plunged inside of her. At that first thrust, her contractions increased. Pleasure poured through her as she wrapped her legs around his hips and held him in place. Again and again, thrusting deep and fast, claiming her.

She held on to him, climaxing until his body stilled and shuddered.

•   •   •

Rafael lay still on the bed. Mia lay next to him. The sound of their breathing filled the quiet of the room.

Once again the power of their lovemaking surprised him. He hadn't thought she would really give in, but now that she had, he felt the first whisper of hope.

Perhaps all was not lost. Perhaps there was still a way to make her believe in him again. Because that is what he wanted. Over the past couple of weeks, he'd begun to see all he had lost with his deceptions and arrogance.

He wanted to make things right with her. He wanted her in his life because she wanted to be there. He needed her.

"Mia," he began, not sure what he was going to say.

She smiled, then stood. "I'll give full points for that one. It was great."

Her lush body distracted him until she reached for her clothing.

"What are you doing?" he asked.

"Getting dressed. I need to get back. I don't want to miss dinner."

"You should stay here," he said. "We can talk."

Talk? Had he really said that?

"I appreciate the invite, but I'm okay." She pulled on her panties and picked up her bra.

"You can't leave," he told her.

"Actually I can and I'm going to."

She quickly finished dressing, then walked to the door.

"It was sex, Rafael. Nothing more. I haven't forgiven you and I'm still pretty sure I don't like you. Unfortunately, I have a mindless reaction to your body. I'll get over it. I did before."

And then she was gone.

17

～

Mia held her bravado until she'd driven out of the hotel parking lot and was confident she was out of sight of anyone watching from a second-story window. Then she pulled to the side of the road and tried to catch her breath.

What had she done? The why was easy—no point in wondering about that. The why was the incredible sexual chemistry that had always existed with Rafael and the things that happened to her body when he touched her. But the what . . . now *there* was a question.

What on earth was she supposed to say the next time she saw him? How was he going to take her seriously if she fell into bed with him every time he smiled pretty? Because the man smiled pretty on a daily basis. He was born to smile pretty.

She leaned back in the seat and did her best to hold back tears. Lately she'd produced as much waterworks as a class 2 hurricane and her emotions were about as unpredictable. She had a good excuse, but still, where was her pride? Bad enough the man could make her come without breaking a sweat, worse if he also got to her heart.

Except her heart was the main problem. Her brain was firmly on the side of "Rafael, bad." Her body was weak, and despite physical evidence of the bones in question, spineless. Still, she could control her body simply by never being alone with him again. Wanting didn't necessarily have to lead to doing. But her heart. Her traitorous still-in-love-with-him heart . . . what was going to happen there?

She wanted him but knew she couldn't have him—at least not again. She hated him and still had to deal with him. She loved him and couldn't trust him.

She wasn't just fighting him, she was fighting herself, and that was one battle she didn't know how to win.

Mia found Joe looking for her when she got home.

"I wanted to give you an update on the—" he started as she climbed out of her car, then stopped. "You look like hell. What happened? Did Rafael threaten you?"

Not in the way Joe meant, she thought, trying to find the humor in the situation and failing badly.

"He didn't see Danny today," she said instead. "At least not for very long. Danny walked in on me having a meltdown and blamed his father. Basically the kid slammed the door in his face."

"I like his style," Joe said.

"It's a little volatile, but that comes with being four. I'm just a little shaky right now, but I'll get over it. What did you want to tell me?"

"That I've been doing regular equipment checks on the tracking system and it's fine. The alarm kicks in as soon as Danny leaves Marcelli land and the GPS instantly boots. It doesn't automatically work on the property, but we can always program it in manually. That wouldn't take much more than half an hour."

"In case Rafael kidnaps him and hides out in the vineyards? I can't see that happening."

"Me either, but it's an option." He stared at her. "Are you really okay?"

"No, but trust me, you don't want to know details."

He sucked in a breath as if bracing to have a fingernail or two removed. "I can listen."

For the first time that day, Mia laughed. "Darcy's done a very nice job with you. You're practically domesticated. But as much as I appreciate that very heartfelt offer, I'll pass. But I do have a question."

He nearly glowed with relief. "Sure. Ask me anything. I know a lot."

"And you're so modest." She hesitated, then asked, "Can men really change?"

The relief faded and his face took on a trapped expression.

"Dammit, Mia, don't drag me into this. As far as I'm concerned, your prince is a real bastard. I don't care if he changes, I just want to beat the crap out of him."

"Which I really appreciate. But that's not the point. He's saying he's sorry, and while I didn't believe him, I kind of do now. Or I want to, which isn't at all the same thing. Can he change?"

"Him specifically? I have no idea. Guys in general? Maybe. If they're motivated. Do I have to get into this with you?"

"Since you're the only brother I have, yes."

"Then it's possible, but not likely."

"How do I know for sure? How do I get proof?"

"Hell if I know. Look, you want to believe him because he's Danny's father and for a couple of other reasons I don't have to hear about. But proof, Mia? How do we prove anything in a relationship? It takes time. Is he going to be there when things get hard? Is he willing to make sacrifices? Are you equals?"

"I can't answer the first," she admitted. "The answer to the second two are probably no. How does a prince make sacrifices? Sleep on two-hundred-thread-count sheets instead of five? As for us being equals, in some ways we're not. He's royal. I'm the girl he knocked up. He certainly wasn't willing to come after me until he found out about his son. Apparently I'm not princess material."

Joe stared at her. "Do you want to be?"

"What? No. Of course not. Nothing about that life appeals to me."

"But you're pissed he didn't come claim you."

"Only in the sense that we'd had a relationship and he ended it by pretending to be dead."

"You have to give him points for creativity."

She punched him in the arm, then wished she hadn't when his muscles hurt her fist.

"I can almost understand that," she said as she rubbed her knuckles. "I mean, I was some American spy and he's got to marry Euro-trash, as Kelly would say. But there's a level of tackiness I just can't support. Plus there's the whole pretending to be in love with me so I'd marry him and he could take Danny. That's annoying."

When she thought of all the things he'd told her, she got mad all over again.

"Do you know he actually implied that I'm the reason he didn't get engaged to any of the appropriate women his father brought around. That he didn't realize it at the time but as soon as he and I were back together, he understood what had been going on."

"You think he's lying."

"As much as I think the sun is going to come up tomorrow."

Joe shifted. "The guy's not married."

"What? You're taking his side?"

"No way. I'm just pointing out that for whatever reason, the guy's not married. He's what, thirty?"

"Thirty-two," she said, fighting the urge to hit him again. Only, seriously, who would get hurt in *that* encounter?

"He didn't know about Danny, so he had to be under some serious pressure to produce an heir. Why isn't he married?"

"I'm sure there are a thousand reasons."

"Such as?"

"He's not willing to give up the babe banquet. Once he gets married, he'll be in a permanent relationship. Rafael doesn't like to cheat. I know it sounds strange, but it's true."

"He told you and you believed him?" Joe asked.

She rolled her eyes. "Yes, and yes. But I have confirmation from other sources. The woman he'd been with before me, plus when I Googled him, all the write-ups indicated he was pretty faithful to his girlfriends. Cheating was never listed as a reason for a breakup. I'm sure part of the reason he's resisted marriage is that the thought of having sex with the same person for the rest of his life is horrifying."

"Not so much as you might think," Joe told her with a grin. "Some of us like it."

She knew that her good-looking ex-Navy SEAL brother had never lacked for female companionship. Still . . . "I'm not sure your babe world compares with a royal one."

"You're saying he didn't come after you because he wasn't willing to give up the possibilities."

"Maybe," she said cautiously.

"So it wasn't personal. He could have been madly in love with you."

"Or not."

"Did you ask?"

She glared at him. "Ask him if he loved me? When, exactly, was I supposed to ask that and why would I believe him now?"

"I'm not saying you should, but the answer could be interesting."

Maybe to him, but to her, not so much. If she didn't care about Rafael, then the question wouldn't matter. But she did, and she didn't want to have him flat out tell her he'd never loved her. Thinking it herself was one thing—she could always secretly hope she was wrong. But once he said the words, all her illusions would be shattered forever.

"I need therapy," she muttered. "Long term. I might have to check myself in to a facility."

"We'll miss you, but I'm sure the Grands will visit regularly."

"Your support is overwhelming."

"I'm here to please." He put his arm around her. "Seriously, whatever you want, I'll do."

"Can you turn back time?"

"Except that."

"Then I guess I'm okay for now."

Rafael walked into Brenna's office without knocking. She looked up from her computer and rolled her eyes.

"You again."

He closed the door and crossed to her desk. "How do I prove myself to her?" he asked by way of greeting.

"The her in question being Mia?" Brenna asked.

He nodded. "She won't listen to me. She won't believe anything I say. How do I change her mind?"

She turned away from her computer screen and faced him. "The first thing that comes to mind is maybe you leaving her and Danny alone until the kid is eighteen."

She toyed with him, he thought impatiently. Didn't she understand he was serious? That he needed help? "Daniel is my son. I cannot ignore him."

"Your government will survive—"

"This isn't about my government. I have a child I did not know about. Now that I have found him, I will not let him go."

Brenna eyed him, then pointed at a chair. "You can sit down if you want."

He sat and leaned toward her. "Mia and I have to come to some agreement. I have already spoken to several members of parliament and they are writing a new law that gives Mia equal rights in Daniel's life. But that will take time. Weeks. Perhaps months. I am willing to wait—I will stay here as long as necessary—but something must change."

"I believe that something you're talking about is you."

He straightened. "What do you mean?"

"Here we go," she said wearily. "The whole 'I'm Crown Prince Blah de blah. You are nothing but dust beneath my feet.'" She sipped her coffee. "It gets old."

He had a feeling she was not referring to her drink.

"I *am* the crown prince."

"No one is unclear on your title. So what? I'm married, but I don't go around referring to myself as the wife of anyone. I'm my own person, separate from that. You're still Rafael, crown prince or not."

"I am not a separate person. My future has created the man I am today."

"See, that's the problem. If you had a little less prince and a little more man, you'd have a shot."

"I do not understand."

"Let's say you and Mia had just met and dated and you weren't a prince. You were just a regular guy. You broke up, she went back to America, and you didn't see each other for five years. Then, suddenly, you discover she had a son, but she had never told you. She didn't want to, didn't think you'd be a good father, whatever. What if she had willfully withheld that information from you? When you found out and confronted her, she had a lot of good reasons, but nothing you really bought. Would you ever trust her again?"

He did not want to answer Brenna's question. He didn't want to understand the analogy. He wanted to tell her that his circumstances were different. That he hadn't done it on purpose . . . only he had. He had let Mia leave Calandria thinking he was dead.

"It was easier that way," he said quietly. "I adored her. She was lovely—bright, beautiful, fearless. But an American with no important family."

"You're rambling, so I won't take issue with that last bit," Brenna said, "but don't push it too far."

"There are traditions," he continued. "Expectations."

"Is one of them for you to wear a condom so there isn't an unexpected pregnancy?"

"I told you. I had used . . ."

Protection. That was the next word. He'd always been careful. Always. Except for two times. The last two times with Mia.

She could be pregnant. Even this second, there could be another child growing inside of her.

He was torn, wanting to experience every moment he'd missed with Daniel, and uneasy at the thought of more complications in an already difficult situation.

"Earth to Rafael," Brenna said. "Where did you go?"

"I must make her understand I am sincere," he said quietly. "That I understand things now."

"Do you love her?"

Love? "It is not relevant."

"That's where you're wrong," she told him. "Love is the biggest relevance there is. It would help a lot, as would humility. Putting her on a stamp would work, too."

"You're mocking me."

"A little. Just for sport." She shrugged. "I like you, Rafael. I don't want to, but I do. Still, I would never advise my sister to trust you again. How could I? You blew it so badly, I don't know how you can recover. It would take a step of faith, and I don't know if Mia's that much of a believer. I'm sorry." She frowned. "Wow—I really *am* sorry."

He had been hoping for a miracle and she didn't have one to offer. "I appreciate how honest you have been."

"It's my strong suit. I live to tell other people what's wrong with them. Come anytime."

Rafael helped Daniel from his pony.

"You are doing well," he told the boy. "I see much improvement."

"I want to ride more," Daniel insisted, and stomped his foot. "Take me out more."

"This would be the imperious child," Mia said lightly. "He's closely related to the overtired one. I like the funny one and the loving ones much better."

"There's just me," Daniel told her. "I'm your only little boy." He frowned. "No more little boys."

"Wouldn't you like a little brother or sister?" Rafael asked, keeping a close eye on Mia as he spoke, but she didn't react.

"No! Just me."

Daniel stalked off to sit on the bottom step by the back door. Oliver led Gaspare away.

"I believe he gets his ill temper from you," Rafael said. "I was a most good-natured child."

She laughed. "Oh, please. You were imperious, too. I'd bet money on it."

She wore a pale summer dress and had bare feet. The loose fabric made him think of what was underneath. Of what had happened the last time they had been together. He wanted her, yet he sensed that making love with her again wasn't the answer. In truth, he didn't know what to do.

Uncertainty was not a familiar or comfortable state of being.

"Mia," he said, his voice low. "There is something we must discuss. About being together."

"No," she said firmly. "It happened, it's over. There will be no recaps or repeats."

"There is another issue that concerns me, although the topics are related."

"What on earth . . . Oh." Her mouth curved up in a smile. "I don't remember you being so carefree before. One could say you were almost fanatical about protection." She glanced at Daniel, but the boy was busy pouting and grinding his toe into the lawn.

"I agree. It has always been an issue with me, just to avoid certain complications."

"And yet here we are, filled with complications."

"Filled?"

"I meant Danny," she said. "It's fine." She moved close and whispered, "I'm on the pill, and it's not something I ever forget to take."

He braced himself for the wave of relief, but it never came. Instead there was a small twinge of regret. Why? Because Mia's being pregnant would have forced them into marriage?

Or would it? Mia was just stubborn enough to refuse him.

He reached for her hand. "How can I convince you I am truly sorry? What words are there? What actions?"

She jerked her fingers free. "None. I don't mean to be cruel. I'm only speaking the truth. There is nothing you can ever say or do to convince me that you're doing anything but playing a game."

He stiffened but didn't retreat. "I will not give up."

"I feel bad, Rafael. I don't want to be a complete bitch. I know about the law you're trying to change. I know that's for me. When it goes through and I've had a couple of lawyers read it over, then we can talk. I won't be unreasonable. In time, Danny has to learn that being your heir is about more than giving orders and getting his way. But not for a while. Not while he's still this young."

"I can't be gone forever."

"I won't let you take him."

"Then come with him. Live with me in Calandria. We can be a family."

"What will your future princess have to say about that?"

"There is no future princess, Mia. Unless you would like the job. We could be married."

He braced himself for the explosion, but there wasn't one. Instead she sighed.

"You're one for surprises, I'll give you that," she said. "Let me guess. It would be a marriage of convenience. We get to share Danny, we have the advantages of . . ." She glanced at her son, then murmured, "The advantages of chemistry without all those messy emotions."

As she spoke, he realized she was wrong. He didn't want to avoid messy emotions. He wanted more. He wanted her temper along with her passion. He wanted her moods, her craziness, her quirks, her beliefs.

Before he could say so, Grandma Tessa opened the back door. "Mia, you have a call from the law school." She saw Rafael and frowned. "I'll stay with him if you want to take the call."

Mia glanced at him and he raised both hands. "I give you my word that I will not attempt to kidnap our son while you're gone."

"I didn't think you would."

"Now *you* are the liar."

"Rafael . . ."

"Take your call. I will be here when you return."

She went into the house. Grandma Tessa came out onto the porch and stood with her arms folded across her chest. Rafael smiled at her.

Daniel stood and crossed to him. "I want to go riding some more."

"Tomorrow," Rafael promised. "Your mother will take you."

"Mom will just say no," Daniel said glumly. "I want to ride when *I* want." The boy leaned against him. "Daddy, can I come live with you?"

Under other circumstances, the question would have pleased him. However, he was now familiar with the mercurial nature of a four-year-old's emotions.

Feeling Grandma Tessa's sharp glare, he said, "You live with your mother and her family. I know you love them all very much."

Daniel stepped back and shook his head. "I want to live with you. I want to ride my pony all the time. I'm the heir."

Rafael knew he had no one but himself to blame for the "heir" nightmare.

"I'm the heir," Daniel repeated, then began to cry.

Grandma Tessa took a step toward them, but Rafael waved her back. Then he dropped to his knees and hugged his son.

"You have had so many changes in such a short period of time," he told the boy. "I think we all need to take a little time and get used to them before doing anything drastic like moving away from home. Besides"—he kissed the top of the boy's head—"your mother would be lost without you. She loves you so much."

Daniel sniffed. "She would cry if I was gone."

"Yes, and that would make you feel bad. Do you like making your mother cry? I never did."

Daniel stared into his eyes. "You could come live here, like before. That was nice."

"It was nice. But remember all the changes? Let's get used to what we have now."

He heard a sound and saw Mia standing next to her grandmother. There were tears in both women's eyes.

He hadn't said the words for her, nor did her tears matter. She'd already made her case very clear. She didn't trust and she didn't want to trust him. He had come so very far only to realize he had lost.

He kissed Daniel again, then stood. "I should be getting back," he said. "I'll see you tomorrow."

Mia groaned at the thought of an eight o'clock class, but it was the only time the stupid subject was offered and she couldn't risk missing out. She entered the number into the box on the computer screen and hit the Enter key. The screen cleared, then offered to let her print out her fall schedule.

She turned on the printer and tried to work up some enthusiasm about her upcoming semester. She was nearly done. Shouldn't she be thrilled at the prospect of finally getting a job in the real world? After all, her compromise with Rafael might have her working in Rome or Paris.

She tried to convince herself that easy access to Italian shoes was going to be fabulous, only she knew she was lying.

"It's all his fault," she whispered to the empty room. Ever since Rafael had left, she hadn't been able to think about anything but his backhanded proposal.

Did the man really think she was willing to play that game again with him? Hadn't she made it clear she would never, ever trust him?

Apparently in his world things like trust didn't matter. He was willing to do anything to be with his son, even marry her. Well, golly, allow her to pause right here and feel the love.

A sharp pain cut through her. All the sarcasm in the world couldn't disguise how much she hurt. Love. Rafael didn't love her. She was a necessary evil in his plan to be a father. Worst of all, she couldn't blame him. Because if their roles were reversed, she would be willing to marry him just to be near Danny.

But she didn't want a duty proposal. That was almost more insulting than a pity one. She wanted the impossible. She wanted him to love her.

"Grow up," she told herself. "Men like him don't fall in love, and if they do, it's not with women like me." Regular women. Oh, sure, there was the whole Grace Kelly thing, but seriously, who would consider her normal?

The library door opened and Grammy M poked her head in. "Is Danny here?" she asked.

"What? No. I saw him about an hour ago. He was watching a video and said he'd come in when he was finished." Her stomach clenched. "He's not in the family room?"

Minutes later it was clear he wasn't anywhere in the house. The Grands were hysterical and Mia wasn't far behind.

"Call Joe," she told them as she threw open the back door and ran outside.

"Danny!" she yelled. "Danny?"

There was no answer.

This wasn't right. He never went outside without telling someone. He never went anywhere on his own. He was a good boy who loved hanging out with his family.

She raced around the lawn, checked the garage, then came to a stop in front of Gaspare's makeshift stable. The pony was gone.

She remembered how Danny had wanted to keep riding. How he'd had a fit about stopping. Oh, God. If he'd taken the pony, he could be anywhere. He could—

Rafael! Danny had wanted them to all be a family again.

But he didn't know his way to the hotel. Sure, he'd seen it but . . .

Panic exploded. He might know enough to try. What if he had? It was hot and he was so small. The hotel was eight or nine miles away, and between here and there were acres of vineyard and a four-lane highway. There were a million places for a little boy to get lost, or hurt.

Or worse.

18

⁓

The fear lived inside of Mia, growing, sucking her strength, making her want to fall to the ground and beg for mercy. Only there was no one to bargain with. She left the prayers to the Grands and their rosaries. She preferred action.

"How long?" she demanded.

Joe typed on the computer. "Fifteen minutes, tops."

"It's hot," she reminded him. "Too hot for a little boy to be out riding. The best we can figure is he's been gone an hour."

She tried to stick to facts because thinking about what could be happening to her son could very easily drive her to madness. She paced the length of Joe's office, then looked out the window.

"Rafael will be here soon," her brother told her.

"I wasn't sure he should come," she said. "Maybe he would do better to search the roads."

"It's too early. There's no way that pony is going to make it through the vineyard in an hour. I'm guessing Danny is lost in the vines, and as soon as the GPS is up and running, we'll find him. Go back to the house, get your supplies, and wait for Rafael. I'll call you in less than fifteen minutes."

Mia nodded, then ran to her car. Three minutes later she was at the house.

The Grands had already prepared a backpack containing a first-aid kit, water, and cut-up fruit. There was also a hat for Danny, to help keep the sun off him.

"You'll find him," Tessa said through her tears. "I've been praying."

"We both have. God protects the wee ones," Grammy M told her.

Mia wasn't so sure God protected little boys who willfully ran away, but she couldn't say for sure either way.

"Keep praying," she said. Maybe it would help.

Tessa touched her arm. "We're sorry."

Mia paused in the act of dropping her cell phone into her shorts front pocket. "What? Sorry?"

She looked at their stricken faces, not liking how fear aged them. "No," she said firmly. "This isn't your fault. Danny was watching a video when I went in the library to finish my on-line registration. I should have checked on him. I didn't know he was still mad about Rafael. If anyone is to blame, it's me."

"You are not to blame."

The statement came from behind her. She turned and saw Rafael standing in the doorway.

"I am the one who encouraged him to do as he pleased," Rafael continued. "He ran off because he is the heir, and the blame is mine."

Without thinking, Mia rushed toward him. He caught her against his body and held her tight.

"I am sorry," he whispered in her ear. "So sorry."

His arms were strong and supported her. He was Prince Rafael of Calandria, she thought. He would insist on finding his son. He would move heaven and earth to make that happen. For once, Rafael's imperious determination was a good thing.

"It's not your fault either," she said. "He got mad. He acted up. Now we have to find him."

"We will," he promised, and she believed him.

Just then, the back door burst open and Brenna came in with an armful of maps. As Rafael and Mia stepped apart, she put them on the kitchen table and unrolled them.

"Once Joe gets the coordinates, I'll tell you what vineyard that is." She traced the road that led to the hotel. "This is where he wanted to go, but hey, the kid is four. Who knows where he actually went."

Rafael bent over the maps. "There are dozens of acres."

"Hundreds," Brenna said unhappily. "Especially if you consider the Wild Sea vineyards butt right up to ours. If Danny headed that way, he would never find his way out on his own."

She squeezed Mia's arm. "But he's got the tracking thingy on, right? So it's okay."

Mia glanced outside and wished it were a little less hot. The weather might be perfect for grapes, but it would be hell on a little boy trapped in the sun.

Rafael traced possible paths. When Mia's cell phone rang, she grabbed it.

"You have him?" she demanded.

"Yes. Put Brenna on. I'll give her the coordinates, then meet you."

Mia handed over the cell phone. Brenna listened, then looked at the map.

"Okay, yeah. I've got it. Uh-huh." She glanced at Rafael. "Are the moron twins joining us?"

He grimaced. "Yes, Oliver and Umberto are waiting by the car."

"We have a team," Brenna said into the phone. "Uh-huh. Sure."

She hung up and handed Mia the phone. "Joe has the location. He's going to stay where he is and monitor the GPS. He'll call every ten minutes with updates. We'll take carts as close as we can, then walk in." Brenna smiled. "We found him, Mia. He'll be fine."

"I'll believe that when I'm holding him."

Five minutes later they were in three golf carts and heading out into the heart of the Marcelli vineyards. The sun beat down mercilessly. Mia drove, closely following Brenna's cart, while Oliver and Umberto maneuvered the last one. Rafael sorted through the contents of the backpack.

"Your grandmothers have thought of everything," he said.

"They feel horrible about what happened. I hate them blaming themselves."

"As do I."

She glanced at him. "I meant what I said. I don't blame you."

"You do not have to. I still blame myself. If he is hurt . . ."

His voice trailed off. Mia didn't want to think about that either. She wanted to find Danny perfectly healthy and safe, and very sorry for what he'd done.

"Thank God for the tracking system," she said. "If he didn't have on that bracelet, I have no idea how we'd find him."

"So my deception has one bright spot," Rafael said grimly.

"Not just that one," she told him. "I can see you're trying to change and I appreciate it."

"But you still do not trust me."

"At least I didn't assume you'd kidnapped him. That's something."

She slammed on the brakes after Brenna did the same. Even as everyone scrambled out of the carts, Mia pulled out the cell phone and tossed it to Rafael.

She had to. She couldn't talk, couldn't breathe, could only panic when she saw the pony standing alone in the center of the path.

"Are you sure about the location?" Rafael asked into the phone. "We have found the pony and Danny is not here."

He listened, then looked at Mia. "Joe still shows Danny about a half mile from here." His face paled.

"What?" Mia demanded. "What?"

"Danny's not moving. He hasn't moved since Joe first found him."

"Oh, God," Mia said, pressing a hand to her stomach. "Oh, God."

Rafael hung up and handed her the phone. "We must hurry," he yelled to the others. "Umberto, the pony."

The bodyguard raced to Gaspare and led him out of the way. Rafael guided Mia into the passenger seat, then pushed the backpack into her arms and got behind the wheel. Brenna took off at full speed and he did the same. Oliver came up behind.

"He's fine," Rafael said, as much to convince himself

as Mia. "It is very hot. He stopped to rest and Gaspare ran off. That is all."

Mia rocked in the seat. "Please, God, let him be all right. Please."

He heard the pain in her voice and felt it himself. At that moment, he would have given anything to have Danny in his arms. All his money, all his privilege was useless in finding one small, lost boy.

A few minutes later, Brenna came to a stop. She jumped out of the cart and pointed to a vineyard.

"In there," she yelled. "Joe has the coordinates, but we don't exactly have street signs, so we're going to have to walk through. It's this vineyard, though. It has to be."

Rafael took the backpack and stepped out. Mia hurried to his side.

"We'll split up," she said. "Brenna, go with Oliver. You have a cell phone, right?"

Both held one out.

Rafael reached for Mia's hand. "We will go this way," he said, pointing to the right section of the vineyard.

Mia squeezed his fingers. "What if he fell off? What if he's hurt?"

"Then we will take him to the hospital."

He spoke with a calmness he didn't feel, but there was no point in upsetting her more.

"Danny," she yelled as they stepped between the rows of vines heavy with ripe grapes. "Danny, where are you?"

"Danny," he called, hearing Brenna and Umberto in the distance. "Danny."

He paused to listen. There were only the sounds of insects and the rapid beating of his heart. If something had happened to his son . . .

He pushed the thought away. He would not consider it. Danny was fine. He had to be fine. Rafael could not imagine any other possibility.

They walked deeper into the vines. Both called. Brenna's and Oliver's voices came from farther and farther away. Beside him, Mia stumbled, then began to cry.

"Why isn't he answering? What if he has sunstroke? It's hot and he's so small."

"We will find him," he promised, then yelled, "Danny? Can you hear me?"

For a moment, he thought he'd heard something. Mia stared at him.

"Was that a cry?"

They listened again. Sure enough, in the distance came a small sound.

"Danny?" Mia screamed. "Danny, is that you?"

Rafael began to run. He pulled her along with him. "Danny," he called. "Danny, answer us. Answer us so we can find you."

"Over here. I'm over here. Mommy? D-Daddy?"

Rafael heard the voice more clearly now and he knew his son was crying.

"He'll be fine," he promised Mia and himself. "He's just scared."

He saw a flash of color and broke through one of the neat rows. Danny sat in a small patch of shade. His T-shirt was torn, his face dusty and red, and his eyes filled with tears.

"Danny!" Mia dropped to the ground and hugged the boy. Rafael sank next to her and put his arms around both of them.

"Are you all right?" she asked. "Are you hurt?"

"My head hurts and I'm thirsty."

"Of course," she murmured. "We have water."

But she didn't let him go. Rafael slipped off the backpack and pulled out the water. He gave one bottle to Mia, who offered it to the boy, but only let him take small sips, and used the other to dampen one of the washcloths the Grands had packed.

"Put this on the back of his neck," he instructed. "It will help cool him down. He might have heatstroke."

Mia did as he told her. He saw her hands were shaking. His weren't that steady either. Relief joined with the fear of what could have been.

Danny stared at them both. "I'm sorry," he whispered. "I was bad."

"Yes, you were," Rafael told him. "We'll talk about that later. Right now, let's get you back to the house."

He opened Mia's cell phone and called Brenna. Next he phoned Joe. Once they had been notified, he picked up Danny and carried him back to the cart. Mia walked with him, constantly touching Danny's hand and arm, as if reassuring herself that the boy was really all right.

Rafael understood her actions. Had he not been carrying the child, he would have needed reassurance as well. Danny was no longer just his heir. Danny was a piece of Rafael, as much as his arm or his thoughts or his heart. They could never be apart. Not him from Danny or Danny from his mother.

Which made for an interesting quandary.

"Wine and cookies," Katie said as she sat in the chair by the desk. "This is the good life." She nodded at Mia's barely touched glass. "You okay?"

"No," Mia admitted. "Every time I think about what nearly happened, I start to shake."

"It'll take a couple of days to feel better," Francesca told her. "The doctor said he was fine and Danny said he was fine. You need to start believing that."

"When I think about what could have happened . . ." Not that she wanted to, but she was having trouble thinking about anything else.

"Let it go," Brenna said. "We found him. You may not be drinking, but I am. Pass the wine, please."

Francesca handed the bottle over to her twin. They were sprawled on Mia's bed. Mia sat in the window seat and did her best to forget the horrible afternoon.

"You guys didn't have to come all the way over here," she told her sisters. "Katie, that's such a long drive."

"I was already on my way," Katie admitted. "More details for David's wedding. But I'm happy to stay and offer support. You must have been terrified."

"That's as good a word as any," Mia admitted. "I felt desperate and unable to cope. I know none of you like him, but Rafael was really there for me today."

To her surprise, her sisters didn't say anything. Instead they exchanged odd glances.

"What?" she demanded.

Brenna shrugged. "We don't hate Rafael so much. You're right. He was great today. He even called the kid Danny. Who knew a royal could unbend that much?"

Mia had noticed that as well, but in the trauma of the moment, she hadn't thought to mention it.

"I appreciate what he did with Kelly," Francesca admitted. "He saw what none of us could. What if he hadn't been here? How long would Kelly have gone on hating her life because she was too embarrassed to tell us the truth?"

"Good question." Brenna cleared her throat. "You know, he's, ah, well, come to see me a couple of times."

This did cause Mia to gulp her wine. "Why?"

"To talk about you and how to make things right. The first time I told him exactly what I thought of him."

"Wish I'd been there," Katie said with a grin.

"Me too," Mia said. Brenna being totally honest was always entertaining.

"Yeah, it was fun," Brenna told them. "But the second time he was . . . I don't know. More sincere, I guess. I'm kinda willing to give him the benefit of the doubt. Not totally. Just a little."

Who would have guessed, Mia thought. She looked at Katie. "What's your excuse? He hasn't saved your world."

Her oldest sister smiled. "How can I hate the guy my baby sister is in love with?"

Ouch. "You noticed that, huh?" Mia had been hoping she'd kept her feelings to herself.

"You can't turn off love," Katie reminded her. "You've loved him for over five years and you two have been apart. Being together would either destroy your feelings or make them stronger. It didn't seem to me you were any less interested."

"Great. So he's not horrible all the time and I'm still in love with him. Now what?"

She thought of mentioning his "marriage of convenience" proposal, but decided it would only make things more complicated.

"You have to decide if you trust him," Francesca said. "He should have to earn it, of course, but are you willing to let him try?"

"I don't know," Mia admitted. "How can I make myself that vulnerable again? Okay, he's getting the law changed in Calandria, which means he won't be able to keep me from Danny, but still. What's real and what's lies? How do I know he's not playing me for a fool again? He was a total sleaze."

"Total," Brenna said.

"But he's Danny's father."

"And he's not going away," Katie said. "You're stuck with him. So how stuck do you want to be?"

Mia leaned back against the window. "I don't know," she admitted. "My head tells me one thing and my heart says the opposite. Which should I listen to? How do I figure it all out?"

"You need a sign," Francesca said.

Brenna rolled her eyes. "Gee, Dr. Marcelli, is that your professional, psychologist opinion?"

"Sure." Francesca smiled. "It's as good a way to pick as any."

"I had a lot more respect for our higher education system before she said that," Brenna muttered.

Mia laughed. "Okay, fine. What kind of sign?"

"A really big one?" Katie offered.

They were all laughing when the loud noise cut through the quiet of the night. Darkness faded into an ever-growing bright white light.

"Oh, my God," Brenna said as she scrambled to her feet. "It really *is* a sign."

The four of them put down their glasses and ran downstairs. The Grands were already there, as was Rafael, who was spending the evening with Danny.

They stepped outside and saw a large helicopter setting down on the driveway.

"That can't be good," Mia muttered, wondering if something had happened to Darcy's father. She couldn't imagine anything but presidential disaster bringing a helicopter.

She heard another engine and turned to see Joe driving toward the house.

"Do you know about this?" she asked over the rising noise of the helicopter.

"No, but I'll guess he does."

He pointed at Rafael. Mia felt herself go numb.

"No," she screamed as she ran back to the small crowd. She shook Rafael by the arm. "You can't. You can't. I won't let you."

"Mommy, see the helopter? It's so big."

She reached down and picked up her son. "You can't," she repeated.

Rafael grabbed her. "I'm not. I swear. I have nothing to do with this. Mia, look at me. I'm not taking Danny away."

She tried to think, tried to breathe. Where could she go? How fast could she run?

The helicopter touched down. As the wind kicked up, she pressed Danny's face into her shoulder and wondered if it was possible to get to her car in time. Only her keys were inside the house and if she stopped to get them, it would be too late.

"Mommy, don't be scared," Danny said as he peered over her shoulder. "I won't let the helopter hurt you. Oh, look. There's people."

She turned to watch two soldiers step off the helicopter. Next a set of steps appeared. Overhead, the blades slowed to a stop.

Mia stood there clutching her son as an older man walked off the helicopter and onto her front lawn. She'd never seen him in person before, but she recognized him from the pictures.

King Xavier of Calandria.

"Rafael, there you are," the king said. "You are well?"

"Yes, Father."

The king glanced at all of them, then settled his gaze on Danny. Mia took a step back.

The king nodded at Danny. "Is that him?"

Rafael took a step forward. "Yes, he is my son."

"Good. Take him and we will leave."

19

❧

"*L*iar!" Mia screamed as she thrust Danny at Brenna, who stood closest, then charged Rafael. "Liar. You son-ofabitch."

She clawed at his face, and when he easily avoided her assault, she pounded on his chest.

"You lied."

She couldn't believe it. Again. She'd been a fool again and this time the price would be her son.

"I trusted you," she sobbed. "It was all lies."

He grabbed her wrists. "I did not lie. I have no part in this. Mia, listen to me."

Mia tried to twist free. She looked at Joe. "Don't let him take Danny."

Umberto and Oliver hovered in the background, but Rafael didn't call them closer. However, that didn't stop the king's guards from looking menacing.

"Enough of this," Rafael said. He released Mia and pushed her toward Joe. Her brother caught her easily. Brenna carried over Danny. Joe took the boy.

"No one is taking Danny," Rafael told his father. "We

are not taking him away. Not without the consent of his mother, and she will never give it."

The king glared at him. "I have been patient long enough. The boy belongs in Calandria, as do you. Come with me now."

"No," Rafael said calmly. "Not without Mia, and until the law is changed, she will not set foot on Calandrian soil. I will not allow it."

"*You* will not allow it," the king repeated, obviously furious. "Until I die, I am ruler of Calandria."

"That doesn't mean you're right about this, Father."

Mia didn't know what to think. Was it possible that Rafael was really taking her side? That he was standing up to the king for her? Protecting her and Danny?

"The child belongs with his people," the king said coldly. "He needs to be trained."

"He needs his mother," Rafael said flatly. "He needs to grow up knowing he is loved. It is easy to learn a history of a people, but much harder to replace family. He's only a boy. I will not allow his life to be destroyed because you want to turn your grandson into a miniature version of yourself."

The king stiffened. "You forget yourself."

"I remember everything," Rafael said. "I remember more than you realize. I was wrong to come here and attempt to deceive these people. I was wrong not to speak to Mia in good faith. The law will be changed, and when it is, she and I will come to terms."

"You allow yourself to be dictated to by a mere woman?" the king bellowed.

"Hey," Katie snapped. "Watch it. Not just any woman. Not a mere woman. A Marcelli."

Rafael glanced at Mia and smiled. "She is right. A Marcelli. Smart, funny, irreverent, beautiful, and capable of so much love." He returned his attention to his father. "She is far too verbal, but it is a flaw I can live with."

Mia hated that her brain, which so far had been the rational one in all this, instantly focused on the "beautiful" part of his sentence.

"Rafael, everything about this situation is unacceptable," the king announced

"Then you will need to learn to compromise. Danny stays with his mother and I stay with them both."

Stay? Mia stared at him. "You're staying?"

"No, he is not," the king said, glaring at her. "He belongs in Calandria."

"I belong with my family." Rafael took her hands in his. "I belong with you, Mia. With you and Danny." He stared into her eyes. "I have changed. I know you do not trust me, and I accept that I am the reason. I will have to earn my way back into your good graces. I am more than willing to do so. I will wait patiently and then perform whatever tasks you set out for me. I want you to believe that I am the right man for you."

She'd spent a lot of the past couple of months in a state of disbelief, but this was certainly going for the record.

"I don't understand," she said.

"Nor do I," the king announced. "You are Crown Prince Rafael of Calandria. You do not humble yourself in front of a woman."

"You are wrong, Father," Rafael said, never looking away from Mia. "I humble myself in front of *this* woman. Have you ever wondered why I refused to marry those others? Did it ever occur to you that the reason was my heart was engaged elsewhere? I didn't understand until I came here and nearly lost the only thing that has ever mattered."

She hung on to his hands because the world had started to spin. There were no words, no way to do anything but stare at him and pray this was all really happening.

"I will stand against my father for you," he said sincerely. "For you and for Danny. I will be there for you, and seek your counsel, and love you for always, Mia. I love you."

At that exact moment, the helicopter blades shut down and his words echoed in the sudden silence.

"I will not have this," King Xavier said. "Rafael, take the boy and get on the helicopter immediately."

Rafael ignored him. "I see doubt in your eyes," he told her. "I know why. I have earned that doubt. There is no reason for you to believe me now. Just accept that I am staying."

"You are not staying," the king said.

"Can someone shut him up?" Brenna asked.

"It's so romantic," Grammy M breathed. "Oh, Mia, it's so romantic."

"I don't know," Mia admitted as she pulled free of his touch and stepped back. "There's too much happening."

"You see," the king said. "She doesn't even want you."

Rafael ignored him. "Mia, I understand. No one is asking you to say anything. I want you to know I love you and Danny."

Mia hated how much she wanted to believe him. He was saying all the right things—especially the part about not going back to Calandria until the law had changed. But what about Danny being the heir? And how was she ever supposed to take that step of faith?

She looked at Katie. "What do you think?"

"That your life is never boring." Katie held up both hands. "I'm not weighing in on this. Are you crazy?"

"You must have an opinion."

"I'm keeping it to myself."

Mia looked at Brenna, who had never been one to stay silent. Her sister sighed.

"He's not a slug," Brenna admitted reluctantly. "I thought he was, but he isn't. He's standing up to his father and when Daddy's the king, that can't be easy. I don't think he's lying. Xavier there looks ready to have a heart attack and no one is that good an actor. I say give him a chance."

The king glared at Brenna, "I will have you arrested."

She smiled. "You'd have to catch me first, your highness."

Mia looked at Francesca. "And you?"

"He was great about Kelly. I think being with Danny has changed him. Is it enough? Only you can answer that, Mia."

Grandma Tessa sniffed. "I still don't know about him. He hurt you, Mia, but when he thought Danny was lost, he was devastated."

Mia looked at Joe. He shook his head. "I'm only on your side, kid. Rafael doesn't matter to me."

"You will stop this immediately," the king demanded. "You will not speak of my son or myself this way. It is unspeakably rude."

Grandma Tessa moved toward him. "What would you

call swooping down in the night and trying to steal a child? Good manners?"

The guards took a step forward, then hesitated, as if unwilling to take on a woman pushing eighty.

"This is not for you to decide," the king said. "Daniel is heir to the throne. He belongs in Calandria and he is going there now."

"No he's not," Rafael said. He looked at Mia and smiled. "I know what to say," he told her. "I know how to make you believe."

She was torn between wanting his words to be true and knowing it wasn't possible.

"Rafael, don't do something you will regret," the king said.

Rafael took her hand and then faced his father. "I have regrets, but none of them have anything to do with this. You only want Danny because he's your heir. Allow me to solve that problem. I, Rafael, Crown Prince of Calandria, do hereby abdicate as heir to the throne."

Mia's mind went blank. "You can't," she and the king said at the same time.

"I can and I do," he told his father. "I am tired of living with all the rules and restrictions of office. I am not interested in an arranged marriage. I love this woman and I will spend the rest of my life proving myself worthy of her. I'm hoping that, in time, she'll be willing to marry me. I told you, Father, I'm staying here."

Mia felt her heart stop. As far as gestures went, this one ranked right up there with going through time. "You'd give up the throne for me?" she asked, her voice a squeak.

"You are more than worth it."

She wasn't sure about that.

The king's face turned the color of a tomato. "Rafael, you dishonor me and our country. No woman is worth the throne."

"You're wrong. I'm not the first man to walk away from his duty because of love."

The king glared. "Do not compare yourself to an English ruler." His eyes narrowed. "What is it about American women?"

"We're sassy," Francesca said.

Rafael turned to Mia. "If I'm not the heir, there's no danger to Danny. I can stay here permanently."

"Oh, you will get a job and live in the suburbs?" the king asked contemptuously.

"Perhaps."

Mia pressed her hand to his chest. "I can't let you do this. You can't walk away from your heritage. Being the crown prince is who you are."

"Who I am is the man who loves you," he told her gently.

"You will be king," his father insisted. "You must be. There is no one else."

"My cousin."

"Quentin? A gay clothing designer?"

Brenna snorted. "There's a coronation I'd want to see."

"Mom loves his clothes," Katie whispered to Mia.

Mia ignored everyone else and stared at Rafael.

"You can't do this. You can't give up your future."

He kissed her. "I give up only my past. You are my future. I think I would like to study medicine and be a doctor."

"Never!" his father yelled.

"Rafael, no," she told him, sure she would wake up at any second. There was no way this was happening. "Trust me, you're not going to like living in the ordinary world."

"I will enjoy it as long as I have you."

She bit her lower lip. "I don't know what to think, let alone say."

"Arrest her!" the king yelled, pointing at Mia. "Arrest this woman. All of this is her fault."

The guards didn't move toward her. If anything, they seemed to be inching toward the helicopter.

Rafael sighed. "Father, you cannot arrest Mia. You're on American soil and she has broken no laws. Even if she had, I would not allow it. You have lost. I'm staying here. Quentin will be king next."

"Never! You are my son. I command you to return to Calandria with me."

Rafael shrugged. "I'm sorry, Father. No. You made me choose and I have made my choice. I want to marry Mia and be Danny's father."

"She hasn't even said she loves you. She hasn't accepted. You've been the one baring your soul and what has she done?"

Rafael smiled at Mia. "I owe her."

"You are Crown Prince Rafael of Calandria! You owe her nothing."

Mia pressed a hand to her stomach. It was all too much. "I think I'm going to be sick."

"Then we should get you inside." Rafael put his arm around her. "Father, we will end this discussion for now. Perhaps we can talk later, when we are more calm."

"I am the king. You do not dismiss me. I dismiss you."

Katie shook her head. "I'll bet he was a real tight-ass when you were growing up."

"Arrest that woman, too!" Xavier insisted. "Arrest them all."

"He was a good king," Rafael said. "But a distant father."

"I'm sure it's how he was raised," Francesca said. "People often find it difficult to break with tradition. It's comfortable and there's a sense of guilt in forging a different path after so many years. In your case it would be what? A thousand?"

"Something like that."

They all started for the house. The king continued to rage, but no one paid attention.

Once they were inside, Brenna opened bottles of Marcelli wine. The Grands did another of their instant meals-on-demand tricks. In a matter of minutes food covered the kitchen table. Mia sat with Rafael on her left and Danny on her lap.

"Are you really staying?" Danny asked tentatively.

"Yes," Rafael said. "I will always be in your life."

"Are you going to live here?"

Mia wasn't sure how he would answer the question, but Rafael jumped right in.

"Not for a while. Your mother and I have to get to know each other again. That takes time. But we're still a family. You're my son and I love you very much."

"Do you love Mommy?"

"Yes."

Mia still had trouble getting her mind around that one.

"You abdicated," she said.

"I am aware of that."

"How could you? You're supposed to rule your country."

He shrugged. "I'm not losing you, Mia. I have waited my entire life to find you. What is a kingdom when compared with that?"

"It's a kingdom! It's being king. Your face on stamps and having buildings named after you."

"None of that is important."

"Fine. Then it's about fulfilling your destiny. You were born to rule. Your people deserve a good leader. Do you really think Quentin is up to the task?"

"He can learn."

"But—"

Rafael leaned in and kissed her. "Stop. If I am an ordinary man, you will see me as someone worthy of a second chance. As Prince Rafael, I will always be the man who deceived you. I am content."

She found herself getting lost in his eyes. On a scale of one to ten, abdicating had to at least be in the twenties.

He picked up her hand and kissed her palm. "I will court you, Mia Marcelli. I will be here no matter what. I will love you with a devotion that leaves you breathless. When you are ready to trust me again, tell me, and then I will convince you to marry me."

There were five other women in the kitchen and Mia heard every single one of them sigh. She would have, too, except she was already breathless.

"Rafael," she whispered. "You know I never stopped loving you."

"I know. I was a fool to let you go and a bigger fool to try to trick you. My time would have been much better spent realizing what was in my own heart and then convincing you we belonged together."

"I'm sort of convinced."

"Good."

Grandma Tessa reached for Danny. "What would you like to eat?" she asked. "Some pasta? It's your favorite."

"That one," he said, pointing. "Mommy? Daddy? Where are you going?"

"They're just going upstairs," Grammy M said as she pulled out a chair for the boy. "To, ah, talk."

Katie poured him some milk. "They'll be talking awhile. But that's okay. After we eat, we can watch a video. Or play a game."

"Can I go talk with them?"

Francesca smiled. "Not this time. It's grown-up talking."

"Talking, huh?" Brenna said with a grin. "Who would have thought it would come to this?"

Grammy M sighed. "I always liked that man."

Tessa rolled her eyes. "If the devil had a title, you'd like him as well."

"That I would."

Hours later, when the house was quiet and stars filled the sky, Rafael leaned over Mia and kissed her.

"You're not saying much," he told her.

"I don't know what *to* say. You abdicated, said you loved me, proposed, and then walked out on your father in a matter of twenty minutes. My head is still spinning."

He kissed her again. "Good. I always want to make your head spin."

She rubbed her hands across his bare chest. "Do you mean it? The not-being-king part?"

"Yes. I have no desire to change my mind." He smiled. "I love you, Mia. I would do anything for you."

"Even walk away from everything you are?"

"I am more than just a prince. It is time to discover the man."

She believed him. There were no doubts, no questions. She opened her mouth to tell him so but what came out instead was, "You have to be king."

He laughed. "Mia, no."

She sat up, not caring she was naked. "Rafael, I'm serious. You have to be king. It's what you were born to be. Plus I think you'd be a good king."

"No. I'm serious about wanting to study medicine. Besides, you don't want to be a queen, do you?"

She grimaced. "Not really, but I would. You owe yourself, and your people. And Danny."

He pulled her down next to him and bent over her. "I think it would be best to discuss this later."

She sank back onto the bed. "Fine, but don't think for a moment I can't change your mind."

He lowered his head. "Mia, I have long since learned never to doubt you."

Epilogue

One year later

"I swear, if anyone from the press tramples through my grapes, there will be hell to pay," Brenna muttered as she adjusted the front of her dark green sheath. "I will kill anyone who so much as bruises a grape."

Francesca rolled her eyes. "Mia, I told you to wait until after harvest. Brenna, you're like an old woman about those grapes."

"I am a protective bear mother of twins," Brenna muttered. She walked to the window and stared out toward the vineyards. "I can feel them inching closer to the grapes. I hate the press. Have I mentioned that? Mia, you should have gotten married in the spring."

"I suggested that, too, but Rafael didn't want my law school graduation eclipsed by wedding plans. He wanted both days to be special."

"I think I liked him better when he was a jerk," Brenna said. "He's so nice now. So caring and thoughtful. It's not natural."

"Ignore her," Katie said as she adjusted Mia's veil and fingered the tiara. "These are real diamonds, aren't they?"

"That's what I'm told," Mia said. "About thirty-five carats."

"Cool," Kelly said with a grin. "Can I borrow it when I get married?"

"Maybe."

Amber turned sideways in front of the large mirror that covered one wall of the bride's room. "I look huge."

Mia smiled at the pregnant woman. "You look beautiful. Radiant."

"You're barely showing," Brenna said. "At six months, I was a cow. Trust me, you're lucky."

"You were a beautiful mother-to-be," Colleen Marcelli said. "I'm a mother and I know about these things."

Darcy walked into the room, closed the door behind her, and leaned against it. "It's done. The president and the king have officially shaken hands. It was a beautiful moment. Joe looked surly, but he often does. I tried to get him to come up here, but he was afraid there were too many women in one place and the estrogen would asphyxiate him." She looked at Mia. "You're gorgeous."

"Thanks. I owe a lot to you guys."

"You're right about that," Francesca said, coming up to stand beside her. "Do you know how many hours of beading went into this thing? I bled quarts on your dress."

Mia stood in front of the mirror and tried to convince herself this was all happening. That she was really getting married to Rafael in front of eight hundred of their closest friends.

The guest list had been just one issue to be dealt with. There had also been the logistical nightmare of housing so many foreign dignitaries and their families. Something, the king informed her on a regular basis, that would not have been a problem had she been married in Calandria, like every other princess.

But then he'd smiled, because after all this time, he'd gotten used to the fact that Mia wasn't like other princesses.

Rafael had resisted revoking his abdication for nearly six months, but after the law had changed allowing Mia equal say in her children's future, he had agreed to once again be heir to the throne.

She stared at herself in the mirror, at the yards and yards of beaded silk. The design for the dress had come from a modified version of an eighteenth-century ball gown. The infamous Quentin had flown out himself to fit Mia. He'd directed the Marcelli women on the beading, which had taken months. Now it was finished and she was about to marry Rafael.

She smiled at the thought. He truly had changed. He was a good, caring father and supportive of her. He had moved into the house and taken care of Danny while she'd crammed for finals, and he had been patient as she had then tried to learn a thousand years of Calandrian history in just two months.

Her father walked into the bride's room. "It's time," he said.

The women collected their bouquets and hurried out. Mia's mother lingered.

"My baby is getting married," she whispered as she kissed Mia's cheek.

"Don't make me cry," Mia pleaded. "We don't have time to redo my makeup."

"Or mine." Her mother lowered Mia's veil over her face. "I'm glad you're happy. That's all I ever wanted."

Her father grinned. "Sure. We don't actually care about being related to royalty. Although I've been thinking. Now we have the perfect in for the European market."

His wife slapped his arm. "You will *not* discuss exporting Marcelli wines during the reception. Do you understand me?"

Marco grinned again.

Then Mia was alone with her father. He squeezed her hand. "You can still get out of this if you want."

She laughed. "Not even on a bet. I love him, Daddy."

"I've offered the same escape to each of my girls and you have all refused. I guess that means you're really in love."

"I am."

"You put him through the wringer. I'm not saying he didn't deserve it, but he came through."

"He did. He loves Danny and me."

"He's a good man," her father said. "I like that I can say that about all my sons-in-law. Come on, Mia. It's time."

They walked down the wide staircase and through the arched doors that led to the wide expanse of lawn. She could hear the royal Calandrian orchestra playing and smell the thousands of flowers arranged for the event. Then she and her father turned and she could see the dais where the ceremony would take place, the beautiful arch, and a seemingly endless sea of guests.

"Katie outdid herself," her father murmured.

Mia nodded in agreement. Her sister had worked with the Calandrian protocol officer to pull off a massive wedding in far too short a time. Everything looked perfect.

"I'm ready, Mommy," Danny said as he stepped in front of her. He held a pillow with two gold bands clipped in place.

"You look very handsome," she told him.

"I look like Daddy." He grinned and tugged at his miniature bow tie.

"All right, kids," Katie said, motioning Danny to join his cousins. "Let's go. Just like we practiced."

Mia watched her sisters' children begin the long walk down the aisle to where Amber, Darcy, and Kelly waited. The girls scattered rose petals. Brenna and Francesca stepped up next.

"Thanks for the great dresses," Brenna said with a grin.

"Thank Quentin," Mia told her.

The twins started their walk.

Katie squeezed Mia's arm. "I love you."

"I love you, too," Mia swallowed to hold back tears. "You did an amazing job with the wedding."

"I loved it. And there isn't a single daisy anywhere."

Mia laughed.

Katie turned to face the arch, then began her walk. Mia slipped her hand into the crook of her father's arm.

"Ready?" he asked.

She nodded, her gaze drawn to the handsome man waiting for her. Her eyes locked with Rafael's and she felt the warmth of his love surround her.

A handsome prince. Who would have thought it would ever come to this?

The music changed to the traditional wedding march. The guests rose and turned toward her and her father. He covered her hand with his and squeezed her fingers. Then they stepped onto the petal-covered path.

Once again, she found Rafael and let him draw her in. Everything about this moment felt right—as if she'd finally found her destiny. Today she would be his wife, and Calandria's new princess. In time, she would be queen.

Today Calandria . . . tomorrow the world.